Learning the Ways of Coyote

Learning the Ways of Coyote

A Novel
By

Fredrick Zydek

Rag and Bone Books
Connecticut

Also by Fredrick Zydek

Poetry

Lights Along the Missouri (1976)
Storm Warning (1981)
Ending the Fast (1983)
The Conception Abbey Poems (1993)
Dreaming On the Other Side of Time (2002)
Stumbling Through the Stars (2003)
This Is Not a Prayer (2005)
T'Kopachuck: The Buckley Poems (2009)

As Editor

Close to Home (1981)

Non-Fiction

Charles Taze Russell: His Life and Times (2010)

Cover design by Eric Hoffman

This book is published by Rag and Bone Books, a division of Winthrop Press, Connecticut.
ISBN No. 1452803552 / 9781452803555
First Edition

Acknowledgments

I must thank Sara Jo Holmes and Barbara Smith for all their work proofing earlier drafts of this novel. Special thanks to Garold Storm who patiently listened to every revision of every page for the better part of two years. And I am grateful to the real people I have known who contributed to the fabric of the story.

While this is a fictionalized version of growing up in a small town in the Cascade mountain range, many of the characters are based on real people - sometimes more than one.

I am again grateful to my editor, Eric Hoffman, who not only read this novel read this novel many years ago - but had sufficient faith in it to repay it a visit this many years later.

I would be remiss if I did not mention the name of my literary assistant, Andrew Dillon. Without his help in this pile of books and papers I call a study, work on this and other literary projects would not be possible. Special thanks to Mark Chavez for the proofing of this novel. I am indebted to his careful read of this book. He has become my hero.

The cover design was taken from an early post card of a Street in Buckley, Washington. The third house from the right was the Zydek family home when the author was growing up. The earlier name for Buckley, Washington was Perkin's Prairie. It was while living in this house and on this street when the author learned the ways of coyote.

Dedication

This book is dedicated to William and Cecil Garfield who became boyhood chums and remained friends of mine all through life. Their parents allowed me to travel with them on many trips to the Quinault and Muckleshoot reservations when they visited members of their family. My relationship with Bill and Cecil and their kin taught me about a way of life to which most American kids never have access. They were great experiences for which I will always be grateful.

Contents

1	The Meeting	1
2	Scalps from the Whitman Massacre	35
3	Shamans in the Family	70
4	The Dog Dance	103
5	The Whale Dance	147
6	Chases Rainbows	186
7.	Talks with Eagles	214
8.	The Orchid Appreciation Society	242
9.	The Sawdust Trail	275
10.	Polish Pilgrims	315
11.	Ten New Houses on the Hill	357
12.	Good Magic	402
13	Testing the Spirits	447
14.	Troopers on the Flats	489
15.	Assault of the Weasels	526
16	Learning the Ways of Coyote	565
17.	Dancing With Kwatee	599
18.	Three Yellow Finch Feather	632

Chapter One

The Meeting

PERKINS PRAIRIE, a small mountain town nestled in the foothills of the Cascade Mountain Range east of Tacoma and Seattle, began as a mining town with a lumber mill. In the early days of its history, it didn't boast of much more than a trading post, six saloons, and a few miners' shacks down by the creek. But by 1938, the year I was born, the small community had become a model of post-Victorian America at the end of the great depression.

Although it had only a three block main street business section, the town laid claim to its own newspaper, library, movie house, hotel, and all the small businesses that make small towns autonomous. Most of the town's men worked in the woods or the mines. A few owned small shops, taught in the local schools or functioned as the town's doctors, lawyers, and city personnel. The few women who worked held jobs as grocery store clerks or as ward attendants at the Cascade Custodial School for the Mentally Retarded.

One woman in town was almost fully self-employed. Evangeline Murphy. She gave piano lessons in her little white house on the edge of Stump Lake at the end of Main Street and sold tickets at the Cosmo Theatre weeknights and Saturdays. The rest of the time she took care of her invalid mother. Everybody in town knew that Evangeline and the town barber were having an affair. The barber's wife had been bedridden since their oldest son was killed in the war but rumor had it that the piano teacher and barber had been seeing one another long before the war effort began.

Very little of what happened in the rest of the world had much to do with Perkins Prairie until World War II came along. The war changed everything. Most of the town's young men went off to defend their country. Many of the miners and lumberjacks left the low paying jobs in the woods and mines for work in the shipyards or at the quickly growing Boeing Aircraft Company. Many of the wives took jobs that supported the war effort as well. Everybody in town knew who Mussolini, Hitler and Emperor Hirohito were.

The war was good for Perkins Prairie. Its citizens suddenly had more money to spend, and by the time I was born the town was easing out of the depression. By 1948, the year I turned ten, even my parents were able to sell the little house on Perkins Street and move across the tracks to a lovely white-framed home across from the high school on A Street.

My tenth birthday party was to be held at my grandparents' farm just outside of town. I decided to get there early so I could watch the preparations and greet cousins and my aunts and uncles as they arrived. Discovering that my grandfather and his dearest friend, Allah Ben Borgstine, a goat farmer who owned a small ranch just beyond Spikton Creek, were deep into one of their many debates was an added bonus. I loved their lengthy discussions and often went to the bedroom above the living room where they usually

2

talked, sprawled across the wrought iron heating vent and eavesdropped on their philosophical and news filled conversations below. I learned most of what I knew about the outside world from their discussions. I knew lots of stuff other kids my age didn't know. For example, I knew the state of Israel had just come into existence, who Mahatma Gandhi was, and that a fellow by the name of Mao Tse-Tung was leading a split between China's Communists and Nationalists. Grandma said that Mr. Borgstine was half Muslim and half Jew. I figured he came from some sort of aristocratic background because even though he raised goats in the foothills, he always came calling dressed in a rumpled but clean suit.

I raced upstairs, settled myself comfortably on the warm wrought-iron vent above them and began listening. "The Federal Government has decided to move some Indians from the Quinault Reservation into town as part of their relocation project," my grandfather told Borgstine in his thick Polish accent.

"I hear that. Seems the government is not only paying to move them to towns but has also given them money to open shops," Borgstine observed.

"There's a family comin' to Perkins Prairie. I heard tell they've given them enough money to open a dry-cleaning shop and buy a little house over by the grade school," my grandfather said, blowing a long blue puff of cigar smoke into the air above his head.

"It doesn't seem to matter much to the government that we've already got a dry- cleaning shop here run by the Orloski family. Small town like this might not be able to support two dry-cleaning establishments," Borgstine mused.

"Don't matter to the government," Grandpa said, taking another puff of cigar smoke into his mouth. "They just want that land on the peninsula. I hear they want to turn it into a tourist hotel and camp sight."

"I heard that too. They're settin' that poor bastard up. He'll lose his rights to his land on the reservation and go broke," Borgstine commented.

"I don't think the town is gonna much care for having redskins livin' in the community either," my grandfather warned.

Suddenly I was all ears. Cowboys and Indians was my favorite game. I always chose to be one of the Indians. My dad's parents both came from Poland. On that side of the family I was European through and through. But that wasn't true on my mom's side of the family. Her mother moved from England to Little Bedeck, Nova Scotia, as an indentured slave when she was just fifteen. After she worked off her passage to the New World she met and later she married John Brune, my mother's father. John was a half breed, Scottish and half Micmac. The Micmacs are a branch of the Algonquin people living up and down the seaboard of North America. John's father had been a fur trapper for the Hudson Bay Company. Somewhere along the Great Lakes, he met and married an Algonquin woman and took her back to Little Bedeck as his bride. The woman died giving birth to my grandpa John. Great Grandpa married an Irish woman after that so my Grandpa John didn't know much about his real mother - and neither did we. But it was enough for me to know there was real Indian blood flowing in my veins. It seemed to me to make me special - more American somehow. And now I was going to have a chance to meet some real full-blooded Indians. I could hardly wait for my birthday party to be over so I could ride my bike over to the Wickersham Grade School and see if I could locate the people from the Quinault Reservation who were moving into our small town. I was busy thinking about how wonderful it would be if the Indian family had boys my age when something my grandfather said troubled me.

"It ain't gonna be easy for them in this town," he said in a low voice, leaning towards Borgstine to emphasize the seriousness of his words.

"Yeah, there's a lot of old-timers here who still remember the Whitman Massacre like it was yesterday. I don't think this is a good idea. Could be trouble," Borgstine observed.

"Maybe not. You and me know a lot of people in this town. We could tell folks we think this is good for Perkins Prairie. We're property owners. People respect us. Maybe we can change the way people look at the Redwings," Grandpa commented.

"I don't know. We're a small town and everybody likes the Orloskis. I don't think there's enough dry cleaning to go around. You gonna take your clothes to the new people?" Borgstine asked.

"Well, we all know you won't. When was the last time you had that suit pressed?" Grandpa joked.

"I keep my money for important things and havin' my suit pressed ain't one of them," his friend grinned.

5

§§§§

We seldom went to church in our family. Mother's people had been English Jews but she herself had dabbled in Unity teachings before she married my father. Dad was baptized a Catholic, but he only went to church for funerals and weddings. This meant that Sunday mornings were free. I got up early and peddled my bike to the Stump Lake side of town in hopes of finding one of the Redwing family doing something outside their house. I wanted to get a glimpse of the first real Indians to move into Perkins Prairie and secretly hoped I would get a chance to actually meet them and become their friend.

On my third trip around the block I saw a man come out of the house and head for the woodshed. I was instantly disappointed that he wasn't dressed much differently than my dad. I didn't really expect to see anyone wearing full-face war paint or a bonnet of feathers, but I had hoped there would be something about their dress that set them apart. The man who walked from the house to the woodshed might as well have purchased his clothes at Madden's General Store.

Still, he was a real Indian. I peddled my bike up the driveway, leaned it against the corner of the garage and followed the man to the shed. "I'm Fritz Harding," I said.

"I'm Clarence Redwing," the man responded without stopping or turning around. "We just moved into town."

"Yeah, I know. My grandpa was talkin' about you guys yesterday," I said, walking a little faster to keep up with his wide steps.

"Well, I hope your grandpa had favorable things to say," Clarence said, stepping slightly into the doorway of the woodshed and picking up a hatchet from the chopping block.

"My grandpa thinks you'll go broke in this town and that the government wants to change your reservation into a resort town. But I was thinkin' that if you charged cheaper prices to dry-clean clothes than the Orloskis, you might do okay."

Clarence Redwing picked up a chunk of cedar and began chopping it into kindling. For the first time he looked directly into my eyes. "Well, let's hope you are a better prophet than your grandfather," he smiled.

"How come you decided to leave the reservation? My dad took me to see the one up on the peninsula . . ."

"The Quinaults . . ." Clarence interrupted.

"Yeah, the Quinaults . . . and I thought it was a perfect place to live."

"Better schools here. The old ways can never come back. I want my kids to have a better chance at a good life than I had. Our way of life will never come back. Moving to town is the right thing to do." Clarence went back to splitting kindling from the chunk of cedar in his hands.

"That's the same reason my grandpa Harding says he decided to move from the old country to America."

"Your people are Polish?"

"I'm Polish on my dad's side, English and Scottish and Micmac on my mother's side," I answered proudly.

"We're Quinault on my wife's side, my people were all Nootka. But I was raised on the Muckelshoot Reservation just outside of Auburn," Mr. Redwing informed me.

"My dad and mom took me to the Provincial Museum up in Victoria, Canada. They had totem poles being carved right there by Nootka carvers. Are you a carver?" I asked.

"Probably would have been if I'd been raised up there. Nope, I'm not even a very good kindling chopper. I was raised by the Muckelshoots. But I do plant and raise great vegetables."

Raising vegetables didn't sound very Indian to me. I was beginning to think the Redwings were going to be very disappointing but I didn't let on that I was surprised to learn that Mr. Redwing raised a vegetable garden just like my dad did. "Have ya ever eaten whale meat?" I asked.

"Oh, many times. It's sort of like beef but stringier. It's very good."

"Do you have any kids my age?"

"I have two boys just about your age. Their names are Willie and Randy. They'll be out in a few minutes to help me carry some wood into the house. They're just finishing up their breakfasts. If you want to hang around for a few minutes, I can introduce you to them."

"I'd like that a lot," I told him just as the

8

backdoor to the house opened and two boys appeared.

"This is Fritz Harding. He stopped by to introduce himself. Fritz, these are my sons, Willie and Randy." Willie was the taller of the two boys and slightly on the plump side. I assumed he was the older of the two as well. Randy was as thin as I was but a little shorter. They were what my mother called cute. Both boys were dressed in jeans and long sleeved plaid shirts neatly tucked in. It looked like they were both wearing cowboy boots. I was a bit disappointed about that. I wasn't expecting buckskin and beads but had hoped there would be something that set them apart. They seemed as excited to see and greet me as I was to meet them.

After exchanging greetings we began picking up the kindling as Mr. Redwing shaved it from the chunk of cedar on the chopping block.

"You lived in this town all your life?" Willie asked.

"Not yet," I answered.

Randy looked up at me and laughed.

"I'm part Indian myself. My great-grandmother was an Algonquin woman," I blurted out, trying to fit in.

"Which tribe?" Willie asked.

"Micmac," I answered.

"You speak any of the language?" Randy inquired.

"I can't even speak any Polish and I'm only second born in this country," I answered.

As soon there was enough wood in our arms to pile in the wood box on the back porch, the boys led the way back to the house and up the steps. Mrs. Redwing came out and introduced herself and invited me into their house to meet the rest of the Redwing children. Now I was really excited. Maybe it was disappointing to discover that Mr. Redwing dressed like my father and that Willie and Randy looked as if they had just stepped out of a Sears Roebuck catalogue, but I was sure that once I got inside the house I would find all sorts of things indicating that this was an Indian home.

What I found dismayed me. I might as well have been standing in my aunt Veronica's living room. The only thing Indian about the room was the people in it.

After being introduced to the rest of the Redwing children, an elderly Indian woman shuffled into the living room from the kitchen. She wore a gingham dress pulled together at the waist by a beaded belt revealing traditional Native American designs and a pair of comfortably worn beaded moccasins. Her hair was long, gray and worn in a ponytail held together by a thin strand of leather tied in a bow.

"This is my mother, Stella Sunfield. She's staying with us until I have the house in order," Mrs. Redwing said. "Mother, this is Fritz Harding who came over to meet the family. He helped the boys and Clarence bring in kindling this morning."

Mrs. Sunfield glanced down at me without smiling. "How do you do?" I responded, extending my hand.

"I do okay," she replied without taking it. She turned around and shuffled back into the kitchen.

"Grandma don't much like whites," Randy

whispered into my ear.

"Will you join us for some cookies and milk, Fritz? Mother and I just finished pulling a batch of chocolate chip cookies out of the oven. I made the batter but it's my mother's recipe." Mrs. Redwing said.

"Yeah, Grandma makes the best chocolate chip cookies on the planet," Willie told me.

I was beginning to lose confidence in American Indian-ry. Chocolate chip cookies? Levis and plaid shirts? "That'll be great," was all I could muster.

We walked into the kitchen and sat around a large table in the center of the room. It was a typical country kitchen - plenty of cupboards, a double sink, and a nice big wood stove with warming ovens above. Somehow I ended up sitting between Randy and his grandmother. As I looked at the huge platter of cookies being set on the table by Mrs. Redwing, the whole scene looked so utterly American I was beginning to think Indians just weren't all they were cracked up to be in the movies. Suddenly Mrs. Sunfield, who had all but ignored me until that moment, reached over, rested her hand on my arm, and said: "My husband took part in Whitman Massacre and was killed by white-eyes. Wanna cookie?" Everyone else at the table went silent.

By the time you get to the fourth grade, you know all about the Whitman Massacre. That was the time when several West Coast tribes fell upon the settlers just north of Perkins Prairie, killing most of them. The battle started at the Whitman farm and had been called the Whitman Massacre ever since. There was still a Whitman living in Perkins Prairie. He owned

11

the funeral home on Main Street. "I'm sorry your husband lost his life," I said.

"He took three scalps before they got him. I've got them in a box under my bed back home. Three scalps!"

Remembering what my grandfather and Mr. Borgstine said about not wanting to start the war all over again and not being sure how I should respond to her comment, I decided to change the subject. "What are white-eyes?" I asked.

"That's you," the old woman replied, folding her arms over her bosom and looking at me as if she expected me to draw a knife or something.

"Oh, Mother . . . please," Mrs. Redwing chided, picking up the cookie dish and offering me another.

"The old ones call Europeans white-eyes," Mr. Redwing explained. "My wife's mother doesn't approve of our moving into town, so she isn't in a very good mood," he continued.

"Fritz is part Algonquin," Randy interjected in an attempt to come to my defense. Mrs. Sunfield's expression softened at once. "What kinda Algonquin?" she asked.

"Micmac," I answered with a pride that surprised me.

"You not look Micmac, white-eyes, but little bit Algonquin is better than nothing. You want more milk? We got plenty," Mrs. Sunfield said, looking at me from behind squinted eyes and a wrinkled face that seemed on the verge of offering a real smile.

"Yes, please, ma'am, more cold milk would be great," I said, making sure I used my best manners but being careful not to break contact with her eyes. My dad once told me that if I came upon a bear in the woods I should stare it down rather than run because if I kept staring at it, the bear would think I wasn't afraid of him and take off for fear I knew something he didn't know. Mrs. Sunfield wasn't a bear but I somehow knew it was important to remain in eye contact until she looked away.

§§§§

After we finished our cookies and milk, Mrs. Redwing asked if I would show Randy and Willie around town. I was ecstatic over the idea. So were the guys. They both had bikes of their own. Pushing them to the end of the driveway, I said, "What do you wanna see first?"

"Let's drive over and see the grade school," Randy suggested.

"Any place you want is okay with me, just so long as I'm home for lunch," I responded.

"Same here," Willie agreed.

"You guys miss the reservation?" I asked as we began peddling our bikes in the direction of the grade school.

"I miss my friends," Willie said.

"I think Perkins Prairie is too big," Randy added.

"We ain't even got a thousand people livin' here," I replied.

"Well, that's five hundred more people than we got on the reservation right now," Willie told me.

13

"That surprises me. I thought reservations were big places with lots of people."

"There was in the olden days. But lots of young people move away even before they get married. There ain't no jobs on the reservation. People gotta have money to live," Randy said.

"They didn't have money in the olden days. They just lived off the land, didn't they?" I asked.

"We had wampum before we had money like you know it. Lots of people used to trade wampum for stuff," Willie informed me.

"What's wampum?"

"Beads and shells," Willie answered.

"Beads and shells?"

"To decorate stuff with. That shows wealth," Randy answered as we drove our bikes onto the blacktop that covered the Perkins Prairie Grade School's playgrounds. "Monkey bars!" he shouted. Randy brought his bike to a screeching halt and ran to the bars. Willie and I stopped and watched.

"He loves the monkey bars," Willie said.

"I'm not very good at them, myself." I said.

"Grandma Sunfield will like you forever now," he informed me.

"'Cause I'm Algonquin?"

"That helps a lot, but mostly because you didn't back down when she stared at you. Grandma believes that if a person backs down or looks away when she stares at them, it means that person can't be trusted. Grandma Sunfield trusts you now. She'll be lots nicer to you from now on. Can you speak any Micmac?"

"Nope. The Algonquin lady married my

grandpa's father. He was a Jew. She converted to his religion and kept kosher. We don't even know her American Indian name."

"I should tell ya, Fritz, we don't like being called American Indians. Christopher Columbus didn't really discover this country. It was here all along. He thought he had discovered a new way to get to India and that's why he called the people here Indians. But we're not Indians. We like to be called Quinault. We're part of the Salashan Nation just like you Micmacs are part of the Algonquin Nation. But we ain't Indians. I'm just tellin' ya so's you won't open your mouth and put your foot in it first time we take you up to the reservations with us."

"You'd be willing to take me up to the reservation?" I asked excitedly.

"If ya wanna and your mom and dad say it's okay . . . sure."

"Where you guys wanna go now?" I asked.

"I don't know. Where do you suggest? We gotta learn where everything is. We know where Main Street and the shops are. We went shoppin' with Mom and Grandma for groceries the other day and we saw where Dad's shop is gonna be," Randy answered.

"We could go out and you could meet my grandma and grandpa."

"Our grandfathers walk with the spirits now," Willie noted.

"You mean they're in heaven?" I asked.

"I'm not sure if Quinaults go to the same place as white-eyes," he answered.

"I'll bet we all go to the same places. Grandpa

15

says there's only one God no matter what we name him. Grandpa says we either go to heaven or hell or purgatory."

"I didn't know Jews believed in purgatory," Randy noted.

"My dad's folks are Catholics. My mom's people aren't Jews anymore. I don't know how's-a-come. They mostly don't go to church or if they do, they go to the Presbyterian.

"When Quinaults and other native peoples die, we go to the Great Spirit. He's an . . . what you people call an Indian. Once a missionary lady told Grandma Sunfield that if she didn't believe in Jesus, she wouldn't get into the Christian heaven and would go to hell. Boy was Grandma mad. She told the missionary lady she didn't want to spend eternity with a bunch of white-eyed land stealers anyway."

"I think there's only one heaven but it gots lots of names," I suggested.

"God never made one of anything!" Willie argued. "There are many clans, many tribes, many nations, just like there are many different kinds of fish and flowers and trees and rocks. What makes you think God would make just one heaven?"

"Because all the people of the earth are one family," I said. "We're all related to Adam and Eve."

"Oh, that's silly, Fritz. If we're all one family, how come you can't just drop into any house in town at dinner time and sit down and eat? There is lots of families," Randy noted.

"I'll have to ask Reverend Willis about that one over at the Presbyterian Church," I said, hoping to

16

change the subject.

§§§§

On the way to my grandparent's farm we stopped along the banks of Stump Lake. I wanted to show them one of my secret places just three blocks from the grade school.

"How come they call this Stump Lake?" Randy asked as we made our way down a steep path leading to the water below.

"Its real name is Lake Woolery. Back in the twenties, Old Man Woolery sold what was called Woolery's hollow to the city for a place to empty a flume diverted from White River to produce electricity and catch salmon and other fish that needed help gettin' upstream because of a big dam farther up the river. But everybody calls it Stump Lake because it was a hollow filled with trees. Now it's filled with stumps. There's real good fishin' in here but a lot a quicksand patches too . . . so us kids ain't allowed to fish down here."

"Any quicksand near the path?" Willie asked.

"Nope. I just wanted you to see my hidin' place. It's a great spot to get away from people. Hardly nobody comes down here."

"What's your grandpa's place like? He got animals?" Randy asked as we reached the bottom of the trail.

"Yup. He and Grandma have cows and pigs and

chickens, and pigeons and a couple of horses. They even got a mule but he's too old to work anymore. He just grazes all day. Once in a while Grandpa takes him greens from the garden. Grandpa says he's retired now."

"Grandma Sunfield has a little farm on the Muckelshoot Reservation. She lives in a government house but she's only got a few chickens," Willie added.

"Grandma Redwing lives in a Quinault house," Randy said with pride.

"What's a Quinault house?"

"It's a sort of converted tribal smokehouse down where the village used to be when Grandma Redwing was a little girl. Hers has two rooms. She had my dad build her a little lean-to made of cedar outside the back door that she uses like a woodshed and pantry. Grandma Redwing doesn't like white-eyes' houses. We have to wear moccasins when we visit her. She doesn't like white-eyes' shoes either. She likes the old ways," Randy said, tugging at some small fern-like plants growing from the moss on a tree beside him. "Want some wild licorice?" he asked, stripping a little dirt from the root of the plant and handing it to me.

"Licorice?"

"Taste it," he urged, handing some of the roots to Willie and putting what was left in his mouth.

I put the tip of the root between my teeth and bit into it. A sudden burst of licorice flavor filled my mouth. I pulled the remainder of the small root into my mouth with my tongue and began chewing it. "This does taste like licorice," I said.

"There's lots of good tasting things in the woods

and they're lots better for your teeth than candy," Randy said, looking around at the trees for additional ferns.

"Show me how to find them," I pleaded, walking over to a tree covered with thick moss.

"You look for these little frail ferns growing from the moss," Randy pointed out.

"Like these?" I asked, locating a small batch of the tiny ferns on a tree next to me.

"That's it," Willie said from his perch on a fallen tree beside the lake.

I pulled the fern from the moss and shook it clean. When I popped it into my mouth, I was pleased to find the flavor of licorice rekindle itself over my taste buds. "What other stuff is good to eat?" I asked.

"Most of it is good for something. Lots of it is medicine. Our grandmothers know about all of them. That watercress down there makes a great salad. Mom uses it in soups too. Did you ever eat baked cattail roots?" Willie asked, getting up to indicate he was ready to go out to my grandparent's farm.

"I don't think the English or the Polish know anything about baking cattails," I replied, starting back up the path towards our bicycles.

"It tastes a lot like sweet potato, only its better," Randy said, falling in beside me.

"How come your grandma Redwing doesn't want to live in a government house?" I asked as we climbed back up on our bikes and headed towards the Harding farm on the other side of town.

"She's not the only one. There are ten families still livin' in the old village. The government knocked down the longhouses back in 1935 but left the communal smokehouses standing. The majority of the tribal members moved into the government houses in what they now call New Quinault. But a few families and a few old single people converted the smokehouses into small dwellings. Some of their kids moved into the government houses as soon as they got married. Grandma says she will never leave her little shack," Willie explained.

"Aren't the government houses nicer?" I asked.

"Nice don't got nothin' to do with it," Randy said. "Grandma Redwing wants to live out the remainder of her days where the spirits of her ancestors still walk. It's as simple as that."

As we peddled our bikes through town, I pointed out the important stores like the Sweet Shop, the Dime Store, the Movie House, and which shops had the best selections of penny candy. When we reached the edge of the business district and the beginning of the residential area, I pointed out the Perkins Prairie Banner building where the town newspaper was published and the public library. "You guys wanna meet my folks and then peddle out to see my grandma and grandpa's farm?" I asked.

"Sounds good to me," Willie answered.

When we rode up to the house, Dad was sitting in his rocking chair on the front porch. Mom was sitting on the steps watching my sister Sonja play on the lawn. Dad was reading his hunting magazine. "This here's Willie and Randy Redwing," I announced, bringing my bike to a stop just before my front tire hit the front step. "Willie and Randy Redwing, this is my mom and dad."

"How do you do," my mother said, shading her eyes to get a better look at the two boys.

"We're just fine," Willie said, getting off his bike. He pushed down the kickstand with his foot and parked his bike in a standing position.

"What do you fellas think of Perkins Prairie by now?" Dad asked.

"This is the first chance we've had to see much more than what Dad showed us when we drove around town," Randy said.

"You boys hungry?" Mother asked.

"No ma'am. We just had cookies and milk at our place," Willie replied.

"Indians bake great chocolate chip cookies, Mom . . . and I met their Grandma Sunfield. She don't like white-eyes much but I told her we're part Algonquin except for Dad. We're gonna ride out around the custodial school and over to Grandma and Grandpa's farm," I said, trying to lump the day into one statement.

"What are white-eyes?" Mother asked.

"Europeans," Dad answered as if surprised she didn't already know the term.

"I'll tell you what. I'll promise not to call you redskins if you'll promise not to call me white-eyes," Mother smiled.

"That's a deal, Mrs. Harding," Willie was quick to respond.

"You boys watch for cars when you ride out around the school," Dad cautioned.

"We promise," the three of us said almost at

once.

"And ask Ma if she has any extra butter. We don't have any for lunches in the morning," Dad added, resuming his interest in the magazine.

The Cascade State School for the mentally retarded was built in the late 20's on land my grandfather sold to the state. All the buildings were white with red Spanish-styled roofs. There were covered walkways to all the buildings and beautiful lawns that stretched out from all directions from the complex which was set back about half a city block from the road. There were also several beautiful homes on the property that housed the superintendents, doctors and a few teachers. The place was considered a showpiece as far as institutions went. People drove from all over the state just to see it. By 1948, over half the town worked at *The School* as it came to be called. We seldom saw any of the residents who lived at the school except when a few of them came into town for a fieldtrip. Cascade State School had its own stores, sweet shop and movie house. It was like a small Spanish city built in the foothills. It had its own dairy farm, vegetable garden and orchards. All the chores were done by the residents who lived there under the supervision of state employees.

"My Grandpa Harding says that anyone capable enough to tend a garden or milk a herd of cows is capable enough to live outside the institution. He don't much like the place. He says it's more like a prison than a school and says he's sorry now he sold them the land," I commented as we peddled past the main entrance.

22

"It's kind of like a reservation then, huh?" Randy speculated.

"Except folks on the reservation can leave whenever they want to. The people who live there never get to even come out on the lawns as far as I can tell," I informed them.

But Willie and Randy had never seen anything like it. From the road the place looked like a collection of gleaming white mansions. The grounds and lawns were so well manicured the place looked like a resort where only wealthy people could afford to stay.

"It's hard to think of any place this lovely being like a prison. Surely nothing so pretty as this place could be as sinister as a prison," Randy speculated.

"I'm just tellin' you what my grandpa thinks," I answered.

When we arrived at my grandparent's farm, we rode our bikes into the north yard over the little wooden bridge Grandpa built to cross the stream surrounding their property on its north and western boundaries. The stream started in the foothills beyond The School and didn't end until it joined Spiketon River near Lower Bernette. It was one of hundreds of small creeks that moved down the mountains to join the awaiting waters of the sea.

Grandma and Grandpa Harding were sitting on lawn chairs under the big walnut tree between the root cellar and milk house. Grandpa was smoking his pipe. Grandma was plucking a chicken for dinner. We rode our bikes down the wooden sidewalk and parked them around the big chokecherry tree near where they sat. "This here's the Redwing boys," I announced as we walked up to them.

"They got individual names or do they just go by The Red Wing Boys?" Grandma asked without missing a pluck.

"The tall one's name is Randy but he's one year younger than Willie here.

"Well, how do you do Randy and Willie," Grandma said. She stopped her plucking as she spoke but resumed the task as soon as she finished speaking and formed a smile on her lips.

"Pretty good. Lots of new experiences," Willie smiled back.

"Where's your father going to put his cleaning establishment?" Grandpa asked.

"Next door to the Dime Store, sir," Randy answered.

"That's a good locations. There's good parking there and it's two blocks away from Orloski's shop," Grandpa replied.

"Their grandma on their dad's side of the family lives in a smokehouse on the Quinault Reservation, and their grandma that lives in Auburn doesn't like white-eyes," I blurted excitedly.

"Well, I hope it's a much bigger smokehouse than the one we have," Grandma commented.

"You got a smokehouse?" Randy asked.

"Why, certainly. We Poles have been smokin' fish and sausages probably just as long as you Indians have," Grandpa answered.

"They don't like to be called Indians, Grandpa; they like to be called Quinaults . . . even though they're half Nootka," I informed with probably too much pride in my voice.

"Well, actually, we even call ourselves Indian - just because that's the word every body else uses," Randy corrected.

"Really?" I questioned.

"Well, it's sort of like your grandpa and grandma is Polish but they is also Europeans. It's like that" Willie observed.

"Could we see your smokehouse?" Randy asked.

"Built it myself," Grandpa said with pride. He got up from his chair and began walking towards the eight foot wooden fence that separated the farm yard from the barnyard. The smokehouse was located at the end of a rhubarb patch down by the hen house were grandma kept her fryers and a few bantams.

The smoking cabinet is only about three by four by four, but the smokehouse itself was about six foot tall with an A-framed roof and tall chimney. It was made of thick sheets of iron Grandpa purchased from the shipyards years before. It was put together with rivets, just like a ship was done in those days. It had a huge metal door, plenty of shelf space on the inside for about twenty-three foot long poles upon which sausages could be hung or fish spread out to bask in the lavish fumes of vine maple and cherry wood. The entire iron smokehouse was placed on a brick foundation or fire box. The smokehouse had been used for so many years, its pungent smells perfumed the air around it for several feet in all directions.

"This here's one of the finest smokehouses in Perkins Prairie," I told the boys as we stepped in front of it.

"It sure is little," Willie observed.

"It looks more like a closet than a smokehouse," Randy agreed.

"What'cha talkin' about? This is considered one of the finest smokehouses in these parts," I declared.

"Sure is," Grandpa confirmed.

"Quinault smokehouses are the size of small houses. That's why they're called smokehouses. This ain't much bigger than my Grandma Sunfield's broom closet," Willie asserted, opening the doors and peering inside. "But it smells right."

"Well, this one is just for one family. I'll bet the ones on the reservation are for the whole tribe," Grandpa observed.

"That's true," Randy said . . . and Indians never knew how to make steel. Ours are always made of wood."

"There is an old Polish nursery rhyme that talks about smokehouses that were made from poles and skins back in the days when our people roamed the Russian steppes as hunters." Grandpa told him.

"We have a story in the tribe that says the same thing! In the olden days Quinault people made smokehouses with poles and skins too. But the skins finally got too brittle and would fall apart. Then one day Kwatee threw a lightening bolt at an eagle perched high in a tree. Eagle was too quick for Kwatee's throw and escaped but the lightening bolt hit the cedar tree and split it into hundreds of cedar shakes. An old medicine man saw all this while walking back to the village from a vision quest. When he returned to the village, he took the men back into the hills to see what

26

the lightening bolt had done to the tree. The men prayed over this amazing sight and one of them came up with the idea of using the shakes to make the walls and roof of the tribe's smokehouses. It's a very old story. Someone always retells it at Pow Wow," Willie said.

"Who is Kwatee?" I asked.

"Kwatee is the changer. He is a mischievous demon-god who lives on the coasts of Washington and Oregon. Some claim to have seen his antics as far north as Alaska."

"Is he like the Devil?" Grandpa Harding asked.

"Oh, no. He can't condemn anybody to hell. He's changed a few people into rocks and stuff like that but the Great Spirit is much too powerful to let Kwatee be like the Devil. No matter how evil Kwatee tries to be, something good always comes from his actions. There's always a big change of some kind too. That's why he's called the changer."

"I think I like this Kwatee much better than the Devil," Grandpa chuckled.

"We aren't allowed to believe in the Devil," Randy said, very seriously.

"And why is that?" Grandma asked.

"Our family ain't Christians. Most of us Quinaults still worship like in the olden days. It's really the same God but we don't use Jesus for much. He's kinda new to the world by comparison."

"Yes, I suppose he is," Grandpa mused.

"Fritz, when you come back from showin' the boys the farm, bring me three sausages from the milk house. I'll fix your friends a little taste of Polish sausage and give them two to take home for the family," Grandma instructed.

"Oh, that'll be great, Mrs. Harding. Thanks," Willie grinned.

After a tour of the barn and the rest of the outbuildings, the boys and I wandered back towards the house. "I'm gettin' hungry, how 'bout you guys?" I inquired.

"That bike ride sapped all the chocolate cookies out of my system," Willie acknowledged.

"How come they keep the sausage in the milk house?" Randy asked as I opened the door to the small white building under the furthest branches of a black cherry tree.

"The building has real thick walls and concrete floor and a real thick roof too. It stays very cool in here," I answered.

"But don't that make the milk smell like smoked sausage?" Randy questioned.

"Not that I ever noticed. Grandma keeps cheesecloth over the tins of milk. Maybe that keeps the smell from gettin' to them."

"How come she keeps the milk in those tall coffee cans on the counter?" Willie asked.

"She lets the cream come to the top. Grandma makes her own butter. I get to turn the handle on the churn when I'm here. She always skims the cream off the top. Most everybody uses it in their coffee. After she skims off the cream, she pours the milk into one of them big milk cans in the tub," I answered, removing three sausages from the thick wooden poles that started a concrete sink. The sink was filled with cold water and large cans of milk waiting to be taken to the side of the road early the next morning for the milk company to pick them up. From there the milk company takes them, along with the extra milk from other local farms, to the dairy to be pasteurized, bottled and sold to people in town.

§§§§

On the way back to their house, I took the boys by the back end of the feed stores by the old railway station and showed them a secret entrance that led under the warehouses. "This is where everybody comes to smoke cigarettes if they got any. None of the grown-ups know about this place. It's just for kids. But you gotta make sure the senior high boys aren't down here before you come in. Some of them get pretty mean and they'll steal your smokes," I warned them.

"We don't smoke except during ceremony," Willie said.

"I do," Randy admitted.

"You do not. You're just trying to fit in," Willie observed.

"I found half a pack just before we moved to town and I smoked four of them. I still got the rest left. I got them right here. You want one, Fritz?" Randy retorted.

"Sure. I don't inhale yet . . . but I love smokin'. Makes me feel like Cary Grant or John Wayne."

Randy took a rumpled pack of Wing cigarettes

out of his ankle sock where he had hidden it, took out a slightly bent cigarette and passed the pack to me. I pulled out another and handed the pack to Willie. "I'm afraid I'd get sick," he confessed, shaking his head no.

"Not if you don't inhale. We can make it a ceremony," Randy said.

"Quinaults and Nootkas use tobacco for sacred ceremonies. But this ain't no sacred ceremony," Will responded.

"We can make it one . . . a friendship ceremony," Randy suggested.

"I don't know . . . what if Mom and Dad smell smoke on our breaths. We'll get paddled for sure," Willie murmured.

"We'll chew gum. You're just chicken," Randy insisted.

"Oh, all right," Willie conceded.

We lit our cigarettes and blew smoke into the damp air under the warehouse. Willie insisted we make a ceremony of it. We each vowed our faithfulness in friendship. Willie had us stand in a circle and blow smoke into it. "The circle is sacred in all Indian ways," Willie said. "The smoke in this circle comes from inside us and makes us friends until death."

"How about *blood brothers?*" I suggested.

"Blood brothers it is," Randy asserted. He blew a large puff of smoke into the circle. His brother and I did the same.

Just before we arrived at the Redwing home, I spied some wild nasturtiums growing alongside the road and stopped to pick them.

"You like flowers?" Willie asked.

30

"Oh, yes, but I'm picking these for your mother. I thought she might like them," I answered.

Both he and Randy gave a little giggle, but I thought it was just because Indians didn't pick wild flowers to give as gifts. But undaunted by my suspicions, I picked the nasturtiums until I had a large bouquet to give to their mother.

When we arrived Randy and Willie were filled with stories about their tour of town and the family farm. "His grandpa has a really tiny smokehouse but he sure knows how to make good use of it. Just wait until you taste Fritz's grandpa's sausage. He says to boil it in an inch of water in a fry pan until the water is almost gone," Willie informed his parents as he handed them the sausages wrapped in waxed paper held together with garden string.

"Well, wasn't that sweet of Mr. Harding. You be sure and thank your grandfather for us, Fritz, and I'll do the same the first time I actually meet him," Mrs. Redwing said, graciously.

"Fritz brought you something else," Randy said with a sort of giggle.

"Here, Mrs. Redwing, I picked you some wild nasturtiums. I wanted to give you something pretty," I said, blushing because I thought she was pretty too and suddenly afraid she might think I was flirting.

"Why that's very thoughtful of you, Fritz. Between you and your grandpa, you've supplied us with almost half of our supper tonight," she said, taking the flowers from my hand.

"Supper?" I asked inquisitively.

"Quinaults, all Indian people, eat those flowers

and leaves," Willie announced, joining in his brother's giggle.

"Mmm, mmm, good," Clarence Redwing said, smelling the package of sausages.

"You eat nasturtiums?" I asked.

"They're very good. Sometimes I just rinse them and add them to a salad . . . but the leaves are also very good when added to soups and meat loafs," Mrs. Redwing assured me.

"Oh," I muttered. I wasn't disappointed. I was glad she liked the gift. I was just surprised that it would become part of their dinner.

"Oh, my," Audrey Redwing cooed, "I'll bet you brought these to me for a bouquet. I'm sorry, Fritz, it didn't dawn on me that your people don't eat these too."

"That's okay. It looks like I have a lot to learn about Indians," I answered.

"Would you like to stay for supper," Audry asked.

"Oh, no, thank you, ma'am, I gotta go home. Mom's fixin' chicken. My aunt and uncle and cousin are gonna be there, then we're all going to a movie. I'm probably late now. I better get going," I said, looking at my watch and heading for the door.

"You tell your grandpa to bring me one of his suits and your grandma to bring me one of her best dresses. I'll clean them for free," Mr. Redwing said, walking me to the back door.

"I'll tell them, Mr. Redwing, but he's real fond of the Orloski family," I sighed.

"You tell your grandpa I'm not trying to steal

Orloski's business. I just want to thank him for his courtesy," he said. "After that he can take his clothes back to the other fella. This here little town has three grocery stores, two barber shops, three taverns and its own bank. I think it can support two dry cleaning shops. Things will be just fine, Fritz. Don't you worry about anything," Mr. Redwing said, reaching down and mussing up my hair a bit. My grandfather did that all the time. I know it was a gesture of affection and reassurance. All of the sudden I was no longer worried about the tension that might happen in town between the Orloskis and the Redwings.

As I was about to turn the doorknob and open the back door, I realized that Grandma Sunfield had walked up behind us. I turned to say goodbye to her.

"You can tell your mama she done a good job by you, boy. You ask her if you can come with the boys to see my place sometime. I'll show you a Muckelshoot smokehouse big enough to hold a party in," she remarked, giving me her first grin. It revealed that she was missing one lower tooth.

Oh, I will, Mrs. Sunfield. Thank you for the invitation. I would love to visit your place."

"You call me grandma like the boys do, if you like, Fritz. It's the Indian way. Even people not blood related call old women grandmother and old men grandfather. We are all really related in the Great Spirit . . . and it's a way of showin' respect. Okay?" Her smile grew larger.

"Okay!" I smiled back. "I mean, okay, Grandmother."

"That's it. You got it," the old woman said

patting me on the shoulder.

"I told you you were in like Flynn," Willie reminded me.

Chapter Two

Scalps from the Whitman Massacre

I LEFT FOR SCHOOL early the next morning because I wanted to be sitting on the front steps when Clarence and Audrey Redwing drove up in their 1948 black Ford to sign their children into school. I pretended I only wanted to walk them into the building and introduce them to Mr. Baker, our principal, and afterwards walk them to class. I knew that Willie would be placed in the sixth-grade classroom but Randy would be in my class. The truth was that I wanted to walk Randy into the classroom so everybody in Mrs. Montgomery's fifth-grade class would know that the only real Indians ever to attend fifth grade in Perkins Prairie were already my best friends.

It didn't turn out that way though. The Redwings parked their car on the east side of the building and went to Mr. Baker's office by the back door. I was almost late for class. I just made it to my seat when the second bell rang. Mrs. Montgomery was already taking roll.

When she finally calling out our names, she walked to the front of the room and wrote Randy Redwing's at the top and at the center of the blackboard. Then she removed her glasses and held them in her right hand. That's what she always did when she was about to tell us something that wasn't an assignment. Sometimes it would be an announcement that there would be a fire drill that day and we should remember how to exit the building in orderly fashion. Sometimes it was to announce a field trip or special event. I knew that today she was going to tell the class a little something about Randy Redwing.

"Class, we will be adding a new member to the class. I've written his name on the board because it is an unusual name. It isn't a name like Smith or Jones or names with which you've grown up. Randy and his family are American Indians. They have moved to Perkins Prairie from the Muckelshoot Reservation in Auburn. I hope you will greet him as you would any other student coming into this class and make him feel welcome. Are there any questions?" she concluded.

Teddy Finkelman's hand shot up immediately.

"Yes, Teddy?" Mrs. Montgomery asked, pointing her folded glasses at him.

Teddy stood to his feet. "My dad says Indians all beat their wives and can't handle their liquor, and their relatives will probably come into town some Saturday night, get drunk, and shoot up the town." He sat back down.

Teddy's accusations stunned me. They seemed to have stunned Mrs. Montgomery too because before she could address his comments, Doug Wallace, whose dad owned the meat market in the Redfront Grocery Store, began talking without raising his hand.

"My dad says Indians don't pay their bills. He's not givin' any credit to any Indians in his store and he says none of the other stores is gonna either." Doug almost shouted the words.

Mrs. Montgomery looked as shocked as I felt. Before she could regain control of the class, Sarah Baker stood and began talking. Sarah always had perfect manners. She was the principal's daughter and I guess she was told to set a good example. "My dad says we gotta let them into the school and we gotta educate them . . . but we don't have to play with them if we don't want to. I don't play with everybody in this class and it won't be no different when they're here." She sat down without waiting for a comment from Mrs. Montgomery.

"Our priest told Mama they are pagans. Mama says we aren't to play with any damn pagans," Ray Neuronski said without raising his hand or standing up.

"I ain't sittin' by no damn Indian!" Archie Malone shouted from the back of the room.

"Me, neither," Norbert Ronne, who was teacher's pet, said from his front row seat.

I raised my hand but began speaking before being acknowledged. "I like them," I said. "I spent part of yesterday showin' them the town and playgrounds. My grandpa sent the Polish sausage for dinner last night and I think it's cool that we have real Indians in our town," I blurted.

"I think we have to give them a chance," Margie Olson chimed. She was the one whose mother was supposed to be part Eskimo.

Mrs. Montgomery tapped her ruler on the desk. That was our sign to quiet down and pay attention. "You children will be polite to the Redwing children. You will not call them names. They will be included in all supervised games on the playground, and you are all expected to treat them just like you would anyone else moving into Perkins Prairie. Failure to do so will be reflected on your deportment grade. I don't care if you're an "A" student in every subject I teach. If you can't behave like moral, civil human beings to the Redwing children, that fact will be reflected in your grades. Anyone showing discrimination toward any of the Redwing children can expect an "F" from me in social skills and deportment," she declared.

Most of us were speechless. Mrs. Montgomery was always strict but never stern. Today her voice took a much different tone and everyone understood that she meant business.

"But they're Indian!" Teddy Finkelman cried, raising his hand but speaking before he was recognized.

"I know they are Indians, Teddy. Remember your Sunday school lesson . . . *yellow, black, or white, they are precious in His sight . . . Jesus loves the little children of the world.*" Mrs. Montgomery also taught the Sunday school class where Teddy attended church, and while she didn't usually mix religion with school . . . today it seemed more than appropriate. "I will remind you that our holiday called Thanksgiving is a day of feasting we inherited from the American Indian. There were more Indians present at that first Thanksgiving than Europeans. If it weren't for what the Indians knew about surviving the harsh winters on the East Coast, the first pilgrims would probably have all died off. If you like eating beef jerky and squash . . . I will remind you that those foods, and many more, were introduced into the American diet by American Indians. You even speak words from local Indian languages . . . Seattle,

Snoqualmie, Enumclaw . . . those are all towns given Indian names. But whether you like it or not . . . the Redwings are here to stay and anyone in this class discriminating against them can expect an "F" in deportment on their report card and that's final." Her face looked red with anger although her voice was under amazing control.

At just that moment Randy was escorted into our classroom by Mr. Baker. I wondered if the same commotion had gone on in Willie's class before he got there. And what of his little sisters? Had their classmates protested as well. I felt very uncomfortable but didn't know what to do about it. I was flabbergasted. I had been so excited about the prospect of having real Indians finally living in our town, it never occurred to me their presence in our community would be disturbing to anyone. The moment Mr. Baker walked into the room, we all dutifully rose to our feet.

"Mrs. Montgomery, children, I would like you to meet Randy Redwing. He and his family have moved to Perkins Prairie from Auburn. Please welcome him," he said in his booming voice.

The phrase *please welcome him* was our cue to applaud. Sarah Baker and I were the only ones who clapped with much enthusiasm. Everyone else followed the rule but with reluctance I felt sure was sensed by Mrs. Montgomery, Mr. Baker and Randy. Randy smiled at the class but when his eyes met mine, I could tell he was uncomfortable.

Mrs. Montgomery assigned Randy to the empty seat just in front of me and next to Sarah Baker.

Randy and I were both pleased with the seating arrangement and winked at each other as he carried his books down the aisle to his seat.

All this time, my best friend, Jerry Cotton, who sat right behind me, had remained silent. But as soon as Mrs. Montgomery turned her back to begin writing our assignment on the board, he leaned forward and whispered in my ear. "I can smell Big Chief Brown Blanket of the Poo-Poo Tribe from here, can't you?"

I was stunned. It hadn't occurred to me that Jerry wouldn't like Indians. I wanted to turn and snap at him but remembering what my grandmother always said about catching more flies with honey than with salt, I decided to ignore his comment for the moment and discuss the issue during recess.

At Perkins Prairie Grade School, children had four options at recess. They could play heavily supervised games and sports in the gymnasium, decide upon a multitude of play equipment and games outside the building, and remain in the basement to play tag or hopscotch, or go to the library and look at books, read, or do homework. A lot of us liked to slip into the bushes running alongside the school building to gossip. I was so intent on speaking to Jerry Cotton about his comment, I didn't realize until after I got outside that none of the Redwing children came out of the building. Jerry caught up to me just as I approached the bushes alongside the building. "How come you stood up for those damn Indians?" he blurted out between gasps for breath.

"I like them and their whole family. I rode my bike over to their place yesterday and met 'em. They're just people. Their other grandmother lives on the Quinault Reservation in a real cedar shake Indian house. They're just people! Why wouldn't I stand up for them?"

"They're Indians! They killed off half the town. Mom was a Whitman before she married Dad. I suppose you've heard about the Whitman Massacre," he retorted.

"That's ancient history. Besides, we also had a war with Germany . . . but there's lots of kids whose parents or grandparents moved here from German. What's the difference?" I was genuinely perplexed by his attitude.

"They're god-damn Indians, Fritz. Perkins Prairie is a white man's town. You let one Indian move in and pretty soon the whole damn tribe will move in and they'll start shootin' out our windows and smokin' salmon on the sidewalks."

"Where did you ever here anything so dumb?"

"From my dad . . . and it ain't dumb! You're dumb! Indians ain't civilized enough to live in towns. That's why the god-damn government put them on reservations in the first place. They eat dogs, Fritz. They're animals!"

"That's just crazy talk. I visited their home . . . they don't even have any bows and arrows. Their house looks just like anybody else's on the inside. My folks met them. So did my grandma and grandpa. They liked the boys just fine. Grandma and Grandpa sent home some Polish sausage as a welcome-to-town gift. Indians are no different than Polish people or anybody else. Besides, Indians have been livin' here long before our people got here. It was their land first."

"My dad says I'm not supposed to play with them and I ain't gonna, no matter what Mrs. Montgomery or Mr. Baker say," Jerry insisted.

"Well, I'm gonna play with them. Their grandmother, Mrs. Sunfield, invited me to visit her home on the Muckelshoot Reservation and my dad says I can go and I'm gonna," I asserted.

"You're just tryin' to be difficult," Jerry declared. "You're always tryin' to be different than everybody else."

"That's nuts. I'm pleased they wanna be my friends."

"How you gonna be friends with them when we're best friends?" The words sounded more like a threat than a question.

"You got lots of friends besides me that you do stuff with," I noted.

"Yeah, but they ain't Indians!"

"I'm part Indian," I said with pride.

"You are not! You're English and Polish. I met you're grandma on your mother's side. She's got an English accent."

"That's true but my mom's real dad was half Scottish half Micmac. He was born in Nova Scotia. His dad married a Micmac woman."

"What the hell is a Micmac?"

"It's one of the tribes that live on the East Coast. They're part of the Algonquin Nation."

"You're makin' all that up!"

"I am not. It's true. You can ask my mom."

42

"Then how come you never told me before?"

"I guess I didn't think about it. But when we play cowboys and Indians, I'm always the Indian. How come you didn't tell me you were an Indian hater before?"

"You're a damn liar, Fritz Harding. You know damn well you ain't no part-Indian. You're Polish and English!"

"I'm one-eighth Micmac and damn proud of it," I assured him.

""Well, I'm gonna ask your mother and if you're lyin' to me, you gotta give me a quarter," Jerry threatened.

"I ain't givin' you no quarter and I'm going back inside to see if I can find Willie and Randy," I said, turning back toward the building.

"If you're gonna be friends with them god-damn Indians, you can't be my best friend anymore!" Jerry shouted after me.

"Don't say anything you might be sorry for later," I retorted.

"I ain't gonna be sorry . . . especially if you ain't nothin' but a damn Indian yourself," he snarled.

I whirled back around, looked him in the eyes and began singing the words to the song Mrs. Montgomery recited for us in class. *Be they yellow, red, black or white, they are precious in His sight. Jesus loves the little children of the world.*

"That's because Jesus' folks weren't killed in the Whitman Massacre. Maybe if he'd been born in Perkins Prairie, he'd feel a whole lot different," Jerry snapped.

"You're just full of crazy talk today," I shouted over my shoulder as I headed into the building.

"And you ain't nothin' but a god-damn Big Chief Brown Blanket in the Poo-Poo Tribe," Jerry shouted after me.

§§§§

I found Randy and Willie in the library with their sisters looking at magazines. "What's up?" I whispered.

"We're lookin' at magazines," Randy whispered back.

"I can see that. I meant how come you guys didn't go outside?"

"Mom and Dad asked us to bring the girls into the library and sit with them at least for the first week or until they meet some kids they like," Willie told me in hushed words.

I looked over at Amy-Lynn and Darleen. They were so engrossed in their magazines, they hadn't noticed I had joined them. I got up and selected a couple of National Geographics and joined them at the table. We browsed through our magazines in silence.

When I got home from school, I started doing my chores. I was carrying in my third load of wood when Dad drove up in his pickup. "How was school?" he asked, grabbing a handful of kindling to carry with him into the house.

"Not so good."

"Hard day with math?" he asked.   Arithmetic was never my favorite subject.

"Nope, I did okay today. But some of the kids in my class said terrible things about the Redwings . . . especially Jerry Cotton. He's a real Indian hater."

"To their faces?" he inquired.

"No . . . but before Randy got to class, some of the kids said terrible things when Mrs. Montgomery talked to us about him joining us."

"What kind of terrible things?"

"Like they would get drunk and not pay their bills and pretty soon the whole town would be overrun with Indians."

"Jerry said stuff like that?"

"Especially Jerry. He called Randy *Big Chief Brown Blanket of the Poo-Poo Tribe* . . . but only in my ear . . . and later on the playground . . . and when I told him I was part Indian, he had a fit."

I elaborated on the comments of the class and Jerry as we made our way to the kitchen. Dad got a beer from the refrigerator and a small Kraft cheese glass from the cupboard. He always liked to take his beer in a small glass, and the glasses the Kraft cheese spreads came in were just right. We had a whole collection of them. Mother also used them for juice glasses. She even made high mountain blackberry jam in them, sealing the stuff with melted paraffin. Everyone on both sides of the family always got a jar of Mom's famous high mountain blackberry jam. It was a tradition.

"I'm sorry you and Jerry had such a big fight. I can see you're pretty upset about it," Dad said, pouring the little glass full of beer.

"He don't like Indians . . . and if he don't like Indians, we can't be best friends anymore. He said so . . . but even if he hadn't said it . . . I would have to stop being his best friend. How you supposed to be friends with somebody that hates the very blood ya gots inside?"

"Hell, you ain't got enough Indian in you to get a free feather at an eagle catch. But if Jerry don't want nothin' to do with Indians, there ain't nothin' else you can do about it. The important thing is that you stood up for what's right. I'm real proud of you," Dad said, extending the half-filled glass toward me. None of us kids ever got a sip of beer very often. When we did, it was for a very special reason. I took the glass in both hands, being careful not to spill any of it, and took a small sip like you see people in the movies do when they're first served a fine wine at a restaurant, then handed the glass back to him.

"Go on, take a second sip. This is a special day. We're drinking a toast," he said, pushing the glass back toward me.

"What' we toastin'?" I asked, taking my second sip. I didn't really like the taste of beer . . . but I knew grown-ups did, and it was very important to me to do grown-up things whenever I was allowed.

"We're toastin' doing what's right," he said, filling the glass back to the brim and lifting it to his mouth. He drank down the contents in two quick swallows. "To the little guy," he said.

"To the little guy!" I affirmed.

After finishing my homework, I rode my bike

back to the Redwing home. Randy and Willie were roller skating on the sidewalk. They were amazingly good. I asked them if they knew they were allowed to skate on the tennis courts over at T'Kopachuck High School. They didn't even know we had tennis courts in Perkins Prairie. Within minutes they had secured permission from their parents to try their skills on the courts and we were on our way. We stopped by my place to pick up my skates.

Both of them could skate backwards, do pirouettes like ballet dancers, jump over things, race and do a dozen other tricks that demonstrated they had practiced their skills for a very long time. "Where did you guys learn to skate like that?" I asked, feeling embarrassed by the fact that all I could do was skate forwards without falling down.

"We have a skating rink at both Muckelshoot and Quinault," Randy said, using his toes to bring himself to a complete stop. "We used to practice a lot."

"Wish we had good wood floors to skate on. We have much better skates in our closets at home but they can only be used on wooden floors," Willie said, sitting down beside me on the bleachers.

"On Wednesday nights, they allow us to skate in the grade school gymnasium. It has a special wooden floor and they have a huge Wurlitzer jukebox in there filled with great skating music and some popular stuff too. Perkins Prairie and Thunderclaw and some of the other small towns around here have a skating competition every year. Nobody from these parts ever wins, although sometimes Jerry Cotton comes in third or gets honorable mention. He's pretty good but you guys are better than anyone I've ever seen take home the grand prize. I'll bet you could win the trophy if you tried," I said, unable to contain my excitement over the idea.

At school Tuesday and Wednesday, things stayed pretty much the same as they had been on Monday. Jerry Cotton didn't speak to me in class, and each recess I spent my time in the library with the Redwings. As far as I could tell, I was the only student in school speaking to Willie and Randy. But Wednesday night things changed in a big way for everyone in Perkins Prairie.

We waited to bike over to the grade school gymnasium until after I thought the long lines formed while kids plunked down their quarters to rent a pair of shoe-skates had subsided. There didn't seem to be any point in setting them up for abuses from Jerry or anyone else while standing in line.

"I see you boys have your own skates," Mrs. Baker, who collected the entrance fees, said.

"Yes, ma'am," Willie responded.

"Ten cents with your own skates, twenty-five cents if you use ours," she said without smiling.

We placed our money on the little table and went in. I walked over to the skate renting stall and handed Mr. Baker my green ticket which showed I had paid to rent a pair of indoor skates. By the time I returned to the side bench where Randy and Willie headed to put on their skates, they were already standing in them and eager to get out on the floor. I glanced at some of the kids skating past us. Most were giving disapproving looks to the boys and me as they passed by.

Once I had my skates on, we glided to the jukebox. Willie slipped a nickel in while Randy glanced at the selections. Number twenty-seven," he told his brother. "That's *The Skater's Waltz* by Strauss."

We stood around the jukebox watching the other skaters go around and around the rink. There were a few kids I didn't recognize who actually skated fairly well . . . nothing fancy, just good steady skating. When Jerry Cotton skated past us, he tried to show off by turning to skate backwards, but he lost his footing and crashed to the floor looking indignant. He did not look our way.

As soon as the introductory music to *The Skater's Waltz* began, the three of us skated onto the floor. Randy and Willie quickly moved ahead of me and took their places in the flow of skaters moving around the rink.

At first, they just skated around the building with the general flow of skaters. But gradually they began doing little extras that hinted in the direction of their real skills and nimbleness. I didn't see any obvious cue pass between them but at a certain point in the music, both began executing complicated graceful moves no one else in the room could come close to executing. Each demonstration of their skills became more complicated than the one preceding. Soon they were like dancers being ignited into a new and exciting choreography by nothing more than the rhythmic and melodic strains of the great German waltz

Soon all the other skaters including Mr. Rufus Twin, who supervised skate night and coordinated the yearly competition, and I were standing or sitting along the sidelines watching Randy and Willie execute their graceful and stylistic skating interpretations of the waltz. It was as if Strauss had written the music just for them. They moved from one end of the rink to the other displaying their abilities with such polish and perfection, some of their artistry was awarded by applause and whistles from the circular crowd gathered about the rink. Randy and Willie seemed oblivious of the crowd watching and applauding them. What they were doing was art. Nothing but the end of the music would interrupt it.

As the waltz moved toward its final movements, the two adept skaters pirouetted the length of the gymnasium, then glided to the center of the rink to a graceful stop. Then, to everyone's surprise, just as the music ended, both boys did the splits, lifted their arms gracefully above their heads and bowed from the waist.

The crowd was stunned and speechless. I glanced across the room to Jerry Cotton. From where I stood, his face appeared to reveal a mixture of extreme hate and envy that were at the boiling point. Mr. Twin rushed out to the center of the rink extending his hands to help both Randy and Willie to their feet. "Take a bow, guys, you deserve it," he said in a voice loud enough to be heard throughout the gymnasium.

The place went wild with applause and whistles. I started skating over to them to offer my congratulations, but before I could reach them they were surrounded by kids offering them accolades or asking for advice on improving their own skills. By the time I made my way through the crowd to where they were standing, Mr. Twin's loud and burly voice asked for everyone's attention.

"Providing their parents give their okay, Randy and Willie Redwing have just agreed to represent Perkins Prairie at the skating competitions this fall, and I have told them they can use the gymnasium to practice any night of the week. They in turn have agreed to give free skating lessons and demonstrations to anyone who shows up while they are practicing."

The crowd went wild again. I gave a thumbs-up and quick wink to them and returned to one of the benches along the wall. This was their moment and something in me knew I should not try to step into their spotlight. Eventually they both skated over to me, gave a brief thank you, and skated back into the throng of kids moving to the music around the rink. I became so engrossed in watching them show Teddy Finkelman and Doug Wallace how to skate backwards, I didn't notice when Jerry Cotton seated himself next to me. "You think they'd be willing to give me some pointers, Old Buddy?" he asked.

"Why don't you ask them. They don't know you called Randy and me Big Chief Brown Blanket of the Poo-Poo Tribe," I retorted, perhaps more sternly than I intended.

"That was before I knew how good they could skate," he offered weakly.

"Oh, I see. As long as dirty old Indians are especially talented . . . then you want to be their friends," I said, looking over at him for the first time.

"I've been thinkin' about what Mrs. Montgomery said. Maybe my dad is wrong about Indians. When I told my mom about Randy being in my class and reminded her about the Whitman Massacre, she told me that was ancient history and that I should move beyond it."

"Your mother is right."

"Yeah, I know. So you think they'd give me some pointers?"

"Mr. Twin said that anybody who showed up while they're practicing can get help. I guess all you have to do is show up."

"I was hopin' for some extra help."

"You'll have to ask Randy or Willie about that."

"And maybe you and me could do something together sometime . . . maybe even invite the Redwings along."

"Why, Jerry Cotton, you mean you still want to be friends even though I'm part Micmac . . . just another Big Chief Brown Blanket of the Poo-Poo tribe?"

"Ah, come on, Fritz. I never think of you as an Indian."

"Well, I am part Indian and from now on I'm gonna talk about it lots more because I'm gonna be Randy and Willie's best friend too. I wanna know as much about being Indian as I can learn."

"Okay . . . then we can all be best friends."

"You're sure this isn't just because you want them to teach you to be a better skater?"

"Nope. Havin' you as my best friend is more important than learning to skate better."

"Then, I say yes," I told him.

Jerry slipped his arm over my shoulder and gave

me a quick hug. Then we both got up and joined the other skaters on the floor.

§§§§

The next day Grandmother Sunfield asked to be driven back to her home on the Muckelshoot Reservation. I was invited to go along for the ride. Mother wasn't exactly keen on the idea of my going with them but Dad felt the experience would be good for me. The only thing he asked was that Clarence call him so he could make sure Mr. Redwing actually wanted me along for the weekend and that my inclusion wasn't a plot cooked up among the boys and me.

Clarence Redwing did better than telephone Dad, he dropped by the house late Thursday afternoon. Dad had just gotten home from work so he invited Clarence in for a beer.

"Our two boys are very fond of Fritz. We all are. He's a fine boy," Mr. Redwing began.

"We're pretty fond of him too . . . but he can be a pushy kid. I just wanted to make sure he didn't invite himself along this weekend. He did mention something about Mrs. Sunfield not taking much to white-eyes," Dad confessed.

"Well, that's true. My wife's mother has her prejudices. But she is genuinely fond of Fritz. She actually extended the invitation herself. She doesn't like most people . . . it's not just white-eyes . . . hell, there are times when I'm not even sure she likes me,"

Clarence laughed.

"She sounds a lot like my mother-in-law," Dad said, lifting his little Kraft glass filled with beer in a toast. "Is there anything special Fritz should bring with him?"

"Just a change of clothes and his toothbrush," Clarence answered.

Once it was clear I was actually going, I didn't listen to the rest of the conversation. I dashed into the dining room where we kept our telephone and dialed 3734 to tell Randy and Willie I could go.

Friday seemed to last forever. The day literally limped from morning to afternoon. All I could think about was being on a real Indian reservation. Even though all the Redwing children played outdoors during recess for the first time, I was oblivious to everything except the slow ticking of the big clock on the west wall of Mrs. Montgomery's classroom.

The last bell of the day finally rang. The Redwing boys and I walked their little sisters back to their house and helped Clarence pack his mother-in-law's things in the trunk of the family car.

"Us guys will sleep in the attic at Grandma's," Randy told me as the three of us jumped in the back seat of the Redwing automobile. "She has all sorts of neat stuff in the attic."

"What sorts of stuff?" I asked

"She's got a big old trunk up there with tomahawks and arrows and leather clothes from the old day. It's just full of stuff," Willie affirmed as the Redwing's 1948 Ford headed down the river road that lead past Perkins Prairie to the Muckelshoot

Reservation.

We played the alphabet game during our drive. Grandma Sunfield began the game by pointing out an "A" on a sign that read *Auburn 37 miles*. By the time we pulled off the main highway onto the road that led to the reservation, we were stuck on the letter "Q." I kept hoping we'd see a Quaker Oil sign but none came into view

""Game over," Willie announced as we drove past a large hand-carved sign informing us we had just passed onto the reservation

"How come?" I asked. "We haven't gotten to "Z" yet."

"We don't put up signs on the reservation except for street signs," Grandma Sunfield told me.

I sat in silence watching out the car window expecting to see something Indian to pass before me but all I saw were woods and fields, an occasional small farm, or groups of houses. "It doesn't look much like a reservation," I said with more surprise than disappointment.

"What did you expect to see?" Willie asked.

"I don't know. Teepees, I guess," I answered as I pressed my nose to the window thinking that if I got closer to it, I might see something decidedly Indian.

"Northwest Indians don't live in teepees, silly," Randy giggled.

"They don't?"

"No. We mostly lived in longhouses and lodges," Clarence answered from the front seat.

"Big houses built of cedar," Grandma Sunfield added.

"You mean that in the old days Indian people lived in houses with four walls and a roof just like the houses in Perkins Prairie?"

"Well, they weren't exactly like the houses in Perkins Prairie. Several related families might live in a lodge or longhouse. But for the most part they were just big houses made of cedar logs, boards and shakes," Mr. Redwing explained.

That seemed far less romantic than the images I had conjured up in my mind when all of the sudden some totem poles came into view.

"Those are totems of the clans that live along this road," Grandma Sunfield explained.

"Is one of them yours?" I asked.

"Oh, yes. The one in the middle. The tall one. That belonged to my father. I had the tribal council bring it here in nineteen and five when my husband and I moved to the reservation. Slow down, Clarence, so the boy can get a good look at it," she instructed.

Mr. Redwing brought the car to a standstill just across from the totem poles and told me to get out and take a better look if I liked. I was out of the car before he finished his sentence. "They're wonderful!" I exclaimed. Each of the poles was carved with the faces and bodies of great bears, wolves, whales, great birds, and occasionally animals I couldn't name. Each animal was painted a different color. "Who painted them?" I asked.

"That's not paint. The wood is stained with natural colors from berries and roots, Willie said from the car.

I reached into the car and grabbed my Kodak

56

Brownie camera. "Would you take my picture standing next to your grandma's totem pole?" I asked.

Willie took the camera and quickly began directing me into different poses. For one picture he lay down in the grass and pointed the camera upward so he could capture me standing next to the full length of his grandmother's totem. I was suddenly aware that not only was Willie a talented skater, he also knew more about photography than I did. I began to secretly hope his grandmother had a piano or a pump organ in her house. I was pretty good at both instruments and found myself hoping I could show off a little of my talents too.

§§§§

After a quick tour of the grounds and house, Grandma Sunfield instructed Willie and Randy to go down to the pond and get some watercress and cattail roots for dinner. The prospect of foraging for our supper in the woods fascinated me.

"If you see some really tender dandelion leaves, pick those as well, she added, turning to go up the stairs to a generous back porch which sported all sorts of potted flowers and trays of herbs. It reminded me of Grandmother Brune's back porch in Tacoma. For all her dislike of white-eyes, Mrs. Sunfield's farm was decidedly American in appearance, right down to the old-fashioned outdoor water pump at the end of a gravel path that stemmed off from a much longer path leading to a woodshed and outhouse.

I had done a lot of harvesting from family gardens but I knew nothing about gathering vegetables from the woods. Gathering cattail roots and watercress for our supper seemed exciting. I felt like a child born to ancient times that predated even the cultivation of small family gardens. Randy and Willie showed me how to select the best cattail roots, at what spot to cut them away from the stem, and how to rinse off the fine-haired outer layer of the root without dislodging the tender skin and exposing the inner meat to the air which Willie said would damaged the flavor. Gathering watercress and dandelion leaves was a much easier task. Before long we had the wicker basket Grandma Sunfield gave us filled with a good supply of roots and wild greens.

"My Grandma Brune makes tea from dandelion leaves and she dries and grinds up the roots for a kind of tea too. Does your grandma do that too?" I asked.

"Sure . . . but these leaves are for salad. She'll add them to the watercress and some other stuff. You'll like it." Randy answered.

"Grandma makes a salad dressing from homemade vinegar, sweet cider, honey and herbs that's better than anything you'll get in a restaurant," Willie added.

When we reached the farmhouse, the old woman was chopping the white, tender root ends from some thick wild grasses that grew along her driveway. Once she rinsed the dandelion and watercress under some cold water from a pump at her kitchen sink, she added them to the chopped grass stems and put them in a cooling cupboard above the sink. The outside wall of the cupboard was covered with screening to keep insects out, but otherwise it was exposed to the side of the house that was kept in shade all day by an enormous cedar that grew just feet away.

When the boys went outside to gather wood for the fire, I asked if I could stay behind to see how the cattail roots were prepared. Mrs. Sunfield pointed to a stool next to the sink and told me to sit down so I'd be out of her way. I watched with avid interest as she spread butter and honey over the cattail roots before sticking them in the oven of her wood stove to bake along with some cornmeal muffin batter she had evidently prepared while we were out gathering the greens.

Once the items were in the oven, Mrs. Sunfield opened a cupboard and produced what appeared to be two quarts of home-canned beef. "My Grandma Harding cans beef and chicken but she smokes and salts her pork," I said as if we'd been carrying on a conversation about food.

"This is home-canned elk. Tastes better than beef," she muttered, flipping back the pressure bars that kept the glass lids pressed in air tight seals against the rubber rings on each of the jars. "I used to just smoke my elk but a white lady showed us how to can food when I was younger. She was a nutrition specialist the government sent to the reservation. I like the canned meat. It's more tender than dried meat and you don't have to soak it in water to soften it up." She added the elk meat to a pot into which she was already stewing sliced carrots, onions, potatoes and a few of

59

the cattails she had chopped into chunks.

"Potatoes and carrots ain't Indian," I said, looking into the pot with some disappointment.

"Sure they are. Where do you think you people got the potato?" she mumbled.

"Indians make Mulligan stew?" I asked.

"Well, we don't call it that - but it's the same thing. People is people, Fritz, and stew is stew."

"Well, the stewing pot ain't Indian," I noted.

"Neither is a cold water pump at the kitchen sink but it sure beats the hell out of luggin' water from the pond," she said, sticking a long wooden spoon into the pot to churn the bits of canned meat into the cooking vegetables

I must have looked particularly confused as I walked back to the stool by the kitchen sink because Clarence, who was chopping nuts at the kitchen table, began explaining the mishmash of Indian and European traditions unfolding in the stew pot on the stove. "Lots of the new ways are good for us, Fritz. I like my car and my telephone . . . and taking the family to the circus. Indians like hot dogs and ice cream, just like you. Electricity? Good thing. Medicine? Good thing. We Indians know a good thing when we see it. Mother Sunfield here would love to have electricity and running water. Someday those things will come to this end of the reservation too. Those are good things. Indians have always expanded their horizons by learning new things. The Quinaults knew nothing about building whaling boats until they met the Nootkas. Before that, the only time Quinaults ate whale meat was when one or two beached themselves near their village. Whaling boats? Good thing," he said, resuming his task.

"It is not Indians who refuse to learn new ways. It is white-eyes who refuse," mumbled Grandma Sunfield without turning around.

"We know many good things Europeans could use to improve their lives," Clarence continued. "We know many healing herbs and roots. The white doctors only laugh at us. So, when whites get sick on the reservation, we cannot help. The woods and fields are full of free medicine and foods. Cattails and watercress are just the beginning of what's out there. We Indians have been eating a balanced diet for hundreds of thousands of years. How many times have you seen a really fat Indian? Not very often unless they've moved from the reservation and do all their shopping at the A & P. We've been eatin' healthy foods without planting a single garden here in the Northwest . . . yet all your people eat are the berries and nuts they remember from the old country. We even know of trees from which fibers can be taken and used immediately as thread. The woods are full of the bounty of the earth . . . and all it takes to get it is a little elbow grease. We use the best from both worlds. Sometimes it hurts our feelings that so many of your people ignore the good things of our ways," he concluded.

"It makes me downright mad!" the old woman said, taking a taste of her stew from the long wooden spoon. "The arrogance of those people thinkin' we managed to live here for thousands of years without learnin' a thing or two. Look at the mess Europeans make where ever they live. Their cities are practically cesspools. Every place you look they've destroyed the forest. We been livin' here just fine and until the white-eyes got here, things was in the same shape they was in when the Great Spirit first put them in place."

§§§§

Soon dinner was ready and on the table. Grandma Sunfield asked everyone to rinse his hands at the sink before sitting down to her meal. Before we ate, she offered thanks for the food.

"We thank you, Great One, for this day and the things it has given us," she said without bowing her head or closing her eyes or ending the prayer in the name of Jesus.

The salad was great. It was served with the dressing Randy had told me about earlier but also garnished with shaved hazelnuts. The bake cattail roots were tender and good tasting, and her stew was as good as anything I had eaten in my life. "You're a really good cook," I told her, reaching for additional wild honey for my next muffin.

"You go down and pick some cattail roots down by the pond for your grandma before you go back Sunday . . . and tell her how to fix them the Indian way . . . and tell her how much we enjoyed her husband's sausages," she responded, ladling a bit more stew onto my plate.

After dinner the boys and I did up the dishes from hot water Clarence boiled on the stove. When we finished, we joined the two adults in the living room. Clarence had lit several kerosene lamps and put out a Monopoly game. It turned out to be Mrs. Sunfield's favorite, and before long she owned Boardwalk and Park Place and had skunked all of us. "Getting late," she remarked, getting up to put the game back in a cabinet.

"Tell us the story about how you met Grandpa again," Randy begged.

"You know that story good as me," she noted.

"But we love it . . . and Fritz has never heard it before," Willie pleaded.

"Okay, okay," she agreed. "Clarence, you put some water on for tea. I'll make some daisy tea so we'll all sleep good and I'll tell the boys the story one more time."

I could hear Clarence pumping up fresh water for the kettle as she began.

"His name was Proud Eagle Standing in a Sunny Place. It was a good name to have. He was like that. He was a very proud man . . . and he was like an Eagle. Sunny is another matter. When the white-eyes came, he lost his sunny disposition and was angry most of the rest of his life. He was Nootka on his father's side and Nez Perce on his mother's. We met at a potlatch at what is now the small town of Tahola. I was a girl of 14. He was a carver and hunter and at 16 years of age had already earned the esteem of his tribe because of his ability to . . . "

"Because of his carving?" I interrupted.

"No . . . not altogether . . . although he was as good as any and better than most at carvin'. Some of

63

the poles he carved are still in the Nootka village where he was born. We got one here too . . . but he was also greatly esteemed because of the way he danced. That's what I noticed first. That boy could dance."

I was spellbound.

"Like all potlatches, guests came from all the neighboring and some from the more distant tribes. The giving of gifts was always accompanied by several days of feasting, dancing, singing, and athletic contests by day . . . and some good-natured gambling and story telling by night. Each time I saw Proud Eagle, my heart trembled . . . and when I saw him dancing . . . I knew he was for me. He was the best lookin' young man at the potlatch. He had the soft eyes of the Nootkas but the lean build of the Nez Perce. He was somethin' to see. So . . . when it came time for the girls to dance, I borrowed a blue blanket my mother had received as a gift from a Hopi woman who had come with her clan to the celebration. It was a long way for her to come . . . but she had relatives up here and wanted to see them one more time before she died. It was the only blue garment at potlatch that year. I knew it would catch Proud Eagle's eye. And before we lined up to dance, I made sure I knew where he was standing with the other single young men so I could line myself up to dance right past him. When I got to where he was standing . . . I broke one of the rules of the dance and looked up from the floor into his face and smiled."

"Unmarried young people weren't supposed to look at one another until they were formally introduced by their parents or tribe members," Willie interjected.

"That's true," Mrs. Sunfield said. "But I knew

my mother didn't care much for the Nez Perce. Her sister had married one and he wasn't a good man. She had to kick him out of her lodge . . . and then she moved back with us because his family started being rude to her even though it was her right to kick him out. So, I decided it was up to me to begin the introductions. It was actually a very brave thing to do. I could have gotten a real tongue lashing if my mother had seen me do it. My father wouldn't have cared. He liked my independent spirit . . . but Mother liked to follow the rules and she wanted all of her children to follow them too. I was always a rule breaker."

She closed her eyes and laughed silently to herself before continuing.

"The next day Proud Eagle visited my father's camp and brought my mother a big basket of freshly picked blackberries - not them fat sweet ones that grow down here. He brought her those tight tart ones that grow up in the hills. We all knew he had'ta get up real early and run into the hills to find them. It was a special gift. Somehow, he learned they were her favorites. She looked at him and the basket of berries for a long time before accepting them. I don't think I took a single breath from the moment he arrived until she finally extended her hands in acceptance. She knew his gift meant he wanted an introduction and to walk with me along the beach."

"Boys and girls who like each other were allowed to walk alone on the beach as long as the grandfathers and grandmothers or other adults were sitting on the sand hills above them to make sure walking was all they did," Randy explained.

"Rules for dating were very strict in those days - not like today. Today the boys and girls are all mixed up together in school like the white people. That is not the Indian way," she mumbled.

"Walking along the beach together was one of the few ways of dating and getting to know one another," Clarence said, rejoining us after putting the teapot on the stove to boil.

"The old people made sure they were in their places above the beaches by early afternoon so we young people could walk together. I could feel the spirit of reluctance in my mother's voice when she introduced me to Proud Eagle . . . but I could also tell from the smile on my father's face that he approved of the young man. Later, when Mother was out of earshot, he told me he had seen me lift my eyes and smile at the boy and decided at that moment it was okay. *'Don't worry about your mother,'* he said, *she'll come around. I'll see to that.'* That's the way it was between me and my father. I was his favorite and could always count on him to back me up."

"And you fell in love right there on the beach?" I asked, dreamingly.

"We both fell in love at the dance . . . at first sight. Oh it was hard to just walk on the beach with him. We couldn't hold hands or nothin' like that in those days. But I wanted to."

She got up and walked to a small chest next to the horsehair couch at the other end of the room and began rummaging in it. Clarence got up to bring cups to the table. I watched as the old woman took what appeared to be an animal fur from the chest and bring it back to the table.

"We was married a few months later. He moved down from his village to where we lived. He and my father and some other men built us a small lodge of our own. Mother said we could move in with them. It was the custom. But it was also okay to have your own place if you wanted. I was always independent. I think my mother was a little angry about my decision . . . but she said nothing to me about it. That could have brought a bad spirit to our union. And she finally came around because when the women of the village brought baskets and blankets and other gifts for the new lodge, my mother brought me a special basket with a bag of herbs and roots and things for cookin' and for medicine. It took her a long time to get all that stuff. It was an unusually generous gift because most girls were expected to gather their own. Sometimes you would get small batches of herbs in' stuff . . . but never anything as elaborate as the complete set my mother gathered for me. It was her way of giving me her blessing. I was very pleased."

"And you lived happily ever after?" I asked.

"We lived happily for a time. But the white-eyes kept takin' more and more land and there was lots of fights. It got to be hard to make a livin' from the woods . . . and when they started puttin' us on reservations, it got harder and harder to trade with other tribes for goods. Proud Eagle was killed, when he was only thirty, tryin' to defend our sacred places from being settled by that Whitman fellow. But before they shot him, he had taken three scalps. His good friend, Spotted Bear, brought them to me several months later after he himself recuperated from the wounds he received during the battle. They are all I have of Proud Eagle now except in the attic where I keep his moccasins and some clothes he wore at potlatch celebrations", she crooned, unfolding a bit of the fur before her.

"You have us," Willie reminded her.

"That's true . . . and I have your mother . . . but I still miss him." She finished unfolding the fur to reveal three scalps.

"May I touch them?" I asked.

"Sure," she said, approvingly.

I don't know why it didn't seem gruesome to me to pick them up and look at them more closely, but it didn't. To me, they were proof that a man named Proud Eagle had tried to defend a sacred place and lost his life for the cause of that sacredness. It seemed to me that Proud Eagle was very much like Jesus. He had died for what he believed.

"When I go, these scalps will go to Willie since he is the firstborn," she said, reaching out to reclaim the scalps. She handed them to Willie. "You put them back the way they belong, boy . . . you know how."

Willie took the scalps and placed them ceremoniously at the center of the unwrapped fur and carefully folded it back around them.

That night, just before the three of us fell asleep on our cots in the attic, Willie whispered, "Our parents want us to live in the world that is and not the world that slips away. When I am older, I will give those scalps to one of the Indian museums."

"Really?" I whispered back.

"Really. I think the old ways are good and fine . . . but the world has changed and my grandmother has not changed with it. Those scalps belong in a museum . . . but don't say anything."

"I won't," I promised.

Sometime during the night, I dreamt I was a Nootka carver living among the tallest cedars on the coast. It was my job to carve the symbols of the world that are in the totems of all Indians who took European names. For Randy and Willie, I carved totems of skaters and Monopoly players, and at the top of the totem I carved the image of a 1948 Ford sedan with three fine scalps tied to the radio antenna.

Chapter Three

Shamans in the Family

The next morning the boys and I helped Clarence spade a small garden plot for Mrs. Sunfield. For lunch we all drove into Auburn and ate at the Dairy Queen. The old woman was especially fond of vanilla soft ice cream and hamburgers although she claimed hamburgers tasted better when made from freshly ground elk or bear. She was genuinely surprised when I told her my dad often hunted bear out behind my grandfather's farm and that our family ate it with some regularity.

"I would be willin' to bake your father two high mountain blackberry pies for just a sliver of good bear meat taken during the fruit and berry season," she said as we climbed back into Clarence's Ford to return to the reservation.

Before returning to Grandma Sunfield's farm, we drove to the Indian Center at tribal headquarters. I was surprised to see an office for the United States Government Bureau of Indian Affairs located there as well. "I thought this as sovereign Indian territory," I said, getting out of the car and heading for the small complex of buildings with everyone else.

"Your government is everywhere," Grandma Sunfield said after giving a loud harumph.

Once inside the Indian Center, I found a wall of

pictures and posters, some of them reproductions of very early photographs, lining the walls. They told the story of the Muckelshoot Reservation. I learned that its people had come from several tribes including the Snoqualmie, Snohomish, Quinault, and Puyallup.

"Most of the Indians who settled here were renegades and wouldn't stay on the other reservations for one reason or another. This was sort of a prison reservation at first. It had guards all around it. But eventually our people figured out that there wasn't any place for them except on one of the reservations. By then people had intermarried or made friends. The Muckelshoots are kind of like Heinz Catsup . . . 44 different varieties all in one," the old woman beside me, said.

I learned that the word Puyallup wasn't just the name of a small town and river. It was originally the name of an important Salishan tribe that lived along a river that had been named for them. "In the Salishan language, Puyallup means *generous people.* They was a bit too generous with old white-eyes, if you ask me," she continued.

I found it particularly interesting that the word *Snoqualmie* meant *People who came from the moon.* "Is that some kind of science fiction Indian legend?" I asked.

"It ain't science and it ain't fiction," Grandma Sunfield corrected. "Everybody knows the Snoqualmie people came here from the moon. My own grandmother told me the story when I was a little girl. The moon used to come very close to the earth. It came so close people could move back and forth between the two just by climbing trees. They did it all the time. The people from the moon use'ta come here to exchange goods and have celebrations and pick berries and sometimes to hunt. They would come from one full moon to the next. This had been done for many generations . . . clear back into the beginning time. But one year, the moon did not come close enough for the Snoqualmie people to climb the trees and jump back into their own villages. The moon never came close enough again. The poor Snoqualmie people have never been able to get back. They are moon people. Even their language is different from ours . . . though today the vocabularies of the Salishan and the Snoqualmie have intermingled just as their seeds have intermingled. Eventually all the green things died on the moon because the people weren't there to honor their spirits. The moon turned white after that," she said, matter-of-factly. Then, directing my attention to a picture of a handsome young brave, she leaned forward, kissed the glass above the photograph, and said: "This is Proud Eagle. Wasn't he pretty?"

"He looks like Clark Gable with a suntan," I noted.

"Yeah, he did. I think that's why I like Clark Gable movies," the old woman said with a sudden sparkle in her eye.

For a moment I contemplated this quite amazing woman. She was truly one of the old ones, a person who still believed the ancient stories of her people and yet, at the same time, was perfectly comfortable going to a movie and buying a bag of popcorn.

§§§§

From that weekend on, Randy, Willie and I were inseparable. I showed them every nook and cranny of Perkins Prairie and they showed me things in the woods surrounding the town that could cure my ailments, ward off mosquitoes and other insects, act as sun-tan lotion, or be eaten cooked or right where we found them. I was amazed at how many flowers could be eaten like fruit and the number of leaves that tasted good was absolutely amazing. I used to take some of them home for Mother to try in a salad and everyone agreed that they tasted just fine.

By the end of the school year, even our parents were becoming friends. Dad and Clarence began fishing together up at Beaver Creek and Mom introduced Audrey to her circle of lunch and card ladies. My sisters and the Redwing girls got along well too. My oldest sister and Marlene Redwing used to play paper dolls together for hours. By the end of that year, the Redwings were part of everyday life in our small town.

The next May both Randy and I turned eleven. A week after our birthdays the three of us, along with Jerry Cotton, who had come in from his parents' farm to spend a Saturday with us found a stash of war mementos in the barn that one of my uncles had brought home with him after the war. Uncle Ronald had been stationed in Germany and France. Among the treasures he had hidden in the barn, we found a

German luger, a cap that once belonged to a Nazi captain, a brown shirt upon which was sewn a swastika, a Nazi flag, a bunch of old newspapers, some buttons and gurky knives, and a small metal box.

"What do you think is in the box?" Jerry asked.

"How would I know," I muttered, attempting to open it.

"Might be bullets for that gun. Maybe we shouldn't open it. We could get in trouble," Willie warned.

"Is it locked?" Randy asked.

"No, I think it's just stuck," I answered.

"Maybe it's full of old money," Jerry suggested. "You know, German paper money and stuff."

"Maybe there's a map of hidden treasure," gasped Willie who was always sure there was buried treasure in the hills behind my grandparents' farm. He had good reasons for thinking such things. There had once been a mining town just the other side of Spikton Creek. Rumor was that the man who once owned the hotel buried his fortune in metal boxes in hills behind the town because he didn't trust banks.

"How stuck is it?" Randy asked, impatiently.

"Pretty stuck. I think it's locked, after all."

"Now what do we do?" Jerry mumbled.

"In my grandpa's workshop there's about a million old keys on a big ring hanging from a nail by the old typewriters. We could get them and see if any of them fit," I suggested. The four of us climbed down out of the hayloft. I asked them to wait in one of the horse stalls while I slipped over to the workshop and storage shed to get the keys. Grandpa didn't like anyone in the long storage shed next to the barn. He kept all sorts of things in there. Extra sacks of oats for the horses, plowing equipment, an old Model T Ford truck, and benches full of all sorts of one-armed-bandits from the days when Grandpa ran a speakeasy in Seattle, rows of old Olivetti cast-iron typewriters, wooden filing cabinets, and a wide variety of tools and other things. It was one of my favorite places to sneak into and snoop around. I knew every item in it like the back of my hand. It took only seconds to slip in, grab the big ring of keys and return to the boys waiting in the barn.

There were keys of every size, shape and description on that ring. I was sure one of them would fit. Finally when one of them did, the lock clicked open and I lifted the lid of the small metal box so we could all see its contents. To our utter amazement and shock, it was filled with dirty pictures and postcards of men and women doing all sorts of things to one another. We began passing around the pictures and did a lot of giggling. I didn't know whether to be excited or embarrassed. I was a little of each. I'm sure it was the same for the other guys, too. "I didn't know ladies did things like that to guys! Did you?" Randy said, wide-eyed and gasping.

"It's called a blow job. All girls do that when they grow up," Willie told us so calmly he might as well have been telling us how to mow the lawn.

"How do you know about stuff like this?" Randy asked.

"I don't think my mother does anything like that," Jerry insisted.

"Everybody does it. It's called foreplay. Ask your dad. He'll tell you. That's what I did," Willie responded.

"You asked Dad about stuff like this!" Randy said. He sound stunned.

"Of course," Willie answered his brother.

"Well, what do you call this?" Jerry Cotton asked, passing a picture to me of two men doing the same thing to each other.

"These must be French postcards," Willie noted. "I heard someplace that everybody does oral sex in France."

"Whoever told you that?" Randy questioned.

"The Shaman on Grandma Redwing's reservation," Willie snapped back.

"Boy, sex sure looks messy, doesn't it?" I reflected out loud.

"Too messy for me," Jerry agreed.

"We won't think it's messy when we're older," Willie advised.

"I don't know," Randy mused. "The whole thing looks pretty messy and embarrassing to me."

Embarrassed or not, we became so engrossed in looking at the pictures and making snide comments about them, none of us heard the barn door open or my grandmother walk up behind us. None of us realized she was there until her hand reached down in front of my face and took the postcards I was holding out of my hands. The four of us jumped up. We were so embarrassed we didn't know what to say and a little scared at having been caught looking at pictures we knew we weren't supposed to have in our possession.

The four of us stood shaking in our boots as we watched my grandmother slowly look at a few of the postcards. After a long silence, she finally spoke. "Where did you boys find these?" she asked quietly.

"In the hayloft along with a bunch of Uncle Ronald's war stuff," I answered, looking down at my shoes for fear I would absolutely melt with shame if I looked into her eyes.

"Hmm," was all she said for a few seconds. I was sure my face was going to burst into flames any moment. Then, extending her hand and the cards back to me. "Here," she said, dryly.

I was afraid to reach out for them for fear she would grab me and give me a swat I was certain I deserved.

"Take them," she insisted.

I reached out and took the cards from her hands and glanced quickly to my left at Randy and Jerry for reassurance. I couldn't catch their eyes because they were both looking at the ground. I glanced to my right. Willie had his eyes closed so tight his whole face was wrinkled. I could see that he had peed his pants. Finally with great fear and trembling I lifted my eyes to my grandmother's and looked her in the face.

"When you boys have finished looking at these, put them back where you found them and don't mess with your uncle's things again after this. I'll have Ronnie take them to his house. He shouldn't have hidden them in the barn in the first place. He's probably forgotten about them."

"Yes, ma'am," I said. I could feel tears of embarrassment coming to my eyes.

"Don't cry, Fritz. You boys are probably old enough to know about such things. I was just three years older than Willie when I got married. You boys are old enough to know what goes on in the world. This isn't how I thought you would find out . . . but now that you have . . . so be it. When you've put them back, you can all come up to the house and I'll fix you some bread and jam," she said. She starting walking towards the barn door.

"Yes, ma'am," I said again.

She turned and looked at us before she stepped through the door into the barn yard. "You boys should wait until you're older to try such things. I will tell your papas' that it's time to talk to you about the birds and the bees. I won't mention the box of dirty pictures. I'll just tell them it's time to have a little man to man talk with you. I don't plan to mention this incident to anyone but if you have questions, I think you should ask your fathers. Okay?"

"Okay, Grandma," I said, trying to force a smile.

"Thank you, ma'am," Willie choked out.

Randy said nothing, neither did Jerry. Grandma slipped through the entrance to the barn as quietly as she had come in. We heard a few chickens cluck in surprise when she walked passed them.

"Whew. That was close!" Jerry whispered.

"It wasn't close, it was right on target. We got caught lookin' at dirty pictures!" Willie corrected.

"I thought we were goners for sure," Randy said, falling down in the hay as if exhausted.

"I can't believe we're not in trouble," I said, sitting down next to him.

"I peed my pants," Willie moaned. "What am I gonna do now?"

"Let it dry. That's what I'd do," Jerry answered.

We didn't finish looking at the postcards. We stuck them back into their metal box and put it back where we found it in the loft. After a lot of hemming and hawing around and debating whether we should go up to the house for bread and jam or just make a break for it, we decided it was better to go up and face whatever music might still be in store for us. But when we walked into Grandma's kitchen, all that was in store for us was bread and jam and lime Kool Aid. She didn't say a word about the postcards or the wet spot on Willie's pants. She did ask us to carry in a couple of loads of wood for her. We filled the wood box to overflowing that day.

§§§§

One evening in late June while Randy, Willie and I were helping their father paint the girls' bedroom, Clarence suggested I ask my parents if I might attend Tahola Days with his family over the Fourth of July holiday.

"What are Tahola Days?" I asked.

"It's a three day celebration that coincides with your Fourth of July but it has no connection. We celebrate the bounty of the earth. It is a time when all the Salishan tribes and many people from visiting tribes as far away as South America gather at the mouth of the Quinault river to feast and celebrate. It's like the world's biggest Potlatch. It's a time of dancing and games. In the old days, marriages would be arranged by the elders during Tahola Days. It's a very old tradition. We thought you would enjoy seeing it," Clarence explained.

"I don't know. We always have a big family reunion at my grandparents' place on the Fourth. It's a big family thing. Even my uncle from California comes, and lots of the people from Grandma Harding's side come too . . . the Talindas and the Jejicks and the Orloskis . . . I don't think my parents would want me to miss it," I said, disappointedly.

"You could ask. But it's up to you. We wouldn't want you to miss out on one of your traditions in place of one of ours . . . but if you come you'll meet our other grandmother, Grandma Redwing. She always comes down from her home at Lake Quinault to join the party. It's just about the only time our two grandmothers see each other," Willie told me.

"The Queets will be making their shellfish soup. It is better than any clam chowder you have ever eaten," Randy said.

"Who are the Queets?"

"They're a small tribe, a sort of subdivision of the Quinault, who live along the Queets River. It is the Queets who actually host Tahola Days. It has been that way for as long as our people can remember," Clarence responded, dipping his brush into the paint can.

"It's really a lot of fun, Fritz. There's all kinds of games, even gambling. Grandma Redwing always makes a lot of money at Tahola Days. She likes the bone game best," Willie said, standing back to check his

80

work along a windowsill.

"What sort of game is the bone game?" I asked.

"It's sort of like musical chairs except there are no chairs. A small bone, usually that of a coyote, is secretly passed from participant to participant. It's the job of the boners to know who is left holding the bone when the drums stop beating. If you know, you win money. If you lose, you give money. In the old days people gave like at Potlatch . . . you know . . . things. But since the whites came and the reservations, money is used," Clarence explained while checking Willie's work. He gave him thumbs up in approval.

"Why do they use the bone of a coyote?" I asked, trying to pay attention to what I was painting.

"Coyote is the prankster. To find one of his bones in the forest is considered very good luck. But it usually only brings about a series of comic events. You know. Good luck . . but in funny little things. So, because of the good fortune associated with Coyote bones, they are always used for the bone game," Clarence explained.

"It sounds like a lot of fun . . . but I don't think I can get out of the Harding reunion. Besides, I always like seeing all my cousins and aunts and uncles," I said, honestly. Mind you, I didn't want to miss out on Tahola Days, but I didn't want to miss spending the Fourth of July at my grandparents' either.

"Let me show you something," Randy said, putting down his brush and leaving the room. When he returned he held up the most beautiful Indian attire I had ever seen. There was a headdress of plumes and feathers, a vest covered with fine beadwork, embroidery, and small shells, moccasins covered with bead symbols of the Sunfield totem I'd seen at the Muckelshoot Reservation, and assorted other handmade things like ankle and wrist bands.

"It's the most beautiful thing I've ever seen, even in the movies," I exclaimed, putting my brush down so I could touch the costume.

"This is what I wear when I'm dancing. Willie's is even better, and Dad's has won a prize more than once. Of course, we keep adding to our costumes and sometimes make brand new ones," Randy informed me.

"What kind of dancing?" I asked.

"Competitive dancing. We do traditional Indian steps. The dances tell stories about our past. Sometimes guys from other tribes bring costumes and dance too. One year a fella come all the way from Peru. We didn't even know they had dances in Peru," Willie informed me.

I didn't need to hear any more. My interest in Tahola Days couldn't be dampened no matter how many cousins might arrive at the Harding farm to celebrate the Fourth of July. I had to go with the Redwings and see the boys dance in their beautiful costumes.

I expected my parents to object. To my surprise, neither of them argued very much on behalf of the Harding reunion.

"You won't see your cousins from Portland until Christmas, you know," Mother pointed out.

"But he will see them in December . . . and that's soon enough," Dad responded.

"First thing I know you'll be wearing feathers at the table," Mother teased.

"It will be a good experience. Be sure you take your Brownie and get pictures for us," Dad instructed.

For the next week, all I could think about was Tahola Days. I peppered the Redwings with questions about the meaning of certain symbols and articles on their costumes. I learned that the dances not only told stories but also joined the spirit of the dancers to the spirits of their ancestors. They believed that during the celebrations the ancient ones could once again be among their people. Audrey told me that a good dancer, one able to lend all his or her concentrations to just the ancient movements of the dance, could actually take the form of an ancestor of the clan, and that in the old days some even gave messages from the other side of time. "There is a lot of magic in these dances," she concluded.

"The drums are very important too. The drums help us hear the heart of the Great Spirit. Some clans have drums that are older than any living person. A few have drums that have been with our people for hundreds of years," Clarence added.

"How does one become a drummer? Do they have schools for it?" I asked.

"It is handed down like the dancing. My father taught me to dance just as I have taught my sons. Each family has its own dance. When you have been going to these things as long as I have, you can tell who is a relative of who by some of the steps they use in their dances. And, of course, each generation adds new steps to the dance. That's how the story grows. It is the same with the drummers. A father teaches his son. When the father dies, his drum is passed along to the oldest son in his line. If there are no sons, then a daughter is given the drum but her husband or son must become its drummer. And sometimes the son and the father play the drum at the same time," Clarence continued.

"How come girls can't be drummers?" I asked

"Oh, they can. But they only play for the dances of the women. The music of women is not the music of men and their dances are not the same either. But at Tahola days the women and the men often play their drums at the same time. Things have changed."

"Our grandmothers don't approve of the girls playing their drums along with the boys . . . but that don't keep them from attending," Randy interjected.

"Do men and women dance together like at the Eagles Hall on Saturday nights?" I asked.

"Men and women of the tribes do not dance together except, of course, for the Dog Dance," Clarence said, getting up to get some more coffee for himself from the kitchen. You want more, honey?" he asked his wife who was mending socks at the other end of the couch.

"No thanks. I'm coffeed out for one day," she responded. "But you didn't really tell Fritz the truth about the dancing. After the traditional dances are over . . . we have a small band that plays swing music and fox trots and a few polkas . . . so men and women and boys and girls do dance together."

"Times change," Clarence shouted from the kitchen.

"So what is the Dog Dance?" I inquired.

"Can I tell?" Randy begged.

"By my guest," his mother answered.

"Well, the story goes that in the beginning time, coyote was in the form of man and man was in the form of coyote. Coyote lived in villages with many rules. Man lived in the forest, free as the wolf and the great bear. His rules were the seasons and his stomach. Coyote became jealous of man's freedom and prayed to the Great Spirit and asked that all the coyotes could change places with all the men and women of the forest. And so Grandfather Coyote began to dance and all the coyotes in his tribe danced with him. First the magic seemed to go wrong. Coyote almost became a bird with long gangly legs, but all of a sudden the feathers fell to the ground and coyote became a human being. Humans took the form of coyote at the same time . . . and so it has been ever since. We commemorate the story with the Dog Dance. One person begins the dance wearing the costume of a coyote. When the person becomes a man, all the men and women join in the dance until the drums stop. Then we all feast and eat. After that we play modern music either from the band or the jukebox when they take a break. It's really a lot of fun."

"Mom and Dad won first place in the Dog Dance when I was five," Willie mused absentmindedly as he worked on a large puzzle with his two younger sisters at the library table in front of the window that looked out onto Lumberlost Street.

What do you win when you get first place?" I asked.

"You get first place," Clarence said.

"No trophy or twenty bucks or somethin'?" I queried.

"Not all trophies can be put on shelves or in the pocket," Audrey commented. "Last year a Makah couple from Ozette won first place. The Dog Dance isn't really part of their tradition . . . so it was quite an accomplishment," Clarence continued.

"Who are the . . . ," I began, but before I could finish my question, Clarence gave a warm-hearted laugh. "The Makah . . . and why isn't the Dog Dance part of their tradition?" he said for me.

"Yeah, that's what I was gonna ask."

"The Makah are a tribe who live on the extreme northwest corner of the Washington Cape. That's what their name means: *People of the Cape.* They are the only Wakashan Indians living in the United States. All the rest live up in Canada. Actually, they have lived on the cape for as many years as the Quinaults have lived on the peninsula. That land was always Makah land and they protected it fiercely when they needed to. It is only the synthetic division between Canada and the United States that separates them from the rest of their tribe," Mr. Redwing explained.

"You think the border between Canada and the United States is synthetic?" I asked.

"It sure is . . . just like the border between Washington and Oregon or the border between Perkins Prairie and Thunderclaw or, for that matter, the border between my backyard and Mr. Finkelman's backyard. Indians don't believe in borders and fences. We don't believe people should own land. It is only there for our use but it belongs to the Great Spirit. The earth is everybody's mother," Audrey said, setting her mending to one side.

"But isn't Quinault territory different than Sioux territory?"

"Yes . . . but unless tribes were at war . . . no one claimed sovereignty over a piece of the planet. Not much of that began happening until Europeans started fencing off the land. The more our land shrunk, the more European we became about borders," Clarence explained. "But before that one tribe would go visit another to trade things and sometimes to look for a wife or husband for their kids. Back in them days the borders sort of merged together. It was language that separated people, not synthetic lines drawn on a map."

"Grandma Sunfield has fences," I noted.

"The government built those fences and told her the land on the inside was hers. To the south, it belongs to whites and isn't even reservation land anymore. Grandma Sunfield lives at the southern edge of the reservation," Randy responded.

"That's sort of how the Whitman Massacre started. Somebody built a fence and the Indians tried to tear it down," Willie said, holding a piece of his puzzle over several possible places to insert it.

"So the Whitman family was killed because of a fence?" I asked.

"That particular fence blocked the Puyallup Indians from the most sacred of their holy grounds. They were also sacred grounds to the rest of the Salishan tribes. That's how Grandfather Sunfield became involved. Each time the Puyallup would tear an opening in the fence so they could get to their holy places, Whitman and his friends chased them off with guns and rebuilt the fence. Finally there were daily armed patrols along the fence. Not even the shamans could sneak in to conduct the sacred ceremonies that kept the tribes free of evil spirits," Clarence explained.

"What made them such holy grounds?" I asked.

"It was the place our first ancestors were buried. They were like your Adam and Eve. It was there the spirits of our ancient ones waited to bless us. Our shamans tried to get the spirits to come from the Puyallup River area to the Queets River. But, of course, not all of them would move. Indians on both sides of this life are very independent people," Audrey explained, biting off a thread with her teeth and setting her mending aside. "I'm thirsty for some root beer. Anyone want to join me?" she added.

We all got up to follow her into the kitchen.

"What happened after the massacre? Did you ever get your land back?"

"In a way. The Whitman family sold an easement path through their land to the sacred grounds of the Puyallup tribe. It was an insulting transaction because as far as the tribe was concerned, the land was already theirs, and as far as Indians are concerned, all the trails and paths in the woods belong to everyone, even the animals. Today it is Indian land again. The Indian Hospital, just outside of Tacoma, stands on that land. The spirits of our ancestors still roam that hill and every shaman worth his feathers visits it at least once a year," Clarence answered.

"We were taught in school that the Indians killed

the Whitmans because they were jealous of their prosperity and were drunk on firewater," I related.

"Is that really what they taught you in school?" Willie asked, sounding puzzled and in disbelief.

"It really is. It's right in the text book."

"It was not about prosperity, it was about the sacred land. The tribe had offered the Whitmans many other spots along the river but they would have none of it. The Puyallups and others who attacked the government troops and the Whitmans weren't drunk either. That's a lie," Clarence told me.

"You gotta remember, Fritz, to those of us who had lived here for thousands of years . . . the coming of the Europeans was seen as an invasion. Lots of human beings from other tribes came into this area over the thousands of years the Quinault and others lived here. But they weren't invaders. They came to share the bounty of the land and were taken into the tribes. They got married and had kids. But the Europeans didn't want to share the prosperity of the land . . . they wanted to own it . . . they wanted to take it away from us. That's why they forced us onto reservations and put up fences. Indians never put up fences. The Indians that attacked the Whitmans was just fightin' for their land, for the ways, for the sacred ground they had honored from the beginning time." Audrey explained. She took a deep breath, then turned to her husband and said: "I think a few of those Indians may have been drunk, Clarence. But it was Europeans who gave them firewater in the first place. And I'll wager you more than a few Europeans took a shot of whisky to boost their courage too."

Clarence gave her a quick glance of disapproval. "I've heard that story too but I choose not to believe it. Besides, an Indian's wealth is not marked by the treasures he has in his lodge," Clarence began. "That's the whole point of the Potlatch. In the old days some Indian families gave everything they owned away. But everybody was so generous that when the celebration ended, everyone had plenty of everything and nobody went wanting."

"Are you going to give everything away at the Tahola Days Potlatch?" I asked.

"No. Now we live as whites. But we will take some fine gifts to give. Most Indians live as whites now . . . but the gifts they give still tend to be homemade. Audrey has woven three fine baskets and I have worked all year making beaded moccasins as my gifts," Clarence answered.

"Should I take gifts?"

"Not this time. You'll be a guest and a stranger. It would not be appropriate for you to bring gifts. But you may be surprised to get a few," Audrey answered as she got up and headed for the kitchen. "Would you like a glass of firewater, honey?" she asked Clarence.

"That sound good," Clarence responded, picking up the evening paper.

"Is it genuine Indian firewater?" I asked, looking over at Willie.

"I think Mom is just going to get a couple of beers out of the refrigerator," Willie answered.

"Really? I thought I was gonna get to see some real Indian firewater," I said, disappointedly.

"There is real firewater, ya know. We Indians

90

made a kind of beer of our own long before we tasted American Whiskey." Clarence said.

"Really?" I asked.

"Yeah. Indian firewater is a kind of cider; it's made from fermented fruits. It's a combination between a cider, a beer and a wine," Clarence muttered from behind his paper.

"There'll be some at Tahola Days. There's always plenty . . . but you boys won't be able to drink it. It's only for adults," Audrey noted as she walked back into the room carrying two small glasses of beer.

"Can't I even have a taste? My dad always lets me have a taste of his beer. I'm sure he wouldn't mind . . . my Mom either," I pleaded.

"Well, if your dad and mom say it's okay . . . I'll let you have a taste. I've let our kids have a taste. But it's the same with Indians as it is with Europeans . . . kids don't get to drink until they're of age," Clarence answered.

"Sometimes we have wine with dinner if it's a special occasion. Mom puts out her best china and silver and the wine glasses and we always have a special wine for times like that. I get to drink then," I said.

"That's not drinkin', Fritz. That's just special occasion stuff like when the kids drink a little bit of wine at communion over at the Episcopal church. Don't worry, you'll be an adult soon enough," Audrey noted.

§§§§

The day finally arrived for our trip to Tahola. Jerry Cotton was really jealous that I was the special guest of the Redwing family at the celebration. He and I had a fight about it the last time I peddled my bike out to his parents' farm to spend a weekend. He insisted I was a better friend to Randy and Willie than to him. No matter how I tried to tell him that all three of them were my best friends, all he did was get more and more angry at me. I didn't stay the whole weekend. Saturday afternoon I rode my bike back home and explained the situation to my folks.

"Friends come and go, Fritz. Get used to it. That's the way life is. You can't please everyone on the planet and you'll never make everyone happy. If that's the way Jerry feels there is nothing you can do about it," my dad told me.

"I'd much rather you were spending the Fourth of July weekend with Jerry and his family than going to that Potlatch thing. Lord only knows what goes on. There's nothing scarier than a bunch of drunk Indians," Mother said.

"Unless it's a bunch of drunk Englishman," Dad retorted. "Besides, what makes you think the celebration is about getting drunk. I've heard lots of stories about these things. It's a big celebration . . . different than ours . . . but pretty much the same in lots of ways. There's probably gonna be a couple of guys get drunk. There's a Ralph and a Henry in every family. I don't think we have anything to worry about. This is going to be a very educational experience for Fritz, and I don't think we should get him worried about anything. You trust Audrey and Clarence, don't you?"

"Well, of course, I do," Mother answered.

"Well then, stop fussing. Fritz will be as safe with them as any of their kids would be if we took them to the Harding Fourth of July party."

While I was waiting on the front porch for the Redwings to drive up in their Ford, my sister Dinah opened the front door and joined me. She had wanted to go to and was jealous that she couldn't, even though the Redwings said it was only because they had to pick up Grandmother Sunfield and there wouldn't be room for her. "I've decided to save your life even though you don't deserve it," she said in a whisper sitting down next to me.

"What are you talking about?" I asked.

"I overheard them Indian girls, Darleen and Amy-Lynn, talkin' about what really goes on at Tahola Days. They told me one Indian family must kidnap and bring a white boy to the party. They make soup out of him and feed the bones to the dogs. That's why they call it the Dog Dance. They don't even have to kidnap you; you're going along of your own free will. But if a girl goes along it's okay because they never make soup out of girls. So why don't you pretend to be sick or something so the Redwings won't suspect that you know the truth and then I'll go along. I could take your camera a take pictures for you," she insisted.

"Darleen and Amy-Lynn never said anything of the kind. That's just another one of your big lies. You're just jealous because you can't go," I told her. I got up and walked to the other end of the porch..

"It's common knowledge," she hissed.

"The only thing that's common knowledge around here is that nobody on the planet makes up bigger lies than you do."

"They're going to take off all your clothes in front of the girls, then throw you into a big pot of boiling water. But before that, they're going to chop off your head with a tomahawk and stuff your mouth with a big apple!" she snarled.

"You don't know anything about Indians," I said. When I turned to look at her I saw Mother walking quietly up behind her.

"Darleen told me her dad will have to apologize to all the tribes because you're so skinny and won't make a very good stew for the people. She said Mrs. Redwing will have to add whale blubber to the soup to make it taste good. But I don't care. Once they've eaten you up, Mom and Dad are going to give me your bedroom so I won't have to share mine with that brat Sonja anymore. Mom and Dad know the Indians are going to make soup out of you and they don't care one bit because you're adopted and they want to get rid of you anyway," she snapped.

"Dinah Harding, you turn yourself around and go straight to your room and start cleaning your closet. How dare you try to ruin your brother's trip just because you can't go!" Mother ordered in that tone which always suggested a spanking would follow any failure to comply with her command.

"Diana's expression didn't soften. "I hope you all die in a car crash," she seethed.

"You get to your room right now, young lady,"

Mother insisted. Dinah turned on her heel and stomped to her room.

"Don't pay her any mind," Mother said softly.

"She's stupid to think I'd fall for such dumb lies," I said. "Are you going to spank her?"

"It doesn't do any good. Maybe I'll make soup of her," she teased, taking five one dollar bills from her apron and handing them to me. "Here, just in case. Don't spend it unless you have to and don't tell your father," she instructed as the Redwings' car pulled up in front of our house. "Tony!" Mom yelled at Dad. "The Redwings are here. I'm going to walk Fritz to the car."

Dad came out onto the porch. "You have a good time, son, and be sure to mind your P's and Q's."

"I will, Dad," I answered, grabbing my suitcase and heading for the door.

Mr. Redwing got out and put my bag in the trunk with the others, then thanked Mom for letting me go along with them.

"I'm sure he'll have a wonderful time," she said, kissing me squarely on the lips.

"We'll take good care of him, Marjorie," Mrs. Redwing assured her.

We were finally on our way. As their car dove down Colfax Street, I could see Mount Rainier gleaming like a white alabaster monument in the sky. "Can you see the deer head on the mountain?" I asked.

"Oh, sure, Willie answered. "We Indians knew the deer head was there long before the settlers saw him. Kwatee put him there."

"Kwatee?" I asked.

"Remember . . he's The Changer. It is Kwatee

who makes the seasons and makes people grow old. Kwatee put the deer head on the Mount Takhoma," Willie said absentmindedly. He was concentrating on the latest Tarzan comic book.

"Takhoma? You call the mountain Takhoma?' I questioned.

"That's what the Quinault called it before you guys named it Mount Rainier. The Puyallup call it Takkobad and the Nisqually call it Tacobud. Some of the Indians who lived up here on the flats before it became Perkins Prairie called it T'Kopachuck. In each of the Salishan dialects, the word means Place of the Great Spirit. We Salishans believe the Great Spirit lives in the summit of Mount Takhoma," Clarence responded from the front seat.

And how come he put the deer head up there?" I pressed.

"The Great Spirit didn't put it there, Kwatee did. Among the Salishan, our best shamans climb Takhoma and wait for a vision from the Spirit of the Mountain. Sometimes Kwatee is jealous of our shamans. Once, when a great Quinault shaman decided to climb to the summit to get his vision, Kwatee took the form of a giant buck and tried to chase him from the mountain, but the shaman would not be defeated in his quest and endured all the assaults the great buck made on him. Then, because Kwatee could not change the shaman, he changed the mountain and put the image of the giant buck's head into the landscape where it has been ever since," Audrey added as Clarence turned the car from Colfax Street onto Main Street and toward the highway that would take us to the small coastal town of

Tahola.

"Are there any shaman's in your family?" I asked.

"Grandmother Redwing is a shaman," Amy-Lynn informed me.

"Not really," Clarence corrected.

"Not really?" I repeated.

"Grandmother Redwing has many powers. She is a wise and ancient woman. Her generation was taught many healing secrets and great wisdom comes to all who are old . . . but she is by no means the designated shaman for the Quinault tribe," Clarence explained.

"My husband's mother clings to the old ways. That is why she remains in the old village. She claims what magic she has comes from the sacred campgrounds and that it is weakened when she visits friends in the government houses on the hill. But the Quinaults do have a shaman. If he is at Tahola Days, we will be sure you are introduced," Audrey commented.

"No one in our family is a shaman either," I said, as if confessing a tragic flaw in the Harding and Brune legacies.

"Whites have their own magic and medicines and much of it is good. We go to the white doctors when we need them," Clarence said.

"But our doctors do not think of themselves as holy men or women; they just think of themselves as doctors," I said, disappointedly.

"That's only because they have forgotten that the magic of healing is holy. Maybe you will teach them that someday," Audrey suggested.

§§§§

Grandmother Sunfield had packed sandwiches and transparent apples for the trip. "Stop at that little gas station just outside Olympia and we'll buy some pop to have with our lunch," she instructed Clarence as she slid into the front seat next to Audrey.

"What kind of sandwiches did you make?" I asked. My mind was flooded with possibilities. Perhaps sandwiches of smoked salmon or unusual Indian spreads that dated back to the beginning times.

"Two Indian favorites," she said. "Peanut butter and jelly, and tuna fish."

I was beginning to have grave doubts about the ways of the ancient ones.

As we drove through the city of Tacoma, Grandma Sunfield marveled at the sprawling community. "I was only about five the first time my family took me through these parts to attend the celebration with the Queets. Let's see, that would have been 1884. Tacoma was a sawmill and port town in those days. Small compared to now. Lots of Indians still lived in the woods. Whites called them renegades, but they were just people who couldn't bring themselves to live on the reservations. There were always more renegades in the summer. Men and woman would take their children and move back into the woods to live in the old ways for a few weeks. Many times my own father took all of us from the reservation to the woods. That is how I know about the plants out there. Sometimes I think the people of Tacoma are like the Miser of the Mountain," she said, continuing to look out the window at the shops and houses.

"Tell Fritz that story, Mother Sunfield. I'm sure he would enjoy it . . and it will pass the time," Clarence requested.

Grandmother Sunfield turned from the window and began looking at her hands. "I heard this story from an old Nisqually Indian named Hamitchou. He told the story of a young brave who loved to hunt and fish and loved a maiden who became his wife. He also loved to be in the woods. But more than hunting and fishing, more than the woods, and more than the maiden who became his wife, he loved hiaqua - shells from the Northland of great rarity and beauty. He became more and more obsessed with gathering hiaqua. In many places and among many tribes, these shells were used like money. One could trade them for almost anything. Everyone loved hiaqua . . .but no one as much as the young brave in this story. No matter how many of the shells he obtained through trade or by finding them, he could never seem to acquire enough. The gathering of hiaqua took over his life. He stopped attending salmon feasts and other festivals, saying they were a waste of time and kept him from searching for more hiaqua. Soon he even stopped sleeping with his wife and no longer attended to the needs of their lodge at the edge of the forest. One day while trading a fine buck he had killed for three hiaqua shells, Kwatee, The Changer, appeared to him as a wise medicine man and told him that somewhere on Mount Takhoma someone had hidden the largest stash of hiaqua shells known to man. The young brave immediately headed for the mountain and spent the rest of his life looking for what was not there. Finally, too old to live on the mountain anymore, he made his way back to his lodge. For the first time in many long moons, he was back in the forest he loved. He saw salmon in the river but was too old and stooped to net them. He saw buck after buck standing downwind just waiting to be taken . . . but he was too old and weak to pull his bow tight. And if that wasn't enough cause for sorrow, he had found not a single hiaqua shell on Mount Takhoma. He was old and poor. He continued to walk down the mountain and through the woods as quickly as his painful old joints would permit. Soon he came to the place where his lodge had once stood, but everything had changed. The little trees that once surrounded it were now huge and had many branches. His lodge was gone. A new and better one stood in its place. In front of the new lodge, a very old, wrinkled woman sat on the ground attending a kettle of salmon soup, weaving a basket, and chanting a song about the children she never had. She asked the wind when her brave would come down from the mountain to her and her salmon pot. Around her neck and wrists were necklaces made of hundreds of hiaqua shells. The old woman had become rich in hiaqua by trading beautiful baskets she learned to weave while mourning her husband's absence and the lack of children around her fire. After that, he was known as the Miser on the Mountain." As soon as she finished telling the story, she looked away from her hands and back out the window.

"I don't get the point of the story," I said, puzzled.

Old Mrs. Sunfield strained to turn around in the front seat and looked at me. "The Miser's pursuit of the shells kept him from being present to those things that give people real joy. He allowed the pursuit of wealth to take over his life and neglected his wife, his lodge, and cultivating the generations that would have followed after him. The people of Tacoma are like this. They have failed to attend their lodges. That is why they must have jails and policemen. In some ways they are worse than the Miser of the Mountain because they do not just abandon the forest, they eat it up in their sawmills and sell it for hiaqua. Someday, when they are old as a people, they will be like the Miser on the Mountain and realize that the pursuit of hiaqua kept them from enjoying their own salmon pots. But it will be too late for them just as it was too late for the Miser . . . and like the Miser, they will have to answer to the Great Spirit."

"What will the Great Spirit ask of them?" I pressed.

"He will only ask if they became who they were supposed to be. The Miser had to say no. His greed for hiaqua kept him from becoming husband to his wife, father to his children, and a true child of the earth," she responded sadly.

"I shall not waste my life gathering hiaqua," I assured her.

The old woman turned again and looked me

straight in the eyes. "Be very careful, Fritz, be very careful. Anything can become hiaqua if we are not on our guard."

"Anything?" I asked.

"Anything," she confirmed.

"How do I know hiaqua when I see it?" I inquired.

"Any time you feel like a miser about anything . . . be careful," she warned.

"You must have a little bit of shaman in you too, huh, Grandma Sunfield?" I asked.

"Just enough to get by," she said, winking at me. "Just enough to get by."

Chapter Four

The Dog Dance

Mr. Redwing parked his 1948 Ford sedan in a small area a few hundred feet from a large building near the Quinault River. Everywhere one looked, Indians representing tribes from all over the area milled about exchanging greetings, showing off their interpretations of classic Salishan attire, and preparing foods for the feasts that would begin that evening and extend to the last hours of the three-day celebration.

"We have to go in and register," Clarence said, opening his door. "This will take a little time but it's how we keep track of how many people come from each tribe. In the old days, marks were made on a tribal pole, but today we register in logbooks for each of the tribes, and we wear name tags that tell others which clans are ours," he continued.

We all followed Grandmother Sunfield into the building. I was amazed at how many people had blond or red hair. There was something relieving about seeing them. I had worried that I would be the only European looking person at the festival and would stick out like a sore thumb. I suddenly felt more relaxed about it. As soon as we arrived at our registration table, Mrs. Redwing handed me a name tag she had filled out for me and told me to register just as she had filled out the name tag. It read: *Fritz Harding (Guest of Redwing family) Micmac.* When I finished reregistering, I voiced my secret concern. "I thought I might be the only European looking kid here but it looks like there are many guests," as I said Mrs. Redwing pinned the name tag on my shirt.

"You might well be the only guest, Fritz. Lots of the people here are mixed-bloods. More and more every year. The elders worry that the day will come when there will be no more Salishans who look like our ancestors. Back in the old days there weren't a lot of white women out here. Lots of men married Indian girls. And now it goes both ways. Grandma Sunfield worries that my sisters will have white boy friends. Me? I don't care. People are people, that's what I say," Randy answered.

"We've been assigned to area 12, lot B," Clarence announced.

"Oh, that's lucky. We'll be close to the main building," Audrey cooed. "Clarence, you take Mother Sunfield and drive the car down there. The boys and I will walk. It will give us a chance to see a few people," Audrey instructed.

As we walked from the registration building to lot B, Audrey, the boys and their sisters, greeted old friends and any number of relatives. I was introduced to so many people their names had all bumped into each other. By the time we arrived at the campground, I couldn't remember a single one of them. Clarence had set up a tent next to the car using the flaps to actually attach the two at the roof. "Audrey and her mother will sleep in the car. The rest of us will sleep in our sleeping blankets in the tent. If you kids get lost, just remember we're in lot B, camp site number 12. Any of the guys wearing official Tahola Days hats can help you find your way back. There are lots and lots of people here this year . . . and if you get sick, report to the registration desk if you can't find me or Mom. Somebody will get you back here or take you to the nurses' station and let us know. Any questions," he asked.

"When do we eat?" Randy asked.

"After the Dog Dance, but there are still some peanut butter and jelly sandwiches if you're hungry," Grandma Sunfield told me.

"You boys have about an hour before the Dog Dance begins. You can go snoop around if you like but meet us back here no later than five-thirty. I want us all to go into the hall together," Mrs. Redwing instructed.

None of us needed a second invitation. I was eager to see the sights.

"Let's go find our cousins," Willie pleaded.

The three of us set out to explore the grounds. I was very proud of the name tag pinned to my shirt that proved I was also a mixed-blood and not just a plain old white-eyes here by invitation. We had just reached the end of the campground and had just started up a trail that led to another area of the camp when an elderly Indian woman dressed in simple but traditional clothes called out to us. "Randy! Willie! Is that you?" she shouted, shading her eyes to better see who was coming up the hill toward her.

"It's Grandma Redwing!" Randy exclaimed. He and Willie took off running up the hill with me close behind.

She wasn't at all what I expected. Both of my grandmothers looked a lot like Grandmother Sunfield. They were short, plump women. My grandmothers always seemed to wear blue polka-dotted dresses to formal gatherings. Both seemed to be born in aprons and always looked as if they had just gotten a permanent wave. The older Mrs. Redwing was tall and thin. Her hair was long but not in braids. She was dressed in a beaded buckskin dress and wore moccasins beaded in the same design as those on her sleeves. Above her right ear, she wore a single white feather which was tied by its quill to her hair. It hung downwards and appeared to be the feather of an owl or seagull. Her face was cracked with age, filled with wisdom, and slightly stern. The word *noble* might best describe the way she held her head high and her back straight. It was obvious she had once been a striking and beautiful woman.

"Grandma!" Randy shouted affectionately as he jumped into her arms. Willie was close behind.

I stood watching them greet the old woman, fascinated by her. She had stepped from a different age, an age when all the Salishan tribes dressed as she was dressed, an age when the journey to Tahola required days and weeks of travel, an age when there were no mixed bloods at the celebrations.

As soon as the boys had their fill of hugs and kisses, they suddenly remembered I was standing behind them. "This is our friend from Perkins Prairie, Fritz Harding. Fritz, this is my grandmother," Willie said, taking the lead in the introductions.

"His grandfather has a smokehouse and he's part Micmac," Randy added quickly.

She did not extend her hand in greeting and made no sign that I should come so much as a step closer. "The Micmac are known for the delicate softness of their tanned deerskins. It is said that no other people know the secret. Do you know the secret, Fritz Harding of Perkins Prairie?" she asked. The stern expression on her face did not change.

"No, ma'am. I'm only one-eighth Micmac. Great Grandma Brune became a Jew when she married into the family. I know very little about her. I know she kept kosher but no one ever mentioned any secret with buckskin. I don't even know her Indian name," I confessed.

"Too bad. No one here has met a Micmac as far as I know. I would be willin' to trade my stew recipe for the secret of that buckskin," she said.

"Mom and Dad said we can spend part of our summer with you just like always," Randy interjected.

"That's good. I need some help fixin' that lean-to out back. You boys can help me. And how do you like this new town? Is the school okay?" the old woman asked.

"Everything is just great. We like the school. Me and Willie are helpin' some of the kids with their roller skatin' and I'm in the same class room as Fritz, here," Randy answered.

"How's everything with you, Grandma," Willie asked.

"I got trouble on the reservation with them federal fellas again," she told him.

"They still want you to move up the hill into one of them government houses?" Randy asked.

"Yup. Same old story. But I ain't movin'. I told that young whippersnapper it would take government troops to get me out of my lodge. I bought me a gun. I don't know how to use it yet, but I bought one. I told that young whippersnapper about it too. And I already planted me a garden just so he'd know I plan to stay right where I am."

"But you always say gardens are for white-eyes," Willie commented.

"I know . . . I know . . . but this garden is a sign. It lets them federal fellas know I'm serious. They may not understand or respect the ways of the Quinault, but they understand what a garden is. A garden means people stay put and I'm stayin' put," she grunted. There was an obvious anger in her tone.

"Does Papa know you bought a gun?" Willie asked.

"No. I will tell him later when I see him. I had one of the young fellas buy it for me in Shelton . . . and some shells to. I'm gonna take it down by the lake and learn how to shoot it."

"You don't mean to shoot any of those federal fellas, do ya," Randy mumbled.

"Don't know yet. But I'll tell you this . . . I ain't movin' from my lodge!" she asserted, and then in a much softer tone said, "What you boys up to? Shouldn't you be gettin' ready for the Dog Dance?"

"Mama said we have until five-thirty to run around and visit our cousins," Willie explained.

"Most of them are over by those vine maples

down by the river. They're lookin' for white stones. I gotta go visit somebody before the dance begins . . so I'll make my good-byes and see you later" she said.

"It was very nice meeting you," I told her.

She looked at me for a few seconds before speaking. "I'm glad the boys made a friend they like enough to bring to Tahola Days. You are welcome to this celebration, Fritz Harding of Perkins Prairie. You come see me when it's time to eat. Maybe I can fatten you up a bit with some good Indian food," she offered as she resumed her walk down the path towards a group of other older Indian women also dressed in traditional attire.

The boys rushed to a large stand of vine maple along the river with me following close behind. I had a particular fondness for the vine maple tree. With the exception of a few pieces of cherry wood, vine maple was the chief ingredient in the mixture of woods used to smoke the family sausage. The trees were always spindly and seemed to grow along the banks of small creeks and streams. Their branches were sparsely covered with leaves but they had such a vivid bright green color to them that what they lacked in numbers was more than made up for by their verdant beauty.

I was surprised to find nearly a hundred boys and girls our age gathered in small groups among the trees. Willie and Randy seemed to know most of them. Once again I was introduced to so many people, I couldn't keep track of their names until they presented me to their cousin, Lily Whitedove. She was the daughter of Clarence's brother and a first cousin to Willie and Randy. Lily was as beautiful as her name.

She was dressed in white buckskin beaded with pale blue and okra shells. She wore her hair in two long braids and had the most beautiful eyes I had ever seen. Until that moment I had never thought much about girls. Lily changed all that in one second. Almost as quickly, I realized I had become tongue-tied. I think I fell hopelessly in love on the spot and remember thinking how I would never leave her side to seek hiaqua shells, no matter how beautiful or valuable they might be.

But Lily Whitedove was not the focus of my companions' attention. Soon we were headed for the smokehouses out behind the hall. Willie was sure he could cop some smoked salmon to whet our appetites before the actual feast began. I really wanted to stay behind and become better aquatinted with their cousin, Lily, but decided it was better to run off and explore the possibility of a snack of salmon than remain behind sounding like a tongue-tied fool.

As it turned out, Willie was right. Among those tending the smokehouses, he found an uncle who turned out to be the father of Lily Whitedove. He gave us each a generous hunk of smoked salmon but wrapped it in wax paper and told us not to eat it until we were well out of sight of the others. We ran to a small grove of birch trees behind the hall and ate the tasty morsels as if they were candy.

"So, Lily's last name isn't really Whitedove . . . it's Redwing, just like yours?" I commented, trying not to show how interested I had become in their cousin.

"Yeah . . . Lily Whitedove Redwing. She's very smart but wants to live with Grandma down in the old village. She has a real thing about preserving what she calls our sacred heritage," Willie answered.

"She's kinda old-fashioned. She can't get with the times. That's the problem with living on the reservations . . . you don't see enough of the real world to know how important it is to move into it," Randy reflected.

"That's 'cause her dad and our dad disagree about the future. Our dad thinks that the only way for us to survive in the real world is to move into it. That's why he moved from the Quinault Reservation in the first place. Dad wants us to know our heritage but be able to live in the now too. Our uncle pretends like the real world doesn't exist even though he lives in one of the new government houses on the hill above the old village site. That's where Lily gets all her ideas . . . from our uncle and from Grandma Redwing. Don't get me wrong, Fritz, I love my Grandma and I respect her . . . but I also love my dad and I think he is right about this stuff. I want to become something like a doctor or an actor or something really interesting when I grow up. I don't think anything like that can ever happen to me if we stayed on the reservation. My parents moved us from the reservation just like your Grandpa Harding moved from Poland . . . to give his kids more opportunities," Willie explained.

I wanted to pursue the discussion further but suddenly Randy shouted that it was almost five-thirty and time for us to get back to their family's little camp around the 1948 Ford sedan.

By the time we returned, both Mr. and Mrs. Redwing had dressed in full Indian attire. They looked magnificent. I was suddenly embarrassed that I didn't have anything Indian to wear except my little name tag that read *Micmac*.

"Are you guys getting into traditional dress now too?" I asked.

"No . . . we always save our costumes for the dance competitions for young men. That is when our costumes are judged. We'll put on our costumes for the big dance competition tomorrow after lunch," Willie answered.

"Not many of the kids get dressed up for the opening ceremonies and Dog Dance. It's sort of a grown-up thing. And lots of them go back after the Dog Dance and put on regular clothes. It's hard to jitterbug when you've got feathers coming out of everywhere," Randy noted.

I was relieved. I didn't want to be the only young person wearing jeans and a white T-shirt. "You look great, Mrs. Redwing . . . like something right out of a movie," I said as Audrey gathered up her daughters to head for the building that would house the opening celebration.

"Why thank you, Fritz. I hear you have already met Clarence's mother. She liked you and has invited you to come with us when we drive her to her home at the end of the celebration. Of course one of you boys will have to sit on the other's lap for the trip . . . but it is only eight miles up the river from here. Is that agreeable to you, Fritz? It will give you a chance to see Mother Redwing's little home down in the old village."

Agreeable? It was the answer to a dream and a prayer. "I would love to visit her home, Grandmother,"

I said, looking at Clarence's mother who was just getting up from a folding chair next to the car.

"Good. I want you to see a real Salishan house, Fritz Harding of Perkins Prairie. Here in Tahola the people all live in American houses. Maybe you learn something," she declared.

"I would like that very much," I said, excitedly.

"Then we are agreed," the old woman smiled.

On the way to the large hall, we met Grandmother Sunfield. She and Grandmother Redwing greeted one another with obvious affection, took one another's hands and led our small group toward the front entrance of the building. We had gone in through a side door before and I hadn't seen the giant relief of the face of a whale that surrounded the double doors leading into the huge structure. It was as if to enter the hall, we had to pass through the whale's mouth. "This is really neat," I whispered to Randy.

"Our people owe a lot to the whale. Without him we would not have survived. He is one of the primary and most important of the Salishan totems. When we enter the hall through his mouth we are going into the spirit of the whale. It brings good luck to the whole celebration," Willie informed me.

Once inside, we discovered that long tables had been placed along the sides of the huge room. Foods of every kind were already being set out for the feast that would follow the Dog Dance. There were many dishes I didn't recognize but among them were trays of freshly roasted cattail roots with a wide variety of syrups and gravies on them. One entire section of table was filled with slabs of smoked salmon with small signs beneath them listing the woods, barks and herbs that were used in the smoking recipes. On one table I spied several baskets of differently colored, freshly boiled wild bird eggs. Beside them were large platters of jerky, smoked clams and mussels from the sea, and mounds of salad picked from the fields and forests surrounding the area celebration. The fragrances of the food made me feel hungry all over again.

At the center of the room drummers and chanters had already gathered and were just finishing a rehearsal as we entered the building. Hundreds of people had already formed an oblong circle around the performers. Once we had inched our way toward the front of the circle, both grandmothers went about arranging us so that the little girls stood directly in front followed by the Redwing boys and me. Grandmother Sunfield and Grandmother Redwing stood directly behind us and in front of Audrey and Clarence who were the tallest among us. I was suddenly aware that Grandmother Sunfield had leaned down to whisper in my ear.

"What they play now is the welcome and blessing. Once we are all gathered and blessed, the Dog Dance will begin. Once it gets started don't move no matter what happens, okay?" she whispered.

"Okay," I whispered back. A quick chill ran up and down my spine. I wondered what sorts of things might happen that might make me want to bolt from my place at the front of the circle. I wasn't sure if I was filled with a sudden fear or heightened anticipation.

At that moment the drummers and chanters

began to slowly make their way to the southern end of the oblong circle formed by the clans who had entered the hall. Once they reached the farthest end of the circle, both the drumbeats and the chants ended in perfect unison. Silence fell upon the hall except for the shuffling of people's feet as they quietly rearranged themselves in a larger perfect circle. The drummers and chanters made their way to an elevated platform at the end of the hall and took their places.

"The circle explains everything in Indian life," Grandmother Sunfield whispered again. "The circle represents the sacred cycles of the seasons of earth and our walk from childhood into old age. Just as the planets circle around the sun, Indian people circle around the mystery of being part of creation." she continued.

Once the new circle was formed, the silence was broken by what was almost a wail from one of the chanters. "Hoi, ya-ya! Hoi, ya-ya-ya!" the voice began.

"Hoi, ya-ya! Hoi, ya-ya-ya," the rest of the chanters answered.

Suddenly the drums picked up the rhythm while the chanters moved into more haunting refrains and began dancing as a unit towards the drummers' platform. Soon a single dancer appeared at the edge of the circle on the other side of the room. He was dressed in the skins of a coyote and over the top of his head he wore a coyote's headdress which covered his face down to his nose. He stepped into the circle and began sniffing the air as if aware of some essence in the room more interesting than the sounds of the music coming from the platform. As he moved about the circle trying to discover the direction from which the essence originated, his feet began moving to the beat of the drums. Once he was clearly at the center of the circle, both drums and chanters hastened the tempo of their song, and the dance began. The coyote's whole body began to interpret the rhythm and sounds of the music. He was at once primitive and regal, ballerina and stalking hunter, frightening, and in some odd way, funny.

Grandmother Sunfield put her hand on my shoulder, leaned down and whispered in my ear again. "He is now the Ancient One, Brother Coyote, he who first learned the dance that allowed human beings and coyotes to exchange places," she told me.

I stood mesmerized as the single dancer flayed his arms in wilder and wilder gestures as if an invisible wind were lifting him into the very marrow and pulse of the anthem coming from the drums and chanters. All at once the music from the platform stopped and the coyote fell in a heap at the center of the floor. For a few seconds, all I could hear was my own heart beating. Then, as if capable of reading the rhythms of the blood pumping in my veins, a single drum began to beat echoing the cadence pulsating in my heart. It seemed as if the drum echoed everyone's heart.

Coyote began lifting himself from the ground in shivers and convulsions that kept perfect pace to the drum. Each time he attempted to rise to a standing position, he tore at his fur pulling off whole sections of his costume. Eventually a second costume began to appear. It was that of an enormous multicolored bird covered with feathers and plumes of every hue in the rainbow. When the entire coyote costume had been removed except for the headdress, he danced in three small circles, stopped at exactly the same moment the drums stopped beating, and suddenly flung the coyote mask and headdress to the floor. As it landed on top of the rest of the coyote skins, a single chanter repeated the wail that had begun the dance. "Hoi, ya-ya! Hoi, ya-ya-ya!" the lead chanter shouted.

"Hoi, ya-ya! Hoi, ya-ya-ya!" the other chanters echoed.

Suddenly the dance was on again. This time the dancer seemed to imitate the motions and gestures of birds. First he waddled like a duck, then strutted like a hawk. All at once he began moving toward the people on the other side of the circle with his arms stretched out like an eagle about to land. Then he started zigzagging across the circle from one person to another. Before I knew it, he had swooped forward and was standing directly in front of me, flaying his feathery wings so close to my face I could feel the tips of the feathers brush against my brow. I felt faint. Grandma Sunfield, aware of the moment of fear suddenly surging through me, rested her hand on my shoulder again. To this day I'm sure that was the only reason I didn't swoon and fall backwards.

As quickly as he had appeared in front of me, the dancer was back at the center of the circle, twirling so furiously it wouldn't have surprised me if he had spun completely out of existence.

With a sudden shout of "Hoi, ya-ya!" from the chanters, the costume of the giant bird fell to the feet of the dancer leaving him nude except for a loincloth covered with beaded designs, moccasins, and a small leather pouch that hung from a leather cord secured around his neck. I was certain he looked exactly as Adam must have looked on the first day of creation.

"He is now the grandfather of all grandfathers," old Mrs. Sunfield whispered behind me.

The man in the center of the floor began dancing towards us again. As soon as he was close enough, he reached out and touched the onlookers as he danced past them. As each person was touched, they broke from the circle and joined in the dancing. Soon he was in front of me again. As quick as a flash, he reached out and touched my shoulder.

"We dance now, boy," Grandma Sunfield said, behind me.

I don't know how I did it or why I didn't feel intimidated but suddenly I was dancing. I knew nothing about traditional Indian dance, but for some reason I was sure I was doing as well as anyone my age on the floor. I was no longer Fritz Harding from Perkins Prairie. I was a Micmac warrior of the Algonquin expressing my humanity in the sacred circle of the Great Spirit. I was my great-grandmother's son letting her blood flow to the beat of the drums again. I was all the things her people had hoped for her. I was part of the celebration of the tribes, the first Micmac to honor the traditions of Tahola Days and the clan of the Redwings and those who fought diligently to keep the sacred grounds of the Salishan people hallowed.

I danced until there wasn't an ounce of strength left in my legs and finally made my way to the platform and sat down to catch my breath. As I looked out into the hall, I saw the entire Redwing clan, including Grandmother Sunfield, joined in a small circle of their own, their arms over each other's shoulders the way Greek men sometimes dance together. It seemed to me their dance was the most holy thing I had ever witnessed. I wanted to join them but knew that this was their moment to be clan and family and a part of their history that could never be mine.

Suddenly the dance was over and people began clearing the floor making their way to the tables of food waiting for them at the other end of the hall. Randy ran up to me. "Whadd'ya think?" he asked breathlessly.

"It's better than any Polish polka I ever attended, I'll tell you that. This is terrific. I don't think I have words to tell you what I think. It's like magic and Hollywood and ancient history all wrapped up in one big bundle," I told him truthfully.

"You were terrific," he gasped.

"You think so? I didn't really know what I was doin' . . . I just danced. It was almost like I'd done the whole thing before. My feet knew what to do. I just trusted them," I panted.

"That's because you're part Micmac. The spirit of Brother Coyote spoke to you. All real Indians know how to dance," he assured me just as Willie walked up to join us.

"You guys hungry?" he asked.

"I could eat a bear," I answered.

"There's one all roasted and cut up over by the venison tables," Willie told me.

"You're kidding!" I responded.

"Of course not. Your dad isn't the only one who knows how to hunt bear," Randy mused.

"Come on . . . let's get in line with the folks," Willie directed. I didn't need a second invitation.

I followed in line behind the Redwings selecting slices of roasted venison, bear, smoked salmon, fresh berries, clam chowder, and a small portion of a special stew prepared by Grandma Redwing and her friends. I couldn't help but wonder if the chefs in France were aware that indigenous peoples of the Americas also had exotic cuisine.

Everything was delicious, especially the stew. I spooned through it trying to identify the vegetables and meat swirling in the bowl. I could smell the fragrance of herbs I wasn't accustomed to finding in stews prepared by the cooks in my family. I suspected that the meat might be venison, perhaps even whale. Whatever its contents were, it was, quite frankly, the most exquisite and savory dish I had ever tasted. Once I finished my first helping and made sure it was okay to go back for seconds, I hurried back to the enormous pot of stew being served by Grandma Redwing and her friends. "May I have more?" I asked.

"You like my stew?" she queried, handing me the ladle so I could help myself.

"Best stew I ever tasted. Not even my grandmothers fix such a good stew," I told her, dipping the ladle into the kettle.

"Dig deep, Fritz Harding of Perkins Prairie, puppy at the bottom," she said, smiling warmly at me.

"Puppy?" I muttered.

"This is dog stew. It is the specialty of our clan

and only served these days at the Dog Dance," she answered matter-of-factly. She took the ladle from my hand, dipped it deep into the kettle, and topped off my bowl with a second portion.

I was in a state of shock. I didn't know what to say and I had absolutely no idea what to do. I knew only one thing. I wasn't going to eat another spoonful of puppy and I was almost sure I was about to lose the portion I had already consumed. I was suddenly aware that I was just standing there doing nothing while other people were in line behind me waiting to be served. "Thank you, Grandmother," I managed as I turned to leave.

As much as I wanted to celebrate Tahola Days as thoroughly Indian as possible, I was suddenly feeling very Polish and very English and was keenly aware that the dog stew wasn't agreeing with me. Instead of returning to the table where my friends were enjoying their meal, I carried my bowl outside the building and hurried to the grove of trees down by the river. When I was sure no one was looking, I tossed the contents of my bowl into the water, rinsed it out, filled it with the crystal clear liquid rushing over the pebbles and rocks, and drank deeply. I sat there for several minutes positive I was going to regurgitate . . . but before long I realized I would not and returned to the feast determined to ask about the contents of each recipe before taking another portion or slice of anything on the tables in the future.

§§§§

On the second day of the celebration, Randy and Willie put on their costumes to dance and be judged with all the other young men from the visiting tribes. It was wonderful standing on the sidelines watching all the young men model and dance in their costumes. Some of the costumes were very simple - loincloths and moccasins and a few bracelets of feathers or leather thongs. But most were complex and probably more exotic than anything worn during the celebrations held before Europeans moved onto this continent. Along with the white man came the technology for better dyes for feathers. The great plumed hats for women during the American Victorian period had introduced indigenous people to ostrich, peacock and parrot feathers. With the introduction of these new and dramatic colors, costumes became more intricate and lavish. Mrs. Sunfield pointed out that had her ancestors had access to the feathers shipped here from other places on the planet, they would have incorporated them into their own costumes, as well. I was sure it was true.

Randy took honorable mention that day, while Willie's costume won second place and a small container of highly prized tiny shells that could be incorporated into his costume for the following year. Watching the boys perform native dances dressed in their ornate costumes made me covetous of both. Not only was I eager to dance in a costume of my own, I was all the more curious about their traditions and those of other ancient people - the Micmacs whose blood mingled with that of my European ancestors.

That evening we visited the camps of several of their friends. At one, an old man was just about to begin the story of the origin of Potlatch. The boys, having heard the story many times before, were anxious to move on to the camps of other childhood friends, but I wanted to stay and hear the story. They agreed to come back and find me later and introduced me to some more of their cousins who were also remaining to hear the ancient story be retold again. To my absolute delight, I was given a place to sit directly behind Lily Whitedove. Her smile, as I passed by to sit on the ground behind her, almost made me dizzy. In fact, it took almost all my energy to concentrate on the story and not get lost just looking at her sitting in front of me.

The old man reminded me of my Uncle Todd. He was wrinkled with age, thin, but unlike Todd who was bald like most of his brothers, the old Indian had a full head of gray hair which he wore long and pulled away from his face with a traditional headband. He lit a cigarette and began his story.

"Potlatch, which is a celebration of colors, good hunting and many gifts, began with the birds. In those ancient days all birds were of one color. No one to this day knows what that color was. But one day an unusual bird with feathers of every color in the rainbow appeared in the forest. It flew in from the ocean and landed on the totem of the bear clan of our ancient ancestral village. All the young men of the village wanted some of its feathers for their headdresses and tried to shoot it with their arrows, but none was able to hit it. Each day Grandmother Blue Jay, who was not yet blue and who was the wise teacher of Golden Eagle who was not yet golden, watched the young men try in vain to shoot the strange bird of many colors. One day Golden Eagle told Grandmother Blue Jay that his children could catch the strange looking bird if she would give them permission to hunt. Grandmother Blue Jay pointed out to Golden Eagle that all his children were girls and that girls could not be given permission to hunt. Golden Eagle grew mean-spirited and shouted at Grandmother Blue Jay for reminding him of the ancient rule that prohibited women and girls from hunting. But the girls overheard the conversation and decided to go into the woods and make bows and arrows anyway. They reasoned that if Golden Eagle thought they were capable of killing the bird of many colors, they would honor his high opinion of them by proving they could hunt as well as any boy."

"One morning, before daylight, the girls joined the other hunters. Because they were girls, they combed their hair over their faces so no one would recognize them. The older of the sisters killed the bird and took it into the forest and hid it. The girls were all very generous people. They knew the feathers of the strange bird were now the most highly prized possessions in the land. Later the girls told their father of their accomplishment and said they wanted to invite all the birds of the forest to their lodge so they could give the many different colored feathers away as presents so that everyone could share in the bounty of their beauty."

"The next day Golden Eagle invited all the birds in the woods to his lodge and the girls gave away the feathers of the strange bird. They gave the yellow and brown feathers to the Meadowlark, and to the Robin they gave red and brown feathers, brown only to the Wrens, yellow and black feathers to the Finch, red feathers to the Cardinal, and gray feathers to the Dove. White feathers were given to anyone who wanted to decorate themselves with them. And even though Grandmother Blue Jay had doubted their ability to kill the strange bird, the girls still gave her all its beautiful blue feathers. Grandmother Blue Jay was so pleased with the gift she threw a feast in honor of the girls. And that is why Blue Jays are blue to this day, and that is why we must never doubt the ability of women and girls to hunt. It was their ability that brought in the strange bird and their generosity that began the traditions of Potlatch because when our ancestors saw the glorious and colorful results of the girl's actions, the Great Spirit blessed colorful costumes, generosity, and feasting." The old man blew a puff of smoke in the form of a circle into the air and began to get up.

When the boys and I finally returned to the makeshift camp next to the 1948 Ford sedan, everyone else had gone to bed. We quickly and quietly slipped into our sleeping bags for the night. Just before I drifted off to sleep I whispered a question to Willie. "What will you give away?" I asked.

"Randy and I will give our costumes away this year," he whispered back.

"But what will you wear next year?"

"We will make new ones or maybe get one at

Potlatch.   Our costumes are the most prized possessions we own so it is only fitting that we give them away," Willie answered.   "Now let's get some sleep."

I wished I had a costume to give away. I wanted to participate in Potlatch almost as badly as I had wanted to attend the Tahola Days celebration. It wasn't enough to just observe what was going on around me. I wanted to be a part of it.

For my eleventh birthday my parents had given me a West Bend wrist watch and taught me to wind it only once a day just before I went to bed so I wouldn't break the spring. As I reached down to wind it, I suddenly knew what I could give away at Potlatch. The watch was the most treasured possession I had on me.

§§§§

Breakfast the next morning consisted of fried cornmeal mush, wild honey, fresh berries, coffee, and a coffee-like drink made from dandelion roots. It was very tasty but I was a tad put off because my own mother often served the same breakfast at our table back home. I was convinced it was an English breakfast and said so.

"Cornmeal mush isn't very Indian," I complained as I sat down on the grass next to Willie.

"What are you talkin' about, Fritz?" he asked.

"We have cornmeal mush and honey at home all the time. It's English," I answered.

"The English wouldn't have known a cornstalk

from a beanpole if it hadn't been for Indians. Indians on the Atlantic Coast taught your pilgrims how to plant corn with a planting stick. The Indians there always poke a hole in the ground, put a piece of fish or meat at the bottom to fertilize the seed, then cover it with dirt. Corn saved your pilgrims many a winter. Corn is an Indian food. It wasn't seen in Europe until after your Christopher Columbus took it back to Spain. It just so happens that the cornmeal used for this morning's breakfast was sent by a cousin of the chief of the Queets who married a Hopi man and moved to the Southwest. Every year she sends several hundred pounds of Hopi cornmeal as her gift to Tahola Days whether she's able to make it up for the celebration or not," he informed me.

"I never knew that," I responded.

"A lot of what you call *good old American food* was unknown to Europeans until they came to this continent. Squash, prickly pear, the tomato, and the potato were all staples among our people long before they were introduced to people living on the other side of the ocean," Randy volunteered.

"The potato? I always thought the potato originated in Ireland," I said in amazement.

"Nope, the Irish got them from us. But they didn't know how to tend them and I'm told they only planted one or two varieties. If Indians had been tending those fields, the great potato famine of Ireland would have never happened."

Fried cornmeal mush wasn't usually among my favorites for breakfast . . . but discovering that it was a traditional food of Indians from the Atlantic to the

127

Pacific Coast and, therefore, probably a favorite among the Micmac as well, I was suddenly much more impressed with its flavor than ever before. I ate three bowls of it that morning.

Soon after breakfast, Potlatch began. The huge tables that had once been filled with food were now filled with gifts from all the clans and families. All over the dance floor, people had spread out blankets upon which were piled gifts for those who knew in advance to come calling. I decided my wristwatch was earmarked for Lily Whitedove and hoped she would come to the Redwing's blanket. I took it off and placed it carefully next to Willie's costume.

As soon as all their gifts were in place, the Redwings surprised me by leaving them unattended to visit the tables and blankets of other families. I followed them about but occasionally glanced back to make sure my watch was still on their blanket.

As it turned out, there was a system for distributing the gifts at this particular Potlatch. Each family head was given a color assigned by the date of his or her birth on the sacred circle of Indian signs. The Redwing family's color was white because Clarence was born January 15th at the northern end of the circle. His animal symbol was the snow goose and his sacred plant the birch tree. Each family whose sacred color was white visited their friends and family to receive their gifts first. After that, those whose sacred color was red did the same. This process continued until each had an opportunity to give, exchange, and receive gifts from one another.

By the time we visited all the tables and blankets

to which the Redwings had been invited, their arms were loaded with new baskets, bead work, carved toys for the children, foodstuffs, belts, a fine buckskin shirt given to Clarence by Lily Whitedove's father, and many other handmade and occasionally purchased gifts. Before returning to their blanket, each of the items given to them was taken to their car and carefully stored in the trunk. I didn't expect to receive any gifts and didn't, but for some reason, I felt awkward about it. Left out.

On the walk back to the hall, I asked Audrey what my signs and color were on the sacred circle.

"When is your birthday? Aren't you and Randy very close?" she asked.

"Yes. Randy's birthday is the 8th of May, mine is the 18th," I answered.

"Well, let's see," she replied, pouring through her memory. "You would be the same as Randy, except certain of the sacred powers would be more evident in your spirit because you are longer into the month than he is."

"Can you figure it out?" I asked anxiously.

"Oh, yes. You were born into the Moon of Frogs Returning. That means you were born into the eastern side of the circle. Your animal spirit-guide is the Eagle, although your name could be Little Beaver as well since the Beaver is also one of your sacred signs. It means you are a person who loves being at home more than traveling. Your sacred plant is the blue camas which is both decorative and a food among our people. That means you will like fine things that are also useful. Your sacred color is blue. It wouldn't surprise me if it is already your favorite color," she informed me.

"It is!" I exclaimed. "And my Aunt Lucille says blue is my best color. When my parents bought me a blue plaid winter jacket, I hated it at first. I thought it looked like something a lumberjack would wear. But Aunt Lucille said it brought out the flecks of blue in my mostly hazel eyes and that the girls would really go for that."

"Was she right?" Willie asked.

"Not that I noticed . . . but Aunt Lucille lives in a beautiful apartment in Seattle and she's very high class. I trust her opinion in these matters."

"When you marry, you should try to choose another born in the sign of the Eagle or someone of the Grizzly Bear sign, like the Snake, Raven or Elk. They will all prove to be compatible signs with yours," Audrey continued.

"How do you know all these things?" I asked as we approached the entrance to the hall.

"These things are common knowledge among most of our people, but it helps a lot that you share the same sign with Randy. I'm not really up on my signs like some people are. If you weren't so close to Randy in birth, I might have had to send you to the Man of Two Souls. His job is to know all about such things."

"Man of Two Souls?" I asked, jumping in front of her and walking backwards so I could better hear the answer to this new and interesting development.

"His name is Saddles Seatco. He lived in the old village next to Grandmother Redwing for many years. But I understand he has already moved to a government house up on the hill. He is like a priest to us and knows the old ways for giving blessings and naming babies. He also knows the medicine plants best among our people. Many Indians go to him first for healing before they will see the white doctors. Especially the older ones. His medicine is usually very good. Grandmother Redwing never sees the white doctors . . . and you see that she is in perfect health," Audrey said as we entered the hall.

When we returned to their blanket, a few people were already milling about it. Lily Whitedove was not among them. I glanced down to make sure my watch was still there. "How come I haven't met Saddles Seatco here at Tahola Days yet? Doesn't he come?" I asked, finding myself as interested in this new possible source of Indian lore as in the security of my West Bend wristwatch.

"He's been around. He was the old man who anointed the star of the Dog Dance just before it began," Audrey told me.

"Do you remember the man who opened the feast with prayer?" Clarence asked.

"That was before Grandma Sunfield put me in at the front of the circle behind the girls. I couldn't see much before then," I responded.

"No matter . . . he's often at Mother's place. Maybe you'll get a chance to met him at Grandmother Redwing's home if you don't meet him before we leave to take her home," Audrey concluded as she reached down and picked up a gift for a woman who had just walked up to her blanket.

Clarence presented a fishing pole and new reel to

Lily's father. "I give you this gift to honor the bond between our hearts," Clarence said, handing the gift to his brother.

"The first fish will be for you and your family," his brother responded.

"I watched as Willie and Randy gave away their beautiful costumes with similar formality. Even their little sisters had gifts for friends and cousins of theirs who drooped by.

There were only a few gifts left on the Redwing blanket when I finally saw Lily Whitedove approaching us. The twins gave her beaded earrings. Audrey gave her a set of hand-embroidered dish towels. "For your marriage chest," she told the girl.

"May the first dishes they dry be those that serve you and your family a meal in my husband's lodge," Lily responded.

I reached down and picked up my watch from the blanket but found myself suddenly incapable of speech. I did some stammering but, so far as I can remember, not an intelligent word came out of my mouth.

"I think our friend, Fritz Harding, has something for you, Lily," I heard Clarence say behind me.

I stepped forward but not on my own inertia. Someone pushed me. Still, I extended the watch to Lily. I wanted to say something like *May time hold still for you and keep you always as beautiful as you are right now,* but heard myself saying, *this will keep ya from being late to school.* Lily looked surprised but reached out and accepted the gift with a slow smile that revealed a perfect set of pearl white teeth. I could feel my knees

132

going weak and my face flushing. I was sure my face and neck were as red as a blinking stoplight.

"May each second it ticks remind me of your generosity," she responded, lowering her eyes and extending her left wrist.

"Lily wants you to put the watch on her," Audrey whispered.

"I took another step forward and placed the wristwatch on Lily's arm. When I touched her skin, I thought my heart would pound itself right out of my body. I was sure she could hear it. I could tell from the way my ears were burning that my face was now much redder than any stoplight in America. It was probably as red as hot flowing lava.

Lily smiled again, gave a slight bow, and disappeared into the crowd.

"It is time for those of the color of blue to visit the families now," Clarence announced.

"That's you, Fritz," Audrey reminded me.

"I thought first-timers didn't get gifts. Besides, I don't have any invitations. I'll just go outside and get some air," I said, still feeling dizzy from my encounter with Lily Whitedove.

"Grandmother Sunfield has invited you to her blanket. We have something for you too," Audrey said, bending down and picking up a small leather pouch covered with beadwork in the form of a beaver. She dropped it into my hand. "You see, I knew about your place on the sacred circle long before you asked," she smiled.

I could feel there was something inside the pouch. I opened the drawstring and dumped its contents into my hand. A single bluish rock tumbled into my palm.

It is a chrysocolla stone, Fritz. We Salishans call it the Stone of Frogs Returning," Willie told me.

"It's just great! I said.

"You're supposed to say something about the gift that shows how it will further link you to us," Randy quipped.

I cleared my throat, sucked in my stomach and stood at attention. "May this stone and this pouch always remind me that you have found a welcome place for me in your family," I said.

"Good one!" Randy assured me.

"I have nothing for you," I said, apologetically.

"That is not the way of Potlatch, Fritz. No apology," Audrey informed me. "We often give gifts to folks who don't have one for us the same year and visa-versa."

When we walked across the hall to Grandmother Sunfield's blanket I could see that Lily Whitedove was standing between her and Grandmother Sunfield. I could feel my face turning crimson again. After the Redwings received their gifts, Grandmother Sunfield reached down to the blanket and picked up a pair of handmade moccasins upon which she had beaded my name. "May your feet always find rest in your journeys," she said, handing them to me.

"And may I, in all my journeys, proclaim your generosity, Grandmother," I said.

Randy gave me a thumbs up sign.

"May I wear them now?" I asked excitedly.

"Of course, you may," she replied. "But first,

Lily has something for you."

I hadn't expected anything from Lily. I'm certain her gift for me was an afterthought but was pleased that she wanted to share Potlatch with me. Lily reached down to Grandmother Sunfield's blanket, picked up a blue feather that was attached to a leather string, and handed it to me.

"Had you been born to the Salishan, Fritz Harding, this feather would have been given to you on your twelfth birthday. I thought you might like it. It will tell everyone you are born to the sign of the Eagle during the Moon of Frogs Returning," she said, looking deeply into my eyes as she spoke.

Suddenly, I didn't feel embarrassed anymore. but I was still tongue-tied. I felt honored by the gift and wanted to say something like *May the Eagle's wings always fly me to your side,* but all that came out was *I'm only eleven.*

"In Quinault ways, the first year is spent in the mother's belly. In our tradition, you were one year old at birth. In the ways of the Salishan, you turned twelve last May when Randy did," Grandmother Sunfield said, coming to my rescue. "In the ways of our people, you are now almost a man."

Her words worked a magic on me. I was not just an embarrassed eleven year old boy. I was now almost a man. I recalled attending the bar mitzvah of Lenny Steinberg when he turned twelve. The celebration was a sign that it was time for him to give up many of his childhood ways and enter the process of becoming a young adult. I remembered wishing my mother still practiced her Judaism so that I could also get up before the adults and read from Holy Scripture. And now, knowing that the Salishan also considered the age of twelve as a major passage, I suddenly felt like a man. "May this feather be a sign that all your days will have blue skies," I said, giving a light bow to Lily. When I came up from my bow, the faces of both Lily and Grandmother Sunfield had slight blushes on them.

A crowd quickly separated us as others moved in to receive their gifts. I ran over to the dancers' platform and removed my tennis shoes, replacing them with my new beaded moccasins. Then I looked at the leather string with its blue feather and wondered how I was to wear it. I knew, by then, that the position and direction of a feather on a person's head carried as much message as the feather itself. I didn't want to embarrass myself by wearing it the wrong way. At just that second Lily appeared from out of the crowd, sat down beside me, took the feather from my hands, and tied the leather string around my forehead so that the feather hung down beside my right ear.

"You must wear the feather down until you've had your first sacred vision," she told me.

"When will I get a sacred vision?" I asked

"I don't know. You must ask the Man of Two Souls. He will know how to guide you," she answered, smiling. Then she got back up to her feet and disappeared into the crowd.

I made my way to the Redwings feeling more like an Indian than ever before. I was wearing a blue feather that announced to the world I was a man after the manner of the great Eagle born in the Moon of Frogs Returning. I was wearing handmade moccasins that proclaimed my name to all the people. In my pocket was a leather pouch with a blue stone that was guaranteed to ward off any evil spirit that should ever come my way, and I was wearing a feather over my ear that told the world I was now old enough for my first vision quest. I wondered if the Micmac woman whose blood surged through my veins was smiling as much as I was.

§§§§

I wanted Tahola Days to last forever, but before I knew it, Mr. Redwing had packed up his little camp and managed to squeeze us all into his Ford sedan. Because he was smaller than I, Randy sat on my lap.

As we headed down the road that would take us to the Quinault Village, Clarence's mother made a request. "Use the road that takes us south of Tahola so we can pass Point Grenville. I want Fritz Harding from Perkins Prairie to see where Kwatee sits with his blanket over his face and the split rocks near the mouth of the Quinault River that were once the tongs used by Kwatee to kill the monster of the lake," she directed.

"Monster of the lake?" I gasped.

"Here we go again," Clarence muttered.

"In olden times a monster lived in Lake Quinault. He was so big he could take an entire cedar canoe into his mouth even if it was loaded with five warriors," Willie said.

"Kwatee is the Changer. Right?" I asked.

"Right," Clarence affirmed.

"So, if he changed himself into a rock . . . does that mean he no longer exists?"

"Oh, no. It is the nature of Kwatee to change everything in the world, including him. But Kwatee is always Kwatee. The one thing he cannot change is his existence. Only the Great Spirit could do that," Grandmother Sunfield explained. "Don't let no cops see ya with all these people stuffed in this car," she added, reminding Clarence there were more of us in the car than the law permitted.

"How come he killed the monster of the lake?" I pressed.

"Somebody tell him the story," Clarence muttered.

"Since I brought it up, I will tell the story," Grandmother Redwing announced.

"She tells it best, anyway," Randy whispered into my ear.

"One day Kwatee's brother was out on the lake fishin'. Kwatee was gatherin' dry grasses to make a basket on the shore. He looked up to see how his brother was doin' just as the monster jumped up out of the water and swallowed his brother, his brother's canoe, and all the fish he had caught. He swallowed it all up in a single gulp. Kwatee was horrified and furious!"

"Did he change things back to the way they were. That's what I'd do!" I exclaimed.

"It is very difficult to change things back to the way they were . . . even for someone as powerful as Kwatee. But he did try. When that didn't work, he

138

made a knife out of a mussel shell and gathered wood to make a huge fire. When the fire was hot enough, he began heatin' rocks on the fire until he had almost a mountain of hot rocks. Then, using special tongs to handle the rocks, he threw each of them into the lake until the water became hot and began to boil Soon the monster of the lake floated to the top . . . belly first. Kwatee jumped into his canoe and paddled to the monster where he took his mussel-shell knife and cut open the stomach of the monster to free his brother. But Kwatee's brother had been changed into a hermit crab and became the father of all hermit crabs livin' in the world today. Kwatee became so angry he threw his tongs into the ocean and changed them into stone. The tongs were open, the handle pointing to the sky. You can see them, the split rocks at the mouth of the river. Look over there. Can you see them?" she asked, pointing out the window of the car.

I could see two rocks that could easily be taken for the giant handle of a giant set of tongs if one squinted hard and used one's imagination. Within seconds a large rock which vaguely resembled a man sitting by the ocean with a blanket pulled over his face appeared.

"Can you see the man under the blanket?" Grandmother Redwing asked.

"I think so . . . but I don't understand why Kwatee didn't just change the hermit crab back into his brother."

"Because even Kwatee can do only so much. Not even Kwatee can bring back the dead," Audrey told me from the front seat.

"Can the Great Spirit bring back the dead?" I asked.

"Yes. The Great Spirit can do anything . . . but I don't recall very many stories where he did such a thing," Grandmother Sunfield advised.

Soon we were at the village by the lake. The upper village was full of government houses, all painted white, lining two streets of the new village. The houses were set fairly close together. None of them had very large front or side yards, but the lawns between them were all neatly trimmed and mowed. Each house looked exactly like the one standing next to it. I could see additional houses being built just beyond them.

"Those are sure ugly houses, ain't' they?" Grandmother Redwing commented as we rode past them.

Clarence drove his car past the government houses and down a narrow road that ran along side a large hill that dropped down to the shore of the lake. It led to the old village area where a few cedar houses stood. These houses were situated far from one another with fields of wild uncut grasses, bushes, and occasional piles of driftwood between them.

Grandmother Redwing's house was just two small rooms with a lean-to out back exactly as it had been described to me. I thought it looked amazingly comfortable. The largest room served as a kitchen, dining room and living room. The smaller room was her bedroom and closet. The lean-to, which could be entered from the kitchen as well as the back yard, served as a pantry and woodshed. Unlike

140

Grandmother Sunfield's house, I saw no faucet or pump for water. "Where's your pump?" I asked, looking around at the handmade furnishing in her home.

"I get my water from the lake, just like my ancestors did before me," she answered.

"Where do you take your bath?"

"In the lake."

"Do you wash your clothes down there too?"

"It's a lot easier to take the clothes down there than it would be to bring the lake up here," she quipped.

"What about in winter?" I asked.

"If there is snow, I take what you call a sponge bath. But most days it is okay to bathe in the lake," the old woman confided. "It keeps me healthy."

As the adults chatted, I continued to look around. The kitchen area was small. An old-fashioned wooden stove, like the one in my Grandma Harding's kitchen, stood against the wall next to a basin for water. A small table with two wooden chairs stood in the middle of the room. Along one wall was a cot covered with a variety of animal skins. A single kerosene lamp sat on a homemade wooden table next to the cot. There were windows at either end of the room. Except for a calendar above the sink, no other wall decorations were present except for a few additional animal skins and three shelves of dishes, cups and pots above the basin. When I snooped in the bedroom, I was surprised to find her bed directly on the floor. A rope was strung from one wall to the other on which were hung her clothes, a few baskets filled with scarves and shoes, and some herbs that were drying. When I wandered out to the lean-to, I found three rows of neatly stacked wood waiting to be used in the stove. At the other end of the lean-to, a few wooden barrels stood in an orderly fashion. Above them were several shelves of home canned fruits and jams along with baskets of potatoes, carrots, and what I suspected were dried cattail roots. It was unlike any home I had ever been in. Despite its frontier appearance, the place was tidy and well kept.

I had barely completed my tour of Grandmother Redwing's home when an old Indian man, I had seen walking along the road as we drove down the hill to the old village site, came up to the house to greet her. After the two had taken each other by the wrists and bowed to one another, Grandmother Redwing introduced me to her visitor.

"Fritz Harding of Perkins Prairie, this old man is Saddles Seatco. He is known as the Man of Two Souls," she said, patting him on the shoulder. She reached over and kissed him on the cheek. "Saddles and me is very old friends."

"How do you do, Fritz Harding of Perkins Prairie," the old man said.

Saddles Seatco was wearing bib overalls, a plaid shirt, badly-worn logger boots, a brand new hat with three large pheasant feathers tucked into the rim on the right side of the band, and very long gray hair. A hand-rolled cigarette was held between his lips. He reminded me much more of old Ben Borgstine, my grandfather's friend who raised goats in the woods above his farm, than what I had pictured in my mind as an Indian shaman. "I'm doin' real well, thank you, sir. Nice to meet you."

"Fritz was the guest of the boys at Tahola Days," Grandmother Redwing explained.

"And how did you enjoy Tahola Days?" the aging shaman asked, extending both arms to me.

At first I thought he was going to hug me. Then I realized he only wanted to take both my wrists in his hands as he had when greeting the elder Mrs. Redwing. "It was a wonderful experience," I said, taking his wrists. "I was given gifts," I continued, hoping to explain the leather string and feather still tied around my forehead.

"Fritz is part Micmac. He gave Lily Whitedove his wristwatch," Randy noted.

"He had two bowls of dog stew," Grandmother Redwing informed him as if it were a sign of status.

"It was good stew, wasn't it, boy?" Saddles Seatco affirmed.

Before I could figure a way to avoid the fact that I hadn't eaten the second bowl, Grandmother Redwing interrupted my efforts by saying: "I brought some home, Saddles. You want some. I can heat it up real quick?"

"Not now," he replied, to my great relief. I see you were given feathers," he said, looking me straight in the eyes.

"Fritz wants to go on a vision quest," Willie interjected.

"I'd like to be able to wear my feather up," I said.

"Ah! A vision quest! Yes, that's very important if you ever expect to wear your feather up, Fritz

Harding of Perkins Prairie," the old man affirmed.

"We'll be leaving in about ten minutes," Clarence announced. "You kids go outside and go to the bathroom if you need to. I don't want to have to stop on the way home. It's a long drive."

That's what the place was missing. Grandmother Redwing had neither a bathroom nor an outhouse! I was suddenly curious and just a little flabbergasted. I had lots of friends who didn't have running water and flush toilets in their houses . . . but they all had an outhouse in the back. Saddles was still holding onto my wrists. "You come back some day when you can spend three days with us. I might be able to help you with that vision quest you want," he said, giving me an enormous smile which revealed several missing teeth.

"Maybe I can come back later this summer," I suggested.

"We'll be coming up for a visit sometime in August. Perhaps your parents will let you come along," Audrey suggested.

"August will be just fine," Saddles Seatco agreed, finally releasing my arms.

After we came back from relieving ourselves near a small wooded area not far from the little house on the flats, Audrey asked me to carry a sack of hazelnuts to the car. "Mother Redwing never sends us home empty-handed," she said.

"My grandmothers are the same. Every time we visit, we come back with jars of jam, bags of cookies, or stuff from the garden."

"All grandmothers are the same," Clarence said,

144

kissing his mother good-bye.

Saddles Seatco and Grandmother Redwing stood on her little porch and waved as we drove back toward the government houses on the hill.

"Where does you grandmother go to the bathroom?" I whispered to Randy.

"In the woods just like we did," he whispered back.

I tried not to show how surprised I was at his answer and decided to change the subject. "Saddles Seatco is an odd name. What does it mean?" I asked, suddenly relieved that Randy was no longer sitting on my lap.

"Saddles is like when you saddle a horse. That means you have broken the wild horse and made him do your will. Seatco is the name of the most evil of all the spirits living on the Washington and Oregon Coasts. He is greatly feared by all the Salishan. Even the Makah fear him. The Old Man of Two Souls saddled Seatco at the time of his first great vision. That is how he became a man of two souls, and that is when he took his name. Before that, when he was your age, he was known as Catches Rainbows because he liked girl's clothing," Grandmother Sunfield explained as she placed a small pillow she brought with her on Audrey's shoulder and leaned her head on it to take a nap.

After my last question, everyone grew silent and I drifted into sleep. I had strange and unusual dreams. In one of them I had been climbing a tall cedar tree when a giant eagle plucked me from its branches and carried me off to an island somewhere off the coast of the Washington Peninsula. He took me to an enormous nest on the cliffs above the ocean, dressed me in clothes made of feathers and down, and taught me to fly. In my dream I flew to the Man of Two Souls who performed a ceremony that made Lily Whitedove and me man and wife. The first meal she fixed for me was dog stew. I woke up just before I had to eat it. We were back at Grandmother Sunfield's house on the Muckelshoot Reservation and only about thirty minutes from home.

Chapter Five

The Whale Dance

It was 8 o'clock in the evening when Clarence pulled his automobile up in front of my parents' home. Mom and Dad were sitting on the porch. Sonja and Dinah were playing with their dolls under the big fir tree next to the house. Mother got up and walked toward the car as soon as we stopped. This was the first time I had been away from home on my own except when I stayed overnight at a grandparents or cousin's house or with one of my friends in town. It suddenly dawned on me that I hadn't given Mom or Dad or anyone a single thought from the moment I left with the Redwings for Tahola to that very instant. But seeing Mom hurry down the sidewalk to the car to greet me made me suddenly glad I was home.

"Was he a good boy?" Mother asked.

I was instantly embarrassed.

"The best," Clarence answered, handing my suitcase to me and slamming the trunk shut.

Audrey rolled down the window and confirmed her husband's estimation of my behavior. "We'd be delighted to take Fritz with us again any time. He was a perfect gentleman and I think he had a very good time."

"Oh, I did!" I exclaimed. "I had a very good time."

"Well, it looks like he came back half-Indian," Mother said, looking at my feather and moccasins.

"Fritz danced the Dog Dance. He earned that feather fair and square," Clarence boasted as I heard Dad's footsteps coming up behind me.

"That's a pretty fancy pair of moccasins you've got there, son," he said, stepping off the curb to shake Clarence's hand. "Thanks for taking my boy with you. I'm sure he had a great time."

"I met the Man of Two Souls, Dad. He's going to help me have a vision so I can wear my feather up instead of down!" I said, excitedly.

"Thank you for taking good care of Fritz," Mother said as Audrey began rolling her window back up.

"Any time," Audrey told her.

As I walked past Dinah, she whispered, "Looks like I won't be gettin' your room this time . . . but I betcha they eat you all up on your next trip." I ignored the comment and walked into the house hoping I looked like a brave warrior who couldn't be bothered with the silly talk of girls.

"I noticed that neither Randy nor Willie are wearing a leather band with a feather on it right now," Mother noted, walking in the house behind me.

"Oh, it's just something new. Don't fuss about it. It's just another phase," Dad replied.

After taking my bath, I carefully placed the gifts I'd received at Potlatch in the bottom drawer of my dresser but took the leather pouch with the blue stone in it to the kitchen to show my parents. They were both sitting at the kitchen table. Mom was drinking

148

coffee. Dad was having a beer from his usual little cheese glass. "So you had a good time," he said, pushing the glass toward me to see if I wanted a sip.

I took the glass and sipped a bit of beer from it being careful to take no more than I knew was considered appropriate. "Ah, firewater!" I said, putting the glass down and pushing it back towards him.

"Is that what Clarence calls it?" he asked.

"No, that's what Audrey calls it. Clarence calls it beer. Guess what I ate at the Tahola Days?"

"Seal blubber," Mother half teased.

"Nope. I ate dog stew. Can you believe it? Dog stew!"

"I tasted that once when my friend, Hanna, and I visited some kind of Indian celebration. I remember it tasting very good," Mother admitted.

"Did you eat more than one bowl?" I asked.

"I don't remember. I think so. But I didn't know it was dog stew until about a week later. As I recall, I wasn't very happy about it."

"Well, I wasn't very happy about it either. I found out right after I ate the first bowl. I took the second one out to the river and dumped it out. I mean . . . dog stew?"

"I ate fried dog once when your Uncle Sean and I went clamming up near the Quinault Reservation. We bumped into some Indians who were out camping too. I thought it tasted a lot like rabbit," Dad explained.

"Oh, yuk! Did you know it was fried dog when you ate it?" I asked.

"Oh, yeah. The Indians in these parts used to keep whole packs of some sort of big black dogs just in case their hunting and fishing didn't go well. They raised them like other people raise sheep. It's considered a delicacy around here."

"That's awful. I didn't see any packs of dogs on the Quinault or Muckelshoot Reservations. I'll bet they stopped raising them," I said.

"Then where did the dog stew you had come from?" Mother asked.

"I don't know but it's just awful to think about. It would be like eating Butch."

"Not much different than eating bear meat," Mom said, half teasing again. That was the thing about Mom . . . she often did her best protesting and teaching by making a little joke or teasing about something But whether eating dog meat wasn't much different from eating bear meat or not, I knew that no matter how hungry I got and no matter how much I wanted to experience life as an Indian, I would never be able to eat dog again.

It was just at about that minute Dad noticed I wasn't wearing my watch. Where's your West Bend?" he inquired.

"I gave it away at Potlatch," I mumbled.

"You gave your watch away for a feather? Fritz, we're not rich people. That watch cost $13.95. I have to work three whole days at the grocery store to make that kind of money," Mother scolded.

"You traded your nice new West Bend wristwatch for a leather string and a feather?" Dad asked in disbelief.

"You don't trade at Potlatch, you give. It's a celebration of bounty. Mr. Redwing gave away a brand new fishing pole and reel," I noted.

"I can get you a leather shoestring and a feather for nothing. The watch cost real money. You have no appreciation for money yet. We had to do some real sacrificing around here to get that watch for you," Mother continued.

"Mr. Redwing is a working man. He can afford to buy a new fishing pole and reel whenever he wants. How are you going to afford a new watch?" Dad asked sternly.

"Who did you give the watch to," Mother queried.

"To Lily Whitedove."

"You gave it to a girl? But it's a boy's watch," Mother pointed out.

"How you gonna afford a new one?" Dad asked again.

"I'm going to pick berries . . . and Indians don't care whether a watch is for a boy or for a girl . . . a watch is a watch," I answered.

"You'll need all your berry money for the Puyallup Fair and school supplies like always. I don't think you can pick enough berries to go to the fair, purchase you school supplies and buy a new watch," Mother insisted.

"Maybe I could mow lawns like Elmer Dunlap does," I suggested.

"You don't own a lawn mower," Dad pointed out.

"You do," I answered.

"I own half a lawn mower. It's one of the few power mowers in town. Your grandma and grandpa own the other half. That thing cost nearly fifty bucks! That's how's-a come we keep tradin' it back and forth. If you start usin' it to mow lawns for money . . . how you gonna pay for it if it breaks down? And there are expenses to running a lawn mowing business. You'll have to buy gas and oil and there will be customers who don't want the grass left on their lawns. You'll have to lug it away. How you plan on doin' that?"

"I could put the grass in gunnysacks and lug it away in my old red wagon. I can dump the grass clippings out on the farm in the compost heap. All you gotta do is show me how to check the oil and where to put the gas in . . . I can do all the rest."

"How you plannin' on gettin' the lawn mower from one end of town to the other? You sure ain't gonna push it," Dad continued.

"I can lift it up onto my old red wagon and pull that from house to house."

"You should never have given that watch away," Mother grumbled.

"I guess I got swept up in the festivities, Mom. Everybody was givin' stuff away and I didn't want to be the only person there not participating. That would've made me look funny . . . like a real outsider. Audrey made a little tag for me to wear that said I was part Micmac and I wanted to fit in so badly. It just seemed like the right thing to do at the time. I didn't even think about it upsetting you. Besides, I don't really need a watch."

"That's not what you said when we busted our butts to get you one for your birthday. Nope . . . you'll have to do extra work and earn extra money and buy

152

yourself another West Bend that's as good as or better than the one we bought you and that's that!" Dad insisted.

"I'll bet I could make enough money from mowing lawns to get a new watch and pay to get the lawn mower fixed if it broke down. And I could work in the bulb fields this year instead of the berry fields. The bulb fields down in the Puyallup valley pay much better than the berry farms. I could even pick beans this year . . . all you have to be to pick beans is ten years old. In Indian years I'm already twelve."

"Well your still not counting what it's gonna cost to rent the lawn mower from your grandparents and me."

"Rent it?" I said, surprised to hear the word.

"That's the business world, son. If you don't have equipment, you either rent it or buy it. I'm gonna charge you a dollar a day to rent the mower and you'll have to buy your own gas and oil . . . and you'll have to pay half when we have the blades sharpened. Deal?"

"Sounds like a lot of money to me," I answered.

"You'll have to put some real effort into the lawn mowing business. You might even have to do a little advertising."

"I'll just ride my bike from house to house and see who will let me mow their lawns. That's free," I said.

"Yes . . . but that will still cost you time and in the business world, time is money."

"Well, right now I gots a lot more time than money so I'll think about advertising later," I said.

"We've got a deal then?" Dad asked.

"We've got a deal," I answered.

"Then I'll be your first customer. That way I can check your work and let you know if it's competitive."

"He already mows our lawn for free," Mother protested.

"Well, that was before he went into the business. Now he'll get paid. What do you plan to charge for a yard this size, son?" he asked.

"I'd say a yard this size would be worth at least a dollar. That includes flower bed edging . . . and a lawn the size of Mrs. Hovey's would be only seventy-five cents. Houses with corner lots and longer parkways I'll charge them a buck twenty-five. What'cha think, Dad? Are those good prices?"

"Fair enough," he said. "Now listen to me. It was very generous of you to give your watch to this Lily Whitedove at Potlatch. I'm sure that at the time it seemed like the right thing to do. But in the future, you think these things through more clearly before you act upon them. Maybe you could give away something you made or purchased with your own money. It is never a very good idea to give away something your mother and father have worked hard to purchase for you. Do you understand?"

"Yes, sir. Perfectly. I won't do anything like that again."

"Now, it's time for you to get to bed. It may not be a school day tomorrow but there are plenty of things that need to be done around here," Mother instructed.

"Well, I was wondering if I could go with the Redwings when they go back to the Quinault

Reservation next month? They already invited me. Grandma Redwing said it would be okay with her. The Man of Two Souls said he would help me go on a vision quest so I can wear my feather up like the other twelve-year-old boys."

"When in August?" Dad asked.

"They didn't say."

"Your grandmother's birthday party is in August. I wouldn't want you to miss that. But other than that I have to objections," Dad said.

"He's talking about going on a vision quest! Some witch doctor is going to wipe mud on his face and send him off into the woods to wrestle with bears and wolves. I'm not so sure this is a very good idea. Vision quests are not for cultured little English and Polish boys. Vision quests are for full-blooded Indians and people who practice voodoo. I don't think this is a very good idea," Mother said in that tone I had come to know meant there would be no way she would agree to something.

"I'm also part Micmac on your side of the family, Mom. Don't forget that."

"How could I possibly?" she said curtly.

"The boy's right, Marjorie. There's nothing wrong in any of this. I'd rather have him up on the reservation looking for the mystery of life in the woods than on the streets in Tacoma smokin' cigarettes and gettin' into mischief. I say this is a good thing and we should encourage it."

"I suppose but if I start to see bonfires and teepees going up in the backyard, you can expect me to put my foot down," Mother concluded.

That night I dreamed of a new West Bend wristwatch and a new pencil box filled with unused pencils and crayons, and I dreamed of a great eagle who knew how to call my name. I rode on his back as he flew to the village of Tahola, inland to the government houses at Quinault, and over the little cedar cabin with the lean-to out back where Grandmother Redwing and her friend Saddles Seatco waited to help me onto the path of my first vision quest.

§§§§

Although school was out for the summer, that Monday was slated as registration day. As soon as I arrived at school, I looked around for Randy and Willie to let them know I could go with them when they returned to Quinault Village for their next visit. They were waiting in the hall by the main entrance for me.

"Something terrible has happened, Fritz," Willie told me.

"You ain't gonna believe what happened," Randy echoed.

I said nothing as I studied their faces for some hint to the magnitude of the terrible thing.

"Someone threw rocks at the windows in Dad's cleaning shop and broke them. There was a note tied to one of the rocks. It said *Get out of town Redskin or your house will be next. We don't want no Indians in Perkins Prairie.* Isn't that awful?" Willie said.

156

"Did you see the note?" I asked.

"No, Dad told Mom over the phone. Mom said we had to register for class . . . but then we can go uptown and help Dad clean up the mess," Randy remarked.

"Do they know who did it?"

"Nope. Dad called the sheriff and he told him not to touch anything just in case they can find some fingerprints . . . but Dad already touched the rock with the note on it," Willie explained.

"You bring your bike?" Randy asked.

"Yup, it's parked in the racks out back."

"Ours too. You wanna ride up to Dad's shop with us after we register?" Willie asked.

"You bet," I answered.

The moment we finished registering for next year's classes we raced from the building, jumped on our bikes and headed for Clarence's cleaning shop on Main Street. There was still broken glass all over the floor when we walked in. Sheriff Hopkins was surveying the damage.

"Who would do something like this?" I asked as we walked into the shop.

"Beats me," Sheriff Hopkins answered. "As far back as anyone can remember, no crime has ever occurred in Perkins Prairie except for the time Johnny Osgood, who used to own the Perkins Tavern, was shot by his wife when she caught him slipping around with Rosette Kurtwaller . . . and that was almost twenty years ago . . . but whoever did it spelled *Indians* wrong. They spelled it *I-n-d-e-a-n-s*," he concluded.

"You think it was a kid?" Clarence asked.

"Don't know. Lots of folks around these part don't spell none too good," the sheriff answered.

"Any idea when it happened?" Audrey asked, walking into the shop from the sidewalk.

"One of the rocks knocked the electric clock off the wall. It stopped at 3:36 in the morning," Clarence noted.

"Well, that probably rules out any kids," the sheriff observed.

"Who in your town would do this then? We've been very well received here. Until this incident there hasn't been a single hint that anyone in town didn't like us," Audrey stated.

"It's because we're Indians," Willie mumbled.

"Anybody that will break windows because you guys are Indians would break windows of Polacks or Swedes," I suggested.

"Polacks and Swedes don't have brown skin," Randy grunted.

After helping Clarence clean up the shop, the boys and I picked blackberries down by the wood mill most of the afternoon. After taking them to the feed store to sell, we rode our bikes back to the grade school to play on the monkey bars for a while. We were surprised to find Jerry Cotton already there. He was sitting on the top of the bars talking with Clinton Smith. No one played much with Clinton. He was always picking fights with kids on the playground. I was surprised to see the two of them together. The Smiths lived on the outskirts of town in an old abandoned railway building. Their yard was full of broken-down cars and trucks. Except for hunting and fishing and helping his wife keep up a garden, Clinton's dad, Zachary, didn't work. His main occupation was driving his truck around the back roads looking for animals that had been killed by traffic. He tanned their skins and sold them to a fur trader who came through town twice a year. Clinton was the only child of the Smiths in school. The others refused to go. "It's a long bike ride to come here and play from your dad's farm," I said to Jerry as we got off our bikes and joined him on the bars.

"How come you're always playin' with these Indians all the time, Fritz?" Clinton asked.

"It's none of your beeswax who I play with," I said, sitting up as straight as I could on the bars to remind him I was a good four inches taller than he.

"Fritz is part Indian himself," Jerry said. "Didn't you know that, Clinton?"

"I'm part Micmac," I confirmed.

"My dad says the only good Indian is a dead Indian," Clinton hissed.

"My dad says the same thing about drunks," Willie retorted.

"You callin' me a drunk, Redskin!" Clinton barked.

"Nope. I'm just tellin' ya what my dad says about drunks."

"Come on, Clinton, let's go over to the other side of the school grounds and play on the merry-go-round," Jerry said.

"Since when did you and Clinton become such good friends?" I asked.

"Since some people decided they'd rather go

paint themselves up with mud and spend the Fourth of July someplace where they don't even shoot off fireworks. That's really not very American, Fritz."

"Our people were the first Americans and the celebration of Potlatch is much older than your Fourth of July," Willie instructed.

"Nobody's talkin' to you," Clinton snapped.

"It's a free country. One of the things we've got here is freedom of speech, Clinton. If ya don't believe in that, why don't you move to Germany?" I snapped back.

"Are you callin' me a Nazi?" Clinton yelled.

"Zig heil," I shouted, giving the Nazi salute I'd seen in pictures.

"Well, maybe somebody should throw a rock with a note on it through one of your windows," Jerry warned.

"How'd you know there was a rock thrown in a window with a note on it?" Willie asked.

Jerry's face flushed for a few seconds. "I heard about it when I was uptown this morning."

"Come on, Jerry, let's ride our bikes out to your place. I don't feel like bein' around these guys anymore. This school yard ain't big enough for the four of us," Clinton said, climbing down from the bars. Before he could reach the ground, Sheriff Hopkins drove up alongside the school. "We better get out of here right now," Clinton whispered. He and Jerry slid down the bars to the ground and started toward their bicycles.

"Just a minute, you two. I need to talk to you," Hopkins shouted.

Jerry and Clinton stopped in their tracks.

"Good morning, sheriff," Jerry smiled.

"You two boys are going to have to come with me. I want you to go down and get in the back of my car," Hopkins instructed.

"What for? We didn't do nothin'," Clinton said.

"Well, it seems that Old Doc Wilson reported seeing you boys hightailing it down Main Street on your bikes about 3:30 this morning. That's about when the window at the new cleaning establishment in town was broken. We know that because you also knocked the clock off the wall and it stopped ticking. I want you boys to do a little writing for me and if your handwriting matches the handwriting on the note that was on the rock that broke that window . . . I'm going to have to put you boys in jail and call your parents," Hopkins said.

"I told you Doc Wilson saw us," Jerry whispered.

"Keep your mouth shut," Clinton hissed.

"What were you boys doing up so late anyway?" Hopkins asked.

"I got permission to spend the night out in the tent Clinton has in their backyard and we couldn't sleep," Jerry answered.

"So you took it upon yourselves to break a store window and leave a threatening note? That sounds like a lot more than just not being able to sleep. That sounds planned," the sheriff said.

"You guys are in a bunch of trouble," Randy said, finally breaking his silence.

And it was true. It turned out that Jerry had

printed the note but Clinton was the one who actually threw the rock and broke the window. Jerry Cotton's dad had to leave work in Puyallup and drive all the way into town to get Jerry out of jail. I didn't see it, but I hear that Mr. Cotton spanked Jerry all the way to his pickup. Clinton's dad was out hunting so Mrs. Smith had to come and get her son. Both families had to split the cost of having a new window put in and having the name of the shop repainted on it.

Things between Jerry Cotton and me were never the same after that.

When I finally went home for dinner, Dad told me that he had invited the Redwings to attend the Harding family reunion and Grandma Harding's birthday party at Flaming Geyser National Park on August 7th. "I figured, if you were learning a lot about Indian life, it was time the Redwings learned a little something about Polish-American life," he explained.

"Is it okay with Grandma and Grandpa?" I asked.

"You don't think I would invite them without first talking to Ma and Pa, do ya? They thought it was a great idea. And it kind of balances things since you'll be going back to the Quinault Reservation with them toward the middle of the month."

I was very excited about the idea and called the Redwing boys as soon as I finished my supper. I could hardly wait to introduce my new friends to all my cousins and aunts and uncles. "Do you think I should wear my new moccasins and my headband and my feather?" I asked Willie.

"Not unless you're going to supply Randy and

me with some kind of Polish vests or something like that to wear. Fritz . . .Randy and me will just be wearing regular clothes. Feathers and moccasins are for very special occasions and only when we're on Indian land. The whole point in moving to town is to learn how to live in the real world. The world of feathers and moccasins has already been replaced with the world of tennis shoes, Levis and T-shirts."

I knew he was right but deep down I really wanted to show off my new found identify. After all, I was every bit as proud of being part Micmac as I was of being part Polish and part English.

§§§§

Willie and Randy helped me canvas our small town for possible customers for my new lawn mowing business and both helped me pick berries after supper if they didn't have chores of their own to do. By the time the day of the Harding family reunion arrived, I had purchased a brand new West Bend wristwatch for myself, a new pencil box and a Big Chief tablet for school and had almost four dollars set aside for rides at the coming Puyallup Fair. Armed with the knowledge that I would accompany the Redwings back to their ancestral home on the Olympic Peninsula, I was all the more determined that Randy and Willie should have the best time possible at Grandma's birthday party at the park.

At seven in the morning on the day of the

reunion, Dad and I were sitting at the kitchen table eating our breakfast of eggs and fried bologna when the Redwing boys opened the back door and walked into the kitchen. "Are we too early?" Willie asked, sitting down next to my dad.

"Not at all. We'll be leaving in a few minutes so we can put up signs directing the family to our tables and to make sure nobody else gets them. The rest of the family will get there 'bout eleven-thirty or noon. I can use the extra help. Will your folks be joining us?"

"It didn't work out. Dad couldn't get anybody to work at the store, but he said to thank you very much for the invitation. The last minute Mrs. Radford got sick and can't work."

"Well, maybe next time," Dad said.

The four of us loaded Dad's pickup with the dishes and other essentials Mother had packed the night before. She and my two sisters would join us at the park later. Uncle Dan and Aunt Mary, who had no children of their own, would pick them up on their way through Perkins Prairie from their home in Carbonado.

As Dad pulled his truck out of the alley behind our house toward the highway leading to the park, Willie turned to me and asked: "What's it going to be like?"

"Well, it won't be anything like Potlatch. Only Grandma gets presents. But it sort of goes like this: Once everybody arrives, most of the aunts will have set out snacks on their tables. Everybody just helps themselves. The ladies will gather in various huddles and gossip about other members of the family or brag

164

about their kids. The men either play catch or fish in the river. Some of them just sit around drinking beer and talkin' about guy stuff. There's almost always a bunch of men who that play cards. Sometimes Aunt Sophie joins them. She always likes to be with the guys. That's true of my dad's cousin Margaret, too. She often joins the guys for cards. We kids usually play horse shoes, or wade in the river or explore the woods. Then, about one o'clock, everybody goes swimming in the big pool. Kids can't go in the pool until the grownups are there. Grandma always goes swimming but lots of the ladies Mom's age stay behind to prepare the dinner. Mom says they won't swim because they don't want anyone to see them in a bathing suit. But Grandma is heavier than all of them and it don't seem to bother her."

"They have three different diving boards at the pool . . . each one higher than the other. My mom can dive from the very top one. She looks like a bird when she dives. Dad is good at it too. He won some prizes for it when he was in school. Everybody swims until about two-thirty. Grandma leaves first to help supervise the dinner. Then the rest of us go dry off and get back into our clothes and return to the picnic area. By then all the great aunts plus the regular ones have a huge dinner ready for us. There will be tons of fried chicken at the covered stoves, pounds and pounds of Polish sausage, and all kinds of stuff. You just wander around and fill your plate with anything that looks good to you but be sure to get some of my Aunt Maggie's foo-foo salad. It's made of pineapple, nuts, marshmallows, whipping cream, and cream cheese. She brings gallons of the stuff. It's everybody's favorite."

"So the day's pretty much about swimming and eating," Randy chirped.

"Sounds a lot like the feast at Tahola Days to me," Willie said.

"It is . . . but the food is mostly Polish."

"Do they have a dance?" Randy asked.

"Yeah, but it ain't much like the Dog Dance. After Grandma opens her presents and we have dessert, most everybody walks up to the geysers to watch them burn. That's how's-a-come they call it Flaming Geyser Park 'cause they got flaming geysers there. Then, as people walk back down from the geysers, we all wander over to the dance pavilion. Lots of my uncles play musical instruments. They've got a band, sort of . . . and they play fox-trots, polkas, the shadish and waltzes. Sometimes I sing with them. Lots of people take turns singing. Grandma and Grandpa always have the first dance to themselves . . . and then everybody dances themselves silly until it starts to get dark. Then we go back to our tables and pick at the food for a while. About eight o'clock the ladies start packing up their things. By eight-thirty, nine o'clock everybody goes home. Some of the family live farther away than we do. They usually leave a little earlier."

After we helped Dad unload the pickup, we asked if we could hike up to the geysers if we promised to be back by the time Mom and my sisters arrived.

"Most of the family walks up there after dinner," Dad advised.

"Yeah, I know, Fritz told us. But me and Randy ain't never seen the geysers before although we know

166

some stories about them. It's one of the sacred places in the woods. Saddles Seatco visited them once. We wanted to visit the geysers before there was a crowd," Willie explained.

"Well, in that case, I have no objection. But you be sure you're back in about an hour. I don't want your mother fussing when she gets here."

"You know how these geysers came into existence?" Randy asked as we began hiking up the path toward them.

"There's natural gas way down in the earth someplace. It comes up through some cracks in the rocks. It's all about something to do with volcanic activity in these hills and under Mt. Rainier . . . and I think it has something to do with the shifting of the geological plates. I read about it in *National Geographic*," I answered matter-of-factly.

"There's a Salishan story about the geysers that's a lot more interesting," Randy said in a tone that was part sarcastic, part tease.

"We've heard the story lots of times but this is the first time we've ever been able to actually see the geysers. Dad was always going to drive us over here, but . . . well, he got so busy with the new store, he just hasn't had time," Willie added.

"It's about Seatco," Randy whispered.

"Well, are you guys gonna tell me the story or just talk about it?" I asked.

"Let me tell the story, I know it better than you and I'm older," Willie instructed. His brother acquiesced.

"In those days Seatco, the evil spirit, could roam

anywhere he wanted from the shores of the ocean way up into the mountains. He was always looking to cause problems. One day he was trying to hit Kwatee with some lightning bolts. Kwatee ran into the forest to better hide himself from the evil one. Seatco took the form of a thunderbird so he could fly high above the trees and find Kwatee anyway. Each time Seatco spotted him, he threw a huge lightning bolt down through the trees, narrowly missing Kwatee each time. Finally, Kwatee arrived at the place where geyser number one is now. As soon as Seatco began to make a wide circle to come back and shoot more lightning bolts, Kwatee, with the help of Brother Mole, dug down through the earth and rocks until they reached the hidden store of natural gas. The next time Seatco flew above Kwatee and threw down a lighting bolt, Brother Mole, who used his body to plug the hole for Kwatee, jumped out and ran into the underbrush for cover, letting the gas escape. The second the lightning bolt hit the hole it ignited the gas which shot hundreds of feet into the sky following the path of the lightning and singed Seatco's tail feathers. He was one mad bird. Kwatee ran farther up into the hills to hide where the trees were even denser. Once again, Brother Mole helped him dig down to a pool of natural gas. When Seatco spotted Kwatee standing in a clearing above the new geyser hole, he began throwing bolts of lightning down again. Once again Brother Mole jumped out of the hole and ran for cover. This time there was more gas in the geyser and it leaped so high into the sky when the lightening hit it, some of Seatco's wing feathers caught fire. Seatco had to abandon his disguise as a thunderbird to save his life. That is why, to this day, Seatco cannot take the form of a thunderbird and must stay away from the foothills and only haunt the coast lines of Washington and Oregon . . . and that is why, to this day, even though moles are plentiful and used to be a favorite food of the Salishan, Indians never eat them anymore," Willie concluded as we turned a bend in the path and saw a park ranger standing by the first geyser.

The geysers usually let off their gas at three hour intervals. Only the park rangers were allowed to light them. We were in luck. The geyser was just about to let its gas escape. The ranger lit some rags dipped in oil tied to the end of a long stick, reached over the chain barrier and lit the escaping gas. The flames shot up at least twenty feet into the air. I almost expected to see Seatco flying overhead. I think the boys did too.

When we arrived back at the picnic area about half the families had arrived and were setting up their tables with light snacks for those whose hunger wouldn't permit them to wait until the main meal was served. Open faced sandwiches, carrot sticks, stuffed celery, bowls of chips, popcorn, homemade pickles, occasional trays of cookies, washtubs filled with ice, beer and soda pop, and other delectables were everywhere for the taking. One washtub was filled with ice and tall green bottles of Aunt Victoria's homemade root beer. Her washtub was out first stop. Then the boys and I perused the tables for morsels and treats that caught our eyes. "Pickled pigs feet! Oh, I love these," Willie exclaimed as he walked up to Aunt Lucritia's table.

"You've got to be kidding," I exclaimed.

"Willie even likes to nibble on the chicken feet Grandma uses to build the stock for her soup. Sometimes she cooks too many and she pickles them. Willie eats any kind of pickled feet. I'll bet he'd eat pickled bear's feet," Randy said.

"Everybody knows bear's feet are better roasted," Willie answered.

"My dad likes pickled pig's feet too. You sure you don't have a little Polish blood in you, Willie" I teased.

"You don't like these things?" he questioned through a mouthful of brine-covered pig's foot.

"I'd rather have the flue."

"What kind of Polack are you? Besides, you don't really think Poland is the only place on the planet where pigs live. There were wild pigs living all over these parts in the old days . . . probably still a few out there if you really wanted to hunt them out. And Polish people weren't the only tribe on the planet to discover salt . . . so why should you be surprised that Indians like pickled meats? Our people used to pickle, dry and smoke all sorts of meat. We didn't have Mason canning jars and pressure cookers in those days either, ya know," Randy said reaching down to pick up a stalk of Aunt Helen's pineapple and cream cheese filled celery.

"I noticed you didn't take any," I quipped.

"I don't even like dill pickles . . . nothin' sour or too salty . . . except maybe popcorn and potato chips," he proclaimed.

"He'd a starved in the old days," Willie mused.

170

I had my doubts.

§§§§

By early afternoon Grandma was ready for her swim. That was the families' cue to head for the large Olympic-sized swimming pool down by the dance pavilion. I am told that when she was younger, my grandmother could dive from the Spikton Creek bridge into the icy waters below and never show a goose bump, and that when the family first started celebrating at Flaming Geyser Park, she dove from the highest diving boards. But these days she entered the pool by the concrete stairs at the shallow end. She could still swim the length of the pool but no longer ventured any dives.

After racing with some of my cousins in the pool area, the boys and I sat on the edge at the shallow end facing the diving boards as Mom and Dad climbed to the highest of them to show off their skills.

"My mother would never have the courage to do that," Randy said, watching spellbound as my mother stepped out on the edge of the board, flexing it to give her enough propulsion to execute her dive.

"My mom dives like a bird," I said proudly as she suddenly shot up into the air, turned two complete somersaults and dove into the pool below with no more splash than a single pebble might cause. Dad followed her. His favorite was the swan dive. It made me proud to watch how he glided downward toward the pool much the way I imagined the great thunderbird of the Salishan legends came in for a landing. Then, just yards before he hit the water, Dad would point his body downward like an arrow and slip into the water like a torpedo slices through the waters of the ocean.

"I can do that," Willie announced.

"They don't let kids on the high board," I told him.

"What if I told them I'm a champion diver," he pressed.

"Are you?" I asked.

"Damn close," he insisted.

The three of us swam over to the lifeguard and asked if Willie could show off his ability on the high board.

"How old are you, boy?" the lifeguard asked.

"I'll be fourteen on my next birthday . . . and I dive from the rocks along Lake Quinault all the time. Some of them are much higher than that old board," Willie answered.

"Okay . . . but you screw up and hurt yourself and it's my ass. I need this job" the man told him.

The lifeguard made an announcement that let the adults know it was okay for Willie to ascend the ladder to the highest diving board. Randy and I swam back to the edge of the pool se we'd be able to watch his brother as closely as we had my mom and dad. "You sure he can do this?" I asked.

"Willie can do it. He's a very skilled diver. His spirit guide is the King Salmon. He was born to swim and dive," Randy affirmed.

172

After climbing to the top of the tall tower, Willie walked out to the end of the diving board without the slightest hesitation. His bronze body glistened in the sun reminding me of a photograph I had once seen in a *National Geographic* picturing a young Mexican boys diving off the cliffs near Acapulco into the sea below. Willie tested the bounce of the board for several seconds, then returned to the platform behind it. He put his hands down to his side and lifted his head towards the sun.

"Is he prayin' 'cause he's scared?" I asked.

"Nope. He's just praying that the Great Spirit will bless his effort," Randy explained.

Then, with great assurance, Willie took three long, fast steps and sprang into the air executing the most perfect swan dive I had ever seen accomplished at the Flaming Geyser pool. Even my father, who had joined Randy and me at the end of the pool, whooped and whistled his applause for my friend's accomplishment. When Willie came to the surface, Dad led a round of applause for him. Nothing like that had ever been done for a diver at the pool so far as I knew.

"You wanna give it a try?" Willie asked as he swam over to us.

"I don't like high places," I responded without apology.

"Me, neither," Randy echoed.

"Where did you learn to dive like that?" Dad asked.

"It was shown to me in a dream," Willie answered.

"A dream? You haven't practiced that dive before?" Dad asked.

"Of course, I've practiced it before. But the first time, I did it almost as good as this time, and before I actually dove ever, I was shown how to execute the dive in a dream," Willie responded.

"He learned to dive when he was on his first vision quest. His spirit guide is the King Salmon. Willie was born to be in water," Randy explained.

"Well, maybe we Polish people should start going on vision quests of our own," Dad commented.

"This Polish person is going to. That's what I wanna do when I go up with the Redwings to the Quinault village next time. Saddles Seatco said he'd help me," I said excitedly.

Dad didn't say anything. He just smiled and gave me that look he often gave which meant he had discovered something about me he hadn't expected. I remember him giving me that same look when I sat down and played *The Desert Song* on the piano for him. Jerry Cotton's mother had taught me to play it one of the weekends I spent at their place in the country. I liked the look and I think he was glad to wear it. I also liked the fact that there were times I surprised my father with the things I could do or ideas I thought about. "You're a very curious young man," he finally said, reaching out and mussing my hair the way Grandpa did when he was especially glad to see me.

§§§§

The Harding feast was everything I promised. Randy and Willie stuffed themselves with chicken, sausages, perogie, foo-foo salad and a host of other American and Eastern European dishes. One platter of food was especially tasty to Randy who raved over what he thought was an interesting recipe for scrambled eggs. "I can hardly wait to finish what I've got on my plate so I can go get some more. These are the best scrambled eggs I've ever tasted in my life," he muttered through a full mouth.

"I hate to tell you this, but those aren't scrambled eggs. Well, not just scrambled eggs. Those are fried pig brains. I won't eat them. I just don't feel right about eatin' somebody else's brains, even if they're just a pig," I told him.

"But you'll eat pig intestines they stuff the sausage into! What kinda sense does that make? You'll eat their guts but you won't eat their brains? Now that don't make no sense at all!" Willie exclaimed.

I have to admit that it gave me some pause.

"Pig brains!" Randy gulped. A sudden revulsion swept over his face.

"Yeah, they're a family favorite. Grandma doesn't waste anything on an animal once it's been slaughtered. She salts the brains down and keeps them fresh in ice water. Then, just before the picnic, she rinses them off and fries them in leftover fat after she has cooked her chicken. She adds onions and eggs. My dad loves them." From the look on his face, I might as well have told Randy he was eating baby fingers. His eyes grew wide and his face turned as pale as mine. Before I could ask if he was going to be okay, he made a charge for a stand of trees behind the men's outhouse.

"He's squeamish about some things," Willie commented.

"I know just how he feels," I observed without making an actual reference to his grandmother's dog stew.

After dinner the aunts brought out a huge three-layered birthday cake as the clans sang the birthday song for Grandmother Harding. Her big surprise that year was a brand new freezer chest. All the aunts and uncles had gone in together with Grandpa to purchase it. After opening her smaller presents, Grandma was led blindfolded out to the parking lot where the freezer had been loaded on the back of Uncle Dan's pickup. The freezer was hidden under a tarp. When the uncles removed it revealing the gift, Grandma began to cry.

"You is good kids. Pa was just complainin' about havin' to drive to town to the locker all the time just the other day. You is good kids . . ." she told them while dabbing her eyes with a handkerchief she always seemed to have tucked in the ample creases of her bosom for just such occasions.

After the gift wrap was all folded neatly for reuse, Grandma and her two sisters led the group in the family's traditional hike to the flaming geysers. Randy, Willie and I walked backward and in front of them so Willie could tell the Salishan story of the geysers. They listened intently but when he finished, Great-aunt Shelly, the tartest and most vocal of the three old ladies, surprised both of the Redwing boys and me with

176

her comment.

"That's a charming story, young fella, but I much prefer the story my father told us when we was little . . . he insisted the gas comes from the farts of a troll who lives in a subterranean cave somewhere under the geysers . . . and who comes out late at night to eat small children who don't obey their parents," she declared, sounding so much like the mean witch from the *Wizard of Oz*, I had to look twice to make sure it was my regal looking great aunt with her snow-white hair pulled into a French roll and smelling of delicious lilac who was speaking.

"Grandma and her other sister, Great Aunt Marvel, suddenly roared with laughter.

"I forgot all about that story," Marvel squealed through her amusement.

"Is not a story we should tell young boys," Grandma chided, although she was unable to hold back her own deep chuckles.

"It's a story our papa told us when we wasn't knee-high to a grasshopper," Great-aunt Shelly insisted.

"You just like to say the word *fart* in public. You was always like that, sister. You like to shock people . . . even if they're only little boys," Grandma persisted.

"Fart is a perfectly useable word, Madeline. Did you know that Benjamin Franklin, one of the fathers of this country, wrote a book titled *Fart With Pride?*" Great-aunt Shelly argued.

"Well, both you and Benjamin Franklin should have your mouths washed out with soap," Grandma retorted, although I could tell she was still greatly amused.

"You can be such a prude, Madeline . . . and the older you get the worse you get," Great-aunt Shelly told her.

"Ladies shouldn't discuss such things in the company of youngsters," Grandma asserted, although she was still not able to control a few remaining giggles.

"Oh, as if you don't fart, Madeline," Great-aunt Marvel gasped at Grandma through her own ebbing laughter.

"As I recall, Madeline, you don't so much fart as yodel . . . unless, of course, you're at church . . . and then you let out those little church farts of yours so nobody knows where they're comin' from," Great-aunt Shelly cackled, jabbing Grandma in the ribs.

Grandma's face flushed. She looked right at me and said, "Is true . . . I hate to admit it . . . but is true," she acknowledged, flipping her wrists and handkerchief at me. "Shelly, you had far too much wine with your supper . . . maybe me too," she concluded.

In a flash I knew something had passed between us that never happened before. My grandmother had spoken to me not just as her grandchild – but as a friend, someone with whom she felt as ease enough to let them in on the joke.

"Feed that girl beans and she could be the lead yodel in a cowboy band," Great-aunt Shelly moaned as she stopped walking and doubled over in a new fit of laughter.

"Feed her cabbage on the side and she can fumigate the barn at the same time," Great-aunt Marvel chuckled, gasping for air and throwing her arms around my grandmother affectionately.

178

"You two are just as dreadful in old age as you were as kids," Grandma declared.

"And you're still the prude in the family. At least I'm not afraid to be honest about such a fragile little thing as a fart," Great-aunt Shelly quipped.

"Come to think of it, dear," Grandma said, squaring her shoulders and looking directly at Great-aunt Shelly, "if I recall correctly, there isn't much fragile or little about any gust of wind that comes out of you."

"She got you, Shelly, she got you back good," Great-aunt Marvel whooped.

"She didn't get me at all," Great-aunt Shelly articulated sternly. "I never said there was anything fragile about me. The difference between Miss Prude and me has always been that I'm not afraid to admit it. And now, if you don't mind, I should like to see the Troll, or Kwazee or whoever the hell it is that shoots all that gas into the air." She started to giggle again.

"Kwatee," Willie corrected.

"Thank you, young man," she smiled. Then with a twinkle in her eye, asked: "Tell me, does this Kwatee fellow fart?" She and Great-aunt Marvel burst back into uproarious laughter again.

"One of them was so big, it blew down all the trees around Lake Quinault back in the ancient days," Willie answered matter-of-factly.

"Then I shall adore this Kwatee," Great-aunt Shelly noted in an English accent and throwing her nose into the air.

"Is that a real Indian story?" I asked Willie.

"Of course not, Fritz. It was a joke. Your Aunts were telling jokes so I made up one of my own."

179

"Don't that break some sort of ancient rule or something?" I asked.

"Come on, Fritz, Indians fart and Indians tell jokes. It ain't all sacred feathers and vision quests."

§§§

After returning from the hike, some of the women went back to the picnic area to finish cleaning up the remaining mess of the feast while the rest of us walked over to the dance pavilion where the uncles were already setting up their band on the stage. It wasn't until we actually entered the pavilion that I realized Willie was walking with my cousin Lorrain and looking pretty chummy.

"I think Willie is as twitterpated over your cousin as you are with Lily Whitedove," Randy whispered in my ear.

"I thought about that when I introduced them," I whispered back.

In a matter of minutes, everyone was gathered for the dance. A few of the girl cousins practiced dance steps with one another on the sidelines, but no one dared enter the floor until Grandma and Grandpa arrived. The first dance was always theirs and it was always Grandpa's favorite tune, *Dear Old Girl*. As soon as Grandma walked into the hall, the uncles began playing the waltz. Grandpa walked over to her, took her by the hand and led her to the center of the dance floor. It always amazed me how well they danced together. In my mind they were the Ginger Rogers and Fred Astaire of Perkins Prairie. They knew all the formal moves of the waltz and fox-trot and glided over the floor as smoothly and gracefully as ice skaters.

When the song was about half over, they separated to choose different partners for the dance. Grandma always chose her first born son, Uncle Amos. Grandpa always chose his first born daughter, Aunt Ladean. The band continued to play the song while the couples separated again and again to choose new partners until almost everyone in every branch of the family was on the dance floor. I couldn't help but notice that Cousin Lorrain asked Willie to dance. Randy and I were still standing on the sidelines watching when Grandma came over to me and motioned me onto the floor.

"I don't know how to do the waltz yet," I reminded her under my breath.

"Time you learned," she said, pulling me to the center of the floor. "We'll do the box step. It's easy," she said, placing my right arm around her waist and counting out the steps. It took a few seconds but I caught on quickly. Soon we were out among the crowd dancing with the best of them. When I looked back to see what had happened to Randy, I saw that he was dancing with my Cousin Sarah Jo.

Once the song was finished, Uncle Fabien, who played the accordion and led the band, walked to the microphone. "As you know, each year we get together, I always introduce any new members of the family or guests. We have no new children or spouses this year but we do have two guests. Many of you have already met them. They're friends of Tony and Marge's boy, Fritz. Willie and Randy Redwing, would you please come up so I can officially introduce you to the Harding clan. Clan, let's hear it for the Redwing boys."

The boys stepped onto the stage with much less embarrassment than I would have had if leaders of the Tahola Days celebration asked me to come up on a stage in front of every one. A round of applause went through the room as Randy and Willie walked across the stage to where my uncle stood. "It was Willie who won the Perkins Prairie Roller Skating Contest . . . and Randy who has proven to be such a good tennis player. Some time back, Fritz attended a big celebration out on the coast with the Redwing family. He tells me they are both very skilled at Indian dancing. I think that with a little encouragement from us, we might convince them to perform one of their dances today," Uncle Fabien suggested.

The family began to whistle and applaud again. I had the distinct feeling the boys didn't need much encouragement. Randy asked Uncle Charley if he could use his drums. He took the microphone from Uncle Fabien, sat down in the front of the drums and began thumping out a soft beat.

"My brother, Willie, will do the whale dance," Randy announced.

All eyes moved to Willie at the center of the stage. He had just kicked off his tennis shoes and was standing in his stocking feet.

"Hoi ya-ya!" Randy shouted, continuing the rhythm on the drum.

"Hoi ya-ya!" answered Willie. He put his hands

on his hips and began the whale dance by circling the room, appearing to search across the stage for something. His feet moved to the beat of the drum and should have caused his whole body to bounce. But it didn't. His upper torso swayed almost elegantly to the steady rhythm of the drum while his feet seemed to move almost furiously to a cadence no one else could hear. Suddenly his steps slowed and widened almost as if he were gliding on ice in slow motion across the stage.

"The hunter looks for the great whale from his longboat," Randy said over the beat of the drum.

Willie began a motion with his arms that gave the impression he was throwing spears through the air.

"The hunter has spotted the great whale and tries to harpoon him," Randy chanted first in Salishan, then in English.

Willie began to dance in a slow circle with his arms stretched heavenward.

"The hunter prays to the Great Spirit and to the Spirit of the Whale to forgive him for the kill. He tells the Spirit of the Whale he has taken his life only because his family must eat, and he must light their lodge with the rendered fats beneath his skin. He tells the whale that nothing will be wasted, that his death will bring life and nourishment and tools to the whole clan.

Willie began softly chanting in Salishan.

"The hunter is singing a song that reminds the people that from death comes life, that it is the way of the world. The song tells the people that just as soil feeds the grass that brings the seeds for the mouse to

183

eat, so does the mouse become the food of Brother Snake, and Brother Snake the food for Brother Eagle. The song reminds the people that just as Brother Bear eats both berries and King Salmon, mushrooms and spotted deer, and then in old age dies himself lying down to become food for the grasses, we too are part of the sacred circle. As the song concludes, Willie will ask the Great Spirit to bless the cycle of life."

Willie began motions and dance steps that indicated he was pulling the whale onto the shore, then began dancing in a circle going in the opposite direction.

"The hunter dances now for the whale's blessing," Randy chanted.

Willie began dancing furiously in a tighter and tighter circle until he was almost spinning like a top, then came to a stop with his arms extended above his head.

"The hunter now thanks the Great Spirit for his success and vows he will never kill for the joy of killing . . . only for necessity - for food and sustenance and oil and tools," Randy concluded, bringing the drum to its final beat.

The whole family broke into wild applause and more whistles to show their approval to the boys. Randy joined Willie at center stage and together the two boys gave one long deep bow.

I was bursting with pride, not just for my friends but for my family as well. It was good knowing that none of them still harbored bad feelings about past history or the Whitman Massacre. I turned to meet the boys as they stepped off the stage, Cousin Lorrain stepped in front of me and took Willie's hand before I could congratulate him. Randy and I watched as the two of them glided out onto the dance floor to the family band's rendition of "The Tennessee Waltz."

Chapter Six

Chases Rainbows

The day finally came for the Redwing's late August trip back to the Quinault Reservation. I had my bags packed for a week ahead of time. Berry picking and mowing lawns had been a lot of work, but not only had I replaced my watch and purchased my school supplies, I also had enough tucked away to attend the Puyallup State Fair and had opened my first savings account with $7.64. It had been difficult not to spend extra money on records and candy, but I wanted to show my parents I was leaving my childish ways behind me and becoming a responsible young man.

When I arrived at the Redwings' home, I discovered that Clarence wasn't going to make the trip with us. His cleaning business was doing better than expected as people began getting clothes ready for the coming school year, and once again Mrs. Radford wasn't going to be able to work in his shop while he was gone. Grandmother Sunfield had come up from the Muckelshoot Reservation to watch the twins and take care of the house while Audrey and the boys and I were away.

We stopped off in the village of Moclips before traveling on to the reservation so Audrey could visit with an old school chum. The boys and I walked along the beach gathering shells for a while. We had gone only a few hundred yards when Randy stopped in his tracks and pointed to a house on the hill above the beach. "That's Lily Whitedove's home," he announced.

"Can we walk over there and see if she's home?" I asked.

"Sure," Willie answered, heading up a path lined with bunchgrass.

I prayed she would be home but as luck would have it, she had gone that morning to the Queets Reservation with her father to attend an auction and baby-sit an aunt's children while the aunt and uncle dug clams. I was disappointed but eager for the adventure awaiting me in the old village of the Quinault Reservation. I prayed that Saddles Seatco was there and hadn't forgotten his promise to help me on a vision quest so I could wear my feathers up.

In less than an hour, we were at the upper reservation at Lake Quinault. Audrey drove to Clarence's brother's new government house where we would be staying because Grandmother Redwing's home had only one bedroom. As we pulled up in front of the house, it occurred to me there wouldn't be room for us there either. All the government houses were the same - two-story frame homes painted white and each having three small bedrooms. "Do you think they'll have room for all of us?" I asked as we got out of the car.

"Uncle Billy owns a little mobile trailer. Remember, I pointed it out to you when we were at Tahola Days? We'll sleep in it. Mom will sleep on the couch," Randy answered.

Audrey's in-laws came out of their house to

187

greet us. "Isn't this young Fritz Harding from Perkins Prairie?" Bill asked.

"It is indeed. He's come to ask Saddles to help him go on a vision quest," Audrey replied.

"That will please Saddles no end. Not many seek visions these days," Bill's wife announced.

After the boys and I put our gear in the little mobile trailer, we went into the house through the back entrance to get a glass of water. We were suddenly aware that we had stepped into the middle of an important conversation going on in the other room.

"I tell you, Alice, they mean it this time. Grandma won't listen to any of us. Maybe she'll listen to you. They told her she has until the 15th of September to vacate her little house and move into the government house they've provided for her or they'll send in troops and move her forcibly," Alice, Bill's wife explained.

"They told her they're going to bulldoze those little houses in the old village, hers included, whether she likes it or not," Bill added.

"Can you even believe they'd speak to a woman of her rank like that?" Alice said disapprovingly.

The boys and I inched our way to the doorway of the living room to listen openly to the conversation.

"They visited her just the other day, then mailed her a document saying that her house along with the few remaining ones down there have all been condemned because they don't meet government standards. I tell you, they're serious this time. Grandma Redwing is going to have to face reality and move," Alice said with exasperation.

"It should be obvious to them that she is in good health. I just don't understand why they won't let her live out her last days in the old ways," Bill fretted.

"Maybe we should try to speak to the state authorities on her behalf," Audrey suggested.

"We've already talked to them until we turned blue in the face. They won't listen. The people in the government office just say they're following orders from higher-ups . . . and so far, we haven't been able to find out who the higher-ups are!" Bill grunted.

"Later I'll go down to the market and call Clarence and let him know. He might have some suggestions and he may want to come up and speak to his mother as well. He would have been here but he just can't find reliable help right now, and it seems that everyone in town is having his clothes cleaned this week," Alice said.

"Do you want some tea, dear?" Alice asked, shooing us from the doorway as she walked into her kitchen.

"That sounds good," Audrey answered.

"I don't understand why they can't just leave that poor dear alone. She loves it down there. In a few years, she's going to have to move in with one of us anyway. I don't know why they can't leave her alone until time takes its toll. They know Indians never put their old ones in nursing homes like they do. They know she's only got a few more years to enjoy it down there. I just don't understand why these government policies never take the wishes of the people they're supposed to be serving into consideration," Alice shrugged.

"They have never taken our wishes into consideration," Bill grunted.

"You'd think that by now they would have learned that we know what is best for us. I'm so sick of it. They treat us like children. Our people lived on this land for thousands of years without an Indian agent telling us what to do or how to live or where. We didn't need them then and we don't need them now," Audrey asserted.

"I noted you and Clarence didn't have any trouble accepting their money to move to Perkins Prairie and open that cleaning establishment," Bill noted.

"And I notice that you are living in a nice new government house with a flush toilet, central heating, and mail delivery right to your front door," Audrey quipped.

"Let's not fight among ourselves. Times have changed. We know that . . . the point is why do they have to change for Clarence's mother when everyone knows except the government that she'll be just fine where she is? She loves living down there. It's a hard life . . . but I think that's what keeps her going. It's just not fair," Alice sighed.

Has Saddles tried to talk to her?" Audrey asked, accepting a mug of tea from her sister-in-law.

"Of course. He actually likes his new home. He hasn't been well the past few years. He's getting awfully old. I think he actually looked forward to his new house. I haven't visited yet . . . but those who have say it's fixed up like a swank big city apartment . . . lots of pillows, carpets, dried flowers, and some antique

190

furniture he evidently had in storage for years from the days when he was a window dresser in San Francisco," Bill commented.

"Well, I'll go call Clarence. Anything you want from the market?" Audrey asked.

"No . . . but could you drive down and pick up Clarence's mother. I went down to see her this morning. Her arthritis is really acting up today. I told her you or I would drive down and get her for supper," Alice explained.

"Can we go to the market with you?" Willie asked.

"No, I want you boys to go out back and pick some apples for Aunt Alice. If you'll pick and peel them, she's promised to bake two of her famous apple pies for dessert tonight. Okay?"

"Okay," the three of us said in unison.

After Audrey left for the market, the boys and I took a bag and went out in the backyard to pick the apples. "I think we should ask Saddles Seatco to help. Sometimes he can convince Kwatee not to make changes. We'll go see him after we pick the apples if Aunt Alice will let us," Willie said.

With the three of us picking and peeling, it didn't take long to have the apples ready for their aunt's pies. We were just going to ask about visiting Saddles Seatco when Audrey walked back into the house.

"Did Dad have any suggestions?" Willie asked.

"Yes. He said he heard a rumor that young Donald Crowfeather and Becky Cranes-In-Flight are getting married in a couple of weeks. He suggested we ask them to petition the agency for that last available house, the one that's slated for Grandmother Redwing. According to the government's own rules, any new couple has priority on the government houses. If the Indian agent will give the house to Donald and Becky, maybe we can buy some time - at least until spring. I stopped by Donald's house and spoke with his father about the matter. He said he would speak to the kids about it this evening."

"It's worth a try," Alice commented. "You want me to go get Mother Redwing?"

"No. I'll do it. I just wanted to tell you what Clarence suggested and that I spoke with Donald's father before I drive down and get her," Audrey replied, heading for the front door.

"Can we hitch a ride to Saddle Seatco's house," Randy asked.

"Did you pick the apples for your aunt?"

"Picked and peeled and floating in a big bowl of cold salt water. Plenty for two big pies. Fritz wants to speak to Saddles about his vision quest, and me and Randy wanna talk to him about somethin' too," Willie answered.

§§§§

The tribal shaman was planting flowers beside his house when we drove up.

"You boys shouldn't stay much more than an hour. Aunt Alice will have dinner soon. I don't want to have to come over here to get you since my place will be in the kitchen too. Okay?" Audrey warned.

"An hour," Randy repeated, jumping out of the car.

"I hope he has time to speak with us," I said under my breath as the three of us walked toward him.

"Don't worry about that. I've never seen a time when Saddles Seatco didn't have time to speak to young men and boys. If he doesn't have time . . . he'll make it," Willie said with a slight giggle echoed by Randy.

"That's nice," I replied, oblivious of the implications in his statement.

"Greetings, youngsters," the old man said, looking up from his work.

"Plantin' flowers?" Willie asked.

"Yes. I'm transplanting some flowers and a few herbs I had growing around the old house. But my garden is still where it's always been. It's good exercise for me to walk down there each day and it gives me a chance to check up on that old lady down there. I'm growing some squash that's the envy of your good grandmother," the shaman replied. "Now, to what do I have the honor of this visit by three such handsome young men?"

"We wanted to talk to you about Grandma, and Fritz was hopin' you could help him with a vision quest," Willie answered.

"To your latter question I respond with a warm and welcome yes. But before I discuss vision quests, why don't you tell me what's bothering you about your grandmother," Saddles responded, taking a package of Bull Durham tobacco out of his shirt pocket and loosening the string around the opening.

193

I was silently ecstatic and barely paid attention as Willie explained his grandmother's plight and his father's suggestion about the newlyweds.

Saddles took a brown cigarette paper from the package, folded it down the middle with a V shaped crease and sprinkled tobacco into it without spilling a single speck to the ground. Then, with only one hand, he rolled a perfect cigarette, sealed the end paper with moisture from his tongue and lit it up before answering. "Your grandmother is a wise if stubborn woman. We both received our names on the same day. I decided to move without a struggle. I am old. My joints hurt in the winter months. I like having electricity and running water. I was all the time takin' hot baths up at my cousin's house even in the summer the last few years. This change is okay with me. I lived in San Francisco for too many years not to appreciate some of the finer things in life. But your grandmother has never lived anywhere but in the old village. I know she has vowed not to move no matter what. She is as brave as any chief and will put up a real struggle in this matter. I have already told her she cannot win in this issue. But you know your grandmother," Saddles observed, taking a couple of quick puffs on his cigarette.

"Couldn't you work some magic?" I asked.

"Well, there is something we could try," Saddles noted after a long silence

"What's that?" Randy asked.

"There is a prayer we could say up at the agent's office after they leave for the day. You boys would have to go into the woods and get me some special roots to grind into a paste to paint on the corners of this building. I'm just too old to go out in those damp woods and dig up roots anymore. Of course, I can't promise the magic will work. That will depend on Kwatee. He may be behind this change in your grandmother's life. If it is Kwatee's will that she move to the new government house . . . nothing I can do will help. But there is a difference between Kwatee's perfect will and his permissive will. If this is only his permissive will . . . then the magic may just do the trick. Besides, Kwatee can't much care for all these government changes that take away Indian rights. The less Indian we become the less power Kwatee has," Saddles explained, taking an especially large amount of smoke into his lungs.

"What kind of roots do you require, Grandfather?" Randy asked.

"I will require the roots of the salmonberry bush. Three good-sized pieces. There's a stand of salmonberries along the road leading to the new village. You dig them after your supper tonight and bring them to me. Wear something traditional. You don't have to be in full costume . . . in fact it's better that you aren't . . . but you should be wearing something establishmentarian. The magic won't work if you wear only European style clothing. Bring them to me and we'll go to the agent's office and see what we can do. Ask your mother to bring her car. I'm much too old to walk that distance. Besides, there's already a chill in the air." He blew an enormous smoke ring into the air toward us.

"What's *establishmentarian mean?*" Willie asked.

"It's one of those fancy words I learned while living in California. It just means traditional . . . but I like to keep up my vocabulary whenever I can." He threw his head back and produced a perfect circle of smoke with a single puff of breath. For some reason he reminded me of Veronica Lake for a moment. I had seen her do the same thing while talking to a thug in a movie at the Cosmo in Perkins Prairie.

"And what about Fritz's vision quest?" Randy asked.

Saddles Seatco studied me for a few long seconds before speaking. "You still desire to go on a traditional vision quest?" he asked.

"Yes, sir. It's all I've thought about since my visit to Tahola Days," I admitted.

"Tomorrow, when you wake up, eat no breakfast. Be here at dawn. You may bring Willie and Randy with you if you like. They, of course, may have their morning meal. Do you still have the gifts you received at Potlatch?"

"Yes, sir," I replied.

"If you want to give me respect, call me grandfather. The word 'sir' is not customary among our people."

"Yes, sir. I mean . . . yes, Grandfather," I obliged.

"How will you boys pay me for my magic?" he asked with a mischievous smile that caught me off guard.

"How about if we weed your garden for you," Willie suggested.

His mischievous smile faded. "That will be most

196

acceptable," he agreed. "You can weed the garden while Fritz goes on his vision quest."

"Do you need anything besides the salmonberry roots?" Willie inquired.

"Ask your grandmother for a few strands of hair," the shaman told him.

Later that evening, while eating dinner, Willie explained their plan to his grandmother and asked for the strands of hair. "You can get some from my hair brush when your mama takes me back home tonight," she answered.

"You think it will work?" I asked.

"Sometimes the magic works and sometimes it don't. But even if it don't, I will never move from my home of my own volition. They'll have to tie me up with ropes and carry me from my house like a slain deer," she said defiantly.

"Well, don't forget the other option. We're going to ask Donald Crowfeather if he'll make a formal request for the house that's ready now. It will take them another month or so to build the next house. That will buy us some time," Alice reminded everyone

After dinner we passed the Crowfeathers on our walk down to dig the salmonberry roots. By the time we returned with them, so Audrey could drive us over to pick up Saddles Seatco, Donald had agreed to request the government house slated for Grandmother Redwing. It seemed to me that his decision along with the shaman's magic would certainly ensure that the old woman would be permitted to continue living in her home in the old village.

I expected Saddles to grind the roots in

197

something like the bowl and pestle the druggist in Perkins Prairie kept on display in his front window. To my surprise, the shaman put them into a common small meat grinder and ground the roots into a mush. To this he added some dirt, Grandmother Redwing's hair, and a few tablespoons of ashes to help the substance become a thick paste. "There. It's finished. We go now. Did anyone check to make sure none of the agents remained behind to do any late night work?" he asked.

"There were no cars parked in front when we drove by," Audrey told him.

"Well, then I think we are as ready as we're going to get," he replied, heading out the door to the Redwing car.

As we drove toward the government office, Saddles began chanting quietly. It was a different tune than I had ever heard before. Haunting. Something inside told me this was magic that came from a deep and mysterious place. I hoped it would be as strong when the time came for me to enter my vision quest.

Audrey parked the car a block away from the government office building. The five of us walked down the sidewalk together as nonchalantly as if we were out for an evening stroll.

"My Lummi friend came by yesterday. He brought me a whole bag of kouse roots. More than I can eat. I already gave some to Clarence's mother but have lots left. Maybe you would like to take some back home for you and the kids and Clarence," the old man suggested to Audrey.

"Oh my, yes. I love kouse! It's so hard to find

these days. Where did he get them?" Audrey inquired.

"He spent some time camping over on Lopez Island. He found a whole patch of them growing in the woods above Shark's Cove. He said he got a whole gunnysack full. He brought me half. I been doin' some magic for his family and he ain't had nothing to pay me until he found the kouse," Saddles answered.

"How come he didn't just pay you with money?" I asked.

"You do not pay a shaman with money. Money is European. We always pay our shaman in goods and gifts or labor," Willie answered.

"Well, what is kouse?" I questioned.

"Its a root. Sort of like a parsnip, only much better. I think the word is Chinook jargon. It means *biscuit-root*. Some folks grind them and let them dry, then use the powdered root like flour. It can also be used as a tenderizing agent on tough meats, like beaver and raccoon. I like them fried like potato, but they're very good boiled and baked too," Saddles concluded.

As soon as we arrived at the government building, Saddles headed around the building to the back. He turned and cautioned the rest of us to wait for him at the side of the building, "Just in case the spirit of Seatco is behind all this. Sometimes when I chase the evil one from a place, he attacks people standing too close. You wait and watch from here," he muttered.

The four of us sat down on the dampening evening grass and watched. As soon as Saddles reached the corner of the building, he took a small amount of the concoction he had made and spread it on the corner of the building. Then he disappeared out of sight. We could hear him chanting and singing as he made his way around the building. He made several circles around the small office seemingly oblivious to our presence.

Suddenly a gust of wind came up and blew our way, messing Audrey's hair just as Saddles rejoined us. "Kwatee has fixed what he can," he announced.

"Does that mean Grandmother Redwing will stay in her house," I asked.

"For a while," he answered with a confidence that invited immediate belief.

"Would you like to come up to the house for a piece of apple pie with us before I drive you home?" Audrey asked as we walked back to the car.

"Any ice cream to go with that?" Saddles inquired.

"I don't know, but we can stop by the little store and get some. They're open until ten," she suggested.

"Get tutti-frutti, it's my favorite," Saddles said, getting back into the car and allowing Willie to shut the door for him.

"That's my favorite too," I admitted.

"That's because you are part Micmac. All the best Indians prefer tutti-frutti," Saddles said.

"Is that true?" I asked.

"Of course, it's not true. He's teasing you," Audrey answered.

"I've been thinking, boy; it would be better if you met me down at the old village in the morning. You'll start your vision quest from there. I'll meet you there," Saddles said.

"Should I hike down to Grandmother Redwing's home?"

"That would be good. I need to go down to my old house and pick up a few things anyway. But you must be there by dawn."

"I can hardly wait," I said honestly.

§§§§

I woke up the next morning and glanced at my wristwatch. It wasn't quite six in the morning but dawn was already about to nudge its way into the eastern sky. I slipped out of bed, dressed as quietly as possible, and left my two friends sleeping in the tiny trailer. Once I was fully dressed, I took the little brown sack that held my moccasins, the leather pouch with my blue stone in it, and the headdress Lily Whitedove had given me out of my suit case and went outside.

It was a typical summer morning on the coast. A light fog from the sea enveloped everything causing the Douglas fir and pines to take on a mysterious look. Somewhere out on the lake, a whooping crane was hooting to its mate. I headed down to the old village. As I passed the salmonberry bushes where we had dug roots the day before, I almost reached out for a handful of berries but pulled my hand back remembering I was to eat nothing, not even water, until Saddles Seatco said I could. I walked the rest of the way down the hill. Suddenly I saw a figure coming toward me through the fog. At first I thought it might be Saddles, but as the figure walked closer and closer, I saw it was Grandmother Redwing gathering kindling for her morning fire.

"Good morning," I said. Do you need any help?"

"I think I have plenty now, but you can carry them back to the house for me if you like."

I took the kindling from her and we began walking back to the house in silence. I had been struggling with the knowledge that true visions only came to people who were honest-hearted, and I knew I had never told the older Mrs. Redwing the truth about that second bowl of dog stew. "There is something I've been meaning to tell you," I said as we made our way down the center of the dirt road leading to her little house by the lake.

"And what is that?" she asked, picking up a fallen branch along the road to use as a walking stick.

"I didn't eat that second bowl of dog stew. When I found out it had dog meat in it . . . I felt real queasy and took the bowl outside and dumped it in the river."

"I know," she said quietly.

"You know?"

"Yes. Just after I filled your bowl, I went out the backdoor of the hall to get some fresh air and rest my arms from feeding people. I walked down by the river. That's when I saw you dump your bowl out."

But you bragged to people that I ate two bowls," I murmured with great embarrassment.

"That was to see if your heart was the heart of an honest man or that of a man who keeps dishonest secrets. There is an old Indian saying that teaches that a person who will lie about little things will also lie about big things. Actually, Fritz Harding of Perkins Prairie, dumping a bowl of dog stew into the river isn't a very big or important matter. Letting people think you ate both bowls is a lot different. You have told the truth about the dog stew. From this day on, I will trust you in all things. Today you have become my grandson," she said, taking my arm to steady herself for the rest of the walk back to her little house with the lean-to out back.

"Thank you, Grandmother," I said. "I am honored."

"You will honor me further by telling Saddles Seatco the truth about the dog stew," she instructed.

"I will," I told her honestly.

Once we arrived at her home, I carried two loads of wood and stacked them in the lean-to for her, brought three buckets of fresh water to her from the lake, and poured them into the wooden barrel she kept next to the basin in her kitchen. "I wonder when Mr. Seatco will get here?" I asked.

"He lives his life on Indian time. He will show up when he shows up. Thank you for bringing me the wood and water. I have a little gift for your quest," she answered, handing me a package wrapped in newspaper.

"What's this?" I asked.

"Open it up and see. It's something I made for you right after Tahola Days when I learned you would seek a vision."

I opened the package and looked at the

unusually shaped leather garment and an additional leather string. "What is it?" I inquired.

"It's a breechcloth. Sometimes white eyes call it a loincloth. I made it so you can be dressed in more traditional clothing than just your moccasins and headdress. It will cover up your nakedness. You slip into it just like you would a bathing suit, then tie these leather strings just above your hips to keep it in place. The leather string is so you can tie the little leather pouch around your neck. That's where it really belongs, not in your pocket. You should always keep your sacred stones and bones in the amulet hung from your neck. With these and the other gifts you received at Potlatch, Tyee Sahle will know you as one of his own and may be more willing to grant you your vision today," she said.

"Oh, this is great. Can I put it on now? I've got my other stuff with me. How can I ever thank you?

"You have already thanked me by accepting the gifts. But if you wish to do something more, and if you find any yellow finch feathers in the forest, you can bring them to me just in case I need them someday," she answered, patting me on the shoulder.

"You bet. I'll look very carefully for yellow finch feathers. Who is Tyee Sahle?"

"The granter of visions. Some say Tyee Sahle is the purest representation of the Great Spirit we ever encounter on this side of the great divide. You will not see him . . . but if you are very lucky, you will feel his presence. Sometimes he comes in the wind, sometimes in the voice of birds or the baying of wolves and coyotes. I even met a woman once who met him in the rustle of leaves in a great oak tree up in the hills above the lake. Tyee Sahle must open the door to your vision. You must be brave enough to walk through it."

"Have you met Tyee Sahle?" I asked.

"Oh, yes. Men are not the only members of the tribes to go on vision quests. Someday I will tell you how I met the Great Spirit . . . but now it is time for you to think about your own vision quest. Saddles will be waiting for you."

"I thought I was supposed to meet him here."

"No, no . . . he will be up at his old house. He's probably up there now getting things ready for you. You slip into your clothes and walk over there. It's a much better idea to change clothes here than over at his place. I can show you which of the old houses it is from the porch."

I walked into her bedroom, took off my T-shirt, jeans, socks and tennis shoes and slipped into my new breechcloth, put on my moccasins and tied the headband on my head. I looked around for a mirror but finding none, I walked back into the main room of her little house. "How do I look?"

"Like a curly-headed Indian boy," she giggled.

"I'm not sure how to get this leather string through the opening on my amulet. Can you show me?"

The old woman took the string and leather pouch from my hands and carefully wove the leather strand through the small slits at the opening. Once she had it evenly distributed, she tied the two ends of the leather string in a very tiny knot and placed it over my head. "There . . . that will do just fine," she muttered.

"Thank you, Grandmother. How many yellow finch feathers do you want me to gather for you?"

"Two or three will be enough."

"And how will I know if they are finch feathers or those of the wild canary or the meadowlark?"

"It will not matter. If they are pure yellow . . . the magic is already in them."

When we walked out onto her front porch, I was dressed in only my breechcloth, moccasins, headdress, and my amulet hanging from its new leather string. I noticed, at once that the fog had lifted.

"The sun is out. That's a good omen," Grandmother Redwing noted.

"I hope you're right. I'm feelin' pretty anxious about all this . . . and I'm gettin' real thirsty. I wish I didn't have to fast from even water," I complained.

"Don't worry. Saddles will give you a cup of hot tea. That will settle your stomach and take care of your thirst."

"Have you had a vision?" I asked.

"Of course. That's how I knew I would marry my husband and that's how I know I should remain in the old village. It was all shown to me in a vision. I am to overcome a great beast. I believe that beast is the one tryin' to force me out of my home and from this wonderful place where my ancestors lived for centuries. That's why I am stubborn, Fritz Harding of Perkins Prairie. It was shown to me in a vision. Now, you go on over to that old man's real house. It's the second one over there by that little grove scrub pines." She bent down and kissed me on the forehead.

I walked down the slight path through the tall

grass leading to the shaman's home. It surprised me that it had become so overgrown in such a short period of time. As I approached the second house, I could see it was also an old smokehouse that had been converted into a dwelling. Saddles Seatco was sitting on the steps of the porch waiting for me. I wondered how he had managed to get there. "Have you been fasting since midnight?" he asked when I was close enough to extend my hand in greeting.

"Yes, Grandfather," I replied.

"Good," he said, stepping down from the porch. "Now stand where you are with your arms above your head while I remove any evil or controversial spirits that may surround you. Close your eyes."

I did as the old man said. He began walking around me singing a song in Salishan deep from his throat. Occasionally he touched different parts of my body. They were quick touches . . . the top of my head, then both shoulders, my elbows, chest, abdomen, knees, ankles, feet, buttocks, back, and finally the top of my head again. Each time he touched me, he gave out with a heavily enunciated chant, though I would not go so far as to describe them as shouts. When he touched the top of my head for the second time, he spoke again in English. "We have finished the first of the initiation rituals. It is now time for the rain to cleanse you. You may open your eyes . . . but remain standing as you are," he directed, turning to get something from the little porch.

When he came back, he carried a small bowl of water in one hand and a freshly cut pine bough in the other. He began chanting again, then dipped the pine bough into the bowl of water and sprinkled it all over my body by snapping the pine bough toward me each time it left the bowl. Soon I was as wet as if I had been caught in a rain storm.

"You may lower your arms now. I have a pot of water boiling on my old stove and will make you a cup of tea."

"Good. I'm thirsty. What kind of tea is it?"

"It is a vision tea. The secret to the ingredients are passed down from one shaman to another. It is a sacred secret," he replied.

I followed him up the steps into the old house. It was very like Grandmother Redwing's except that it was stripped of everything but the old wood stove, a table and two chairs, a few dishes, a couple of cups on a shelf above the sink and an old crank up Edison phonograph player, well-polished and obviously well taken care of, standing in one corner. "How come you didn't take your record player up to your new house," I asked.

"I have a new electric model up at my new house. I keep this one down here along with a few records so when I come down, I can listen to music while I'm here. I got some friends who will take it up the hill before the government men come down here and bulldoze the old smokehouses. But until then . . . I like to have it down here. I like my new house just fine but if I wasn't so old . . . I would have stayed down here too. That's why I had you meet me here. The magic is much stronger down here than up on the hill."

"What kind of music do you like, Grandfather?" I asked.

"Mostly opera. I have many recordings down here of Galli Curci. Her Rigoletto is still the best I've ever heard," he said, going to the machine and pulling out a twelve inch disk recorded on just one side and handing it to me.

I looked at the label. It was deep red. The word *Victor* was printed in large letters. Above it was a little white short-haired dog gazing into the horn of a small portable record player. Below them were the words *His Master's Voice* and in smaller print below that were the words *Recorded February 1904*. "Boy, this is old," I said, handing the disk back to him with great care.

"I bought this along with other Verdi recordings when I lived in San Francisco. You can buy almost anything in San Francisco," he reflected. He put the record back into its slot and closed the cabinet doors.

"I didn't know Indians like opera, but I think someone did say something about you living in California when you were younger," I observed.

"When I was much younger, I moved to San Francisco. My name was Chases Rainbows in those days. It was a different time and in many ways I was a different person. I lived down there for over twenty years before returning to the reservation," he added, pouring boiling water into a small glass tea pot into which he had already dumped a few selected herbs.

"When did you move back to Lake Quinault?"

"When my father grew ill. He wanted to see me again before he died . . . so I returned to care for him. There was no one else. I was his only child. My mother died in childbirth. I never knew her." He picked up a spoon and stirred the herbs a little.

"And you decided to stay after he died?"

"His illness lasted for several years. Sometimes he'd get better and I'd think about moving back to California, but then he would get sick again. He was the medicine man for this tribe as my grandfather had been and his father before him. My father began to teach me how to prepare medicines, how to perform the sacred chants, and finally how to do magic."

"Why hadn't he taught you all that before you moved to California?"

"I was a different sort then . . . and not very interested in the old ways. I wanted the city life. I became a window dresser. I was very good at it. And I made many wonderful friends. San Francisco taught me its own magic. Opera was just one of its gifts. I met a man who became very important to me. He was a longshoreman. We lived together for many years. He died in an accident down on the wharf just before my father sent for me. It wasn't until I returned to the reservation that I became interested in the old ways again. At least that was part of it. Part of me just didn't want to return to San Francisco if I couldn't be with my special friend. So, when my father grew too ill to function as shaman for our people, the chief sent for three other shamans from local tribes. They sent me on a new vision quest. When I returned I had a new name . . . Saddles Seatco . . . and the chief made me the Man of Two Souls three weeks before my father passed on. It made him very proud to know I would carry on the family tradition after all. Here, drink this," he concluded, pouring me a cup of tea from the little ceramic teapot into which he had poured the boiling water.

I took the cup from his hands and smelled the aroma of the tea. It had a sweet smell to it which I supposed was that of honey. I took a tiny sip of the hot liquid. To my surprise it tasted like licorice. "You put some of the little fern roots that taste like anise in this, didn't you?" I noted.

"It is one of the ingredients. You are most astute. You might make a good shaman yourself someday," he told me.

We sat in silence as I drank the tea. When I finally emptied the contents of the cup, I placed it on the table and pushed it toward him to indicate that I was ready for the next step of my vision quest. "What happens next, Grandfather?" I asked.

"I must now give you the cautions. There will be spirits out in the woods who want to keep you from your vision. If they come to you in the form of doubts, remember I have already placed the armor of faith around your body and washed away any of the places doubts might try to take root. You must also remember that earth is your mother and the sun your father. The Earth is alive. The soil is her flesh, the rocks and mountains are her bones, the trees and grasses are her hair, the wind is her breath, the rain and the snow are her tears. You are the child of Mother Earth and Father Sun. You must show great respect for them always and especially today. You must thank them for life. You must ask them to intercede for you in prayer to Tyee Sahale. Ultimately it is only Tyee Sahale who can grant your vision. Do you understand?"

"I understand everything but who Tyee Sahale is. Grandmother Redwing mentioned his name. I meant to ask her to explain more fully . . . but I forgot."

"Tyee Sahale means *Great Chief up above* . . . sometimes we just say Great Spirit. Tyee Sahale is the true name of God in Chinook jargon. You must ask him for your vision. But don't forget to ask Mother Earth and Father Sun to pray for you as well. They are much older than you and have much stronger prayers than either you or I. You capeesh?"

"What is Chinook jargon, exactly?"

"It is a language made up of Salishan, English and French words. Chinookan is the language of tribes living along the lower Columbia and Willamette Rivers. It is much like our language. Over the years we all learned the Chinook jargon so we could better communicate with Whites. Eventually many Chinookan words became our own. Originally our tribes all spoke various versions of the Salishan tongue. More often than not, those variations were difficult for Whites to understand . . . so, we all took up Chinook jargon to make it easier for us when we traded with them. Now it is used by everyone. It is time for you to go down to the lake alone and stop asking questions. It is time to go into the forest to await your vision. You may take a walking stick with you but you must be careful to kill no animal, not even an insect with it. All creatures are the children of Mother Earth and Father Sun so all creatures are your brothers and sisters. It is especially important that you do not injure anyone today."

Saddles Seatco walked me out to his backyard and pointed to a path that led down to and around the lake. "You follow that path, boy. It will lead you out into the woods and to your vision."

"How will I know when I get to the right place?"

"You will know. You go. When you come back . . . things might be different for you. Things might also be same. I will know before you tell me." The old shaman turned and began walking toward the little shack that had once been his home.

"Any last minute advice," I yelled after him.

The old man turned around. "Yes. I forgot to tell you how to pray. Do not pray the way the missionaries taught us. They wanted us to ask the Great Spirit for things and to thank Him in the name of Jesus once we received them. But that is not the way of the Quinault. We pray very differently. If you want to pray like an Indian, you must learn to be still and listen for the voice of Tyee Sahale. He can speak in the wind or paint ideas in your mind more vivid than anything the eye can see. Tyee Sahale knows our needs before we do. There is no reason to remind him of anything. You will listen for his voice and he will listen for your voice. You will listen together. You need not be still to listen . . . and you do not have to speak to praise him."

"But how will I speak without words?"

"Through the vision and in the vision. Now remember. You listen and you let him listen."

"Yes, Grandfather, I'll remember. Anything else?"

"Nope. You're on your own now," he answered.

I watched as he turned and headed back towards his little house and his precious Victrola.

Chapter Seven

Talks With Eagles

I was halfway around the path that surrounds the lake when I found a good walking stick and picked it up. At about that same point, I came to a fork in the trail. One path continued around the lake, the other veered into the woods. I decided it was as good a place as any to go into the forest. I turned away from Lake Quinault and headed down the trail that led upwards and wound its way through the trees.

The path continued up a slow hill through a thickly wooded area for about a mile. Huge cedar and Douglas fir lined both sides of the path and blocked the morning sun from entering the forest. The trees were so dense I wouldn't have been able to see a deer if it had been standing five yards from me. The floor of the forest was lush with enormous ferns and carpeted with moss and Oregon grape. Except for the occasional sounds of birds singing and those flushed from their perches because of my intrusion, there was nothing but silence around me. There was something cathedral-like about the path as if the only light came from massive but invisible stained glass windows somewhere above me. I had been in the woods many times but never had it felt so sacred and intimidating. After a while I realized I had been praying. They weren't the kinds of supplications ending in the name of Jesus like the ones I had been taught at the Perkins Prairie Presbyterian Summer Vacation Bible School. These prayers were different. They were prayers directed to Mother Earth and Father Sun, to the Great Spirit of the universe.

I tried to use the name Tyee Sahale but it seemed too small a name for a God who suddenly seemed to me to be everywhere and nowhere, to be within me and beside me, to be within the ferns and trees, within the air I breathed and in the light that helped me find my way through the forest. I prayed for signs and wonders, for voices in the wind, for animals who could speak English, for omens in the branches of trees and in the petals of wild flowers I saw growing along the path.

Eventually I came to a small clearing. I stopped abruptly before stepping out from the trees because a small herd of white-tailed deer were in the clearing leisurely munching down their breakfast. I was spellbound by their grace and innocence. I had seen many deer in zoos and once at a family gathering in Rainier National Park, a doe accustomed to mooching food from campers and picnickers ate potato chips from my hand. But this was the first time I had come upon an entirely relaxed herd of deer casually beginning a typical day in the forest. The wind was in my favor. The deer were unaware of my presence. I watched them for the better part of a half an hour before they wandered, one at a time, back into the cover of the trees and disappeared into the foliage.

When I made my way down the path to the center of the small clearing it was filled with tall drying grasses. I used my walking stick to press down a circle in it so I could lie on my back and watch the clouds pass above me. Perhaps I would see my vision in the patterns of the clouds. To my surprise, the first clouds to resemble anything seemed to be in the shape of an airplane with an elephant riding on its back. Since there was nothing Indian about either, I decided to get up and continue my journey. But when I looked back up at the clouds, the airplane had been transformed into a huge eagle. The elephant now looked more like a giant bear, and where its trunk had been, three smaller clouds took the shapes of maple leaves.

The clouds took on many shapes and forms that morning, but before long I grew drowsy and was just beginning to slip away into the twilight of sleep when I was suddenly aware of something running across the clearing headed straight for me. Whatever it was, the wind was obviously behind it because it hadn't caught my scent and didn't know I was waiting in its path. It occurred to me that if the creature was one of the deer I had seen earlier, I might well have my abdomen or lungs punctured by its sharp hooves. I sat bolt upright and leaped to my feet. At that same instant, a bobcat broke through the tall grass and came to an immediate stop in the pressed down grass before me. I don't know who was more surprised or more frightened. We both gave out a yelp. Something dropped from the bobcat's mouth, but I was too intent at staring into its eyes to notice what it was.

For a split second we were both frozen in alarm and fear. I could feel my heart beating wildly in the cavity of my chest but was sure I wasn't breathing. The bobcat neither snarled nor curled its lips at me. For what seemed an eternity, we were two immobile and rigid creatures rendered all but witless by the shock of suddenly being in one another's presence. I tightened my grip on my walking stick, suddenly aware I could use it if the bobcat decided to attack. I debated about using it to threaten him to see if he would leave. He seemed to have read my mind and leaped back into the tall grass, bolting across the meadow into the security of the huge pine and Douglas fir trees that grew all along it.

It took me a few seconds to regain my composure. When I did, I looked down into the grass to see what had fallen from the bobcat's mouth. It was a dead bird . . . a yellow finch. Remembering Grandmother Redwing's request for yellow feathers, I picked up the tiny creature, plucked about six of the best feathers from its wings and carefully slipped them into the leather pouch tied around my neck.

Still shaken by the intrusion of the cat's visit, I decided to follow the path deeper into the woods and put some distance between me and the event in the clearing.

Once again the trail led through the density of the thick forest. I walked about a half hour when I heard the sounds of a small creek gurgling ahead. It wasn't much more than three feet wide and seemed to have tracked its way through the forest for hundreds, maybe thousands of years. Its bed was entirely composed of small pebbles. The body of the creek was lined with ferns and moss, and in the eddies small patches of watercress grew lush and green in its shallows. The water looked incredibly cool and delicious. I felt thirsty and was tempted to quench my thirst right then and there until I remembered the shaman's admonition that I should neither drink nor eat until after the vision had been given. Reluctantly, I moved along down the path and left the little stream and its tempting gurgles behind.

The next half mile was all uphill. I was glad I had the walking stick with me. Once I reached the summit, I came upon another meadow. This one was much larger than the first. I could see the jagged peaks of the Olympic Mountain Range stretched out before me. I wondered how many Indians had seen this same incredible view while hunting or traveling to powwows. It occurred to me that the mountains had a much older name than the one my European ancestors had given it. I made a mental note to ask someone about that as soon as I returned to the village.

Hunger and thirst began to gnaw at me again. I remembered Saddles Seatco telling me such cravings would be preludes to doubt. I tried to flush thoughts of water and food from my mind but the harder I tried, the more often I seemed to see visions of piles of food and ice cold bottles of Hires root beer before me. I decided it was a good time to do some praying. The spectacular mountains would provide the perfect setting for my prayers and perhaps concentrating on my desire for a real vision would dampen my interest in food and water. I stood facing the snow covered peaks of the Olympics, recalling how the old shaman had instructed me to pray. I closed my eyes, lifted my arms over my head and presented my palms to the sun. I

218

concentrated on emptying myself of hunger and thirst, from worry and anticipation, of fretting about the bobcat through whose territory I would soon have to walk again when I returned to the village and from the voices of doubt that spoke as if from behind closed doors, trying to dissuade me from believing that mighty visions, powerful enough to give one a new name and link me inexorably and forever to the natural flow of the planet and cosmos, were even possible.

One by one the intruders left me. I had the feeling that I was no longer just Fritz Harding of Perkins Prairie. I was part of the whole, a part of something larger than myself, perhaps even larger than all outdoors. I wondered if this was what it felt like to be a child of Mother Earth and Father Sun. It wasn't so much that my connection to Perkins Prairie was lost. I knew I was still a Harding, a boy of mostly Polish and English descent who was lucky enough to have a little Micmac blood flowing in his veins. And I knew I was a city boy. Perkins Prairie might have been a small town nestled in the foothills below Mt. Rainier, but it had most of the amenities of a larger city. It had its own newspaper, movie house, restaurants, shops, fire department and sometimes live entertainment. Still, I was equally aware that I was also a meadow creature exalting in the experience of being alive. I tried to quiet my thoughts. I wanted to enter a silence from which I might hear the voice of Tyee Sahale, the Great Spirit, from which and in which all things found sustenance and life and joy.

At that second, I heard the sudden screech of an eagle overhead. I opened my eyes just in time to see him swoop toward the forest and out of sight. Seconds later, he flew back over my head and circled the updrafts above me. I stood up and watched transfixed by his enormous wingspread and the ease with which he rode upon the invisible wind. Without warning he broke from his circle, pushed his wings through the air, then dropped like a missile behind the trees on the other side of the clearing.

I picked up my walking stick and continued my trek through the forest in the direction the eagle had flown. The forest grew darker and darker. At first, I thought it was just a particularly dense section of the woods, but looking up I saw dark clouds blowing in from the ocean. Soon they were everywhere overhead. Before long it began to rain. For a while, the thick boughs of the trees acted as an umbrella. All I felt was an occasional drop of dampness. But soon the branches began to drip with rain and a steady patter of droplets commenced pouring down unmercifully. Dressed in only a breechcloth and moccasins, I might as well have been walking naked in the rain. I was suddenly aware that while in the past a shower of rain might have been perturbing and uncomfortable . . . this time there was something natural, even sensual to the experience. I was also aware that something spiritual was happening to me. The drops of rain reminded me of how it had felt when Saddles Seatco dipped his pine bough in water and splattered it on my body. I couldn't help but wonder if Tyee Sahale was preparing me for the next step in my vision quest.

But despite the agreeability of the experience, the fact that I wore glasses made it more and more difficult to secure a sure footing on the trail. The raindrops on my lenses fragmented my vision. I could no longer see adequately to continue. I had seen a wall of rock a few feet back that appeared to have a slight overhang above it. I decided to retrace my steps and seek protection from the rain until the storm passed. I found a narrow trail leading toward the rock wall. To my surprise, it led directly to a shallow cave not much more than thirty feet deep. The opening was about four feet high. I peered inside to make sure the bobcat or some other creature hadn't already claimed it, then stepped inside. The ceiling stretched some twelve to fifteen feet above my head.

I swiftly learned I wasn't the first human to find the cave or to seek shelter in it. I found the remnants of several small fires and an embanked circle of stones in which a larger bonfire had once burned.

The ground of the cave was dry. I sat down near the entrance with my back to the wall and was instantly aware that I was much more exhausted than I had realized. What happened next is difficult to explain because I really don't know if I fell asleep and had a dream, or if, in fact, what occurred in the cave happened in full consciousness. I remember deciding to pray again after the manner of the Quinaults by emptying my mind and being slightly annoyed that both hunger and thirst were still gnawing away at my thought processes. I tried to concentrate on the sound of the rain falling on the stones outside the cave. I remember feeling drowsy and closing my eyes. I didn't think I was asleep and yet I recall thinking it was perfectly natural that the dripping of the rain seemed to echo the rhythm of my name. *Fritz Harding, Fritz Harding, Fritz Harding*. The more I focused my attention on it, the more clearly I heard the words. *Fritz Harding, Fritz Harding, Fritz Harding* splashing their way to the ground just outside the cave. For a few seconds, I wondered if perhaps Saddles Seatco had come to fetch me from my quest because of the bad weather, but then remembered that he could barely get up a flight of stairs by himself. I decided it couldn't be he. Maybe it was one of the Redwing boys sent up the mountain to bring me back. I hoped not. I wanted to finish what I had begun.

I continued to peer out into the rain. All at once I saw what I thought was the figure of someone or something coming toward me. I adjusted my glasses. When I looked out again, the figure of an old Indian man wrapped in a buffalo or bear robe stood before me at the entrance of the cave. I was suddenly filled with great apprehension but somehow it was void of real fear. The old man entered the cave. At first he seemed oblivious to my presence and set about making a small fire from a bundle of kindling and dry moss he took out from under his robe. "There are some bigger sticks and pieces of wood at the back of the cave, Fritz Harding of Perkins Prairie. Would you be kind enough to get them for me," he instructed. His voice was soft and unintimidating.

I got up and looked for the sticks and chunks of wood at the back of the cave and brought them to him. "How do you know my name, Grandfather?" I asked, placing the wood beside the fire.

"We were introduced during the Dog Dance at

Tahola Days," he answered, taking a few pieces of wood and arranging them above the flames. "This will take the chill from our bones," he assured.

"I don't recall that introduction," I replied honestly.

"It was I who taught you how to dance. Don't you remember how easily your feet and body participated and moved to the magic of the drums? I was also there when you dumped your second bowl of dog stew into the river. If you didn't see me, you can be sure that Grandmother Redwing did. It was also I who gave you the suggestion to give Lily Whitedove your West Bend wristwatch. In fact, Fritz Harding of Perkins Prairie, it was I who placed the need for your vision quest in your heart." All the time he spoke he did not look at me. He stared into the fire.

"Are you Tyee Sahale?" I asked.

"No, no, but I know him well," he replied, taking a thin branch and stoking the fire before placing a few larger pieces of wood on its flames.

"Am I having a vision now," I asked.

"Look into the fire," he instructed.

I did as I was told. The fire was beginning to burn well. A thin stream of blue smoke lifted above the flames to the roof of the cave and slipped out into the rain.

"Look deep into the flames. Study the coals."

As I concentrated on the coals forming below the burning wood, there seemed to be a path leading through them. Suddenly they were no longer coals but steep cliffs on either side of a valley through which a man dressed in buckskin was walking. He came upon a

223

young Indian woman picking berries. The man stopped to talk to the woman and began picking berries and putting them in her basket. Soon they walked off together. I remember blinking to see if I could bring them back. Instead, only the hot burning coals illuminated before me.

"That man was your great-grandfather. The woman . . . she is the source of the Micmac blood in you. She is your link to this cave and to this moment," the old man explained, placing additional sticks of wood on the fire. "Look back into the fire. It is the flames you must watch, not me," he instructed.

I returned my gaze to the flames in front of me and concentrated on the coals again to see if the vision of my great-grandparents would reemerge. The burning coals gave no vision this time. I was aware the old man next to me got up and moved to the other side of the fire. I wanted to remain steadfast in his directive to look into the fire and not him, but my curiosity about the fellow got the best of me. I looked up from the fire to get a better look at him. To my absolute surprise, the old man was gone and in his place stood an eagle with wings outstretched. He was fanning the flames. His gaze moved from the fire to me. His yellow eyes seemed to penetrate so deeply into my being, I began to tremble with fear. "You may ask me three questions," the eagle said. His voice was soft and melodic - nothing like the screech I had heard from the eagle who flew overhead when I was in the clearing farther down the mountain.

"You can talk!" I exclaimed in bewilderment.

"All animals can talk, Fritz Harding of Perkins

Prairie, but men are only privileged to understand our words on rare occasions like this," he volunteered.

"Are you the eagle I saw flying overhead and into the forest earlier today?" I asked, surprised to hear myself speaking to this quite remarkable bird.

"And it was I who took you flying while you slept," the enormous creature told me. He folded and tucked his wings back along the sides of his body.

"That was an incredible dream," I responded.

"That was no dream, Fritz Harding, anymore than being present to the meeting of your great-grandparents was a dream. They are both parts of your vision."

"My vision has already begun?"

You have been experiencing parts of your vision for weeks. One who desires as deeply as you is always rewarded. If you were desireless, you would have only seen the mystery of such things. But because you desire so completely, you have been given the manifestations as well. In that way, the mysteries become yours."

"And will they lead me to my new name?"

"Of course. The manifestations will be like stones upon which you cross the river of your life. Each stone will have a story to tell you and a mystery to reveal. You will learn to explain the revelations of those mysteries. The role of the storyteller is second only to the role of those who have two souls. From this day on, you must tell the stories waiting in the stones, in the flames and in the sky. That will be your payment for the visions."

"But when will I get my new name?"

"Look into the fire. Your new name waits there to be claimed," he instructed.

I didn't want to take my eyes from the eagle for fear he would disappear and I would never see or experience talking with him again. "Will I ever see you again?" I asked, almost pleading.

"Many times," he responded.

I looked back into the flames with some reluctance. I was pulled between wanting to learn my new name and continuing the conversation with Brother Eagle. But the moment I looked into the fire again, I knew the eagle was gone and that the old man had returned to his place across the fire. I searched through the burning coals for some hint of my new name. Nothing spoke to me. The two of us sat there in silence until the last of the flames cloaked over with a dull blanket of ash gray. Only then did I look up from where the fire had been and back into the old man's eyes.

"You may help me to my feet now," he said, breaking the long silence.

I got up from my place on the cave floor, walked around the smoldering ashes, and helped the old Indian stand up.

"It is time for me to go now and time for you to return to the village," he murmured, turning toward the cave entrance.

I followed him outside. The rain had stopped much earlier and the sun was shining again. Most of the rocks were already dry. We walked single file to the main path through the forest. The old man turned to go deeper into the woods. I started to follow him.

"No, no, you must go back to the village now," he said softly.

"Grandfather, " I said to his back, "I did not learn my new name from the fire."

"The old Indian turned around slowly, gave a slight bow and a great smile before speaking. "You have not yet learned to listen, Fritz Harding of Perkins Prairie. The fire told you your new name . . . you just did not hear it."

"Will I ever hear it?" I pleaded.

"It's no secret now. I heard it very plainly. You will now be known among our people as Talks With Eagles," he said, turning again to resume his journey back into the forest or back into whatever magical place he had come from.

"Thank you, Grandfather," I called after him.

He did not turn back around. He did lift his right arm to acknowledge he had heard my words of appreciation.

The name kept rolling and echoing through my mind like an anthem. Talks With Eagles . . . Talks With Eagles . . . the words sounded delicious. I watched until the old man disappeared into the woods. Then with a reluctance to leave the place of my vision but also filled with an excitement about my new name, I turned and started walking back to the old village.

I repeated my new name to myself over and over again. When I reached the largest of the two meadows, I saw the eagle perched high on one of the branches of a tall and majestic cedar tree. "Thank you, Grandfather!" I shouted up to him. The eagle gave several piercing screeches, then caught an updraft and flew out of sight.

§§§§

When I finally arrived back at the old village and made my way up the path leading to the last house to be occupied, I could see Saddles Seatco and Grandmother Redwing sitting in her backyard on a wooden bench. It had been made by resting a thick plank across the top of two parallel elder stumps. I remember seeing it for the first time and thinking what a good use it was for two stumps.

I walked up to them and stopped without saying anything. They were peeling early apples. The elder Mrs. Redwing put her work aside and walked to the barrel of water alongside the house. She dipped a gourd into it and brought it to me. I drank deeply. I don't remember ever being as thirsty as I was that afternoon. "Thank you." I said after drinking my fill.

"I got something fixed for you to eat in the house. You want it out here?" she asked.

"I love being in the little house. I'll eat inside, if it's okay with you," I answered.

"I'll go warm it up. You come inside when you're ready."

"I see you have had your vision," Saddles said from the bench.

"Can you tell just by looking at me?"

"You wear your feather up," he answered.

"I did not put my feather up," I replied with

surprise. I reached up and felt for the feather. Sure enough, it was in an upright position.

"Of course not. Only your Spirit Keeper can turn the feather up. Surely Saddles remembered to tell you that?" Grandmother Redwing said.

"No . . . he didn't mention it," I answered honestly.

"He's gettin' old and forgetful. There is no one to take his place, you know. No one in the village has stepped forward to become his apprentice . . . and, of course, he has no children of his own," she remarked as Saddles put his peeled apples aside and stood up.

"Tell us about your vision," he prompted.

"You didn't tell the boy his spirit guide would change the direction of his feather for him," the old woman chided.

Saddles shrugged his shoulders. "The magic still worked," he observed.

"You come on inside and have something to eat. You can tell us everything that happened while you eat. You must be famished," Grandmother Redwing instructed. She took the gourd from my hand and walked back towards the house.

"You must have found the cave," Saddles asserted as we walked up to the house.

"I did. But only because it was raining and I needed shelter. You didn't tell me to look for a cave," I replied.

"Details . . . details . . . details . . . is that all you two think about. I'm getting old. The important thing is that you found the cave. Besides . . . it is not the shaman who gives the vision or the urge for the quest.

It is Tyee Sahale. I am really nothing but an old man who knows how to do a few rituals and say a few prayers. The real mystery is between you and the Great Spirit. When you go to Him in faith . . . He always finds a way to find you. The cave is the traditional place . . . but it is not the only place. Still, I had my own first vision in that same cave. It is a very fond memory to me."

"So, it rained up in the hills. It hasn't rained here all day," Grandmother Redwing observed.

"It rained in torrents just above the lake. The clouds were so thick it was almost like night up there," I replied.

Once inside, the old woman took a plate from the warming oven above her wood burning stove and placed it on the table for me. "You eat. I caught some quail this morning after you left. I saved one for you. There are baked cattail roots for you as well. I baked them in wild honey. I stuffed the quail with eggs and some special herbs that grow wild out back. You will like it."

I ate ravenously and began telling them about the events of the day. Both listened with rapt attention as I told them about the small herd of deer I had seen in the first meadow, how the eagle had led me further into the forest, and how the rain led me to the cave.

"The trail you chose to take is the traditional path most Quinaults take who seek their vision. They are almost all given at the cave. Saddles and I used to make the trip two or three times a year to ensure there was always dry wood at the back of the cave for fire. I had a hunch your spirit guide would take you to the cave.   That's probably why he made it rain," Grandmother Redwing told me.

"Who is my spirit guide?"

"Isn't that fairly obvious," she mused.

"I think He Who Changes came to him," Saddles interrupted.

"He Who Changes?" I repeated.

"He Who Changes," Grandmother Redwing affirmed.

"Well, an old man did come into the cave and lit a fire. At least I think he did. I brought him wood I found at the back of the cave. He had me look into the coals. I saw my great-grandmother and great-grandfather meet and fall in love. Then the old man turned into an eagle . . . sounds weird, huh?"

"Not to me," Saddles asserted.

"Well, it was kinda weird. The eagle talked to me just like if he was a man. And I didn't even feel dumb talking to a big old bird like that. It seemed like the most natural thing in the world. Well . . . I was a little surprised at first . . . but I got used to it real fast. Now you gotta admit that that's weird."

"He Who Changes has appeared to many of us," Grandmother Redwing assured me. "Now eat some more of this food before you perish."

"Do you think it was the same eagle who appeared to me in the meadow?" I asked, stabbing a bit of cattail root onto my fork.

"Of course. He Who Changes is your spirit guide . . . but Brother Eagle is your spirit keeper. It was he who appeared in the meadow and he who led you to the cave. You can count on that," Saddles said. He reached over with his fingers and picked up a small bite of baked cattail root from my plate and placed it in his mouth. "Can't help myself. I love the way she fixes these," he mumbled.

"How do you like your new name?" Grandmother Redwing asked, motioning with her hand for me to put the food on my fork into my mouth.

"I love it. You wanna know what it is?"

"We already know," Saddle informed me.

"But I haven't told you yet," I said.

"You don't have to. Your new name is Talks With Eagles," Grandmother Redwing stated.

"How did you know?"

"You talked with an eagle! You don't suppose just anybody does that, do you? I have never talked with eagles," Grandmother Redwing teased.

"I have talked with eagles . . . but I talk with all the animals," Saddles pointed out.

"Yes, but you are shaman . . . for you such things are ordinary. In Fritz's case . . . this is extraordinary. Besides, Saddles, you even talk in your sleep."

"Who did you meet in the cave?" I asked Saddles.

"I came to the cave late in life. There were many demons waiting for me there. Seatco himself was the greatest among them. I had to wrestle each of them to the ground and chase them out of the cave one at a time before my spirit keeper could come anywhere near me. Seatco was the most difficult to fight off. To this day I don't know where I got the strength or courage . . . but fight I did. And I won. I not only wrestled Seatco to the floor, I straddled him like a horse and

232

rode him into the spirit world. Even then, because of my many sins, my spirit keeper came to the cave with some reluctance. I can't blame him. I walked into that cave a drunk. I walked out of it a man with two souls and a new name of my own."

"Who is your spirit keeper?" I asked.

"The white buffalo," he answered, smiling almost more to himself than to me.

"Is that good?" I asked.

"Good! It's the best. The white buffalo is the supreme keeper of all the spirit keepers. There is no creature more holy," Grandmother Redwing declared.

"That is why I was able to saddle Seatco. The white buffalo's spirit is stronger than Seatco just as the light from the sun is stronger than the light of the moon," Saddles informed me.

I suddenly remembered the finch feathers in the pouch tied around my neck. "Grandmother, I almost forgot. I brought you something," I said, excitedly opening the drawstring and removing the feathers. I placed them on the table before her.

"My yellow feathers!" she exclaimed. "You remembered. Thank you, Talks With Eagles. I will put them to good use."

"A bobcat brought them to me," I told her.

"I know that bobcat," she said, picking up the feathers and examining them more closely.

"You've seen him in the woods?" I asked.

"He comes as many cats. I was born on the Moon of Big Winds. The cat is my spirit keeper. That old bobcat came during my first vision. I had a demon or two of my own in those days. I fought a little with the bobcat, and I did him a few favors too. He owed me those feathers. I'm glad he got even before the Great Spirit takes me to the other side . . . and I'm very pleased he chose you to bring them to me," she said.

"Me too," I assured her as a knock came at her front door.

"Who could that be," she asked getting up.

"Better hope it's not that fool government agent again," Saddles speculated.

"If it is, I'll run him off with a broom."

It was Donald Crowfeather. "I'm glad I caught you at home," he said.

"Won't you come in, Donald. What brings you down to the old village today?" Grandmother Redwing asked.

"Better yet, how about a ride back up to my place in that pickup when you leave?" Saddles interjected.

"Fine by me," Donald answered.

"I've just fixed Fritz a snack . . . you hungry?"

"No, Grandmother, I'm not. I just wanted to tell you about what happened at the agent's office. Becky told them she and I were getting married and asked for that house they had slated for you. They went along with it. They weren't very happy about it . . . but they didn't have a choice. You don't have to move. At least not right now. The agent said we could tell you they will be building ten new homes this coming spring. They're going to put in the foundations before winter sets in. He said you will have to move then for sure . . . but for now, for this winter, you can stay here in the old village." Donald Crowfeather was smiling.

234

"I don't know how to thank you," the old woman replied. She threw her arms around the young man and gave him an affectionate hug.

"It is Becky and I who should thank you, Grandmother. Had they moved you into the house before we got married, we would have had to move in with one of our parents. Becky really wants a place of her own . . . so do I. So we're really in your debt. If there's anything you need down here, you just ask. Okay?"

"I'm doin' just fine. But you might bring me a nice duck if you get any this fall. I haven't had duck in some time," she said.

"I'll smoke them for you myself," he answered. "But I must go. I promised Becky we'd take a drive along the coast this evening."

"Can I hitch a ride back to the upper village," Saddles asked.

"Of course," Donald answered.

"Me too?" I inquired.

"Long as you can come now," Donald responded.

"Fritz had his vision today. He is now Talks With Eagles," Saddles said proudly.

"Congratulations, Talks With Eagles. How does it feel?"

"I feel much more like a real Indian now," I answered.

"It's a great tradition, isn't it?" Donald noted.

"I feel connected to the ancient times . . . way, way back." I said.

"Well, way, way back I don't know if people

went on vision quests," Saddles commented as the two of us began following Donald out the door.

"Didn't we always do such things?" the groom-to-be asked.

"My father told me we learned about the magic of the vision quest from the plains people. Oh, it goes way back all right . . . and I think we always had spirit guides and spirit keepers . . . but the actual vision quest came later. My father did not know exactly when but he did tell me he had been told the story of a man of the Sioux who came among the coast people. He was a medicine man and a shaman. He brought strong magic with him and taught the people how to talk with the spirits. Before then people named their babies after the first animal they saw. You know, Little Dove, Red Fox, Soaring Eagle, names like that. After we were taught the magic of the vision quest people got to change their names," Saddles informed us as we hugged Grandmother Redwing goodbye and headed for Donald's pickup.

"I heard that story too," the old woman affirmed.

"Ya learn something every day," Donald said, getting into his truck.

"Talks With Eagles, you be sure and tell my grandsons to come see me again before they go back to Perkins Prairie. Okay?"

"I will, Grandmother. And thank you for everything. It's been the greatest day of my life."

"The greatest day of your life was the day you were born. But I am glad today was a good day. May there be many more," she said, waving goodbye from

236

the porch.

§§§§

Everyone was interested in the results of my vision quest. Alice served us lemonade while I told them about the events of my day. I wondered if my own family would accept the story with as much interest and enthusiasm as my Indian friends did. Everyone was filled with questions.

"Did you see He Who Changes actually change?" Willie asked.

"Nope. One second he was an old man . . . the next time I looked up, he had changed into an eagle."

"That's the way it was for me too," Willie whispered.

"Ain't nobody seen him actually change . . . that's what I heard," Randy commented.

"That's not true, dear," Alice interjected. "When my father had his vision, his spirit guide was the Coyote. His Indian name was Hunts With Coyote, and he always had one as a pet . . . but whites just called him Coyote. Anyway, when Daddy had his vision quest, he actually said He Who Changes transformed from an old woman into Coyote . . . he said it was so much more magnificent than the change of costumes during the Dog Dance that it can't be compared. He said the old woman seemed to become transparent for a while, and then she changed into several mixes of animals . . . you know, half bird and half whale . . .

strange stuff like that. Anyhow, she finally changed into Brother Coyote and became completely solid again . . . you know . . . he couldn't see through her anymore."

"That's fascinating," I declared. "Do many people meet a woman in the cave instead of a man?"

"It's about fifty-fifty," Audrey answered.

"Then what makes you so sure He Who Changes shouldn't be called She Who Changes?" I questioned.

"I never thought about it," Alice quipped.

"We have always said *He Who Changes* . . . since the beginning, I think," Willie advised.

"But if He Who Changes also appears as a woman, why do you know it's really a he? Couldn't he be a she just as easily?

"But the Great Spirit is male!" Alice retorted.

"How do you know? That's the same kinda stuff they said at church. God is always a man . . . the Heavenly Father. I don't see how come God couldn't just as easily be the Heavenly Mother . . . maybe even the Heavenly Other," I speculated.

"What to you mean by *other?*" Randy asked.

"Well if God is neither male nor female . . . and that's also what I learned at the Presbyterian Church, then maybe God is something else."

"I think the Great Spirit is a male. At least I've always thought of Him as male," Alice insisted.

"We could say One Who Changes. That would be a name we could all use," Audrey suggested.

"I could live with that," Willie observed.

"Well, just maybe you folks have been living with

238

the whites too long," Alice mumbled. "Anyone for lemonade?"

§§§§

The next morning, after stacking as much wood as we could into Grandmother Redwing's lean-to, I asked her about the possibility of He Who Changes being a woman instead of a man. She was caught off guard by the question because she sat down at her kitchen table and gave off a loud sigh. "I've never even considered such a thing," she admitted.

"Alice told us that when her dad had his vision quest, the Changer came to him as a woman and a coyote . . . not as a man . . . so I figured maybe the Changer is both," I told her.

"Or neither," Willie interjected.

"Audrey even suggested we use the term One Who Changes," I added.

The old woman brought her elbows up to the table, rested her chin in her hands and stared into a bear rug nailed to the wall across the room. The boys and I looked at each other wondering if she was going to answer or become angry like their aunt had done the night before. Suddenly she gave a whistle. "I ain't never thought about anything like that before. But you know, it's possible. Maybe He Who Changes isn't a he. I don't think anyone's ever questioned it. But it seem to me to be a distinct possibility. We'll have to ask Saddles. He might know. Of course, it just might be that it's something he's never thought about either. But wouldn't it just make him laugh like hell if it turns out He Who Changes is really She Who Changes!" she laughed. "It is a very important question. It is probably a question your spirit guide has given you. Maybe that's why you have come to make friends with the Quinault, Talks With Eagles . . . maybe your great-Micmac grandmother is finding a way to share the secrets of her traditions with our people through you."

"That would be great," I said, pleased to have my question taken so seriously.

"And maybe you're full of bear poop too. Who knows?" she answered.

"But you think Saddles will know?" I asked.

"I think so. The question may come as much of a surprise to him as it has to me. But he might just know the answer to it. A shaman does not always tell his friends everything he knows. Saddles is a good shaman . . . very holy . . . I've watched him grow into his office as shaman and medicine man since he was a boy. We were children together, you know. I've known him since I was a papoose. I always liked and trusted him . . . even when he ran off to live in San Francisco. He and his daddy didn't get along much when he was younger. Saddles was always a little different, and his daddy had a lot of trouble with those differences. But not me. When he came back to take care of his father, the old man had mellowed out. Saddles' differences were easier for him by then. When he left for California we all called him Chases Rainbows . . . Chases for short. But when he saddled Seatco and

240

came down from his vision sober as a judge and filled with the wisdom of the ages . . . even his daddy had to give in and accept the differences. I'll tell you this, there ain't a shaman among the Salishan more trustworthy or more holy. If anyone will know if we should change the name of He Who Changes, Saddles will know. And if you're right, Talks With Eagles . . . his differences will suddenly make all the more sense to him. This is a very interesting proposition. I can hardly wait to relate your question to my old friend."

Chapter Eight

The Orchid Appreciation Society

"We were just getting worried," Mother said as I walked into the kitchen from the back porch.

"You're a lot later than we thought you'd be," Dad pointed out.

"We had a flat tire just the other side of Olympia. Somebody spilled a case of pop on the highway. There was glass everywhere," I responded.

"You should have called," Mother quipped.

"I never thought about it."

"That's the problem, not the answer," she chided.

"Well, the important thing is that you're back safe and sound. Did you have a good time?" Dad interjected.

"I had such a great time I don't even know where to start telling you about it."

"There's fresh-baked cookies in the cookie pot. I made oatmeal cookies with walnuts and chocolate chips, your favorite. Why don't you get some for yourself and a nice glass of cold milk and tell us from the beginning about your first big weekend away from home on your own," Mother directed.

"Sounds great to me," I said, opening the cupboard and getting a saucer to put some cookies on.

"Next time, call," Mother insisted.

242

"I promise," I answered. I was glad for the time it would take to pick out four cookies and pour a glass of milk. I wasn't sure if I should tell them about my vision quest or not. Mother wasn't religious and didn't understand anyone who was. As far as I knew, Dad simply never thought about religious matters. He was interested in my mother, his family, his job, hunting, fishing, playing cards with his buddies, and his guitar. Beyond that he didn't seem to give three hoots about much else. If Dad couldn't love it, play it, lug it home in a gunnysack, or earn his living from it . . . things were pretty much ignored. I decided I wouldn't bring up the quest or my new name unless asked.

"Well, tell us everything," Dad said as I sat down at the table and joined them.

"Grandma Redwing almost had to move from her place in the old village up to the new government houses, but Donald Crowfeather and the girl he's going to marry talked the Indian agent into letting them have the house instead. Now Grandma Redwing gets to stay in her house until at least next spring," I said, taking a bite of my first cookie. I decided not to tell them about the ceremony Saddles Seatco had conducted around the government building to ensure that the old woman could stay put if she wanted to.

"That's nice, dear," Mother cooed. "But I can't for the life of me understand why that crazy old woman wants to live down in those mudflats in that drafty little shack without running water or electricity. How does she hear the news down there?"

"She isn't very interested in our news, Mom. Besides, it's the way she likes to live. She tries to live as closely as she can to the way her mom and dad taught her to live. She's very comfortable in her little house. It has everything she needs. She has an old woodstove like Grandma's, so it isn't like she's cooking her meals over a fire in a cave or something. She's a lot like Grandma Harding. She likes the outdoors and keeps a fine garden. She cans jams, smokes salmon, and likes to make clothes. She's not crazy. It's just a different way of living."

"Well, I wouldn't want to live that way," she said, folding her arms under her bosom. It was always a signal to the rest of us that Mother was certain of her opinion.

"Did they feed you good?" Dad asked.

"Real good. Audrey's sister-in-law makes an apple pie to die for."

"Did you dig any clams?" he inquired.

"No, there wasn't time for that. There was a bunch of stuff I wanted to do," I answered.

"What kind of stuff did you want to do?" Mother asked.

"Just stuff. You know . . . explore things on the reservation . . . stuff like that."

"Well, can't you be more specific?" she insisted. She got up and took a cigarette from a pack she always kept on the windowsill next to the kitchen match container attached to the cupboard.

"I went on a vision quest," I said, a little more quietly than I intended.

"What on earth is a vision quest?" she asked.

"It's a thing where Indians try to find out which animal in the forest or sea might be their spirit companion or something like that," Dad explained.

"You know about that stuff?" I asked.

"You don't grow up in the foothills of the Cascades surrounded by Indians and not know stuff like that," Dad answered.

"I don't know stuff like that," Mother muttered.

"You grew up in Tacoma. The only Indians you saw were statues in front of tobacco shops," Dad commented.

"That's not true . . . but I was never told about vision quests. Did you have one?" Mother retorted.

"I got all dressed up like an Indian. Grandmother Redwing made me a loin cloth and Saddles Seatco, he's the shaman for the whole tribe . . . he blessed me in the ancient ways and sent me off on my quest. I saw things in the clouds and in the coals of a fire that reminded me of things, and I saw an eagle flying in the sky."

"Doesn't sound like much of a vision to me. I see stuff in the clouds all the time," Mother mused.

"I saw a bobcat. He was runnin' in a field where I was looking at the clouds. He didn't see me until he jumped into the grass where I was stretched out on my back. He dropped a dead bird from his mouth when he saw me. Then he jumped back into the tall grass and ran away. I took some yellow feathers from the bird and gave them to Grandmother Redwing 'cause she wanted them for something. It was all pretty great."

"Were you out in the woods alone?" Mother exclaimed.

"Yes. I was on my vision quest. You have to be

alone when you go on a vision quest."

"Alone in the woods! You might have been killed."

"He plays in the woods around the farm by himself all the time. I'm sure there was nothing to worry about," Dad said.

"He saw a bobcat . . . are you listening?"

"He wasn't killed. He's just fine," Dad pointed out. Then turning to me, he asked: "Did you find the cave?"

"You know about the cave?" I asked with a surprise.

"I've been digging clams on the beaches up there for more years than I can remember. I know about that cave. I even know about Saddles Seatco. He's a legend up in those parts. I used to buy fish eggs from the Quinaults whenever we went clamming above Moclips. Is Saddles Seatco the shaman who blessed your vision quest?"

"I didn't know you knew any Indians up there," Mother said.

"There's a lot you don't know about me," Dad answered.

"Yes . . . it was Saddles Seatco who blessed me. He's an old friend of Grandma Redwing. They grew up together," I said.

"It must have been very interesting talking with him," Dad mused.

"Well, I met him on my first visit. But this time I got to know him a lot better. He used to be a window dresser in San Francisco. His name used to be Chases Rainbows but it was changed when he became

246

the shaman of the tribe. His dad was the shaman before him and his grandpa before that. They go a long ways back that way," I explained.

"So, did you get a new name?" Dad asked.

"You know about that too?"

"Sure."

"My new name is Talks With Eagles," I said proudly.

"Big Chief Wet Blanket of the Poo-Poo tribe, if you ask me," Mother said, brushing away some wrinkles that didn't exist from her blouse.

"You sound just like Jerry Cotton," I chided.

"Marjorie, the Indians put a lot of stock in their religion. It's very serious stuff to them, just like being a Roman Catholic is important to Ma. Some people are religious and some aren't. Obviously our son is one of the ones who is."

"It's all voodoo if you ask me. Besides, Fritz isn't an Indian," she declared.

"I'm part Micmac, just like you," I corrected.

"Your great-grandmother became a Jew, and besides, everybody knows the Indians in those parts interbred with the Vikings who boated over to get furs and trade . . . you're probably more Norwegian than Indian," Mother muttered.

"I saw great-grandma in my vision. I saw great-grandpa meet her and help her pick berries. I saw it all during my vision quest," I said defensively.

Mother didn't comment. Instead she looked into the sack of things I'd brought home with me from my trip. She reached in and pulled out my breechcloth. "What in the world is this?"

"It's like a loincloth . . . it's what Indian boys traditionally wear during their vision quest," I answered.

"Did you actually wear it?" she asked.

"Oh, yes. It's sort of like being naked or in a bathing suit. It's made of leather. It feels a lot different than Fruit of the Loom," I said, more to Dad than to her.

"Well, that's nice, dear. Now all you need is a headdress and you'll have a full outfit," she said.

"I have a headdress and I get to wear my feathers up from now on."

"I don't mean that little leather strap and those few puny feathers you brought home with you. I mean one of those full headdresses with hundreds of feathers that reach all the way down to the small of the back. Now that's a headdress," she observed, sitting back down at the table.

"You have to earn each feather. I'll be an old man before I can wear anything like that. You have to be a pretty extraordinary person to earn that many feathers," I pointed out.

"Well, I don't understand what's wrong with the name your father and I gave you," she said.

"The name you and Dad gave me is just fine. I've lived with it very comfortably all these years. But when you go on a vision quest, the Great Spirit gives you a name that helps you remember who your spirit guide is. Mine is the Eagle . . . and I actually talked with one. That's why my name is Talks With Eagles."

"It all sounds like voodoo to me," Mother insisted.

"The boy is just trying out his wings in a

different direction, Marjorie. There's no point in mocking it just because it is a direction we haven't gone. The names Indians receive from the Great Spirit are like the names nuns and monks take when they are initiated into religious life. They still go by their real names when they're with their families, but when they are in their religious communities . . . they go by their new names. I've even see graveyards where the gravestones have both names on them," Dad said.

"Well, if it makes you happy, dear. I guess there's nothing wrong with it," Mother said in a conciliatory tone.

"It makes me very happy, Mother," I said.

"Did it rain before you found the cave?" Dad asked.

"It did," I answered.

"That's very good," he said, giving me an especially warm grin.

§§§§

There was a little more than a week left of summer vacation. I didn't see much of Randy and Willie for most of that time because I helped bring in the hay at Jerry Cotton's grandmother's farm. She always paid us $20.00 apiece, fed us three meals a day, and let us sleep in the freshly stored hay out in the barn. It was my favorite way to spend the last days before school started.

I rode my bike out to Jerry's place late the next

afternoon to report for work the following day and catch up on what Jerry had been doing through the summer. Usually we kept in fairly close contact, but I had spent so much time with the Redwings that summer, I hadn't spent much time with Jerry. I did call him almost every night to tell him what the boys and I had been doing and to find out what he had been up to but we hadn't actually seen each other for weeks. Randy and Willie were actually my first close friends living in town. Most of the boys I chummed around with lived in the country and took the bus to school.

Perhaps I should have expected Jerry to feel miffed at me for not riding out to see him before it was time to work in his grandmother's hay fields, but I was so swept up in my relationship with the Redwings, earning enough money to go to the fair, and replacing my West Bend wristwatch, I had neglected many friends that summer. It wasn't that I ignored them intentionally. Circumstances just got in the way of my usual relationship that year. Jerry and I had been best friends since second grade. I should have anticipated that his feelings would be hurt, but I didn't.

"Guess what?" I asked, jumping off my bicycle next to the woodpile where Jerry was chopping kindling.

"What?" he asked, lifting his hand to shade the sun from his eyes.

"Randy and Willie are going to the Puyallup Fair with us this year! Isn't that great? They've never been to a fair of any kind except Potlatch and stuff like that but nothin' with rides and displays like at the Puyallup Fair. We can show them everything! They've never been on the octopus, or a roller coaster, or anything! Won't it be great?" I blurted, excitedly.

"But we always go the fair by ourselves, just you and me. Remember? None of the other kids like the flower displays or the canned stuff awards. That's why we always go together 'cause all the other kids want to do is go on the rides. You and me always try out all the pianos and organs and get free scones and jam at the Fisher Flour display. We always go together. Just you and me," Jerry said. He was pouting.

"But Randy and Willie want to do all that stuff too. I've been tellin' them about it for weeks. Besides, they took me to a big Quinault thing that's sorta like a fair, and I promised," I told him.

"Nobody asked me if I wanted to go to the fair with Willie and Randy. I like it better the old way," he said emphatically.

"I didn't think you'd care. I thought you'd be excited about showing them all the stuff, and you know so much about flowers and orchids and stuff . . . I thought you'd jump at the chance. Besides, I promised them. They've been picking berries and working in their dad's shop all summer earning money to go. They even helped me earn some money. I gave my West Bend away and my folks made me earn enough money to buy another one. Randy and Willie helped me with that too."

"Who did you give your watch to?"

"I gave it to this girl, she's their cousin, Lily Whitedove . . . at Potlatch."

"Why would you do that?"

"Because it was the neatest thing I owned."

251

"Givin' your watch away is dumb and I ain't hangin' out with Randy and Willie at the fair. I don't care how good they skate or how much they teach me. You and I always go together, and I ain't changin' my plans.

"Oh, come on, Jerry . . . I promised them. I can't go back on my word."

"What about your word to me?"

"I never gave you my word we would always go to the fair just the two of us. Come on, don't be like this. I gotta go with them now . . . I promised."

"Then I'll just have to find somebody else to go with," Jerry said defiantly.

"What's goin' on? You always liked Randy and Willie before. Why don't you think you'll have fun with them at the fair? We all go in the school buses anyhow. The whole school goes. Kids always pair off in groups together. Our group will just be bigger. We'll still be there together."

"It won't be the same."

"We always bump into other kids we know."

"But we don't hang out with them."

"They're real excited about seeing the orchids you'll have on display. They like flowers and stuff like that."

"I don't care if they raise their own orchids. They are not hanging out with me at the fair and that's that!" Jerry snapped, slamming the axe down on a chunk of cedar and splitting it in two.

"Well, they're going with me, and that's that!" I said emphatically.

"Well then, I guess you'd rather go with them

than me!" he shouted.

"No. I didn't say that. I love going with you. I always go with you. But it never occurred to me you would be upset if I included Randy and Willie. I don't understand why you're so mad about it."

"You've spent the whole summer with those boys. Twice I rode into town to surprise you and you were off someplace in the woods with them Indians or up to the Muckelshoot Reservation. You were never home. And you didn't ride out here to see me once."

"You're jealous!" I said, finally beginning to understand.

"I am not. I'm not a girl. Only girls get jealous. I don't give a damn who you chum around with. I like Randy and Willie just fine but they've spent most of their summer with you. Now it's my turn. Are we best friends or not?"

"We are . . . but Willie and Randy are my best friends now too."

"You can't have more than one best friend!"

"Yes, you can too . . . it's like a mom and dad that's got more than one kid. They don't love one more than the other. They love them all the same. They're different and that's what makes it easy. I ain't my sisters but my mom and dad love all three of us. And that's how I feel. Now I have three best friends . . . and it ain't fair to ask me to dump two of them any more than it would be to ask your folks to dump your brother and sisters just because you were first born."

"You should have asked me first!" Jerry snapped.

"Okay. I'm sorry about that. Maybe I should have talked to you about it first . . . but I don't need your permission to do anything . . . and if I do . . . maybe you ain't such a good best friend after all," I mused.

"You don't need my permission but you should have at least talked to me about it. We talk on the phone almost every night and you never said a thing about it."

"All I can do is apologize . . . and I've done that," I said. I was getting angry because it seemed to me that Jerry was being unreasonable.

Jerry put down the axe. He was pouting and that annoyed me too. He looked at me without saying anything.

"Oh, screw you," I said. I picked up my bicycle and started to remount it. "You can just pick hay by yourself this year. Twenty bucks ain't worth this kinda grief. I'm goin' home," I snapped.

"Okay, okay, okay . . . they can come," he said in barely audible tones and with an obvious reluctance I decided to ignore.

"I knew I could count on you!" I replied, attempting to put a positive spin to his decision. I leaned my bike back against the wall of the woodshed and began picking up an armload of kindling to take into the house.

"You're an asshole, Harding," he said, half teasingly.

"I'm only part asshole, the rest of me is charm, Polish, English, and Micmac," I teased back. I was careful to smile, remembering that Dad once told me a smiling man can seldom be accused of starting a fight. I hoped my comment sounded more witty than condescending.

"Wanna go down to the river and look for white rocks?" he asked.

"Don't we always," I replied.

"Yeah, we always do," he answered.

§§§§

The morning of the first day of school, Jerry, Randy, Willie and I made arrangements to meet for fifteen minutes before classes on the front porch of the school gymnasium to discuss our trip to the fair. I saw no real need for the meeting but agreed to it as a sort of reconciliation prize for Jerry. I knew he still harbored some hard feelings about the Redwings joining us for our traditional outing. Besides, he claimed he wanted the meeting to help organize our trip to the fair so we wouldn't miss anything. It seemed like a good idea to me.

The Redwing boys and I arrived at school as early as possible the morning we were to ride the school busses to the Puyallup Fairgrounds. Jerry was waiting for us on the steps of the gymnasium. He held three pieces of notebook paper in one hand. "You doin' homework even on the morning of the fair?" I asked.

"Nope. I've carefully printed out our itinerary once we reach the fairgrounds. I've planned the buildings and exhibits we'll visit so that if anyone gets lost from the group, they'll know which building or exhibit to go to next. They pass out free maps of the fair grounds and exhibits when you give the gateman your ticket. So, between the list and the map - we should all be able to stick together for the whole day," Jerry concluded.

I was a little put off by the fact that he had made all the decisions about what we would see and how we would make our way through the exhibits without asking for any input from the rest of us, but I had to admit that it was a good idea. I decided not to argue the point. "Sounds like a great plan to me," I said, just as Mrs. MacDonald blew the whistle that meant it was time to get on the school bus that would take us to the fair.

"How do we know which bus to get on?" Randy asked.

"We can get on any bus we want. Each bus has an assigned teacher who has a list of all the kid's names. All we have to remember to do is get back on the same bus when it's time to come home," Jerry answered.

We were all so excited about actually getting to the fair, we rode in silence most of the trip. I stared out the window as the familiar landmarks leading to Puyallup passed by before me. I was lost in our plans for the day. I enjoyed all the exhibits but was especially pleased that Jerry had slated the commercial building that held the piano and electric organ displays. It was my favorite place to visit. Many of the merchants actually liked having us stop by to play their display instruments. It gave them a break and demonstrated to the crowds walking through the exhibits that even a kid could get some fairly decent licks out of a Hammond console or a Baldwin upright.

As it turned out, both Randy and Willie played too. It soon became clear that both of them played the piano better than either Jerry or I could. I was busy having Randy teach me a song he had just played when I realized that Jerry was irritated by the attention I was giving him so I decided to wander off to try out a player piano I had spotted when we first entered the exhibit. There were so many different pianos and organs on display that year, the four of us spent much longer in that section of the fair than we planned and were already thirty minutes behind our schedule before we left to visit the animal barns. We agreed to make the animal barns a walking tour with the emphasis on walking, although I insisted we slow down long enough to really enjoy the bantam chicken and rabbit exhibits since I raised both and was particularly interested in them. But Randy and Willie had no idea that cows, sheep, horses and goats come in so many sizes, colors, and shapes. They were so interested in the miniature horses, the long-haired cattle from Scotland and the miniature goats, we ended up spending much more time in the animal barns than planned as well. It was almost noon when we emerged from the last of the barns and realized we were all starving. We went directly to the Fisher Flour booth housed under the grandstands and made our way past the quilts, paintings and other collectibles on our way to the lines of people waiting for a free Fisher Flour scone filled with jelly from the Nalley's Valley Food Products company. Willie and Randy had never tasted scones before and picked up a free recipe pamphlet and placed it in the free sack they had been given from the man at the Puget Sound Power and Light booth back in the commercial building we had toured when we first arrived. It was very important to pick up a sack as soon as possible so that one had a place to store all the free samples and pamphlets passed out at the booths. By carrying the sack we became walking advertisements for the Puget Sound Power and Light Company. We were glad to do it because everyone knew they gave away the largest and strongest souvenir bags on the fairgrounds.

After eating our scones we went to one of the hamburger stands to buy a few Puyallup Fair specials, small root beers, and bags of fries. One could get two burgers, the drink and fries for 75 cents. That was almost twice as much as one paid for the same amount of food in town, but everyone knew that food was more expensive at the fair. It was for just that reason that lots of the kids brought sack lunches with them so they would have more money left over for rides. But eating at the fair was part of my tradition. The Puyallup Fair burgers were very different than those sold at burger places in town. Instead of the usual lettuce, tomato and onion, the fair burgers were garnished with fried onions and green peppers and served with only horseradish mustard. Jerry and I were wild about them. Randy thought they looked anemic. Willie didn't like green peppers. They purchased hot dogs instead. Their lunches cost only 65 cents.

Jerry's favorite pavilions were the buildings that held all the flowers and plants. He raised orchids in his bedroom and had a huge stand of bamboo growing in his backyard. He had a real talent for growing plants. He made most of his money by selling orchids to florists. That's why Jerry never picked berries to make money. Between helping his grandmother with the hay and his orchid business, Jerry always had money. He also made candles in his room. He had hundreds of molds. He sold them to the dime store in town. Mrs. Mizenback kept them on a special shelf in the back of the store. There was a little sign that read *Candles by Jerry*. They came in all sizes and shapes and often in the forms of flowers or gourds or snowmen. Jerry sold them to the dime store for 50 cents apiece. Mrs. Mizenback sold them to the public for a dollar. Most people never burned them. They were used to decorate more than anything else. Jerry had a real head for business.

But flowers were not among my favorite exhibits. As it turned out, they weren't Randy or Willie's either. The three of us made a quick tour of the buildings only to discover that Jerry had yet to make it a third of the way through building number one. The rest of us were eager to visit the sideshows and start going on the rides. We had already seen the banners claiming they had a two-headed cow and a lady with three legs. Of course, they had the usual sideshow exhibits that seemed to return every year. There was always a bearded lady, a hootchy-kootchy dancer and huge jars of formaldehyde that displayed a variety of freakish looking creatures. But this year, on top of everything else, they claimed to have a living pair of Siamese twins. Randy, Willie and I were eager to see the twins and get on with the rides. We were almost an hour and a half behind our scheduled itinerary and Jerry was still gathering catalogs and seed samples from the floral displays.

"How about if the guys and I go over to the sideshows while you finish up here . . . we can meet you at the fun house in about an hour," I suggested, looking down at my watch.

"Don't you want to see the free movie about how to make better compost?" Jerry asked. "It's on the agenda. See . . . right there where it says *Free Movie.*"

"Not really. I thought it might be a movie like they had last year . . . remember, it was a movie about how the Wyerhauser company replants the forest. Now that was interesting. But a movie about compost . . . well . . . I'd much rather see the sideshows. Besides, we're just not as interested in flowers and gardens as you are, and we're really behind on the itinerary. The guys don't want to miss the sideshows or rides, and we've only got a few hours left. You don't really like the sideshows anyhow and I want to be sure we get to see the rest of the fair before it's time to go home" I said honestly.

"Me too," Willie interjected.

"Me three," Randy echoed. He said the words coyly, hoping not to offend Jerry. It was obvious to all of us that Jerry was becoming disquieted over the fact that the rest of us were ready to do other things.

"Then who will go to the sideshows with me," Jerry whined.

"You never like them anyway," I reminded him.

"I put up with them because you always stick

260

with me through the flower displays," he observed.

"But this time there isn't just you and me . . . and time is flying by. We'll meet you at the fun house in an hour and a half," I insisted.

"Did you guys even bother to look at the orchid displays?" he asked.

"We did. You won a ribbon. Wanna know what color?" I answered.

"No, I want to be surprised," he muttered.

"Then you don't mind if we go on ahead?"

"Why should I mind. If you'd rather spend time at the sideshow with your friends than observing the flower displays with me . . . why should I mind?"

I decided to ignore the sarcasm in his voice. "We'll meet you at the fun house at three-thirty. That will give us two and a half hours to go on the rides before we have to get back on the busses and go home."

"Three-thirty," Jerry repeated.

§§§§

The Redwing boys and I headed for the sideshows without any further conversation with Jerry. I knew he was miffed again, but secretly I was glad I could forego the usual hour and a half it took to get through the flower displays. The three of us ogled and observed as many of the sideshows as we felt we could afford One could always see the teasers on the stage in front of the tents that housed them. There were plenty of them to see free. But we did pay for and enter the best of the sideshows including the one that displayed the Siamese twins. Randy said he had heard a story about some Quinault twins who had been born the same way . . . but it had been hundreds of years before even his grandmother was born. They were considered sacred by the tribe and had been well taken care of until their death.

By three-thirty we were in front of the fun house waiting for Jerry. We waited nearly thirty minutes but he never showed up. I had Randy and Willie wait there to catch Jerry if he walked by while I returned to the buildings that housed the flower displays to see if he was still there locked in a discussion about some new plant or involved in a conversation with another orchid grower. It had happened before though in each of those cases I was both present and disinterested. When I couldn't find him, I returned to the fun house. "You guys seen him?" I asked.

"No. Willie walked back to the sideshows to see if he could find him in the crowd over there . . . and I waited here. Neither of us saw him," Randy answered.

"Well, if we keep looking for him, we're never going to get on the rides," Willie observed, verbalizing what was already going through our minds.

"He's probably mad because we went to all those sideshows without him. I don't know what to do. I don't want to make him even more mad by not waiting for him . . . "

"We've already waited the better part of an hour," Randy pointed out.

"Let's at least go into the fun house. We've

never been in one. Maybe we'll bump into him once we start going on the rides. I really think we've waited long enough. I'm sorry if we've come between you and Jerry again. Maybe we shouldn't have come with you guys," Willie said.

"No, no . . . the problem isn't you . . . it's him. Let's go in the fun house. You guys are going to love it," I answered. I wasn't pleased about it but under the circumstances there wasn't anything else I could really do. We each plunked down our 25 cents for tickets into the fun house and went in. By the time we were tumbling about in the huge barrels separating the slides from the wind tunnels and distorting mirrors, Jerry was no longer on our minds. We were just three kids enjoying ourselves. Randy and Willie had only been on a small merry-go-round and Ferris wheel that came to the reservation with a small circus each spring. The whip, octopus, roller coaster and other big rides were absolutely new and intimidating to them. Since neither had been in the tunnel of love nor the haunted house, we went through them first. The idea was that we would start out on the least intimidating rides and work our way up to the really scary ones.

We saved the roller coaster ride for last. I never liked it and seldom rode on it more than once. Sometimes not at all. It was Jerry Cotton's favorite ride. In years past I had stood on the sidelines watching him take ride after ride until his store of reserved quarters ran out. Once Jerry was finally out of money, we would go back to the piano and organ displays and play music until it was time to hike through the main gate and return to our bus in the parking lot. I was secretly hoping that Randy and Willie would be as intimidated by the ride as I was. It didn't turn out that way. They loved and were exhilarated by it. I rode on it with them only once, then took my usual place on the sidelines, strategically situated so I could see the looks on their faces as they were swooped down from the highest drop.

During my wait, I spotted Jerry standing in line to buy a ticket for the ride. He was with Teddy Finkelman and Doug Wallace. I began making my way through the crowd to the ticket line, but by the time I got there, Jerry and the other two boys had already boarded one of the cars and were headed up the first incline. Knowing the ride took only a matter of minutes, I hurried to the exit of the ride at the other end of the roller coaster. Jerry and his companions were just debarking when I got there. "I thought we lost you," I said as Jerry and the other two boys walked down the gangplank past me.

"You did," he responded without stopping.

"Don't be like that . . . we waited and waited for you," I shouted as he merged into the crowd. I pushed my way through the crowd until I caught up with them.

"I'm not mad," he said curtly.

"Randy and Willie love this fool thing as much as you do. They're in line for their third ride right now. I betcha they'd let you squeeze in line with them," I suggested.

"I have companions of my own, thank you," he said coolly.

"Yeah, he's got companions," Doug echoed.

"We waited and waited for you, Jerry. What

happened?"

"I went with Teddy and Doug and threw baseballs at bowling pins instead. I won this little stuffed dog for my sister," he replied.

"But you hate sports and all that stuff," I retorted.

"Not anymore," he snarled.

"Aren't you gonna spend the rest of the day with me and the guys?" I asked.

"Look, Fritz, or Big Chief Wet Blankest of the Pee Pee Tribe, or whatever you call yourself these days . . . it is obvious that you are more interested in two headed cows and other birth defects than beautifully cultivated orchids and flowers. It is also obvious that you would rather run around in a breechcloth with your two Indian companions than honor your tried-and-true friendships. Doug and Teddy have invited me to spend the rest of the day with them. I'm going to pay for some of their rides on the roller coaster . . . so why don't you just put on some war paint and find a bonfire to yelp around?" he snapped.

"Do you really want to do this?" I questioned.

"I think I prefer things this way," he answered. He turned his nose up in the air and resumed his return to the long line of people waiting to buy tickets to reboard the roller coaster.

"Yeah, he prefers it this way, Indian lover," Doug snarled.

I watched as the three of them disappeared into the crowd, then returned to the exit of the ride just in time to catch Randy and Willie coming down the exit ramp. "Where's Jerry?" Willie asked. "I thought I saw you standing over there talking to him."

"You did. He's decided to spend the rest of the day with some other kids."

"It's because we're Indians, isn't it?" Randy noted.

"Maybe a little bit. Mostly I think he's just mad because he didn't get his way. He wanted just the two of us to come to the fair like we usually do. I should have discussed going with you guys with him before I spoke to you about it . . . but I thought he would love showing you the fair."

"You should have told us the spot you were in. We would have understood," Randy said.

"Yeah, it wouldn't have been as much fun without you, but Randy and I could have explored the place together. We would have understood," Willie affirmed.

"I know you would. The point is that Jerry should have understood too . . . that's sort of what friendship is all about. My Grandpa Harding once taught me a really important thing about relationships. He typed it up for me. I got it right here in my wallet. Let me read it to you. It's really important." I took out and unfolded the well-worn piece of paper and read from it. *"Your freedom ends where my freedom begins, and my freedom ends where yours begins."* Isn't that neat. Grandpa says it's an old Polish saying.

"It's also an old Indian saying," Willie informed me.

"Yeah, it's because of that saying that our people never expected the Europeans to put up fences and take away the land. Saddles says that when the whites first came, we figured there was room enough for everybody. It's too bad Americans didn't follow that old Polish saying. We'd all be a lot better off if they had," Randy mused.

After I stood watching as they took a few more rides on the roller coaster, the three of used headed back to the Fisher Flour stand to stay our hunger with a few additional scones and wait until it was time to leave the fairgrounds and head for our bus. On the way a group of horseback riders, some dressed as cowboys and some dressed as Indians, made their way from the horse barns to the entrance gate of the grandstands and rodeo show. "I wonder why they don't use real Indians?" Randy asked as they passed.

"Because they do a mock war where all the Indians die. It's sort of a traditional opening to the grandstand show. It started a way back," I answered, apologetically.

"Why do they do that?" Willie asked.

"It's meant to show how the whites were victorious at winning the land from the Puyallup tribe," I told him.

"They won those wars because they never honored any of the treaties we made with them. We were a peaceful people in a place of plenty. Grandma Redwing says that her parents' generation never wanted war and made treaties with the whites just like they did with surrounding tribes. But unlike the surrounding tribes, the Europeans never kept the treaties. The real war was a paper war and we lost it. Our people were always caught off guard because we honored the treaties. Whites just used them to buy time to prepare another attack. We were always caught off guard," Randy explained.

"That's sure not the way they tell it in the history books."

"Yeah, we already noticed," Willie grunted.

"How come you guys didn't just jump on your horses when you were first attacked . . . and run the Europeans off the land?" I asked.

"Well, we did start a couple of battles. And we won more than a few. But we lost the war. We didn't have horses. Europeans brought them to America. When the Quinaults first saw horses, we thought they were big dogs. We called them mystery dogs. That's still the word used for them in the Salishan dialects," Willie observed.

"Well, if you didn't have horses, how did you get around?" I asked.

"We walked or took canoes. That's why most villages were built near lakes or on rivers. The waterways were our roads. We didn't have to bulldoze things or pave anything, we used the rivers. That way, the land stayed in good shape for the animals. There was no such thing as road kill in those days," Randy pointed out.

"But what about all those pictures of the Plains Indians chasing buffalo on horseback?" I asked.

"Before the horses came, the people would start fires to herd the buffalo into pits or from canyon walls. If they didn't die from the fall, they were clubbed to death or killed with spears," Willie answered.

"But how did they get the meat back to the villages?"

"The same way we got elk or deer or bear meat back to the village. We carried it on our backs or on poles carried on the shoulders of several men. Sometimes the meat would be dried so it didn't weigh as much. Drying preserved the meat too. Sometimes the Plains Indians would just move their whole camp to where the buffalo were killed. Don't forget, they lived in portable teepees, not long houses like the Salishan and other coastal tribes," Willie explained.

"Believe it or not, our people got along for thousands of years without horses," Randy said proudly.

§§§§

The three of us arrived back at the bus just as Jerry got into line to have his name checked off by the driver. He was no longer with Teddy and Doug. I stepped in line behind him. "Hi," I said.

"Humph," he harrumphed when he turned around and looked at me.

"Where are your new found companions?" I asked.

"I don't know. Maybe they came on a different bus," Jerry claimed.

"They did not. I'll bet they dumped you when your quarters ran out, didn't they? You wanna sit with me on the way back?"

"I've already made plans to sit with Cybil and Alice. They're saving me a seat with them." He almost hissed the words.

"You don't even like Cybil and Alice," I hissed back.

"I do now. We formed a new club just today," he boasted as the driver placed a check mark after his name.

"What kind of club?"

"The Orchid Appreciation Society," he smirked, removing his glasses and pursing his lips. "I'm going to give them snips and starters and they're going to start raising orchids too. And we're all going to make a fortune and win all the ribbons at the fair next year. And besides that . . . I talked with Mrs. Clogston today. I met her at the Fisher scone pavilion. She's agreed to let me use one of the rooms at the town library to give orchid raising lessons. She's going to put an ad in the Perkins Prairie Banner and a little sign in the front window and everything."

I boarded the bus after him, giving Randy and Willie a sign to indicate I hoped to speak with him a little more. The boys nodded. I followed Jerry to his seat hoping there would be room for the boys and myself in the seat behind or beside him. But once we got back to where the girls were saving room for him, the only seats left were in the very back of the bus.

"Hi, Fritz," Alice Madden smiled.

"Hi, Alice," I responded.

"Are you going to join the Orchid Appreciation Society?" she asked.

"He's much more interested in totem poles and running around in the woods in a breechcloth than in anything so refined as horticulture," Jerry interjected sarcastically.

That made me mad as hell. I had had enough of Jerry's racist comments and jealousy. "My dad says you can lead a whore to culture but you can't make it stick," I quipped.

"And I'm sure your dad knows," Jerry snapped back.

"Did I say something wrong?" Alice asked just as Randy and Willie walked up behind me in the aisle.

"No, Alice, you didn't. Jerry here is just revealing his true colors and I'm on my way to the back of the bus with my real friends."

"It's a pretty sad state of affairs when the only real friends you can make are a pack of redskins," Jerry snarled.

I doubled up my fist and was just about to punch him when Willie grabbed my arm and stopped me. "Let's just go take our seats, okay?" he said, nudging me down the aisle. I was glad he stopped me but I also knew I had taken real delight in the sudden expression of fear that swept across Jerry's face when he thought I was going to hit him.

"We don't need any more Indian wars," Willie whispered in my ear as we took our seats.

"I just get sick of all that petty, self-righteous stuff."

"Well, hitting him is just as petty. The Great Spirit doesn't approve of such things. If you're going to be a true Indian, you have to learn to be peaceful and accept what you cannot change. You aren't responsible for his behavior . . . but you are responsible for your own," Willie chided.

"Besides, Fritz, both Willie and I worry that if we weren't here with you . . . you and Jerry would be gettin' along just fine. We feel terrible. We never wanted our friendship with you to ruin your long relationship with Jerry or anybody else," Randy asserted.

"And it didn't help that we didn't make much of his orchids or his ribbon. He won first place. We could have been more interested in his accomplishment than we were in the sideshows and rides. We weren't really acting very cool ourselves," Willie noted.

"I guess. Maybe we should have spent more time with him . . . but I think he should have understood that there was only so much time . . . and if we hung around in the flower pavilion as long as he likes to, none of us would have ever gotten to see much else," I offered.

As the bus made its way out of the parking lot toward the highway that would return us to our homes, we began going through the souvenirs and free stuff we had dropped in our bags as we toured the various building and exhibits. Randy had managed to secure three fans from the Shell Gas Company. "What you gonna do with three fans? Learn how to do the fan dance like those geisha girls in Japan?" Willie asked teasingly.

"No, frog-head, I'm going to use them as braces for something I want to do with feathers for the new costume I'm thinking up for next year's Dog Dance," Randy declared.

"Could I make a costume too? Would it be okay for me to enter the competition, or do you have to be related to the Salishans in some way?" I asked.

"Oh, sure you can. You don't even have to have a vision to qualify for the Dog Dance," Willie answered.

"As far as that goes, you don't even really need to be an Indian. We once had a Chinese lookin' fella come and dance in a traditional costume from his village someplace in Siberia. It was almost spooky how much alike our dances his were. I think there's some kind of connection between Indians and the Chinese people. Did you ever notice how much the Inuits look like Asians?" Randy noted.

"Yeah, we're probably related to them in some distant way. There's all that talk about Indians coming over from Siberia . . . so maybe our ancestors came from there," Willie commented.

"Who are the Inuits?" I asked.

"Folks mostly call them Eskimos these days," Randy answered.

"I wonder how come Micmacs and other tribes on the eastern coast of the continent look so much more European?" I asked.

"Don't you suppose there was lots of trade and stuff going on between the northern people of Europe and the East Coast tribes. Probably lots of intermarryin' went on. I read once that they think the Phoenicians might have sailed into the Gulf of Mexico and right up the Missouri and Mississippi Rivers, and that's why so many of the Plains People look almost middle-eastern . . . like they were from Iran or something," Randy contributed.

"Boy, you guys know a lot about Indians," I told

them.

"We've been at it all our lives," Willie mused.

I looked out the window as we reached the top of Eli Hill. On a clear day, Mount Rainier always spreads out across the highway looking like a huge ice cream cone sitting in the middle of the road. The sun was just beginning to set. The mountain was bathed in rich pink reflections.

"Tacobud is blushing. It will rain tomorrow," Willie whispered.

"I feel like I'm raining already," I told him.

"You still upset about Jerry?" Randy asked.

"Yeah. I don't know why he has to be such a jerk-off."

"Well, then it is good that you are raining on the inside," Willie assured me.

"Why?"

"The rain washes everything clean. Do what Saddles says, Fritz. Listen to the rain inside you. Find out what sorrow has to teach you," he whispered.

Chapter Nine

The Sawdust Trail

For the next several weeks, the chores of autumn kept me busy at home and at my grandparents' farm after school and weekends. There were apples to pick, nuts to gather, fields to harvest, gardens to pick, and a wide variety of tasks germane to homes that put food by for the winter. The Redwing boys seemed busy too, so except for recess at school, we didn't see much of each other.

By early October Jerry Cotton's *Orchid Appreciation Society* boasted members ranging from as young as eleven years old to Martha Roads, an eighty-five-year old widow who raised blue ribbon roses and iris in the only greenhouse in Perkins Prairie. The town newspaper carried a long article about the club. According to the paper, the club met in Mrs. Road's greenhouse the first and third Saturday of each month and at the library the second Saturday of each month. The club was so popular that notices of their meetings were posted on the town bulletin board and in the windows of certain stores.

Jerry enjoyed talking loudly about the club each time I walked past or near him on the school grounds to make sure I understood how successful and popular he had become because of the club. I was actually glad for him until Randy, who loved flowers and wanted to learn more about them, asked to join the club but was refused on the grounds that it was for orchid growers only. It seemed to go unnoticed that everyone else who asked to join was given an orchid starter by Jerry. Everyone, that is, except Randy. I wanted to make a big deal of it but Randy said that if he wasn't wanted in the club there would be no reason for joining. At that point in time we were not aware that Jerry Cotton had not even discussed the issue with the other club members and that they were uninformed concerning Jerry's rejection of Randy's application.

Not long after Randy's attempt to join the club, I spotted an ad in the Perkins Prairie Banner about a week-long Pentecostal tent revival to be held down where the circus and carnival usually put up their tents along the railroad tracks that separated west Perkins Prairie from east Perkins Prairie. The tent was reported to be large enough to seat 2,000 people. That was more seats than the entire population of Perkins Prairie.

We soon learned that one of the goals of the evangelist conducting the revival was to draw as many people as possible away from the town's traditional Halloween celebration. That seemed especially strange to me and to the Redwing boys. Halloween was a big deal in our small town. I doubted there would be many Perkinites in the evangelist's tent that night. The Eagles held a huge costume judging contest in the gymnasium along with games that rewarded prizes. Once the judging was finished, everyone marched to the high school auditorium where horror movies were shown and everyone was given free popcorn, hot dogs and pop to munch during the film. It was a tradition in our town that almost everyone attended. The Eagles had originally begun the program to discourage the house to house trick or treating after two young girls had been abducted in the early 1920s while going about town to get treats. It became a huge success. Many of the town's businesses set up booths in the gymnasium where they gave out candy, gum, apples and nuts to anyone who dropped by.

So, while Randy, Willie and I weren't at all interested in missing the annual Eagles Halloween celebration, we were curious about the Pentecostal revival. Neither of us had ever been to a revival of any kind. It sounded like a lot of fun, especially after the evangelist went around town playing gospel music over a loud speaker attached to his car while inviting everyone to attend his services under the big top down by the tracks. We made plans to go.

I informed my parents about our plans at dinner the night before the revival was to begin. Mother was instantly opposed to the idea. "We used to call them Holy Rollers in my day. They had a small church down the block from Mother's boarding house. Fanny and I would go down and sit outside and listen to them hoot and carry on. I swear, some of those people used to actually foam at the mouth. I don't want you going. Pentecostal tent revivals are for people who have emotional problems and the IQ of gnats. You can see stuff like that at the movies but I don't want you hanging around those people. I've heard that some of them even make you handle snakes." She picked up her cup and took a sip of her coffee.

I looked at Dad to see if he would speak in my behalf. He was occupied with the usual attempt to get my sister, Sonja, to eat what was on her plate. "Eat your peas," he ordered. She hated peas and always tried to stuff her cheeks full of them, then pretend she had to go to the bathroom where she would spit them into the toilet and flush them into oblivion. Not wanting the ball to be dropped, I assumed my own defense. "They've got a gospel band and a singer that has two 78's out on the Decca label. I heard one of them over at Jerry's once. The guy is a real good singer. Besides, if you and Fanny went, why can't I?"

"It's just more voodoo. I don't know why a nice smart boy like you has to be interested in all this voodoo stuff," she said, picking up her cup to take another drink of coffee.

"If the boy wants to attend, I see no harm in it," Dad asserted, lowering his fork and giving Mother one of his looks. Looks were very important on my father's side of the family. My grandparents and all my aunts and uncles on that side of the family each possessed a series of looks and could say more with a glance than most people could say in five minutes. Grandma Harding even had one we all called the evil eye. If it got flashed at you, you were in big trouble.

Mother's family was just the opposite. They verbalized everything with a sort of deadpan nonexpressive face that only those of English heritage can truly appreciate. I imagined they had all learned this art from my grandmother on that side of the family. She had been born in England and even though she was sent to work as an indentured servant to

Newfoundland when she was only a girl of fourteen, her English accent and ways were still in tact.

"Well, if he goes, I certainly don't want him going alone. Some of those people all but hypnotize some people. Gabriel Heater did a whole story on it," she responded.

"Randy and Willie are askin' their folks tonight if they can go too," I answered. "If they can go, can I?"

"Oh, I suppose so but I don't understand why. If you want to explore religion, why don't you start going to the Presbyterian Church with the Fox kids on Sundays?" she said.

"And you could always attend Mass with your grandmother," Dad commented.

I called Willie right after my evening chores were done and asked if they could go.

"We're going to be at Grandma Sunfield's for a couple of days helping her with some stuff, so we can't go with you," Willie answered.

"Well, I guess I won't be able to go either," I sighed.

"Why don't you call Eben Johnson? He's been after Randy and me to attend for days."

"Eben Johnson?" I repeated.

"Yeah. I told him we couldn't go but I'll bet he'd be happy to take you along. He told us his little church down in South Prairie was one of the sponsors of this thing and they're all supposed to bring somebody with them. I'll bet he'd be real glad to take you along."

"Eben is a religious fanatic. He even brings his bible to school. He never plays with anybody . . . he's always preachin' to kids like he was Billy Sunday or somethin'," I whined.

"Yeah, I know . . . but he might be your only ticket in. I think you should call him."

I didn't know Eben well, although we had been in school together since the Johnsons moved to town when I was in the third grade. All the Johnsons were very religious. Eben and his two sisters never cussed and always made a big show of praying before they opened their sack lunches. I decided to seek him out at school the next day at recess.

I found him reading his bible out by the acorn tree in front of the building. "What'cha readin' about?" I asked.

"Armageddon," he said, looking up somewhat surprised that he had been spoken to. Most of the kids in school avoided the Johnsons because they were always preaching to everybody about getting saved.

"What is Armageddon?" I asked with real curiosity.

"That's when God is coming back to Earth to burn up all the bad people and sinners with a huge fire-breathing dragon," he answered.

"I thought God was supposed to love people. Why would He want to burn them all up?"

"Because they're evil and don't have Jesus livin' in their hearts. If you don't have Jesus living in your heart, God's going to burn you alive and then send you to hell forever. God hates sinners. It's all in the Bible. If your name isn't written in the Book of Life . . . you're on your way to hell and that's all there is to it. Is your name written in the Book of Life, Fritz?"

"I don't even know what the Book of Life is," I

answered.

"It's a big book God keeps up in heaven. He writes down all the names of the saved people in it. If your name isn't in that book, you're going to burn alive at the Battle of Armageddon when Jesus comes back to wage war against the unsaved, the corrupt nations, the Devil and all his slimy, slippery demons. Are you saved, Fritz Harding?" he asked, standing to his feet.

"From what?" I asked.

"From sin!"

"I have no idea. Are you?"

Jesus saved my soul, August 14th, five years ago and washed my sins away, hallelujah," he shouted.

"You remember the date?"

"Of course. It's my new birthday date because I was born again. Praise his holy, blessed name!" Eben stood up and began to twitch and dance around.

"You okay, man?" I asked.

"I'm dance'n in the spirit, Fritz. Jesus saved me from sin. Oh happy day!"

"So does that mean you don't sin anymore?" I asked.

"Everybody sins and comes short of the glory of God, Fritz. That's right in the Bible too," he answered excitedly.

"Then I don't get it. What's the point of being saved from sin if you just go right on sinning anyway. That doesn't sound very saved to me. What's the point?"

Eben looked as if I had slapped his face. He was visibly stunned by the problem my comment presented to him. He stopped dancing and twitching.

The expression on his face slowly shifted from joy to concern. After a few seconds, he spoke again. "I don't know the answer to that one . . . but I'll ask my pastor. Pastor Calvin knows everything in the Bible. I'll ask him at our Wednesday night meeting . . . but that don't change the fact that if you ain't saved, then your name ain't in the Book of Life and you're headed straight to hell in a hand basket," he retorted, snapping his bible shut.

"You going to the Pentecostal tent revival?" I asked.

"Sure. Pastor Calvin is going to give the opening prayer and be up on the platform with the revival maker, and our choir is going to sing during the first offering," he replied with visible pride.

"What's a first offering?" I asked.

"Tent revivals take up lots of offerings to help spread the gospel message all over the world. The revival maker who's coming to Perkins Prairie believes in takin' as many as ten offerings a night . . . one for each of the commandments."

"Oh, kinda like payin' off your debt to God, huh?" I asked.

"Nothing like that! You can't pay your way into heaven. Salvation is a free gift from God through the free grace of Jesus Christ," Eben informed me. He rattled off the words as if he were reading a list of ingredients from the label of a box of Cracker Jacks.

"Well, if you can't buy your way into heaven . . . why take the offering?"

"To spread the Gospel to all the nations, dummy."

"Well . . . I don't have much money to give . . . but my parents said I could go if I found someone to go with me."

"You know me. You can go with us if you want to."

"You sure your mom won't mind?"

"My mom loves to take unsaved people to tent revivals," he assured me.

"What makes you think I'm unsaved?"

"Do you have Jesus in your heart?" he asked as the bell rang indicating that recess was over.

I decided at once that Eben would not count the experiences of my vision quest as having Jesus in my heart so I only said . . . "I think God has spoken to me."

"Well, that ain't enough. He's gotta move in and wash all the sin out. Maybe you'll get saved at the revival!"

"Maybe," I responded.

§§§§

We could hear the music of the gospel band and chorus as the Johnson's car pulled into the parking lot outside the huge tent. I was so anxious to see and experience the Pentecostal revival, I was the first one out of the car. "The Lord is callin' you to the sawdust trail, son," Mrs. Johnson remarked as she stepped out of the car.

A boisterous and bumpy rendition of the old

gospel song *Jesus Saves* filled the evening air. Mrs. Johnson ushered us as close to the front as possible so we would have a good view of the platform upon which a man in a white suit paced back and forth shouting *Hallelujah* and *Thank you, Jeeesuss!"*

"That's Pastor Wally Pots. He's the visiting evangelist," Mrs. Johnson said. Her tone was hushed as if she was in awe of the man. I recognized the tone in her voice. Grandmother Harding often used it when she spoke of the pope.

As we made our way to our seats I took in the sights around me. Some people were clapping their hands to the beat of the music; others had tambourines which they played with the proficiency of a concert timpani player. Those who weren't singing along with the band and chorus were waiving their arms in the air, and every time Pastor Wally Pots shouted out a *hallelujah* or a *thank you, Jeeesuss,* members of the audience shouted back a loud *Amen!* I had never seen anything quite like it before except at the Cosmo movie house where I had seen a news feature about throngs of girls and young women swooning and waving their arms at Frank Sinatra.

Just as we were about to sit in our seats I saw Martha Roads, in whose greenhouse The Orchid Appreciation Society now held the majority of their meetings, stretched out on the carpeted floor of the platform with a dozen people gathered around her shouting things in foreign languages and dancing about her as if she were a campfire. "What's happened to Mrs. Roads?" I whispered into Eben's ear.

"What?" he shouted above the singing and

shouting going on around us.

"What's the matter with Mrs. Roads?" I shouted back.

"Oh, she's just slain in the spirit. Happens to her all the time," he answered as if explaining nothing more mysterious than a hiccup.

The songfest continued until the big tent was overflowing with the curious, the unrepentant, and those who simply loved gospel music played by a ragtime band and a honky-tonk piano. Occasionally pastor Wally Pots would pick up his microphone and shout *Thank you Jeeesuss!*" in one of the thickest nasal Southern accents I had ever heard in my life.

When the music finally subsided, the evangelist threw the cord of his microphone dramatically over his shoulder and walked deliberately, perhaps even solemnly, to the pulpit at the center of the stage. He stared at us for a long time, moving his head and turning his eyes towards the masses of people gathered under his tent. He stared until the crowd grew silent. More than once I was sure he was staring directly at me. "Do . . . you . . . love . . . the Lard . . . tonight?" he shouted.

"Amen!" I heard Eben and everyone around me shout back.

"If the Lard of glory has saved you from your pitiful sins and ya know it . . . let me hear ya shout amen again!" he wailed into the microphone.

"Amen! Praise the Lord," people shouted all around me.

"If you've been warshed in the bloooood of the lamb and ya know it . . . let me hear ya praise His wunnerful name!" he bellowed.

For a while, because I didn't want Eben or anybody else to think I was unsaved, I would repeat the amen myself but with no kind of effort that could be called a shout. Muffled is probably a good way of explaining it. I was glad when all the shouting subsided and the little band and singers began performing again. Each of their songs was followed by what Pastor Wally called *a love offering for Jeeesuss.*

After a while only the guy at the Hammond organ played a sort of accompaniment to Pastor Wally's admonitions and proclamations of faith. Before I realized it a number of people had lined up to be prayed for. The evangelist would lay hands on them and shout wildly. "What's he saying," I turned and asked Eben.

"He's speakin' in tongues and casting out the demons that own the diseases and darkness in the people. Pastor Wally has the gift of healing, the gift of tongues, the gift of prophecy, the gifts of exorcism, and all the gifts of the Holy Ghost. He's a mighty man of God!" Eben proclaimed.

After several people seemed to have been healed of their ailments, the band and chorus struck up another song, and the offering baskets were passed around again. This time Pastor Wally walked to the edge of the platform and shouted: "The Lard loves the color green. That's why he made the trees and grass so green. Give the Lard a great big amen by fillin' those baskets with the color green!"

The swell of music from the gospel band and chorus filled the big top with a rousting rendition of

There's Power In the Blood while the ushers passed the deep wicker baskets down the rows of people praying, or shouting, or singing along with the song being performed. After the ushers brought the baskets up to the platform to be blessed by Pastor Wally, he took the microphone again, looked out in to the throngs of people before him and said, "If your name is written in the Book of Life, I want ya'll to shout amen so loud you'll wake up the cherubs snoozin' up there in heaven!" he roared. I heard an unbelievably loud *amen* lift up all round me. I contributed nothing to it. I wasn't sure if my name was written in the Book of Life or not, but I decided it was best not to lie about such things, at least not to Pastor Wally Pots. I shrank back into my seat as the evangelist began to shout his message of salvation and hellfire and brimstone throughout the big top. I wasn't sure why but I had the strangest feeling he was speaking directly to me. Then, all at once, I was sure of it.

"Tonight I wanna speak just to those of you who aren't positive you're saved . . . to those of you who don't know, without a shadow of a doubt, that your name is written in the blessed book of the lamb. The rest of you can tune out and pray your way to glory for those pitiful unsaved ones among us tonight." He almost moaned the words into the microphone.

I heard a low mumbling rise up around me as people began to pray. Eben and his mother and sisters got up from their chairs and knelt at them as if they were altars. Some lifted their arms and waved them in the air begging the lord to save all the sinners under the big top that night. I didn't know whether to close my eyes and pray for the unsaved or just watch in amazement at the antics and goings on around me. I had been to mass with my grandmother and to the Presbyterian church with friends. Nothing going on inside the revival tend was anything like I had experienced in the past. In a strange way it reminded me of being in the fun house at the Puyallup Fair I didn't know whether to laugh or just watch in amazement.

"Cast the demons of doubt out of them, Lard! Thank ya, Jeeesuss! Bring 'em into the fold! Halleluiah," Pastor Wally Pots shouted over and over again. All at once I remembered something Grandmother Redwing had told me about prayer. *If you want to pray . . . you must learn to listen*, she had told me. How, I wondered, could anyone in the tent listen for anything in the midst of so much clamor and shouting and loud music. How could the Great Spirit speak to anyone in that tent as softly and gently as He had spoken to me that wonderful afternoon when I had stretched out in the tall grass and saw images and visions in the clouds. All at once I remembered the bobcat and how surprised we had both been to suddenly fin ourselves face to face. For some reason, reflecting on that moment made me laugh.

"What you laughin' at, Fritz Harding?" Eben Johnson asked with a disapproving look on his face.

"I was thinking about a bobcat I saw above the hills of the Quinault Reservation earlier this year when I went on my vision quest," I confessed.

Eben's eyes widened and his face paled. "You'd better be listenin' to the word of God and not be thinkin' about no pagan vision quest. Those visions are given by demons and everybody knows it," he hissed.

At just about that same moment, Pastor Wally Pots fell to his knees. His eyes were closed. His face was turned to heaven. There were tears pouring down his cheeks. Both his arms were stretched heavenward. "Lard, I just pray that those who need Jeeesuss tonight will have the courage of their convictions and come down the sawdust trail to this old handmade altar and pray their way into the arms of Jeeesuss." Then, motioning for the choir and band to start up, he leaped to his feet, pointed his right arm and finger directly at me and bellowed into the microphone, "If you want your name written in the Book of Life tonight before you leave here . . . if you know there is something missing in your life . . . you come on down . . . rat now . . . and I'll pray with you."

I looked around. People from all over the tent were stepping out into the sawdust-covered aisles and heading toward Pastor Wally Pots as the choir and band played a rendition of *Just as I Am*. Each time someone stood up, the evangelist or someone would shout, "Thank you, Jeeesuss!" and hundreds of people, including Eben and his mother, would shout amen. Someone behind me touched my shoulder. "Wouldn't you like to go up and get your name written in the Book of Life, Fritz" Eben's mother coaxed.

"I'm not sure," I told her. "All this is pretty unusual stuff for me."

"All you have to do is confess your sins and God will write your name in the book," she assured while easing me out onto the sawdust trail.

"Halleluiah," I heard Eben mutter as I pressed past him.

Before I knew it, I was in one of the long lines inching its way toward the platform. All I could think about was trying to find a sin I could confess. I don't mean to imply that I thought I was a paragon of saintliness, but I had only recently emerged from my first vision quest, and I knew one had to have a clean slate to receive one. Saddles had made it very clear that a vision is as much about what goes on inside a person as it is about what the person sees and experiences during the quest. Try as I might, I couldn't think of a single sin worth confessing. I mulled over the Ten Commandments attempting to discover some fault I may have overlooked. I couldn't come up with a thing. Suddenly Pastor Wally Pots was standing directly in front of me. Mrs. Johnson pushed me closer.

"Have ya'll come to meet Jeeesuss, son?' the evangelist shouted at me.

"I've come to make sure my name is written in the Book of Life," I answered under my breath.

"What's that? I can't hear you!" he shouted back.

"Book of Life!" I yelled at the top of my lungs.

"Hallelujah! Thank you Jeeesuss!" he howled.

Before I knew what was happening, two men led me into a smaller tent attached to the big top. To my surprise, they led me to Eben and his mother. "How did you guys get back here?" I asked.

"We're prayer warriors, son. We're here to help pray you into glory!" Mrs. Johnson thundered at me. The singing and the shouting and the music from the big top were only slightly muffled in the smaller tent.

"I think I'm already into glory, ma'am. I think my name just got written in the Book of Life in the other room."

She grabbed me and pulled me to her ample breasts and began speaking in tongues. After all but suffocating me, she dropped to her knees and pulled me to mine. Eben knelt beside her.

"Tell the Lord Jesus you are a wretched and sin-filled little boy. Tell Him your soul is filled with the spit of Satan himself. Tell Him you're filled with slimy demons and puss-filled devils and all manner of sexual deviations. Tell Jeeesuss you want Him to come into your heart and cast the buggers, every last one of them, into the fiery pits of the raging brimstone they deserve. And tell Jeeesuss you want proof of the pudding. Tell Him you want to speak in tongues so you'll know you're filled with His spirit and can praise Him in the language of heaven instead of the paltry, putrid grunts of human speech! Tell him boy! Lift your arms to Jeeesuss and tell Him," she roared through a fountain of tears and a series of facial contortions no one would believe could happen on a human being.

"Amen and amen!" Eben shouted beside her. His arms were stretched heavenward and tears were streaming down his face.

"Why do I need proof of the pudding? Shouldn't I just trust God?" I asked.

"If ya don't speak in tongues we'll never know if your name is written in the Book of Life or not. You must speak in another tongue, boy!" Mrs. Johnson insisted.

"I took shop instead of Latin, but I know a few prayers in Salishan," I told her.

"We're not talking about any language of the sinful and popish Roman Church or any devil tongue spoken by the wretched and lost savages, son . . . we're talking about the language of heaven!" Mrs. Johnson growled.

"What makes you think the prayers of the Salishan are wretched," I asked, hoping I sounded as offended as I felt.

"Because they aren't prayers from Christian hearts directed to the only true God and Father of our Lord Jesus Christ. Them Salishan prayers is pagan, boy, and so is that Latin those image-worshipping Catholics rattle at their pagan and Babylonianish masses. They were both spun from the pits of hell! I want you to speak in real tongues!"

I stood up and looked her directly in the eyes. "I don't think you know what you're talking about, Mrs. Johnson. I've had the help of a man of two souls, the greatest shaman and medicine man living on the coast. He taught me how to pray and about the Great Spirit . . . and I've already been on my vision quest so I know for a fact there are no slimy paltry demons living in my soul. I think I should go home now." I attempted to step to the side of her but she moved at the same time.

Mrs. Johnson's face turned gray and into one enormous frown. "What kind of vision did ya see, boy? Did you see Jeeesuss?"

"No, I saw my Spirit Keeper, and my great-great grandparents, and the One Who Changes," I answered firmly, looking around for the exit.

292

"Sweet Jeeesuss, the boy's been worshipping Satan!" she shouted. Several other people who were praying with other sinners looked our way in horror.

"Oh, Lord, forgive this miserable wretch, zap him with you power and glory!" Eben all but screeched towards the heavens.

"I am not a miserable wretch, Eben. Sinners don't get visions and can never wear their feathers up. I've been thinking about all Ten Commandments and I can't think of one of them I've broken. How do I get out of this place? I wanna go home now."

"Fritz Harding, I don't think you should move a muscle in your body until we've cast the heathen demons from your soul. The only feathers God is interested in are on the cherubim and seraphim and archangels. If men and women were supposed to have feathers they'd have wings like the rest of the angels. You come with me right now. We're going out to see Pastor Wally Pots," she grumbled while taking me by the nape of the neck and pushing me back towards the big top.

I struggled to get free of her but several other prayer warriors grabbed me by my arms and shoulders and dragged me back in front of the white-suited evangelist.

"This boy didn't get saved! He couldn't speak in tongues because he has been worshipping the devil!" she yelled trying to force me to my knees.

"Is that true, boy?" Pastor Wally asked, trying to place his hands on my head.

I jumped to the left to avoid him. "No, it is not true. I was given a vision by God, the Great Spirit," I told him.

"He was in one of those caves the Indians talk about!" Eben shouted.

"Them caves is of the devil, boy," the evangelist roared, coming at me with his arms outstretched.

I bolted between him and Mrs. Johnson and began running down the sawdust trail to the entrance of the tent. I had to push my way past a lot people but midway through the tent, the crowd thinned out and I was able to dash back out into the cool air of the evening. I continued running toward town and our house like a pack of wolves were on my tail. When I finally reached the safety of our front yard, I lay down in the cool night grass to catch my breath. I glanced at my watch. It was eight o'clock. It was almost time for me to be home anyway. I got up and walked into the house through the back door. Mom and Dad were sitting at the kitchen table listening to the Jack Benny Show. Mom was working a puzzle. Dad had the sports page spread out before him.

"Oh, hello dear. Did you have a good time at the Pentecostal voodoo show?" Mother asked giving me more of a smirk than a smile.

"Marjorie, that was uncalled for," Dad chided.

"It was okay," I said, opening the refrigerator door and reaching for the milk.

"Did you become a Holy Roller?" Mother asked.

"I certainly did not," I said emphatically.

"I was right, wasn't I," she said, looking up and giving me an I-told-you-so smile.

"You were right . . . but the music was sorta okay."

294

"I'll bet that's all you liked," she beamed.

"Well, it was pretty bizarre," I confessed.

"More bizarre than seeing ghosts in old caves up on the reservation?" she quipped.

"By comparison, the caves were Sunday school," I answered.

"Did you *get saved*," she asked with a sarcasm that was thick enough to slice.

"I didn't need to get saved. I've had a vision quest . . . but I did walk down the sawdust trail to see what was going on," I answered, stretching the truth just a little.

"You plannin' on goin' back some other night?" Dad asked.

"Not unless Willie and Randy want company," I responded. Once is really enough."

"Sort of like dog stew, huh?" Mother noted.

"At least the dog stew tasted good," I said honestly.

"Do you want some cookies with that milk?" she asked.

"Gotta have cookies," I answered.

§§§§

Saturday Dad and I drove out around Lake Tapps to gather hazelnuts before the squirrels got them all. The road around the lake was part of Dad's daily drive to and from work. He loved hazelnuts and checked the trees often for the right weekend to pick them. We gathered the nuts form the trees just before they fell to the ground and lost their thick cloaks of a needlelike covering that deterred squirrels and other nut gathers from disturbing their maturation. The prickly blanket that protected each nut was covered with a needle-sharp coat of barbed hair-like spikes that easily penetrated and irritated the skin. We wore thick leather gloves while we picked. Dad always insisted on leaving enough nuts on each tree so the squirrels could also stash away sufficient amounts to sustain themselves through the coming winter. Even at that, we always gathered at least three onion sacks full. Once home, it would be my job to carefully pull off their needle like covers so the sacks of nuts could be hung in the attic to dry. By mid-December, we would be feasting on them right out of the shell or in cookies, Dad's homemade caramels, or Grandma Harding's sweet bread.

I didn't realize I had spent most of the drive out to the wild hazelnut groves silently pondering my experiences at the Pentecostal revival until Dad jarred me from my thoughts.

"What'cha thinkin' about," he asked

"I was thinking about that revival meeting I went to last night. Did you know that Pentecostals believe human beings are born wretched and filled with slimy paltry demons?" I questioned.

"Not just Pentecostals . . . pretty much Christians in general believe that. That's why I don't cotton much to church and don't go," he explained.

"So you agree with Mom that religion is all just so much voodoo?"

"I didn't say that. You can tell there's a God just by lookin' around. This earth we live on, the universe, all the stuff that's alive . . . you can tell just by lookin' at it that there's something holy goin' on. And I think there's some kinda wonderful Spirit or God behind it all. Nope, I don't agree with your mother about all religion - but I think I agree with her about Pentecostals and a lot of other organized religions."

"What about Presbyterians?"

"They're okay. Sort of God's frozen people . . . don't ya think?"

"Well, at least they don't go nuts and call all the other churches bad names," I said.

"Different strokes for different folks, Fritz. It takes all kinds to build a world."

"So you don't think human beings are filled with slimy, paltry demons?"

"No. I think human being are some kind of miracle."

"Me, too. That's what Saddles Seatco says too. He says everything is a gift from the Great Spirit. He says that everything that exists is here to help make the existence of everything else possible. He says that there is a holy process at work called the sacred circle. For the Salishan, all creation is good. Saddles says that everything born around the sacred circle is also sacred . . . you know, people, animals, plants, rocks . . . everything. He doesn't think we're miserable pieces of sin. So why does this Pastor Wally Pots and Eben Johnson and his mother think so?"

"Religion isn't my best subject, son. I don't know why Pastor Wally Pots and the rest of them think the way they do. It ain't the way I think . . . and from what you tell me, it isn't the way Saddles Seatco or you think. The American way is that everybody has the right to his own religious beliefs . . . or to none if that's what they want. If you don't like the Pentecostals . . . maybe finding what you need in Indian ways is best for you."

"I just don't understand how believing you're filled with filthy, slimy demons can be good for anyone . . . or right. That's like saying people are just piles of shit! That's the way Eben Johnson treats everybody. He won't play with anyone on the play field because we're all just too sinful for him. If ya even say hi to him he asks if you're saved so everybody stopped saying hi to him. Then he started wearing a pin in the form of a question mark on his jacket. When kids asked him what the question mark was for, he'd ask if they were saved again. That's all he thinks about. At least Saddles teaches us to have balanced lives. Did you know that Eben and his family don't even go to movies because they think they're full of sinful people telling a great big silver screened lie? Now ain't that dumb?"

"Just stay away from them if you don't like them," Dad advised as he pulled the pickup off the road next to a stand of hazelnut trees. "Sometimes people see themselves they way they think God sees them. Some folks have a self image problem. They don't like themselves so they think God doesn't like them either. I'd just stay away from them if they bother you.

"I told Randy and Willie all about it. They wanna go. I told them I'd go Monday night if it's okay

298

with you."

"Why would you want to go back. I thought it was a bad experience?"

"Because Randy and Willie want to see it for themselves. Besides, it was so bizarre, it was kinda fun. I wanna be there to see the expressions on Randy and Willie's faces."

"You boys might just be asking for trouble but it's okay with me and long as you've got your chores done and your homework."

§§§§

Monday evening couldn't come fast enough to suit me. I had the distinct feeling I was taking the boys to an event every bit as entertaining as the Puyallup Fair. I guess I had stopped thinking about the revival as a religious event and had begun thinking about it as a super sideshow. My anticipation and curiosity over Randy and Willie's experience was mounting as we rode our bikes to the big top. I repeated a few of the highlights of my own experiences from the night before.

"Well, I'm not lettin' them pray over me. All I want to be is an observer," Willie asserted.

"Our dad went to a revival once. He didn't like it much either. He wanted to take us kids, but Mom said we were too young," Randy commented.

"I'm surprised she let you come tonight," I noted.

"We're lots older. Besides, we really wanted to come after hearing all your stroeies about it.," Willie observed.

We parked our bikes just out behind the big top and found seats close enough to the platform to give us a good view but near enough to one of the side exits where we felt sure we could get out in a hurry if we decided to make a fast break for it.

Pastor Wally Pots preached against the upcoming Halloween celebration being prepared by the Eagles for the town's children. He called it *Satan's birthday party.* Randy rolled his eyes. "This guy is nuts . . . he sees demons behind every make-believe ghost and goblin and in every little old lady who passes out candy at her door. What a strange religion," he commented.

"It must be a very rich religion. If I'm not mistaken, Pastor Wally is about to take his fifth offering," Willie whispered as the evangelist motioned for the ushers to come forward to get the offering baskets again.

"Brothers and sisters . . . the Lard has put the call of missions on my heart tonight . . . so I'm gonna ask ya'll to dig real deep for the cause of Jeeesusss. I want you to reach into your right pocket and into your left pocket, and if ya'll don't find enough for the Lard there . . . then reach into the pocket of the person sitting next to ya . . . because the Lard blesses a bounteous giver. In fact . . . the Lard is tellin' me rat now that some of you is strugglin' with the voice of God tellin' you to drop a twenty or a fifty into this special mission love offering," the evangelist shouted. Suddenly he broke into a wild dance and shivered all over as if he had been struck by lightning. When he stopped gyrating, he ran back to the pulpit and yelled . . . "The Lard has just told me that someone out in the congregation is strugglin' with the voice of God that's tellin' them to write a check for $500.00!"

The crowd went crazy with shouts of alleluia and amen.

"Thank ya, Jeeesusss!" Pastor Wally shouted at the crowd. "I want the person who God is tellin' to write that check for $500 to stand up! Rat now! Rat where you are! Stand up and identify yourself! Step out in faith. We're gonna pray you home to glory!"

"He means he's going to pray them into writing that check," Willie whispered.

"Amen to that," I whispered back.

All at once Martha Roads stood up from her seat among the choir members sitting behind the white clad evangelist and began to shout. "It's me! It's me! God is speaking to me!" she shrieked as she opened her purse, took out her checkbook and hurried to the pulpit.

Pastor Wally handed her a pen from his jacket pocket. Martha Roads took the pen and began writing. The evangelist motioned for the chorus and band to play a song. They immediately broke into a rousing rendition of *Jesus Saves*. Martha Roads tore the check from her checkbook and handed it to Pastor Wally. He looked at the amount and began shouting more praises and commenced dancing all over the stage. "Thank you, Jeeesuss," he hollered over and over again.

Everyone under the big top began shouting, dancing in the aisles and clapping their hands for joy.

The boys and I didn't know what to make of them, but I was glad the hullabaloo had started up again because I wanted the boys to see what had gone on when I had attended the revival the night before without them.

Pastor Wally took the microphone again. "Tell these fine spirit filled people how you feel, Sister Roads . . . tell them the kind of blessings God is flooding your soul with right now. Tell them how giving deeply floods your soul with the assurance that you are saved by the blood of the lamb . . . that all your sins have been washed away in the precious blood . . . maybe that will encourage someone else to be as generous to our dear sweet Lard."

Martha Roads took the microphone from Pastor Wally Pots and waited until the crowd settled down before speaking. It was hard to believe that the sweet little old gray-haired lady standing before us was part of the evening. The evangelist leaned into the microphone and repeated his invitation for her to speak. The crowd grew silent.

She smiled sweetly to the audience. "The moment Pastor Pots said that God wanted someone to write a check for five hundred dollars. I knew it was me!" she said softly and shyly.

"Alleluia!" Pots bellowed

"Thank you, Lord!" someone shouted behind me.

"It was a leap of faith!" Martha Roads said. She didn't sound as bashful this time.

"Thank you, sweet Jeeesusss!" Pots proclaimed.

"Amen!" I heard a woman's voice a few seats down from me yell. I recognized it as the voice of

Eben Johnson's mother right away. There was no mistaking that voice. It had a shrill, high-pitched and nasal sound even when she spoke softly. When she shouted it sounded like the shriek of a Siamese cat in heat.

"It was an answer to the call of God!" Martha shouted from the platform.

"Yes, Lard!" Pots whooped.

"It's a miracle!" Mrs. Roads shouted.

"Yes, it was! Pots shouted back.

The big top filled with shouts of joy, tongues, people being slain in the spirit, people dancing in the spirit and the chorus and band playing so loudly I was sure they could be heard as far as my parents' home across from the high school. Over it all the voice of Pastor Wally Pots could be heard shouting, "Thank you, Lard, thank you!" over and over until the crowd grew silent and we were all left watching as the evangelist, his eyes closed, his face twisted with a strange glee, finally turned again to Martha Roads and said, "Bless you, sister." He sounded exhausted and consumed.

"You're more than welcome, Pastor Wally . . . and I just know that now that the Lord has convicted my heart and inspired me to write this check . . . he will also find a way to make it good," she said sweetly into the microphone. With that, she swooned and slipped gently to the floor.

Pastor Wally Pots' face was in shock. The crowd was stunned into a thunderous silence except for Randy, Willie and myself. We were suppressing muffled laughter at the whole scene.

We heard several muffled laughs coming from somewhere behind us. They opened a flood gate. The three of us began to laugh and so did a lot of other people. Pastor Pots looked both defeated and angry. He held up his arms to quiet the crowd.

Suddenly Eben's mother leaped to her feet, pointed her right index finger at us and began shouting. "You'll burn in hellfire for mocking God with your sniggers and laughter, you little demon worshipers, you! And that goes for the rest of ya, too." she bellowed.

I had had quite enough of Mrs. Johnson the night before. Her bellowing, her accusatory tone, and her insistence that by loving God differently than she did, I was to be punished and sent to hell seemed immature and a good reason to get from under the big tent and be about our business. "Let's get out of here," I mumbled to my companions as I rose to my feet. Randy and Willie stood as well.

"Not so fast, you little whipper-snappers," Mrs. Johnson bellowed. "I want you three boys to march right down there so you can get saved!"

"Yes, Jeeesuss. Send the boys down the sawdust trail. Convict their hearts. Send the balm of Gideon!" Pots hollered into the microphone.

"No, thank you!" I shouted. "If this is what your religion is all about, I don't want to have anything to do with it!" I shouted.

"How dare you talk that way, young man! That's blasphemy!" Mrs. Johnson shrieked.

"Young man! Young man . . . you are just the sort of stinking pagan flesh that God had to let his own son die for! You get yourself out of that row and get yourself down here so we can pray ya home to glory!" Pots yelled.

"Amen!" several people shouted around us.

All the commotion woke Mrs. Roads from her swoon. One of the choir members helped her to her feet and off the stage.

By that time Mrs. Johnson was out in the aisle and heading up the bleachers toward us. Randy, who was closest to the side entrance, pulled at my sleeve. "Let's get out of here before that woman eats us alive," he commanded.

We slipped in front of the few people blocking our way and headed for the exit just moments before Mrs. Johnson reached the row in which we had been seated.

"Grab those boys so we can pray for them!" she ordered.

"Anybody touches me and I'm calling the police!" Willie shouted as Randy and I jumped from the bleachers to the sawdust floor and ran out the side exit. Willie was right behind us. I glanced over my shoulder to make sure no one had followed us out of the tent. No one had, but we ran until we reached our bicycles, then peddled back toward town as fast as we could anyway.

"What time is it?" Randy asked.

"Seven-fifteen," I answered, using my flashlight to read my wristwatch.

"We've got almost an hour before we have to be back. How about we coast our bikes down the river road and have a smoke," he suggested.

"A smoke?" Where did you get cigarettes?"

305

Willie questioned.

"I don't have any cigarettes . . . but I do have a bag of Bull Durham tobacco and some papers," Randy answered.

"And where did you get them?" his brother asked.

"From Earl Vanderfleet. He bought them for me. I gave him enough money to buy two bags. One for him and one for me. The papers come with them. His Uncle Ralph runs the confection and tobacco sections of his dad's gas station. His uncle will sell Earl whatever he wants," Randy boasted.

"You don't even know how to roll a cigarette," Willie commented.

"I do too. Earl taught me. I think we should all start smoking. It's very sophisticated. Everybody in the movies does it. Even Saddles Seatco smokes Bull durham. We're old enough. Dad told me he started smoke'n when he was twelve." Randy insisted.

"My mom and dad both smoke. They smoke Raleighs and save the coupons for gifts," I added.

"If our parents catch us, they're going to have a fit," Willie pointed out.

"I'll bet Pastor Wally Pots would call this sinful," I said.

"Well, after all that hullabaloo at the big top . . . I'm ready for a little sin. How about it? You guys with me? Shall we coast our bikes down the hill, slip under the bridge and have a smoke?" Randy asked.

"We're gonna have to push them all the way back. Nobody in Perkins Prairie can peddle up that hill," I said. I really enjoyed coasting down the hill but never looked forward to pushing my bike back to the top of the crest.

"We could ride our bikes down the dirt road through the woods over to the graveyard and come up past the big top again. We can peddle that hill. Come on, guys. Let's put a little sin and adventure in our lives," Randy insisted.

Once we arrived at the top of the hill, we stopped and lined up across the road giving ourselves plenty of room. Randy gave the word and we pushed off and began coasting down the hill. Hardly anyone used the road at that time in the evening. We weren't worried about traffic. The hill road was long and its only curve was wide enough so that we would easily be able to see any cars coming our way. "First one to apply his brakes is a chicken," Randy proclaimed as he and his bike took their usual lead. Randy's bicycle was lighter or more streamlined or more something than mine or Willie's. Randy always took the lead if we were just coasting. But peddling made a difference. I had longer and stronger legs. In a few quick seconds I shot in front of him. The hill did the rest of the work for all of us. The farther down the hill we went, the more speed we gained.

White River Hill Road was steep and long, nearly three miles from the stop sign to the bridge below. I had made the trip many times. It was I who introduced the hill to the Redwing boys in the first place. We all knew that if we didn't meet any cars and gained enough momentum, we would coast clear across the bridge and part way up the next hill before we would have to turn around and face the arduous task of getting back up the hill to Perkins Prairie and our homes.

Racing down the hill was exciting. I felt as if all the weary noise of the Pentecostal revival was being washed away by the force of the river air sweeping over me as we descended toward the bridge below. It was just dusk. A faint tinge of pink leaned across the road from the tops of the trees and the instant nip of damp night air began having its way with my skin. Saddles Seatco once said that Tyee Sahale lives in the wind. If that were true, I was sure the Great Spirit was with me on the ride down the hill.

None of us used our brakes. We coasted well beyond the bridge and up the hill beyond it before our bikes came to a natural stop. "Do you know how to roll the cigarettes?" I asked Randy.

"Sure do. Earl showed me how one night under the feed store. Just watch me," he said, taking a paper from the little pad provided with the pack of Bull Durham. He folded it the long way and creased it with his fingers. Then, while holding the paper in one hand, he used his other hand to take the pouch of tobacco out of his shirt pocket. He lifted it to his mouth, pulled gently on one of the strings of the pouch and opened it. Then he carefully tapped a bit of tobacco out of the opened pouch onto the creased cigarette paper, lifted the pouch back to his mouth, pulled the other string to close it, and placed it back in his shirt pocket. After spreading the tobacco evenly across the creased cigarette paper, he placed both hands on the paper, rolled his thumbs down the edges somehow, pushed them back up . . . and presto . . . a perfectly

308

rolled cigarette appeared. He brought it to his mouth, licked the paper to moisten and seal it and handed the efforts of his labor to me.

"Boy that's pretty good. You'll have to teach me how to do that," I said with envy.

"No need to spend twenty-two cents for a pack of tailor-mades when you can roll two packs for the price of a nickel," he said with obvious pride. After rolling two additional cigarettes he lit his, took a deep drag and inhaled it.

"You've done this before. How long have you been inhaling?" I asked.

"For about a week. Earl taught me how. I was pretty sick the first time. But you get used to it. I like the way it tastes now," he answered, blowing a smoke ring into the night air.

Willie lit his cigarette, took a drag and drew it into his lungs. He immediately coughed and sputtered a couple of times, then gave a deep cough that seemed to rumble down to his toes. "This tastes like shit!" he complained as additional smoke came out of his mouth.

"Does not. It tastes good," Randy insisted.

"It's a nasty European habit and I don't think I like it," Willie retorted.

"It is not. Indians were smokin' long before Europeans came to this country. And Bull Durham is practically the same as Indian tobacco. That's what Saddles Seatco told me and he ought to know . . . he smoked Bull Durham long before he started buying tailor-mades. We Indians used tobacco in ceremony. We're the ones that firt gave it to the Euopeans. They gave us rum and we gave them tobacco."

"I wonder who got the best of that trade?" I asked as I lit my cigarette and took a puff. I was careful not to inhale it. I just let the smoke sit in my mouth for a few minutes, then blew it back out. "It tastes kinda bitter," I said, watching my puff of smoke change shape in the moonlit air.

"Have you smoked before, Fritz?" Willie asked.

"I took a few Raleighs out of my mother's pack. She leaves them on the kitchen windowsill so she knows where they are. I take one once in a while and smoke it up in the top part of our garage," I told him.

"Do you like it?" he asked.

"Not really, but I figure we got to smoke them when we grow up . . . and a fellow's got to learn sometimes. Cigarettes is kinda like coffee . . . they taste terrible, but ya gotta learn to like them or you can't ever become an adult," I mused.

"I suppose you're right," Willie answered, taking another puff.

"Don't inhale it this time. Just taste it. Let the smoke roll around in your mouth and then blow it out," Randy instructed.

Willie took another drag and followed his brother's instructions. "Well, it ain't half so bad that way."

"That's the spirit! Get used to the taste first. You can learn to inhale later," Randy said, taking another deep puff from his own cigarette. We watched in amazement as he took the smoke into his mouth and then blew it out through his nostrils.

"My dad can do that! How did you learn?" I

asked.

"Earl showed me how. He knows everything about cigarettes," Randy boasted. "Besides, it's easy. You just sort of swallow the smoke and breathe out through your nose. You don't even have to inhale to do it."

We watched carefully as he demonstrated the marvelous feat a second time. Willie and I gave it a try. Willie did it right on his first attempt. It took me several trial runs before I finally mastered the art.

"Well, what did you think of that tent revival," I asked.

"Pretty messed up," Randy answered.

"I have a feeling real churches aren't like that. I went to the Presbyterian church with some friends of mine once . . . it was more like a town hall meeting with songs from a choir and a nice talk about how to live the Ten Commandments. It was all very proper and refined. There wasn't any shouting or crap like we saw tonight," Willie said.

"I wonder why that Pastor Wally Pots thinks he's gotta yell at people?" Randy asked.

"I don't know. It must have something to do with not being a Presbyterian. Eben and his mother yell all the time too. It's a very noisy religion," I observed.

"I kinda like their music. It's got a good beat." Willie told us.

"Yeah, but I heard them Holy Rollers don't dance. I heard they don't dance and they don't go to movies and the girls can't wear lipstick. That's real odd, isn't it?" Randy added.

"I guess all religions got their no list. Mormons can drink coffee, coke or tea. Did you guys know that?" I said.

"Where did you ever hear a thing like that. What would God have against Coca Cola and tea?" Willie questioned.

"I know some Mormon kids. They told me all about it. But Mormons can dance and wear lipstick and go to movies." I answered.

"I hear that Seventh-Day Adventists can't eat meat. That really take that really takes the cake, doesn't it?" Willie reflected.

"I guess they all got their lists." I repeated.

"Not the Catholics. They can do all those things." Randy pointed out.

"Yeah but they can't eat meat on Fridays and they can't eat chocolate before Easter. So they got problems of their own. My Grandma is a Catholic. They don't even say their church service in English. They do it in Latin. Now that's an odd religion if ya ask me." I told them.

"What'cha think about Jerry's Orchid Appreciation Society?" Willie asked.

"I think he made up the whole thing to make us jealous. I don't think it's got a damn thing to do with wanting to spread the good news about orchids around town . . . I think he just wanted to create something he could use to exclude us. He's just trying to get even," I answered.

"Me, too," Randy agreed.

"I think we should start our own club," Willie suggested.

312

"What kind of club?" I asked, blowing a smoke ring into the moonlit air.

"I think we should start *The Vision Appreciation Society*. I'll bet there are lots of kids in town who would like to go on a vision quest. They're not just for Indians, ya know. Anybody who really wants to be in tune with the Great Spirit can do it," Willie observed.

"Do you have to have a vision to be a member?" Randy asked.

"I don't know. We can talk about rules once we've got some people together who are interested in the idea," Willie answered.

"I think it should be for anyone who believes in visions," I said.

"Maybe we could get Saddles Seatco to come and speak at the town library for us," Randy suggested.

"That's a great idea," Willie responded enthusiastically. "There might be a lot people in town interested in Native American culture – even if they aren't interested in going on their own vision quest."

"That's why I'm your brother . . . so you can have a few great ideas." Randy teased.

"Should we talk to the lady at the library about letting us use a room some night of the week?" I asked.

"Definitely," Willie responded. "And maybe we could make some posters and get the guy who runs the town news paper to do an article about Saddle's visit."

"Should we invite Eben Johnson?" Randy asked.

"He'd probably burst into flames just at the thought of seeking a vision," Willie chuckled.

"Or meeting a real shaman," I added.

"Then we're gonna do it?" Randy asked.

"I think we should," I said.

"Then we will," Willie smiled.

By that time we had smoked our cigarettes so short it was time to put them out. As I recall, I felt very much like an adult that night.

Once the cigarettes had been dropped into the river below, we began peddling our bikes back across the bridge to the little gravel road that would take us along the river and through the forest to the new cemetery road which was far less steep and easily traversed by bike riders eager to get home and put their tired bodies to bed.

Chapter Ten

Polish Pilgrims

Eben Johnson handed me a mimeographed pamphlet as I walked onto the school grounds the next morning. "Here, demon worshipper . . . read this. Maybe it will convince you to get saved," he said politely but with an arrogance that made me want to slap him.

I glanced down at the neatly folded piece of paper and was jolted by its title: *End Devil Worship in Perkins Prairie!* I tucked it into one of my books and hurried to my classroom. As soon as I was in my seat I took out the brochure and read it in its entirety. I was flabbergasted by what it suggested.

END DEVIL WORSHIP IN PERKINS PRAIRIE!

Did you know that Halloween is the Devil's birthday party? It's true, friends. Halloween is an ancient celebration that has its roots in the sinful history of ancient Babylon.

Don't let your children dress up like demons and monsters from hell. Don't let your children put on the shameful attire of witches and ghosts. Don't even let them dress as characters from fairy tales. My friends, the word fairy is just another term the demons use to hid themselves from us and work their evil ways into our lives.

If you love the Lord Jesus Christ, if you want to keep your children and family free from devil worship, don't let them attend the Halloween party in your town this year.

Don't let them dress in costumes that mimic the dead. If you do, there is a good chance one of those demons will move right into the soul of your child and lead them down a path of certain sin. Their souls will be forever lost

In **hellfire and brimstone!**

Instead, dear ones, I invite you to join me and my friends down at the revival. The Lord is blessing us every night with His power and glory.

Boycott Halloween for Jesus!

"What are you reading, Fritz?" I heard the voice of Mrs. Saunders ask. I had been so engrossed in the reading the pamphlet, I wasn't aware she had walked down the aisle and was standing by my desk.

"This pamphlet. It's written by that evangelist fella who's got the big top just outside of town. He wants everybody to boycott the Halloween party this year," I answered.

"Let me see that," she requested.

I handed it to her and watched as she read. Her usual friendly smile quickly changed to a frown. "Where did you get this?" she asked.

"Eben Johnson handed it to me when I came to school this morning," I answered.

"Was he standing on the school grounds when he gave it to you?" she asked.

"I don't really remember," I said as Randy slid into his seat next to me. He had one of Pastor Wally's pamphlets in his hand too.

"Did you get that from Eben Johnson?" Mrs. Sanders asked.

"No, ma'am, I got it from one of his sisters. She's passing them out on the front steps of the building," he answered.

Mrs. Sanders handed the pamphlet back to me and walked to the head of the classroom. Most of the students were in their seats or at least in the room and headed for them. "How many of you children were handed a pamphlet denouncing the Eagle's Halloween party this year?" she asked.

Almost every hand in the room went up.

"If you haven't already read it . . . I want you to

take a few moments and read it right now. Those of you who have read it may take a few moments to talk quietly among yourselves about the pamphlet. It will be the point of our first discussion on current events this morning," she announced.

"Did you read that thing yet," Randy whispered from across the aisle.

"Yeah," I whispered back.

"What did you think?"

"I think it's nuts."

"Me too."

After everyone had read the pamphlet, Mrs. Sounders led a discussion on its contests. Sally Johnson, Eben's sister, tried her best to defend the pamphlet by telling us that Pastor Wally was just trying to warn us concerning what the Bible says about Halloween.

"Can you show us in your bible where Scripture, either in Old or New Testament, actually condemns the celebration of Halloween?" Mrs. Saunders asked.

"Well, no I can't, ma'am . . . not right now . . . but I'll ask my mom when I get home," she answered.

Jerry Cotton's hand went up next.

"Yes, Jerry. What is your opinion of this pamphlet?" Mrs. Sanders asked.

"I think it's just stupid to say that we become demons if we dress like one. I went as Frankenstein to last year's party and I didn't become Frankenstein . . . and Johnny Ecclesberg went as Rita Hayworth and he didn't become no girl," Jerry noted.

"Any girl," Mrs. Saunders corrected.

"Ain't there some law against mixin' religion with

318

public education?" Ray Bomkowski asked.

"There certainly is . . . only the beginning of that sentence should have begun with *isn't there some law.* But you are quite right. This school is funded by the state of Washington. The state of Washington is a government. It is illegal for the government to mix in the affairs of religion and equally illegal for religion to mix in the affairs of government. The Halloween party isn't just sponsored by the Fraternity of Eagles; it is also sponsored by the Perkins Prairie Volunteer Fire Department, its Police Department, the Public School System, the Perkins Prairie Chamber of Commerce, and the Ladies Town Auxiliary. So even Halloween itself, at least in Perkins Prairie, is a quasi-governmental function. And Pastor Wally Pots' pamphlet because it is a religious opinion has no business being passed out on school grounds because the school is a governmental institution. I am licensed to teach by the state. Even my teaching degree was earned at a state college. But we can discuss the issue of the religious pamphlet because it is a current event and an event happening in our own community."

"What about freedom of speech?" Sally Johnson asked. "Don't religious people have the right to freedom of speech just like governmental people do?"

"Everyone has the right to freedom of speech, Sally, but with certain legal and moral bounders. Let me ask you this, Miss Johnson. Do you think this Pastor Wally Pots would approve of a Buddhist or a Hindu being allowed to stand around on our playgrounds trying to convert little Christians to a different religion?"

"Of course not, Mrs. Saunders . . . because them other people are pagans themselves and headed straight for hell."

"And who says so, Sally?"

"The Bible! It's all in the Bible, Mrs. Saunders."

"And does the Bible represent a religion, Sally?"

"Of course it does . . . it represents Christians."

"Or if one only believes in the Old Testament . . . .it represents Jews and Muslims, isn't that correct?"

"Yeah, but they're all pagan too . . . headed for hell just like them Chinks and Japs," Sally responded.

"And yours is a religious opinion, is it not?" Mrs. Saunders asked.

"Well, of course . . . it's right in the Bible . . . so it's both a religious answer and the truth," Sally answered.

"It is merely a religious truth . . . and probably one with which other persons who call themselves Christian might disagree. Thus the law. The state has said that there can be no mixing of religion in a state's event because that is why our forefathers left England and other European countries in the first place - to escape the state's persecution of certain religious ideas. In America everyone's religious ideas and ideals are protected by the law. That is to say that the law insists that the government may not persecute anyone for what he believes religiously. By that same token, no religion may make itself a state religion, as it still is in England, Norway and other countries. In this nation the two may not be mixed. That is a law. And on the moral side of the discussion, even though people have

320

freedom of speech, it would not be moral to shout fire in a crowded theatre when you knew full well there was no real fire. Doing so could cause a panic and a stampede and someone could get very hurt. So, there are parameters within which freedom of speech may be practiced. Now I would like you to go down to the principal's office. I have a strong suspicion that your sister and brother will either be waiting for you or will join you shortly. I will be down to discuss this issue with you and the principal just as soon as I have given the class an assignment."

§§§§

After dinner, chores, and a quick look at my homework, I rode my bike over to the Redwing's house. Randy and Willie had promised to help me with ideas for my costume and I had promised to help them with theirs.

"Did ya hear what happened to Eben and his sisters for passin' out those pamphlets?" Willie asked as I walked into their living room.

"Didn't hear a thing. I had a lot of chores to do today and Mr. Storm assigned a whole chapter in world history. I went right home after school so I'd have some time to come over here tonight. What happened?"

"The principal called Mrs. Johnson. I guess she went right over to the school and had a real shouting match with Mrs. Baker. Carl Fudd, the janitor . . . he lives just across the street . . . he told Mom that even

Eben and his sisters were shouting at Baker . . . you know . . . stuff like *Praise God!* and *Thank you Jeeessuss!* and stuff like that. Mrs. Johnson called him a devil worshipper and told him if her kids couldn't pass out the word of God on school grounds, they'd pass it out from the sidewalks surrounding the school. I guess she started prayin' for him out loud and all kinds of stuff. Mr. Baker's secretary had to call the police to make her leave. I guess she was bound and determined that Mr. Baker was gonna get saved right then and there! You know he's already a deacon or some such thing over at the Presbyterian church. Anyway the kids were all suspended for three days and Mr. Baker said that if they pass out any more pamphlets to school kids on the school grounds. . . he'll expel them."

"But they can still pass them out from the sidewalk?" I asked.

"There's nothing Mr. Baker can do about that. The sidewalk is not considered school grounds. That's what the policeman told him. Carl Fudd heard everything when he was dusting and cleaning the front office."

"I think they're nuts," I said.

"I don't understand why that woman is so eager to push her religion down everyone's throat," Audrey noted, looking up from some sewing she was doing.

"Beats the heck out of me, Mrs. Redwing. I was wonderin' if it would be okay for me to wear my breechcloth and stuff to the Halloween party this year . . . do you suppose that would be okay or should I make up another costume and save my real Indian stuff for when I go to the reservation?"

"Well, there would certainly be nothing wrong in doing so. A costume is a costume is a costume . . . but I would think the weather would keep you from just wearing your breechcloth. I don't know if you have noticed, young man, but winter is swiftly approaching. The weather report says we might even get a little snow Halloween night. You try running around in just a breechcloth, a feather, and moccasins, and you'll freeze your little fanny off. I've got a lot of stuff in trunks up in the attic . . . if you want to go as an Indian, I'll help you go as a warm one. How does that sound?" she responded.

"Great! You guys goin' in full Indian dress too?" I asked the boys.

"I'm goin' as Mae West," Randy answered excitedly.

"Mae West! But she's a woman!" I noted.

"So are witches . . . did you ever go as a witch?" Randy questioned.

"Nope. I went as a werewolf once though. But Jerry Cotton went as a witch one year. He won first place and nobody knew it was him until he got up and spoke over the microphone. That was really something. But lots of the guys called him a sissy after that. Aren't you afraid some of the guys might call you a sissy? I responded.

"Well, I'm really going to be something too. Mom is workin' on my costume right now. And besides, Jerry Cotton is a sissy. He raises orchids and makes candles and raises peacocks," Randy retorted.

"I don't think of him as a sissy," I said honestly.

"Oh, for Pete's sake, Fritz, we're all sissies. None

of us even like football or most other sports. We like swimming and tennis and roller skating," Willie said.

"You think that makes us sissies?" I asked horrified. "Do you think we're sissies, Mrs. Redwing?"

"Well, I'm not sure what a sissy is. But I would say you three are much more gentle than many of the boys in town. You'll all grow up to be gentlemen and the others will be grease monkeys or lumberjacks. Don't worry about it. I like you just the way you are," she responded.

"But you'll be goin' as a girl!" I repeated to Randy.

"Oh, Fritz, don't be such an old prude. It's just a costume. It's Halloween. Get into the spirit of things," Audrey said. The tone of her voice was playful, but I could tell she was also giving me a mild scolding.

"What about you, Willie, you goin' as a woman or as an Indian?" I asked.

"Neither. What would be the point . . . I am an Indian, and I'd feel funny in a dress. I'm thinking of goin' as a pilgrim."

"That's a great idea."

"His Grandmother Sunfield doesn't think so . . . but Clarence and I see no harm in it," Audrey commented.

"And I was think'n of going as Howdy Doody – but he's got red hair." Willlie mused.

"How can you tell if he's got red hair. He's in black and white?" I asked.

"I saw a picture of him in a magazine. He's got red hair alright and I don't wanna color my hair. So I think a pilgrim will be fun."

§§§§

I didn't show my parents the costume Audrey loaned me until right after I put it on Halloween night. It resembled what one might think an Aztec Shaman who worshipped the sun god might wear. The costume included a cape made of red feathers, a white buckskin shirt and trousers made the traditional way, decorated with tiny shells on the front of the shirt and along the sides of the trousers. The moccasins were topped with a plumed ring of red feathers that matched the cap. The headband was decorated with bear teeth, but Audrey said that if anyone asked I should tell them they were the teeth of a black South American panther. "It will add mystique to your character and costume," she insisted. I was sure I would win first prize. I borrowed a makeup kit from the drama teacher and put a brown tan on my face, arms and hands.

When we arrived at the gymnasium, I left my parents and sisters to find Randy and Willie right away. I wanted to be sure Mom and Dad saw them before we were gathered together in specific groups for judging and were herded over to the main auditorium for the prizes, snacks and a movie.

Willie looked the perfect pilgrim. His mother had found an old broad-rimmed black hat at the Salvation Army shop in Tacoma that looked like something right out of the 16th century. He also wore a buttonless and collerless white shirt, black pants and coat, a traditional pilgrim belt buckle, and black shoes. His costume was topped off by an old-fashioned powder and ball rifle his father had borrowed from someone on the Muckelshoot Reservation. His costume was so believable, I began having doubts about my chances at first prize.

Randy was a shock. He made a very pretty Mae West. He had purchased an old red sequined floor-length gown, long black gloves, and high heels from the same thrift shop. Willie found his hat. He had stuffed pillows under the dress to give himself the perfect hourglass figure Mae West made popular and painted long black lines on the back of his legs with an eyebrow pencil to make it look like he was wearing silk stockings. His mother had applied his makeup, he told me, and his grandmother loaned him a fox stole to slink around his shoulders. To top off the effect, Belle Jackovitch, who waited tables at the only cocktail lounge in town, had loaned him a pair of long dangly rhinestone earrings and a huge blond wig. "My God, Randy, you're the prettiest girl at the party!" I said with honest enthusiasm.

"Why don'tcha come up and see me sometime," he cooed, giving me the once-over, placing a hand on his hip and striking a typical Mae West pose.

As we headed over to show my parents their costumes, we bumped into my grandparents. "Why, Fritz, don't you just look like something right out of a Cecil B. De Mille movie? What a great costume. Have you seen your mom and dad?" Grandma asked.

"Thanks. Audrey Redwing loaned it to me. Isn't it great. I'm supposed to be an Aztec shaman. We're just goin' over to show Mom and Dad our costumes right now. They're over by the piano. Just follow me," I instructed.

"Your pilgrim costume looks great," Grandpa told Willie.

"Thanks. Mom made it for me . . . but it was my decision to come as a pilgrim."

"And is this lovely child one of your sisters?" Grandma asked Willie.

"No, it's Randy!" I exclaimed.

"I'll be damned," Grandpa quipped.

"Why, Randy Redwing, you make a more beautiful girl than half of my daughters!" Grandma chuckled.

"Willie, your costume gives me an idea. What do you and your family usually do on Thanksgiving? Do you all get together for the day on one of the reservations or what?" Grandpa asked.

"We don't much celebrate Thanksgiving, sir. Too many treaties were broken between the whites and Indians. We never do much special on Thanksgiving. At least we didn't when we lived on the reservation. I don't think my folks have anything planned," Willie answered.

"Well, we've never broken any treaties with you," Grandpa pointed out.

"That's true, sir," Willie responded.

"Well, if your parents are here, I'd like to extend an invitation to them. Grandma and I would be right proud to have you folks celebrate the day with us. The first real Thanksgiving was celebrated by Europeans and Indians. Both of them brought food for the meal.

We could do a real Thanksgiving - and maybe change things a bit for you and your folks. After all, you aren't living on the reservation anymore and you have talked a lot about living in the real world. What do you think?"

"You can ask my parents, Mrs. Harding . . . but they have pretty firm convictions about all this. They're with Fritz's folks right now," Willie answered.

"Let's go ask. The very worst that can happen is that they'll say no. I can live with that. But who knows . . . they might just say yes."

The five of us walked over to our parents. After a series of informal greetings and a little small talk about costumes, Grandmother Harding's face took on a serious look. "Clarence and Audrey, my husband and I would be very honored if you and your family would join us at the farm this coming Thanksgiving for dinner. Your boys have already explained to us that you don't usually celebrate Thanksgiving. And I understand all the treaty stuff . . . but my husband and I haven't broken any treaties with you . . . and it would mean very much to us as immigrants from Poland to have Thanksgiving with real natives of this country. What do you think?"

"Oh, that's very sweet of you, Mrs. Harding . . . but the reason my mother lives on a reservation and cannot feel free to put up her lodge where your root cellar stands is because of broken treaties. Thanksgiving Day usually reminds us that our country has been taken away from us," Clarence responded.

"Our country was taken away from us too, Clarence. That's why we fled Poland. There were no jobs, no way to get out of poverty . . . no way to have the best possible life for our children. That's why we moved to America and here to Perkins Prairie. I thought that was why you moved here too . . . for a better life. Can't our two families get together and be thankful for that. I'm sure it was not easier for you to make the decision to move than it was for me and mine. But out of that choice we have a better life, and out of that choice we have met you. I am thankful for that," my grandfather said. His words made chills run down my back. I was touched by what he said and proud of him. More importantly, I learned something I had not known before. I learned why my grandparents had moved from the old country in the first place. Until that moment it had not ever occurred to me to ask.

"You speak great wisdom, Grandfather. I am touched by your words," Clarence said.

"I hope you are touched enough by them to join us," my grandmother interjected.

"A real peace and spirit of thanksgiving between our people must begin somewhere, Clarence," Audrey whispered to her husband.

"Oh, please, Dad, say yes. I wanna wear my Mae West costume to the Harding's Thanksgiving party," Randy pleaded.

"The only place you're going to wear that costume is over to the auditorium and back home again," his father noted.

"What do you say, Clarence?" my grandfather pressed.

"I think we must say yes, Clarence. This is a good idea. Now that we have moved into the mainstream of American life, it is probably time to move into the day that celebrates that life. I say yes," Audrey asserted. She reached up and took her husband's arm.

"You are a people of two souls. If you were Indians, you would both be great medicine people. All the village would come to you for advice," Clarence declared.

"Then you'll come?" Grandpa asked.

"We will come. You provide the turkey, we'll provide the deer," Clarence answered.

"Deer?" Mother asked with a surprised tone in her voice.

"Have you forgotten that both meats were eaten in celebrating the first Thanksgiving. I may not have celebrated that day before . . . but I did read about it in school," Audrey noted.

"Then it's a done deal and we can let the kids enter some of the games and contests before we go over for the judging and movie? Dad asked.

"It's a done deal," Clarence affirmed.

The boys and I wandered around the gymnasium looking at other costumes and playing some of the games to see if we could win a few prizes. Randy won a pair of sunglasses which he immediately put on, saying they made his Mae look more Hollywood. Later, when the judges requested those in costume gather in specific areas on the gymnasium floor, we were all assembled according to type. All witches and warlocks were placed in one group, ghosts and goblins in another, animals, monsters, cartoon characters, historical figures, hobos and a category called miscellaneous. Randy was originally sent to join Willie and me in the historical figures area, but when the judges learned that our Mae West was actually a boy, he was rerouted to the miscellaneous group. I was a little jealous. Everyone knew that the miscellaneous group always had the most interesting costumes. I craned my neck to see what sort of competition Randy would have. Someone had come as a fire truck and ladder. Other costumes included a palm tree, a tap-dancing pack of Chesterfields, an enormous potted orchid made of crepe paper and metal clothes hangers, a cigar, and our Mae West. Randy had some pretty stiff competition.

The judges moved among the contestants making notes and conferring in small huddles from which they would eye specific costumes. It was an intense half hour.

Once the judges had made their final decisions, we were permitted to adjourn to the high school auditorium where some of the other townspeople had already gathered . There we would each parade across the stage by group and be individually introduced. After the introductions, ascending prizes were awarded. That last prize to be awarded in each group was always first prize. Willie and I received only honorable mention for our efforts. Honorable mention received a gray ribbon and a five dollar bill. We were outclassed by Billie Smith, who won third prize and ten dollars as George Washington, and Berdette Franklin, who won second prize and fifteen dollars as Little Bow Peep. As Berdette went back to her place everyone was holding their breath to hear the name of the first prize winner.

Not only did the prize bring with it a large fancy white ribbon edged in gold, but it also came with a crisp twenty dollar bill. The main judge picked up the beautiful white ribbon and showed it to the audience. "Now, ladies and gentlemen, boys and girls, we are pleased to announce the first prize winner in the historical category, Harry Loomis, who came as Jesus carrying his cross, wins the coveted first prize ribbon and a twenty dollar bill. Let's have a big round of applause because it shows that despite that evangelist's attempt to separate this town . . . even Jesus came to our party!"

The place went wild with applause, whistles and shouts. Harry Loomis went up to get his prize, bowed to the audience, then returned to his place on stage. Next came the miscellaneous category.

But it was Randy, not Jerry Cotton, who won first prize in the miscellaneous category. The fire truck and ladder won second place in the miscellaneous category, the tap-dancing pack of Chesterfields won third, and the palm tree won one of two honorable mentions. Of course Jerry's honorable mention was announced first. Unlike the two boys who came as a mule, Jerry did not step forward to receive his prize. He just stood there as the other prizes were awarded. Finally, after Randy went back to his place on the stage, the announcer spoke again to Jerry. "Will the orchid, Mr. Jerry Cotton, please step forward to receive his prize?"

The orchid, who had been standing on the side of the stage with other contestants whose costumes were too large to fit on the main part of the stage, was furious. The enormous potted plant turned away from the judge's table and headed for the exit.

"Don't be a poor loser," the announcer said over the microphone.

The orchid whirled around. Jerry Cotton's muffled voice came from inside. "If the judges are more interested in female impersonators than the natural beauty of one of God's most exotic flowers . . . I don't want a damn thing to do with this so-called party. As far as I'm concerned, you can keep your damn old gray ribbon and your five bucks. I may go out and knock over some outhouses," he shouted from inside the orchid. I doubt that anyone heard him except those of us standing on the stage near him.

§§§§

A few days after Halloween I was surprised to learn that Grandmother Redwing had accepted the invitation to celebrate Thanksgiving on our farm, providing Saddles Seatco could come along so she would have company on the long bus ride to her son's home in Perkins Prairie. My grandfather called Mr. Seatco long distance to personally include him in the invitation and to ask that he pass that message along to the elder Mrs. Redwing, who was still making her home in the old cedar shack along the flats of Lake Quinault.

Grandmother Sunfield was another story. That surprised me. I had thought that if anyone was going to refuse the invitation it would be Grandmother

Redwing.

"Why won't she come?" I asked Audrey one afternoon when I stopped by with the boys on my way home from school.

"She says that if she attends, it would be a betrayal to the spirit of my father who died at the hands of the whites. She's very upset that we've decided to attend. I even told her that Clarence's mother and Saddles will be coming down for the event. I was sure she would want to see Saddles. She doesn't see him unless she attends Tahola days. But she only grew more angry when she learned that people of her own generation would go."

"That's awful. Do you think I could talk to her? She likes me. Maybe I could talk her into it."

"No, no, Fritz, that would never work. Clarence and I are going to take the kids up there this weekend and see if we can talk her into it face to face. So far we've just spoken on the telephone. I think maybe face to face we'll do a better job. Maybe havin' the kids there will soften her."

I was at my grandparents' farm picking up milk and butter for Mom a few days later when Audrey drove into the barnyard. Grandma and I were just coming out of the milk house when we saw Audrey walking down the wooden walkway from the barn toward us. The moment she saw my grandmother, she broke into tears. Grandma took her in her arms and comforted her. "What's the matter, child? Has something happened to one of the children?" Grandma asked.

"No, Mrs. Harding. It's my mother. She simply

334

refuses to attend your Thanksgiving celebration. I probably shouldn't even have invited her . . . and I'm afraid that Clarence and I have pressured her so severely about it, she won't speak to either of us right now. I think maybe it would just be better for everyone if we didn't attend either," Audrey sobbed.

"You take me to your mama. I got time right now. You wanna drive me? I go tell Papa . . . he can handle things here while we're gone. Auburn ain't that far away. You got time?"

"That might make Mother even more angry."

"Sometimes two old ladies can talk better together than an old one and a young one," Grandma suggested.

"I've never fought with my mother before. Not like this. She was pretty upset when we decided to move the boys to town, but she is really upset this time. I'm afraid that if I take you up there, she'll just get all the more angry at me."

"It don't sound like she can get much more angry. Besides, she ain't angry at me."

"But I'm not even sure she'll speak to me," Audrey worried.

"Then you sit in the car and I'll go talk to her by myself. Okay?"

"Can I go too?" I asked. "We could drop off the butter and stuff at home on the way."

"Why you wanna come for?" Grandma asked

"Mrs. Sunfield likes me a lot. Maybe me being there will help," I asserted.

"It might help," Audrey admitted.

"Okay, okay . . . let me get a scarf. I take her a

pie. I just baked a blackberry pie."

When we arrived on the reservation, I pointed out the totem poles to my grandmother. To my surprise it wasn't her first trip there. "I used to come with your grandpa when he would buy fish eggs from some old guy up here," she informed me.

The two of us walked up the path to Grandmother Sunfield's house leaving Audrey to wait and worry in the car. I saw the old Indian woman watching us from behind a lace curtain as we climbed the steps to her porch. Grandmother knocked on the screen door. Mrs. Sunfield opened the main door to the house but left the screen door closed.

"Good afternoon, Mrs. Sunfield. I am Martha Harding, Fritz's grandmother. He has told me many good things about you. I brought you a blackberry pie. Is high mountain blackberry pie. The tiny tart ones."

"Good morning," Mrs. Sunfield returned without further comment.

"Audrey tells me how upset you get over my idea that we all celebrate Thanksgiving together this year. She is so unhappy because she has upset you that she has decided no one in her family should attend."

"Good. Then she is finally thinking like an Indian again."

"Well, I cannot think like an Indian, Mrs. Sunfield, but I can think like an immigrant to this country who suffered very much to get here. My own hometown was taken over by other people . . . just like your land was. But they didn't even bother to make reservations for us. They just took over our homes. My parents had to run for their lives and were lucky enough to get to America. I was just five years old when we come by oxcart from the Missouri River to these hills here in the Northwest. It looks a lot like the area of Poland we were from. Of course it's not Poland. But to me it's been a good life. I have a good husband. He is from Poland too. We had seventeen kids. I got lotsa grandchildren already. I wanted to celebrate and give thanks for all that with some of the good people who made room for me and mine," Grandmother explained. Even with her thick Polish accent, I thought she was eloquent.

"We didn't make room for you willing, you know," the old Indian woman grumbled.

"And my parents didn't come here willingly. They would much rather have remained in Poland. They had land there. But what happened here was not my fault. It is not part of my history."

"It is part of mine," Mrs. Sunfield said.

"I know. I even think I know how you feel. I know what it means to make changes you don't want to make. Could I come in and speak with you? It is chilly out here on the porch."

"It would be bad manners for me to show you hostility when you have been so polite, and I have a soft spot for your grandson. And I am partial to high mountain blackberry pie. You can come in if you want." Grandmother Sunfield opened the screen door for us.

We followed her into the house. Mrs. Sunfield sat us down at the kitchen table and offered to make tea. "Tea would be good. I need to warm these old bones," my grandmother smiled.

"You want me to cut the pie now?" Mrs. Sunfield asked.

"I have another at home in the kitchen window. This is for you and your friends."

"Then I can do with it whatever I want?"

"Of course."

"Then I slice us some when the tea is hot. Tell me, did Audrey ask you to come and see me?"

"No. Coming here was my idea. She didn't think I should come but she did drive me up here. I don't drive anymore and Pa doesn't like to drive this far. She's out in the car right now."

"I know. I saw her," Mrs. Sunfield said, sliding her teapot from the warming side of her stove to the top of one of the burners. "Maybe I should call her in."

"Maybe. I'm hoping you will reconsider. Did our daughter tell you that my invitation is wrapped in the hope of this being a real Thanksgiving between our two families? Me and my husband were born in Poland. We're like the first pilgrims. You are Muckelshoot. If we eat together we can redo that first Thanksgiving and this time I promise you I will break no treaties."

"We ain't' got no treaties between us. You want honey with your tea?"

"Just a little, thanks."

"I always fix it with milk and honey for Fritz. He likes it that way," Grandmother Sunfield smiled as she placed three cups on the table.

"I do the same with his coffee," Grandmother responded.

Mrs. Sunfield poured hot water over some herbs and leaves she had placed in the teapot. "In all due respect, ma'am, Europeans took our land from us and put us on reservations. Where Perkins Prairie is now use'ta be our huntin' grounds. That prairie was full of elk and deer, quail, pheasants, squirrels . . . and the streams and ponds were so full of fish you could tickle them out of the water with your bare hands. Now it's all roads and houses and stores. We were once a free people. Now we must live where we are told. We can't even hunt anymore except on the reservation unless we have a huntin' license to go up into the hills. A hunting license. Don't that beat all. I see no reason to be thankful for any of that. Don't get me wrong, I understand why my daughter and her husband have moved into town. Times change. My grandchildren must live in a different world than the one I grew up in. I accept that. But I do not have to celebrate it. Can you understand that?"

"A little. But I am not an Indian. I'm an old Polish woman. I'm from peasant stock. I got no real education. I can't even write in English good. My girls write my letters for me. My husband was a city boy. He is better educated. But we both came to America because someone took our land away too. My mother became so ill from the hardships of getting out here, she died a year after we arrived. We couldn't even speak good English when we got here. Now, none of my children speak enough Polish to ask how the weather is. I haven't seen my home country for seventy-five years. Yet this place has given me life and many good things. I was hopin' that one of those good things would be the opportunity to meet some real Americans. I don't mean the children of immigrants who got here before we did . . . but real Americans. Indians. I wanna know what life was like before we Europeans got here. Maybe if we celebrate together and eat a Thanksgiving meal together . . . maybe you and me could become friends or at least as friendly together as you are toward my grandson. Won't you reconsider?"

"I did not know you came to this country because you lost your land," Mrs. Sunfield said, pouring my grandmother some tea.

"They were hard times. I was very young . . . but my father told me the stories many times," she answered, lifting the cup to her mouth and tasting the tea. "Looking back, I don't know how he kept his sanity and his good humor. He had to finish raising us kids alone until I was old enough to take over with the boys."

"Sometime I don't know how I keep my sanity and my good humor," Mrs. Sunfield confessed. She finally sat down at the table across from my grandmother.

"I know. It is hard to be human in a time of change. Maybe that's what life is all about . . . because that old pest *change* is always with us. This is good tea."

"Kwatee! That scoundrel!" Mrs. Sunfield scoffed.

"Kwatee?" Grandmother questioned.

""He's the changer in Quinault and Salishan legends," I explained.

"So you know him?" my grandmother asked,

directing her question to the old Indian woman.

"Far too well."

"Mrs. Sunfield, your daughter loves you very much. She is a fine woman. During all those hard times you managed to raise a truly wonderful daughter. I would be proud to call her my own. She is a good woman. Won't you at least forgive her. It was I who convinced her to do this thing. She was against the idea when I first suggested that your family might join mine for Thanksgiving. It would be far better if you asked me to leave your home but repaired your relationship with Audrey. She has already told me she no longer thinks she can celebrate with us. She has rejected my invitation to please you . . . not herself. She has earned your forgiveness . . . and a cup of this delicious tea. Daisy, isn't it?"

"You know it?" Mrs. Sunfield asked with a surprised tone in her voice.

"Of course . . . it is a favorite of our people. I have gathered and dried daisy blooms for tea since I was a child."

"I also make a jelly from daisy blooms. You wanna try some on a biscuit?" Audrey's mother asked.

"I certainly would. How do you get the bitterness out?"

I use wild honey instead of store bought sugar . . . just like my mother and her mother before her did," Mrs. Sunfield answered, bringing a platter of cold biscuits and a small jar of clear golden jelly to the table.

Grandmother Harding and I watched as the old Indian woman split a biscuit and spread her sweet concoction over it. "Here . . . you taste," she smiled.

I had eaten her daisy jelly many times before and knew how good it was. I watched with anticipation as my grandmother bit into it and tasted Mrs. Sunfield's culinary talents. "Mmm, this is very good. I've never had this before. Is there a hint of mint in it?" My Grandmother asked.   "Yes! Just a hint . . . that adds a pleasant mystery to the flavor, don't you agree?"

"Oh, I do. I would love to have your recipe."

"I'll have Audrey copy it down for you. I don't write myself. I can read pretty good, but I don't write too good."

"Me neither. English is too hard to put on paper. I talk my letters and one of the girls write them for me."

"Fritz, you go down to the car and get my daughter. Tell her I want her to have some tea and warm up and she can write something down for me too," Grandmother Sunfield commanded.

"You are a good mother, Mrs. Sunfield," my grandmother mused.

"Please call me Stella."

"Thank you. Please call me Martha."

"Like Martha Washington?" Mrs. Sunfield asked.

"I never thought about that . . . it was my name before I knew who Martha Washington was. I am named Marta after a great aunt on my mother's side. The guy at the immigration office wrote down Martha when I told him my name . . . so even that got changed. I couldn't even keep my own name."

By the time Audrey and I made it back to the house, the two old women were exchanging humorous stories about raising children.

342

"Audrey, would you be kind enough to write down my recipe for daisy blossom jelly for Martha? She was just telling me how much like you her third daughter is. It's your lucky day, Audrey . . . Martha likes the third daughter."

The two old women broke into laughter. It was obvious they were already privy to a secret only grandmothers were permitted to share.

"I'd be happy to, Mother," Audrey answered over the few remaining giggles flowing between my grandmother and Mrs. Sunfield.

"I like your Mrs. Harding, Audrey . . . she knows a lot about Kwatee. You want some tea, girl?"

"Then you're no longer angry at me?" Audrey asked.

"No, child, I am no longer angry. I wasn't really angry with you in the first place. I think I was angry at history. But now that I have met this old woman with a rich history of her own . . . a history not unlike mine . . . I do not see how I can keep her history and my history from merging. I would be proud to share history with such a fine woman. No wonder Fritz is such a good boy. He has good roots."

My grandmother smiled at Mrs. Sunfield, lifted her cup of tea as if in a toast.

"And if Martha will forgive my hard heart and stubborn ways . . . I would very much like to join you when you go to her farm to celebrate the first Thanksgiving between the tribe of the Hardings of Perkins Prairie and the Redwings of Muckelshoot and Quinault."

"I will forgive your stubborn ways . . . but I do

not think either of us has to forgive history too much. Better to remember it. What is the old saying?"

"He who does not remember his history is doomed to repeat it," Audrey said.

"Yes. That's it. I forgive you for being stubborn, Stella Sunfield, if you will forgive me for being such a pushy old woman."

"It's a done deal," Grandmother Sunfield said, lifting her own cup of tea in a toast. When she had taken a sip, she put the cup back down on the table, stood up, went to her daughter and enveloped her in her arms and said: "Your mama is sometimes a very heavy rock to lug around . . . you must forgive her."

Grandmother Harding gave me a wink and took another sip of her tea.

§§§§

About a week before Thanksgiving, I learned that several of my aunts and uncles were opposed to having their traditional Thanksgiving at the family farm changed by inviting the Redwings. It had never occurred to me that any of them might react in that way. I don't think it ever occurred to my grandparents either.

When I overheard my father inform my mother that Grandpa had called a family meeting, I knew the matter was far more serious than I had imagined. Family meetings were never called unless something truly important had affected the family . . . like the time my grandparents learned that my cousin Raymond was a homosexual living with a male hairdresser in Seattle. It took several family meetings before the whole clan finally agreed to at least be civil to Raymond and his friend, Cecil, when they came to family functions even if they didn't approve of their relationship. My grandparents had insisted. Eventually everyone acquiesced and by the time the Redwings moved into town, most of my aunts and uncles actually liked Cecil. In fact he often accompanied my father and Uncle Bert on fishing trips.

They had another family meeting when one of my aunts came home for a visit in big fancy car and two standard French poodles and announced that she wasn't going back to her Hollywood husband and was filing for divorce. She sent the dogs back with the chauffer. I never understood that. I loved those dogs.

I was determined to be present at the meeting about the Redwings even though children were usually not allowed. I always found a way to eavesdrop on the proceedings. About a half hour before any of the aunts and uncles were scheduled to arrive at the farm, I rode my bike out and hid it in the barn.

"Whatchu doin' here?" Grandma asked as I walked into the kitchen.

"I was just out for a ride on my bike and thought I'd drop in to give you a hug," I answered.

"Okay, you give me a hug and get back on your bike. You know the rules. No kids during a family meeting. This is adult stuff. You get a piece of candy if you want and get your butt out a here. Go on! Get goin'."

I hugged her and kissed her on the cheek, went into the dining room and took a piece of licorice from the candy dish, then slipped under the long white table cloth of the dining room table. Once there, I slid myself between the four center pillars that supported the middle of the table and waited. I could smell kielbasas steaming on the stove in the kitchen. Family meetings always included an old fashioned Polish lunch.

By the time lunch was over and the topic of the discussion for the family meeting was finally presented by my grandfather, both my knees and butt were sore. I was more than relieved when I heard him finally open the conversation.

"Now, what is all this fuss about the fact that your mother and I have invited the Redwings here for Thanksgiving?" he asked calmly.

Uncle Amos spoke first. He was the oldest. "Some of us just don't think it's a good idea to invite outsiders, Pa. It's always been just the clan."

"It's a family affair," Aunt Ladean echoed. She was second to the oldest.

"Besides, what will people say if they find out we've had a bunch of Indians over for dinner?" Aunt Victoria asked.

"And what did they say when the two Redwing boys came with Fritz to Flaming Geyser Park for my birthday?" Grandma asked.

"That was just two little Indian boys . . . you're talking about a whole tribe," Uncle Amos answered.

"We are just talking about the Redwing family. The mama, the papa, the kids, and the grandmothers," my grandmother corrected.

"I heard tell there's some old medicine man is comin too." Aunt Mary contributed.

"A friend of the grandmothers and a companion for the elder Mrs. Redwing so she won't have to take the long bus ride from the coast to Perkins Prairie by herself," my grandfather replied.

"But they're Indians," Aunt Victoria sulked.

"Now, hold on a minute," I heard my father interject. "My wife is one-fourth Micmac . . . and you know it. I didn't hear any complaints when I started dating her."

"We didn't know she had any Indian blood in her until after you married her. And just because you didn't hear any gossip about it doesn't mean it wasn't going on behind your back," Aunt Mary quipped. She was the youngest.

"What?" my father snapped.

"Oh, for goodness sakes, Tony, it's not like Marjorie looks like an Indian. You know we've all grown to love her. She really isn't enough Indian for it to really count anyway."

"Even she only claims to be English," Aunt Maggie said, throwing her two cents onto the table.

"I think we should keep this a family affair," Uncle Lawrence asserted.

"So, if my old friend, Tony Kowal should drop by, like he usually does . . . I should chase him away?" Grandpa asked.

"No, of course not, Pa. Tony is like family," Aunt Victoria answered. "And he's Polish."

"And how about if your mama's friend, Mrs.

Hermison, should drop by with a couple of her huckleberry pies . . . should we shoo her away?"

"Mrs. Hermison and Tony Kowal are family friends . . . they don't count," Amos said.

"It's for damn sure Mrs. Hermison isn't Polish," Grandma quipped.

"Well . . . so the only people I can invite to my home are friends you already know. Is that what you're saying?" Grandpa asked.

"You can invite anyone to your home you like, Pa . . . you know me and mine like the Redwings and hope they'll be here and be made to feel welcome," I heard my father say.

"You kids gotta remember that Mrs. Hermison and Tony Kowal were friends of ours long before you met them. I don't see no difference right now. I am already a friend to Mrs. Sunfield. I like that old woman. She is just like me in a lot of ways. But before I talked with her, she was like you kids. She didn't want to be with no white people on Thanksgiving," my grandmother explained.

"You mean she didn't think we were good enough for her?" Uncle Sean asked.

"White people took her land from her, killed her parents and her husband, forced her to live on a reservation. I guess she was just a little disquieted by all that," Grandma said sarcastically.

"We had nothing to do with all that," Aunt Victoria noted.

"Nor did you have anything to do with uprooting yourself from your home in the old country because your land was taken away from you. I didn't see any of you kids in that oxcart that brought me to these hills. You wanna see hardships? You should watch you mama die from the hard ride from Council Bluffs over the Cascades. Your pa and me . . we seen real hardships . . . just like Mrs. Sunfield and, I suppose, Mrs. Redwing whom I have yet to meet. We are here on this nice farm that provided for each of you and gave you dignity and sustenance because people like the Redwings and the Sunfields lost their land and their dignity in battles that happened before Pa and me cleared this land. Now Clarence and his wife come to Perkins Prairie so their children can make their way in the new world like me and you papa. If you can't be thankful for that . . . if you can't see how much they have lost so that you could have such gain . . . if you can't do what Grandmother Sunfield is going to do . . . come here and celebrate the first Thanksgiving between her clan and mine . . . then you go to your in-laws for your feast this year . . . because I did not travel halfway across this planet so I could raise kids that turned out like the sons-a-bitches that ran my daddy from his land back in Poland!"

I had never heard my grandmother speak so harshly to her kids before. It surprised me, and for reasons I could not pinpoint, gave me a sense of pride.

"Mother! What are you saying?" Aunt Victoria yelled.

"I'm saying that what the Austrians did to the Poles - even what Hitler did to the Jews is the same thing you are doing to the Redwings. You make them less than human because they are native to this country and not filled with immigrant blood. It was racism that forced your papa and me to move away from our homeland. It is racism that killed Jews and Poles and it is racism that would exclude friends of mine from my very own table and I won't have it. Maybe you should all take your kids and go by oxcart back to Poland, 'cause you sure ain't actin' like no Americans as far as I can see!" Grandma shouted back. With that she scooted her chair away from the table and left the room.

"I had no idea Mother felt so strongly about this," Aunt Maggie quipped.

"We feel the same way, your mama and me," Grandpa assured her.

"You'd rather have Indians here for Thanksgiving than your own children?" Uncle Sean asked.

"We didn't say that. We love you kids. You're our flesh and blood. But if you had been through what your mother and I have been through . . . maybe you would better understand. If we had stayed in Europe . . . we would probably have all been dead a long time ago and none of you would have been born. This country changed all that. Your ma and me want to celebrate Thanksgiving and make peace between the Redwings and us. It will be just a little bit of peace between the red man and the white man . . . but it will be real peace.

"Well, I'm not eatin' with a bunch of Indians. I think me and mine will go to the in-laws this year," Uncle Charlie asserted.

"You do as you like, Charlie," Grandpa mumbled.

"Not me . . . my in-laws are all Swedish. I can't stand Swedish cooking. If it means so much to you and Mother, we'll come," Aunt Victoria yielded.

"Count us in too," Uncle Dan agreed.

"You know me and mine will be here," Dad said.

"How about the rest of you?" Grandma asked, coming back into the room with a coffee pot in her hand.

"It don't make no never-mind to me. I wasn't upset in the first place . . . this family is so big I never get a chance to visit with everyone anyway . . . I just came to the meeting to hear what everybody else had to say. The more the merrier, if you ask me," Uncle Rufus said.

So, with the exception of Uncle Charlie, everyone agreed to attend the Thanksgiving celebration. Not all the affirmations were as positive as they might have been - but they were affirmations.

Many of them hung round visiting for longer than I expected. I had to pee something terrible and didn't think they would ever leave. When the last of them went into the kitchen, I crawled on my hands and knees to the front door, slipped out onto the sun porch and out the front door.

§§§§

We had an unusually warm Thanksgiving that year. The temperature soared to the mid-sixties. That permitted the children to play outdoors and many of

351

the adults to wander around the farm gossiping and reminiscing about their own childhood' on the place.

Dad drove Audrey, her mother, and the girls out to the farm so Clarence and the boys could pick up Saddles Seatco and his mother at the bus depot. As soon as Audrey and Grandmother Sunfield arrived at the farm, Mother introduced her to a few of the aunts and uncles. She was just about to take the younger Mrs. Redwing and her mother into the house to introduce Grandmother Sunfield to my grandfather just as he and my grandmother came down the back steps of the house to greet her.

"I'm so glad you come," my grandmother told the old Indian woman as they exchanged hugs.

"I am glad I come. I brought two salmonberry pies," Mrs. Sunfield smiled.

"Salmonberry pie. I don't think I've every had it," Grandma commented. "Stella Sunfield, this is my husband, John Harding. John, this is Audrey's mother, Stella," my grandmother beamed.

"It is a pleasure to meet you, ma'am. I have grief that because of history you cannot introduce me to your brave and wonderful husband. I hope it is not offensive of me to tell you that I believe he is here with us in spirit," my grandfather reflected.

"No wonder this fine woman has lived with you all these years . . . you're a good talker, John Harding of Perkins Prairie. I am not offended. I am warmed by your sentiment and all the more glad I've decided to come here today," Mrs. Sunfield responded.

After a few additional introductions to other family members, Grandpa excused himself to check on a batch of freshly-stuffed Polish sausages that were cooking in the smokehouse. Grandma turned to Mrs. Sunfield and said: You wanna tour the farm, meet some more people, see the house? How can I make you feel welcome and comfortable?"

"What was you doin' before I got here, Martha?"

"Helpin' in the kitchen. Those girls make such a mess when I don't supervise, even as old as they are now."

"Then, that's what I will do . . . providing you can use an extra pair of hands," Mrs. Sunfield suggested.

"A woman's work is never done, " Grandmother said, taking her arm and walking toward the house.

As they started up the stairs, I saw Clarence's car drive past the little bridge that led from the road to my grandparent house. I ran to the barnyard to meet them. By the time I swung the big gate open and went out to greet them, they were already out of the car. Grandmother Redwing was dressed in traditional Indian attire. Saddles Seatco looked no different from the last time I had seen him. Saddles always looked as if he had slept in his clothes and used his hat to catch fish. There was little of San Francisco left in the old shaman. He carried a covered aluminum cake dish. After hugging both of them I turned to Saddles and asked: "What'cha got there?"

"I baked an angle food cake with lemon frosting," he answered.

"Can I carry it for you?" I pleaded.

"Of course, child. I'm always delighted to be helped by handsome young men," he responded.

"Can I ask you a question?"

"Certainly, child. What is it?"

"Do you think The Changer is a man or a woman?"

"I told you that would be his first question," Grandmother Redwing chuckled.

"Well, Fritz, I never thought much about it until this old lady told me about her conversation with you about it," Saddles answered.

"Have you had time to think about it?" I asked eagerly.

"You gotta admit it's one hell of a good question, Saddles. Who knows . . . it may even explain why you are a man with two souls," Grandmother Redwing cackled.

"Well, what'cha think, Saddles. Is the One Who Changes a man or a woman or both?"

"I did a lot of thinking about this, boy. It's a question I never thought about before. I don't think any of the shaman before me ever thought about it either or my father would have said something to me about it. But I have figured it out, I think. It came to me in a dream. I think The One Who Changes is like the Great Spirit - neither male nor female but something other than just that. It's the same with Kwatee. We've always assumed that Kwatee was a male spirit . . . but I'm no longer convinced that is true. I went down to the Tahola Reservation and met with some of the other shaman down there and talked about this. They were intrigued by the question as I was. We talked long into the night."

"What did you decide?" I asked.

354

"We decided we must now call The Changer *One Who Changes* instead of *He*."

"It sure makes better sense to me" I admitted.

"It makes good sense to me, too," Grandmother Redwing interjected. "What did some of the other shaman have to say?"

"There was a lot of debate . . . but you know, many of those guys are just like me, Bertha . . . it made a lot of sense to all of us."

"So, even after we are put on reservations, the history of our people continues to develop just as if the Europeans had never come here," Grandmother Redwing mused.

"I'm not so sure of that, Bertha," he responded. Suddenly he put his hand on my shoulder and said: "Fritz Harding . . . I mean, Talks With Eagles, you have opened a new door for me and the other shaman with this question. The Thanksgiving meal we will share later with you and your family will be the first big party I've every attended without harboring a sense of old guilt, the nature of which you are too young to understand yet . . . but let me tell you this . . . as a person of two souls, I have always wondered how I came to be. If you are right . . . if we are right, then the mystery of my life now make sense to me. I must thank you for your question." When I looked to smile back up at him, there were tears in his eyes.

§§§§

No one was ever sure how the Perkins Prairie Banner got wind of the Harding and Redwing Thanksgiving, but old Ed Darrenger, editor and publisher of the paper, showed up and asked permission to talk with folks and take a few pictures. In the end he convinced everyone to pose for one huge photograph which was placed on the front page of the Banner the following week under headlines that read: ***Polish Pilgrims and Local Salishans Authenticate Thanksgiving.*** At the center of the photograph, in the front row, was Grandmother Harding flanked by my grandfather. Grandmother Redwing was seated to the right of my grandmother, and to her left, Grandmother Sunfield. The three old ladies looked almost like sisters, and it was obvious from their smiles that the day had been a complete success. To my surprise, Saddles was standing next to Cousin Raymond and his friend from Seattle, and on the far right of the front row was Aunt Victoria standing behind the Redwing twins with her arms around both of them.

Chapter Eleven

Ten New Houses on the Hill

That Christmas was the eve of the 1950's and the first time I exchanged gifts outside my immediate family. It was also the first opportunity I had to understand that the holiday could be celebrated without any emphasis on Jesus.

Mom and Dad paid lip service to the religious aspects of the season. Mom liked the few cards she sent to have some sort of image of the nativity on them and always took us to church the first Sunday before the 25th.

For Grandma Harding, Christmas was Jesus' birthday. The celebration started for her with Advent. She began the season by setting out the figures of her nativity set all over the house. The manger was always kept as the center piece on the library table in the living room. She would cover the table with mounds of cotton to represent snow, then place evergreen boughs over them. She would place the little barn at the center of the table surrounded by small hand-carved farm animals and an occasional camel. Each day of Advent, she would move the other figurines from one room to another until they were closer and closer to the little barn on the library table. The afternoon of Christmas Eve, she would place Mary and Joseph, surrounded by shepherds and all the little animals on the table as if waiting for the coming of the baby Jesus. It was a silent play done in miniature. An enactment of the biblical story the reminded her to focus more on the religious aspects of the holiday than the commercial.

Little Lord Jesus, as Grandmother called him, was never brought out of his hiding place in her lace handkerchief drawer until after she returned from midnight mass at Saint Aloysius Catholic church. Then and only then would the small figurine, wrapped in swaddling clothes, be set carefully in his place in the nativity scene. The next morning, long before anyone was up, Grandma would take the three wise men bearing gifts of gold, frankincense and myrrh to the nativity scene. It would also be the first time the candles on the Christmas tree would be lit. Grandma and Grandpa had been given several sets of electric lights for the tree including a full set of bubble lights. But they preferred to maintain their tradition of using real candles. They were very small candles, painstakingly clipped to the very ends of branches where they could burn without fear of catching a bough above them on fire. It was a spectacular event, and although I only witnessed it on the few occasion I had stayed overnight with them, I am still convinced that their Christmas tree was the most beautiful I have ever seen.

At the top of the tree Grandpa placed an angel with a large star in her hands. A few of the large round ornaments with pictures of the saints painted on them had been brought to this country by my grandmother's parents when they immigrated from Poland. These were considered very special. Only Grandmother was allowed to place them on the tree. Two of the ornaments had portraits of popes on them, and twelve had images of the twelve apostles. Grandmother Harding always insisted that it was important to remember that Christmas was a day set apart to celebrate the birth of the baby Jesus but Santa Claus and his elves were also present. Grandma said that Santa Claus was really St. Nicholas who had been a bishop in ancient Denmark exiled from his native country by a pagan king. She said he was only allowed back into the country on Christmas Eve to celebrate midnight mass and that each time he returned to his flock, he arrived in a sled pulled by reindeer with a huge sack in which he brought gifts of food and toys for the children. Even Santa had religious significance at the Harding Christmas.

The tree and decorations in our house on Colfax Street were a mishmash of folk legends, mild religious trappings, and multitudinous departures from Grandmother Harding's vision of the season. Mother was especially fond of Santa and Rudolph the Red-Nosed Reindeer. She had one of each in every room of the house. Instead of a nativity scene, Mother kept a Santa and his reindeer at the center of the buffet table in the dining room. The only specifically religious symbol was that of an angel at the top of our tree. I thought she looked remarkably like Snow White because she had raven black hair and wore an apron. Mother insisted she was an angel, but I've always had my doubts, especially since the seven dwarfs were also ornaments on the tree.

For the Redwings, Christmas was a totally secular

celebration. As far as they were concerned, it was more like a winter Potlatch than a religious event. The Redwings still practiced the religion of their ancestors and after our experience at the big top revival with Pastor Wally Pots, none of the Redwings took much stock in the efforts of missionaries and well-meaning folks in town who kept inviting them to church.

Mormon missionaries had once visited Clarence telling him that *The Book of Mormon* was all about Jesus visiting American Indians after his resurrection. Clarence accepted a copy of the book and read it from cover to cover. I asked him what he thought about it one day while I was helping pick apples from their tree to store in their root house. "It's a great story, Fritz, but I like my religion better. Me and God have a great arrangement. I don't do no miracles and He don't pick no apples."

But even though Christmas was considered a secular event, it was an event thoroughly enjoyed by all of them. They too had a tree in the living room. Theirs was topped by Frosty the Snowman. He, along with tinsel, was the only purchased ornament ever placed on their tree. The rest of the decorations were taken from nature. At some point in their marriage, Clarence and Audrey had hand-painted a variety of pine cones in different sizes and shapes gold. They made up the majority of their tree's ornaments, although they also used a few dried gourds, strings of beadwork, and small hand-carved totems and spirit guides of the two tribes their family now represented. About the only thing the Redwing's tree had in common with Grandma and Grandpa Harding's tree was the chains of hand-strung popcorn draped in half loops around the tree.

The Redwings practiced their gift exchange differently too. They drew names. That was only for purchased gifts. Handmade presents were also exchanged and there was no limit on them. At our house, Mom and Dad showered us with all sorts of presents. So did our grandparents. We always had three package opening celebrations. One with my mother's family on Christmas Eve in Tacoma, one at our house on Christmas morning, and one later on in the afternoon of Christmas Day when we all gathered at the Harding farm. The idea of drawing names and buying only one present was new to me, but I was delighted and genuinely touched when the Redwings included me in the drawing of their family names. It would never have occurred to the Brunes or the Hardings to include an outsider in their gift exchange. But the ways of the Salishan were different.

I drew Audrey's name out of the hat. It made me a little nervous because I knew mine would be the only store-bought gift she got that year. To make matters even more complicated, the Redwings had a rule . . . no present could cost more than five dollars. I hunted the two dime stores and other shops along Main Street but found nothing that truly caught my eye as something Audrey Redwing would take exception to and prize as a Christmas gift. For a while I considered getting her flowers. A beautiful bouquet of fresh flowers in the dead of winter might be a perfect gift. But after realizing the flowers wouldn't last very long, I gave up on the idea and began searching for other possibilities.

But the flower idea made me think of Jerry Cotton and his orchids. Maybe a living plant would be something Audrey Redwing would truly enjoy.

The next day at school I passed Jerry a note in class asking if he had any plants for sale, explaining that I wanted to give one as a gift that year. I didn't know whether he would respond or not since we hadn't spoken much since the Puyallup Fair incident. But he passed a note back telling me to met him at his grandmother's farm the following Saturday at about two in the afternoon.

"Are we speaking, then?" I whispered across the aisle after reading his note.

"No!" But business is business. Meet me about two and I'll show you what I have for sale," he whispered curtly.

I talked Dad into driving me out to the Cotton farm that Saturday afternoon because a light snow had begun to fall that morning making it dangerous for me to ride my bike out there. He had his own agenda set for the day but agreed to drive me providing I did my business quickly so he could get back to town to do his own shopping.

I was excited about the trip to the Cotton farm. I hadn't been there in a long time and was very fond of the peacocks the Cottons raised. They had a flock of nearly 100 birds. Most nested at night in the huge cedar trees that lined the farm, although some slept in the rafters of their enormous barn. During the day they all walked freely about the farm's yards and fields. The males strutted their beautiful plumes, and the hens pecked among the flower beds for choice worms and insects. Jerry's grandmother also fed them just as she did her chickens just before she served lunch to the farm hands. I loved going with her and throwing handfuls of feed on the ground to them. The flurry of peacocks competing for their lunch was always a high point to any visit. But arriving at two in the afternoon meant missing the event. I couldn't help wondering if that was why Jerry asked me to come in the afternoon. He knew how much I enjoyed feeding the peacocks. Perhaps it was a privilege he wanted to end.

When we arrived at the Cotton farm, I was surprised to discover that Jerry's grandfather had built him a small greenhouse adjacent to the barn. It came equipped with an electric heater, several tables and workbenches for plants and its own cold water faucet. "Wow! When did you get this?" I asked as he opened the door to his greenhouse for me.

"It was an early Christmas present. My folks don't much like having me over at Mrs. Road's too much. They paid for the materials but Grandpa built it," he answered dryly.

It was like a jungle inside. Jerry had ferns and plants hanging from hooks all over the ceiling. The tables were filled with all sorts of plants including bamboo and tomatoes that were about to be picked. There were even plants and ferns under the tables. "How come those plants under there don't die from lack of light?" I asked.

"Dad installed grow lights for me on the bottom of the table . . . but most of those are plants that like to live in the shade. They get just about all the light they need. Once in a while I give them a little splash of artificial light just to keep them especially happy."

"This is just great. It's like a small arboretum. What kind of plants are those over there?" I asked, pointing at some long willowy spears jetting up toward the ceiling near a small pond at the center of the building.

"That's a special bamboo from the Amazon Rain Forest. The orchids are over here," he answered in a somewhat officious tone.

"I looked at the orchids and felt my heart sink. The flowers were beautiful but the plant itself were decidedly ugly. Still, if Audrey could get one to thrive, she might have a steady supply of orchids to enjoy. "What are you asking for the orchids?" I inquired.

"I get $7.50 for the small ones, $10.00 to $12.00 for the larger plants," he replied.

"My limit is $5.00. I never realized that orchids were so expensive," I told him.

"You can't buy an orchid anywhere on the planet for $5.00 except maybe from some jungle dealer in deepest Africa. These plants are very hard to raise and very expensive to keep up. I have to duplicate a tropical environment in here at all times. That costs money," Jerry responded.

"$7.50?" I repeated.

"That's for the whole plant and it comes with a small bag of special plant food. But after that you have to buy the plant food when you run out. You could, of course, buy just a blossom for $5.00 . . . but not the whole plant."

"Couldn't you make an exception?"

"Business is business, Fritz . . . besides, it isn't like we're still good friends or anything."

"Have you any other living plants for sale?" I asked.

"I'm in the orchid business. The rest of the plants are my hobby. I collect them. No other plants are for sale here except orchids. If you're not purchasing anything, the shop is closed . . . let's go," he sighed sarcastically.

I turned toward the door and began following him when I spotted two brown paper grocery bags filled with long luxuriant peacock feathers. "What'cha gonna do with all those feathers?" I asked.

"I sell them to a guy in Tacoma for $2.50 a bag. I usually wait until I have about eight bags before Mom drives me in to sell them. Why?"

My mind was swirling with the things I had seen Audrey do with feathers of local birds. What might she be able to do with the vibrant and multicolored feathers of the peacock. The Cottons also had pure white peacocks on their farm. One of the bags was over half full of them. "Would you sell those bags to me. I'll give you $2.50 a bag and you won't have to drive in to Tacoma."

"Why would you want to buy peacock feathers? You gonna dress up like Mae West for the next big Halloween party and see if you can that sissy Randy?"

"Maybe I just want to make bouquets of them. They're really beautiful and since this is just business . . . will you sell me these bags or not?"

"I'll bet you're going to do something Indian with them, aren't you. When are you gonna realize that the whole town thinks you're nuts runnin' around in all that Indian getup and hangin' out with those Redskins all the time."

"I plan to do something with them for Christmas," I said, hoping I didn't sound as defensive as I felt.

"I once glued some of the plumes on Christmas ornaments. They turned out real nice. But since we all know you don't have any talents like that, I can't imagine why you want to spend your hard-earned money on two bags of feathers."

"What do you care as long as you make your money off them? You gonna sell me these feathers or not?"

"Show me your money," Jerry snapped.

I reached into my back pocket, pulled out my wallet and handed him the money.

"Sold to the female impersonator with the five dollar bill," Jerry mocked, taking my money with one hand and motioning for me to pick up the two bags with the other.

Once the bags were securely in my arms, I followed Jerry back to the house. When we were within eye shot of my dad's pickup, I decided it was a good time to see if we might yet repair our friendship. "Are you going to the Eagle's New Year's Eve party for kids?" I asked. A lot of the kids who attended the affair did something to entertain the others. Jerry and I usually played a piano duet or sang something together.

"What if I am?" he responded.

"I thought we might sing *Auld Lang Syne* together like we always do."

"If I sing with anybody, I'll sing with members of the Orchid Appreciation Society who show up," he said, jerking his head as if to put a period in the air just in front of his nose.

"Just thought I'd ask," I replied, turning toward the truck.

"Thank you for your business," Jerry called after me. He sounded no more sincere than one of the barkers at the sideshows of the Puyallup Fair. I turned to tell him he was welcome, but he was already headed back up the driveway toward his grandparents' house.

"I thought you were going to buy orchids?" Dad noted as I got into the truck.

"The plant is really ugly and they cost more than I wanted to spend. I bought these feathers instead. Audrey will really like them. She does wonderful things with feathers on their costumes."

"What'cha pay for these?"

"Five bucks . . . but I got them wholesale," I replied.

"Well, there's a mercy, " Dad quipped. "Do you really think feathers are an appropriate Christmas gift for Mrs. Redwing?"

"I don't think I could have picked a better gift if I'd thought of it even before I came out here," I answered.

"I suppose you're right. You know your mother is going to look at you like you're crazy," he said with a wink.

"I'm gettin' used to it," I said, winking back.

§§§§

As soon as we finished opening our gifts Christmas morning and I had properly thanked my parents for them, I reminded Dad of his promise to drive me to the Redwings with Audrey's present so I could exchange gifts with them before we left for the Harding family celebration. I had secured a large empty Modess carton from Mr. Packard at the Red Front Grocery Store into which the two sacks of peacock feathers fit without being pressed for space. The box took two whole packages of wrapping paper to cover it completely. Mom had helped with that . . . though, as predicted, she fussed about the suitability of the gift.

When I arrived, the Redwing were just finishing brunch. "You want something to eat, young man?" Grandma Sunfield asked as I walked into the kitchen with the enormous box.

"I'm starved," I admitted.

"Well, I hope that box is for me. That's the biggest Christmas present I've ever seen in my life," she teased.

"Sorry, Grandmother, but I didn't draw your name.

"You're always starved! Go put your package by the tree. We've been waiting for you before we open our gifts. I'll fix you a plate. You want toast?" Audrey asked.

"That would be great," I answered.

After devouring a plate full of scrambled eggs, bacon, hash browns and toast smothered in

368

Grandmother Sunfield's famous salmonberry jam, we went into the living room to exchange gifts. The littlest children got dolls. Darleen got a baseball bat from Willie. She was very athletic and liked sports better than either of her brothers. Amy Lynn received a pair of fur-lined handmade gloves from Grandmother Sunfield. Willie was given a new pencil box filled with colored pencils from his brother and Randy got a paint by number kit from Darleen. I thought I had managed to save the big box until last but had forgotten that there would also be a present under their tree for me. I slid the big box on the floor across the rug and let it come to a stop in front of Audrey.

"For me? You drew my name?

"I hope you like it."

Audrey leaned over to pull the box a little closer. "This is as light as air. What in the world?" She took off the wrapping paper with great care. "I can use this next year. I hate to waste pretty paper like this. I always save it if I can," she said.

"My mom does the same thin,." I told her.

After the wrap was removed, Audrey lifted the lid from the box and looked inside. "Feathers! Peacock feathers! Oh, my God, look at all these beautiful feathers. Where in the world did you get these?" she squealed with delight.

"You like them?" I asked eagerly.

"I love them. I've wanted some for years. Where did you get these. They cost a fortune. There's a place in Tacoma that sells them . . . just too much money if you ask me. They wanted a dollar a feather at that place. You didn't go over the agreed limit, did you?"

"No, ma'am . . . I got both bags for five bucks from Jerry Cotton. I think he sells them to that shop you visited in Tacoma, 'cause he said he sells them to some guy there."

"Talks With Eagles, I just can't imagine a better gift. Sometimes I think you are a better Indian than my own boys," Audrey exclaimed. She got up from the couch and gave me an especially warm hug. "Look at all those beautiful feathers, Mother."

"I see . . . they are beautiful. I could use a few of them myself," the old woman commented. "Maybe you'll draw my name next year, boy. I culd use me a bag of feathers like that."

"You take some . . . there's plenty," her daughter responded, holding up one of the bags as if she had found a pot of gold at the end of the rainbow.

"I have something for you under the tree, Fritz. It's your turn to get a present now. You sit down on the couch next to Audrey and I'll bring it to you," Clarence directed.

I had been so anxious to see the look on Audrey's face when she opened her gift of peacock feathers, I had forgotten about the fact that one of the Redwings had drawn my name. I dutifully took a seat next to his wife. "I had forgotten that I'd get a gift too," I said, wondering if my face revealed the intense anticipation I was suddenly feeling on the inside.

Mr. Redwing picked out a tiny box from under the tree and brought it to me. It was wrapped in aluminum foil and decorated with a blue ribbon. "From me to you," he beamed.

370

I couldn't imagine what might be inside the little box. I knew that the large teeth of wolves, bears and mountain lions were considered sacred among the Salishan. They were said to give their owners the wisdom, hunting skills, and protection of the animals of whom they were once a part. I found myself hoping it would be such a gift. If I could add the totem spirit of one of the other great hunters of the forest to that of the Eagle who already protected and guided me, I was assured of an even more powerful second journey quest, than my first. I removed the blue ribbon, took off the aluminum foil, and opened the box. Whatever was in it was covered with a layer of cotton. I lifted it from the object below it and found a perfectly carved arrowhead. Beneath it was a note. I looked up and smiled at Mr. Redwing, then picked up the arrowhead and examined it more closely. It was carved from a jet black, shiny stone that looked almost like glass. I placed it on my knee, took out the note, unfolded it, and read:

Christmas 1949

Dear Talks With Eagles:
This arrowhead belonged to my father's
father's father. It is carved from lava
glass. Keep it in your leather pouch along with your blue stone. It bonds you in a special way to my lodge and those of my ancestors.
Merry Christmas - Clarence Redwing

I was at a loss for words. I looked up at Clarence remembering the first day I met him in his driveway. I could not have imagined back then that the day would come when he would actually count me as one of his family. I absolutely did not know what to say. I do know this: I was so touched by the gift my eyes were tearing-up and my throat felt thick and useless.

"Do you like it, boy?" Mrs. Sunfield asked.

"Like it? I love it. But are you sure you want me to have this. It must be sacred to you. Wouldn't you rather give it to one of your boys?"

"It is sacred to me and I have a few others. Enough for my boys. That stone is rare but somewhere in my family's past, they found a big bunch of it someplace. I must have inherited twenty of those arrowheads. Many members of the tribe also have them. The old ones say they came with our people when they moved from the northlands down here to the coast. Mountains sometimes make that stone when they make fire. My father told me that it was the preferred material for arrowheads and spears because it is so sharp. Today we know it is actually a form of natural glass . . . a very hard glass. Don't you fuss none about me givin' it to you. I wouldn't have done so if I didn't want you to have it. Just remember to keep it in the pouch you wear around your neck. That will keep it holy for you."

"Oh, I will . . . I will," I promised.

Later that day, after we returned from the Harding Christmas celebration at the farm, I opened my amulet and showed my parents the arrowhead

Clarence had given me. Dad looked at and handled it with real admiration. Mother wasn't as impressed. "I don't know what the world is coming to when people start giving feathers and rocks to one another at Christmas. I much prefer the Evening in Paris perfume and earrings you gave me. The only feathers I like make up the down in my pillow, and the only rocks I like are diamonds!" she said, reaching out to muss my hair. I winked at Dad. Like me, he knew she was only half kidding.

A few quick days after Christmas, the Forties were lost to us forever. We were suddenly in the Fifties. I made a New Year's resolution to make up with Jerry Cotton if at all possible. We had been home on Christmas vacation for a number of days and with all celebrations going on, I hadn't taken the time to call him. Besides, I felt any attempt to reconcile should be done face to face.

I finally had an opportunity to speak with him just minutes before midnight at the party the Eagles had thrown for the children of Perkins Prairie. It was held in conjunction with the usual adult bash at the Eagles Hall, although we minors were not allowed downstairs where the dancing and drinking were going on until thirty minutes before Old Man Time handed over his hourglass to the child of the New Year. Many of the younger children, my sisters and the Redwing girls included, had fallen asleep long before eleven-thirty rolled around. When one of the sitters, hired to watch over us and keep us busy with games and treats, announced that those who wanted to could go downstairs and join their parents, Randy, Willie and I were among the first to go.

We found our parents standing together just off the dance floor near the stage watching the band play. After greeting them and being handed a bottle of ice-cold Coca Cola by one of the many wandering waiters, I spied Jerry Cotton making his way across the dance floor toward us.

"Good evening, Mr. and Mrs. Harding. I just thought I'd drop by and wish you a happy New Year", he said loud enough to be heard over the band.

"Why thank you, Jerry, the same to you," my father responded.

"And if we don't get a chance to see your parents before we leave, you be sure and extend our best wishes to them for us, won't you?" Mother added.

"I sure will," Jerry answered.

"Wouldn't you like to extend greeting to Mr. and Mrs. Redwing as well?" Mother more instructed than asked.

"Happy New Year," he said somewhat blandly. Somehow he had managed to ignore the Redwing boys and me by not making eye contact.

"What's your New Year's resolution for the year, Jerry?" Dad asked, I think in an attempt to make small talk.

"Happy New Year, Jerry," Willie interjected before the young Mr. Cotton could answer.

"Jerry looked at Willie as if surprised he had been spoken to. "Happy New Year, Willie," he said with obvious curtness. He ignored Randy and me.

I was just about to extend my greetings to him when he turned back to my father and said: "My

374

resolution is to expand my orchid business. I know now it is what I want to do the rest of my life. I plan to put all my energy into becoming the king of orchid growers in America. And to ensure I don't become sidetracked, I'm only going to associate with people who either buy orchids or who raise them," he announced, turning slightly so he could glance directly into my eyes.

Mother looked at me too. Then, turning back to Jerry, asked, "Doesn't that somewhat limit your social mobility, dear?"

"If one hopes to succeed in life, it is sometimes important to limit the people with whom one is seen," Jerry quipped with a devilish smile. "I'll give your greetings to my folks," he added, slipping back into the crowd.

"Looks like you're going to have to give up on that one" Clarence advised.

"Unfortunately, I think you're right," I answered.

§§§§

In late February of that year, another skating competition was held in town. I was very eager to attend the event because I knew that Jerry had been secretly practicing a skating routine for months. According to a few of our mutual friends, Jerry was positive he would walk away with first prize. Rumor had it that his uncle had been driving him to a skating rink in the valley three nights a week where he had practiced his new routine.

The afternoon of the competition, Jerry was the second to the last of the performers. The Redwing boys were scheduled to skate right after he was finished. Jerry entered the spotlight wearing the same orchid costume he had worn at the Halloween party, but this time he was wearing skates. He skated around the rink to the song *I'm a Lonely Little Petunia in an Onion Patch* and gave what I thought was a pretty good demonstration of skills. He was certainly a better skater than I was, and it was clear that he had worked very hard on his presentation. His act including four cousins dressed in onion costumes. They did not skate with him but acted as props for his performance. He was graceful, didn't fall once and somehow managed to be as amusing on skates as the song itself. I thought he did a great job and rose to applaud him along with many others when he finished. He saw me stand and was glad because I thought it might help sooth things between us. And I could tell from the smirk on his face, when the act ended and he took his bow, that he was very confident of being among the winners that afternoon.

It didn't turn out that way. Randy and Willie skated as a team to a Glenn Miller rendition of *Indian Love Call*. They wore lavish costumes decorated with peacock, turkey, canary, cardinal, robin, and blue jay feathers. They were almost iridescent under the lights as they glided over the floor doing a modern version of the traditional Quinault whale dance. Once again they were vivid, graceful, and walked off with first prize. To make matters worse, Ebbie Olson took second prize for her rendition of a hula dancer on skates, and the third prize was given to Teddy Wilson and his sister Alice from Enumclaw who skated as the scarecrow and Dorothy from the Wizard of Oz. Their performance was so funny it brought the house down with laughter. Honorable mention went to Brandon Salish and Gregory Caviezal, both from South Prairie, who came as the Carnation Cow and skated to a rendition of *Old MacDonald Had a Farm* by Spike Jones and His City Slickers. Competition was very high that year and while Jerry received an enthusiastic applause for his performance, he didn't even win honorable mention.

The next week the Banner displayed a picture of all the winner including a large one of the Redwing boys in their costumes holding the trophy between them. Enormous headlines above them read simply, **The Best!** They were eager to take a copy of the paper and the trophy to Grandmother Redwing to show them off.

Later that week I bumped into Jerry when I went to get some books from my locker at school. "I thought you skated real well at the competition," I told him honestly. "You deserved that standing ovation."

"The whole thing was rigged," Jerry said without looking up.

"Rigged? How do you figure?"

"I think the judges were afraid to give me a prize because it would have been like giving me free advertising for my orchid business and the Orchid Appreciation Society."

"That's just so much bull, Jerry. The other skaters got the prizes because the judges liked their acts better. Some of those kids have been skating for years. You did a great job but you should say it was rigged. Why on earth would the judges pull a stunt like that?"

§§§

As we drove onto the reservation, we could see the ten new houses being built on the hill just above the road that led to the old village and Grandmother Redwing's.

"They're sure not wasting any time," Audrey commented as we passed the workers and equipment being used to construct the new section of the village.

"I wonder which one they have slated for Grandma," Randy pondered.

"I guess time will tell," his mother answered.

"I don't understand why we even have to have time. If it weren't for time, our people would still be living in the old ways and Grandma wouldn't have to worry about having to change," Willie mused.

"Time isn't the villain," Audrey said.

"I don't know, Mom. But I sure wish time would stand still for a while," he answered back.

"That's just plain dumb, Willie. We gotta have time. If we didn't have time, every thing would happen at once. Can you imagine what a mess that would be?" Randy proclaimed. We all laughed but somehow I knew that Randy had unwittingly voiced a philosophical view that would change the way I looked at everything.

The moment we pulled up in front of the old

Indian woman's house, she came out on the porch to greet us. "What'cha got there?" she asked as Willie pulled the trophy out from behind his back.

"Me and Randy won the skating competition again this year. They put our picture right on the front page of the paper again. We brought you a copy," he blurted. His voice was filled with well deserved pride.

Randy, running alongside his brother toward his grandmother, handed her a copy of the town paper.

"Your daddy wrote me about those costumes. Peacock feathers! Boy, I would sure like to get me some of those," the elder Mrs. Redwing responded, taking the trophy in her hands and admiring it. After giving it a thorough moment of visual praise, she handed it back to Willie and pulled both of the boys into her arms. "Congratulations, my beautiful grandchildren. You have taken the strange shoes of white eyes and conquered the wind. Audrey, you must be proud as a peacock," she said, smiling at their mother.

"Oh, I am, Mother Redwing. And I have some of those peacock feathers for you in the car. The boys can bring them in when they unload it."

"Oh, bless you, girl. I was hopin' you wouldn't forget me."

"Don't be silly, Mother Redwing. Besides, there are plenty for all of us. Fritz gave me two grocery bags overflowing with peacock feathers. Even some white ones – for Christmas. I brought you some of those too."

"White ones! I once saw a white peacock at the zoo. I'm sure I could find some good uses for white ones.

"Fritz was very generous.

"You're a thoughtful young man, Talks With Eagles. And how have you been," the old woman asked, opening her arms to draw me into the hug.

"Very well, thank you. How are you, Grandmother?"

"Fussin' and frettin' about those damn new houses goin' up on the hill. Other than that, I'm just fine. Of course, it wouldn't hurt if some strong young arms went out and gathered me some wood for my stove and some fresh water from the lake."

"We'll be happy to help, Grandmother," Willie said.

"Audrey's mother sent up a jar of her salmonberry jam for you," Clarence noted, kissing his mother on the cheek.

"We'll get some fresh oysters for you to take back to her before you go home. If I recall correctly, your mother is partial to oysters, ain't that right, Audrey?"

"She is indeed, and the oyster beds are badly depleted near where she lives. She'll love that," Audrey answered, kissing her mother-in-law's other cheek. "Two of those houses look almost done."

"Ah, them damn houses is drivin' me nuts. Come on inside, I got hot water on for tea . . . and I made some lemonade for the kids," the old woman responded.

Randy, Willie and I carried up several buckets of water until the barrel was full, then carried enough wood to last several days for her fire. After

380

refreshments were served, the boys and I sprawled out on the floor to play a game of *Sorry* while the adults visited.

"You wanna know what that damn whippersnapper of an agent told me the other day?" Grandmother Redwing asked as she and Audrey did the dishes.

"Nothing would surprise me," Clarence answered.

"He told me they gonna let me pick out which one of those new houses I want instead of just assigning me one like they're doin' to everybody else. Like that's gonna get me excited enough to agree to move. Everybody knows that each of those houses is just like the other ones. There ain't no difference. The nerve of that white-eyed, arrogant, little piss ant! I told him I ain't pickin' out no house, and I ain't movin' into no new house. I chased him right off my porch with my broom. I'll teach him come to round here makin' me fuss and fret about all this."

"Mother, you know you are going to have to move this time. That's just the way it is. I don't like it. I wish there was something I could do about it but there isn't. You're just going to have to accept the facts, hold up your head with pride, and give in," Clarence asserted.

"Don't you be so sure, mister smarty. I went to the cave in a dream. I had a vision that I overcame an evil spirit and was able to add three yellow finch feathers to my headdress at Tahola Days. I talked to Saddles about it. He thinks the evil spirit is that damn little house on the hill."

"Saddles shouldn't be encouraging you to be stubborn about this anymore. You're just going to have to face it, Mother. You will have to move into one of those little houses so you might as well pick out the one you would rather have. At least you'll get to choose what you look at from your backyard," Clarence rebutted.

"Saddles says it's a very reasonable interpretation of my dream. He's not encouragin' me, he's just interpreting my dream. That's what shamans do or have you lived so long in Perkins Prairie you've forgotten the ways of our people?"

"I haven't forgotten anything, Mother, but you know how Saddles likes to make you happy. There could be many interpretations to your dream."

"Well, maybe I'll move and maybe I won't! I got a lot of fight left in me and I ain't been thinkin' about anything else."

"Mother, the agent told me that if you aren't out of this house on the day you're supposed to be . . . he'll send state troopers down here to move you. They'll pick you up and carry you bodily out of this house. Is that what you want? I know this is all very difficult for you but there are no maybes about this." Clarence's words were gentle but firm.

"Don't give in so easily, boy!" his mother snapped.

"I'm just facing reality and so should you."

"I'm thinkin' about goin' up to the cave in person. Saddles says I'm too old but I think I could make it," his mother whispered as if she were telling him a secret.

"That's not a very good idea. Mother Redwing. You are far too old to make that trip anymore," Audrey interjected.

"Don't you kids understand? This is my place. This ground was the lap and bosom of Mother Earth to the Quinault long before the Whites came among us. My spirit will wilt and die if I am forced to cook my meals and sleep where the white man tells me to. I wanna sleep here where the spirit of the great whale, silver wolf, and the sacred otter guard our traditions. Saddles should have stayed down here too. That old fool doesn't do anything but listen to his records these days, and I hear tell he's gettin' some new electronic contraption up there. Besides . . . I got me some new magic!"

I looked up just in time to catch her eye. The old woman winked at me. I knew in an instant that the new magic had something to do with the Redwing boys and me.

"There is no magic that will work this time, Mother. This time, as sad as it makes me to say so, this time you will be moved to the new village whether you like it or not."

"You sound like a white man, Clarence . . . what's the matter with you? Isn't your skin still just as red as mine?"

"Mother . . . everyone in the Quinault Village has moved to the new houses except you. All your family live up on the hill now . . . even the tribe's shaman has moved. You've got to move into the future. Things can't be like they used to be anymore and that's that!" Clarence had raised his voice a little but knew better than to shout at his mother.

"We Quinault lived for thousands and thousands of moons without the white man's houses . . . and we could live for thousands more without them. I ain't gonna move and that's that. I don't give three hoots and a holler what the rest of the tribe does . . . ain't nobody up there old as me . . . they don't remember like I do. I wanna cherish and keep the way of the people until I die. I don't want anybody but death itself to try and stop me. You're beginning to make me mad, Clarence!"

"Mother, when I was born . . . why did you name me Clarence and not a regular Indian name?"

"I liked the sound of it," she answered.

"But it's a white man's name! If you don't want to change things, why did you change the tribal traditions when you named me? Wasn't it so I could fit in better in the new world? Isn't that why you did it?"

"Whatchu talkin' about, Clarence? You're gettin' me all dizzy with this talk, talk, talk. When you was born, I didn't hardly speak no English. *Clarence* was just a noise to me. I liked the way it sounded. It was like the wind slipping over the ice. You were a winter baby. I thought the sound of that word would be a good omen for you. If I had known it was going to make you run off to live in one of those damn towns with paved roads and sidewalks where the deer used to bed down for the night . . . I might have named you Skunk Who Squats and Poops in His Own Cave." Grandmother Redwings tone was livid. I could tell she was furious.

"What kind of new magic do you have?" I asked,

384

trying to change the subject a little.

"I had Saddles write a letter to Audrey's mother asking her to send me her three scalps from the Whitman Massacre. Saddles knows a sacred dance that needs three scalps taken in battle. He's gonna come down here the next sunny day after they get here and do some magic for me. You watch . . . it will give me much power."

"I hope you're right, Mother, but we've got to get up to the village and get these kids fed their dinner. You're comin', aren't you?" Clarence asked.

"Of course. Maybe I'll get a chance to see Saddles and talk to him about my magic," Grandmother Redwing responded.

"I think we should drive past the new houses too. I know you don't want to . . . but just in case . . . it wouldn't hurt," Audrey pressed.

"Okay. I don't care. They all look the same anyway. We can drive by if you want. But I ain't gettin' out of the car to look at them and I ain't gonna choose one of them. You can drive anyplace you want. It won't change my mind one bit."

We all squeezed into the Redwing's Ford and drove up the hill to the new village. The street for the ten new houses had yet to be paved. Each house was an exact copy of the others. Clarence drove slowly down the street, turned the car around once we had seen the houses, then drove back up the street in the opposite direction. "Which one would you like to see more closely?" he asked.

"I don't wanna see none of them more closely," his mother mumbled.

"Well, if you did want to see one of them, which one would it be," Randy asked, trying to help his dad.

"I would choose the last house on the lakeside of the hill at the other end of the street," his grandmother answered somewhat curtly.

"Why that one?" Audrey asked as Clarence stopped the car and began backing up.

"There was a bunch of trees on the other side of the house and the woods start there. If I had to live in one of these houses, I would want to live nearest the woods and where I could look down on the flats and my old home. But you needn't be backin' up, Clarence. I said I wasn't gonna look at any of these damn houses and that's what I meant."

"Clarence stopped his car in front of the house the elder Mrs. Redwing had chosen. Nobody knows where the Indian agent came from, but Clarence had no sooner parked the car than he appeared alongside the passenger seat.

"Good morning, Mrs. Redwing . . . and how are we today?" he said pleasantly.

"I can't speak for the rest of these kidnappers, but I'm a little hot under the collar right now, Albert, and I'd just as soon Clarence would pull the car away from this house and let us get about our business."

"Aren't you here to pick out your house?" he asked.

"Nothing of the kind. We're on our way to my other son's home so these kids can get some dinner. Clarence has driven me here against my will."

"Well, as long as you're here, Mrs. Redwing . . . why not come in and take a look around?" the young man asked politely.

"Yes, Mother Redwing . . . why not. It's not as if you haven't been inside any of these houses before," Audrey added.

"Come on, Grandma, lets take a look at it," Willie pleaded.

"You've all ganged up on me. This isn't fair at all," the old woman pouted.

"Life isn't always fair, Mother, but it is real," Clarence offered.

"Let me take a few minutes to give you a grand tour of your new home," the agent added enthusiastically.

"Albert Radford, I don't believe this will be my new home and I will not have you usin' that term around me. But I guess I wouldn't mind seeing what kind of view of the lake the backyard has," she conceded.

"Fair enough," the agent responded.

"Well, if you don't want to see the inside of the house, I do," Audrey said, getting out of the car.

"Oh, for Pete's sake . . . I'll go inside the house. It's bound to have a back door. I'll walk through the house to get to the backyard. Will that shut everyone up?" the old woman grumbled as she got out of the car.

"It will shut everyone up," Clarence promised.

Albert Radford led the way on the little cement sidewalk and up onto the front porch. He opened the door to the little house, pushed it open, and stepped aside so that Grandmother Redwing would be the first to step over the threshold. "We're going to call this street Redwing Avenue, did I tell you that?" he asked as he followed her through the door.

"Don't be tryin' to butter up my ego with such nonsense. I don't need no street named after me," the old woman grumbled as she stopped to look about the room.

"We're actually naming it after your husband and his family, Mrs. Redwing. Your husband died a hero. We thought it was important to honor him by naming the street after him," Albert said quietly.

"Oh," she answered. I could tell by the look on her face that she was genuinely touched by what he had said.

"Your people complained there weren't enough electric plug-ins so we put four in each room in these new houses. There were also complaints that the houses were too dark. If you'll notice, we've enlarged the windows and put two in the living rooms of each new house," Radford explained.

"Two windows," Grandmother Redwing repeated under her breath.

"We also had complaints from a good many mothers that the kitchen sinks were too high so we lowered them and the drain boards accordingly. And if you'll step this way, I'd like to show you something in the new bathroom we've had installed," he said, guiding her toward the bathroom. "Your people complained because the other houses had only showers built in them . . . so we installed bathtubs with overhead showers in each of the ten new houses. You can keep real clean here," he beamed.

"I like to bathe in the lake or the rain. If I bathe

in that tub, I gotta wash my face with the same water I wash my ass with . . . that don't sound too clean to me, Albert," she responded.

"And look here . . . we put in Crane fixtures. Nothing but the best. Why that Crane porcelain toilet costs over twenty-five dollars all by itself," the agent pointed out, ignoring the comment about the bathtub.

"Humph!" Grandmother Redwing retorted as she left the bathroom and walked through the dining area toward the kitchen.

"Your people complained because the houses didn't have a dining room . . . so we put one in each of the new houses. You can get a big table in here along with a buffet table and some other furniture . . . and there's room for another table in the kitchen," Radford pointed out.

"Big table," Grandmother Redwing mumbled as she stepped into the kitchen.

"Of course, this room isn't complete yet. When we're done, we'll have installed an electric stove and refrigerator. Not only that, but because your people complained about not having trash burners in the other houses we built, a brand new trash burner will sit right next to your new electric stove. You can take the chill out of the room on a given morning and not have to heat the whole house if you don't want to. How's that for cooperation?" he exclaimed.

"It seems my people do a lot of complaining," the old woman responded. She turned abruptly away from the young agent and walked out the back door.

"We appreciate healthy criticism," he answered. "Don't you want to see the bedrooms. This house has two and each one has a very big closet. Lots of room for storage. There's a nice attic too . . .lots of room up there . . . "

"Then may I give you some healthy criticism?" the elder Mrs. Redwing asked.

"Be my guest. We aim to please," he answered.

"I think it is wicked and cruel of you to make an old woman leave her beloved home to spend what few years she has left living someplace she doesn't want to live. You've been given' me a heartache and a pain in my ass for ten years over this . . . when I should be usin' my energy just to stay alive and be a good Quinault! You're fixin' to make me a good European. What do I care if there's room for a nice buffet table? Do I look like I got fancy silver and silk napkins to store in the fool contraption?"

"Mrs. Redwing . . . all the houses on the flats were condemned by the United States Government. The Health Department says they're not fit for human habitation. And I've only had the job as agent here for three years. I'm just doing my job, and I must say, you aren't making it very easy for me," Albert Radford answered.

"I was not put on this planet to make your job easy for you! I was placed on this planet to be a Quinault woman . . . not a European! Houses like mine have been fit for human habitation for more years than there's been a United States Government. Besides, I thought this reservation was Indian territory . . . what is the United States Government doing nosing around in my business on sovereign Indian land? Answer me that one, Albert!"

390

The young agent looked long and hard at the old Indian woman before speaking. "Mrs. Redwing, I do not make the rules. I am hired to ensure they are followed. Your house on the flats is scheduled to be bulldozed to the ground on June 15th. If you have not moved into this house or one like it by that date, state troopers will be sent in to do the moving for you. This house will be ready to occupy by the end of April . . . no later than the first of May. After that, you have about forty-five days. No more. No less. Good day to you, Mrs. Redwing." The tone in Radford's voice was neither crisp nor officious. It was just matter-of-fact, even pleasant. He turned, walked back through the house and returned to his car.

"Mother, I wish you would learn to be more diplomatic," Clarence whispered.

"Bullshit. Bein' diplomatic ain't gonna get me nowhere. I tried that when all this invasion of my privacy first began. They didn't listen to diplomatic talk . . . they don't listen to nothin'. I might as well be a dog . . . so if I want to bark, that's my business. Just be glad I didn't bite that little son-of-a-bitch!"

"Mother Redwing, you shouldn't speak that way in front of the children," Audrey complained.

"And government agents shouldn't talk about bulldozin' down a grandmother's house in front of children . . . life is life, Audrey. What? Are you gonna try and take away my freedom of speech now too?" She stepped defiantly off the porch and walked out into the backyard.

"My mom says *son-of-a-bitch* all the time," I whispered in her defense as we followed her to the edge of the property that looked out over the lake below.

"It's a grand view, isn't it," Clarence noted, walking up behind us.

Clarence was right. It was a grand view. One could look down on the old village site and see the lake shimmering in the distance. And there on the flats not far from the lake, one could see Grandmother Redwing's house standing like a sentinel guarding the last stronghold of her people.

"At least back here I could sit on the grass and see the lake," the old woman said with a tiredness in her voice I hadn't heard before.

"Maybe the magic will work this time," Willie offered.

"Maybe, boy . . . maybe."

We all stood in silence for a long time looking out over the lake. In some ways I felt as if we were attending a funeral. I looked up at Clarence's face. He had tears in his eyes. Suddenly I had them in mine as well.

Our silence was interrupted by the sound of the back door of the house opening behind us. At first I thought it was the government agent come back to add more fuel to the fire. I was relieved to see Saddles Seatco when I turned around.

"I thought that was your car, Clarence," he said, waving to us and he stepped down from the porch and began walking toward us. Saddles had a very distinctive walk about him. It was brisk but not manly. It reminded me of the way lady models walked when they were showing off new clothes or swim suits, except

392

that he was always in bib overalls and usually wore penny loafers. I often thought that brogans might make his walk more manly.

"We're just lookin' at the new houses," Audrey told him.

"I'm glad you're up . . . I got something I want to show you," Saddles beamed.

"I heard you got some newfangled electronic contraption," Grandmother Redwing remarked.

"That's true. I want you to come and see it," Saddles coaxed.

"The man plans to bulldoze my house to the ground on June 15th! We better forget about your newfangled contraption and get started on the magic," Grandmother Redwing responded.

"We can do both. I've got a kettle on for tea and some biscuits baking in the oven. You folks come on over. I really want you to see this," Saddles pleaded.

"What about my magic?" Grandmother Redwing insisted.

"I've got magic brewing at my place for you too. Come on . . let me show you my new toy," Saddles squealed.

Clarence drove the girls, his wife, and mother to the shaman's house. The boys and I walked back to it with him.

"I hear you have an electric herb grinder," Willie said as the four of us walked up the middle of the street.

"That's true. I just have too much arthritis to grind things by hand anymore. I bought me an electric grinder and an electric juicer too. I just love all these gadgets. And I have something else. Wanna guess what it is?"

"An electric blanket?" Randy answered. "I saw some in the Sears catalog."

"Yes . . . I got me one of them too . . . but I got something else you ain't guessed yet."

"A new record player," I suggested.

"I had that in the house the last time you visited. Nope, it's something else."

"An electric smokehouse," Willie ventured.

"No . . . not an electric smokehouse . . . but that's a great idea. I wonder if they make anything like that? Nope . . I bought me a brand new Zenith television set!"

"A television set? the three of us shouted, stopping dead in our tracks.

None of us had ever seen a television set except in pictures in magazines and the one that was on display at the Puyallup Fair. No one we knew owned one and they were the last things on our minds that day.

As we approached Saddles' house, he pointed out a huge television antenna attached at the top of a tall fir tree in front of his house. Its fingers were pointed toward Seattle. The boys and I ran ahead of the shaman. When we arrived at the steps of his front porch, Clarence and the others were already getting out of the car.

"Saddles Seatco has a television set!" Randy squealed, running up to his grandmother.

"Nonsense!" she grumbled.

"But it's true. It's true. Look over there at the big fir tree in Saddles' front yard . . . look way up at the

394

top, you can see the antenna," Randy instructed. He was jumping up and down while pointing toward the glistening structure of metal tubes and bars looming in the Quinault sky. "It looks like the tuning fork of technology, doesn't it!" he observed, breathlessly.

Everyone looked up at the aluminum edifice swaying gently in the breeze at the top of the tree.

"How come you put the antenna way up there?" Clarence asked, shading his eyes so he could see better.

"The signal gotta come all the way from Seattle. I tried it up on the roof . . . but it wasn't tall enough. Some of the young men workin' for that loggin' company down by Tahola is Quinault. I got two of them to come and put it up in the tree for me. You should see them kids climb that tree. They got spurs or cleats or some kinda spikes on the heels and soles of their boots. They climbed up that tree like they was monkeys. It took a lotta wire to reach down to the house but I pull in King TV pretty good. Some days it's a little fuzzy and sometimes if the wind is blowing, the picture rolls a lot, but I get a real good picture most of the time," Saddles explained.

Grandmother Redwing leaned against her walking stick, furrowed her brow, made snapping noises with her tongue, and shook her head in the negative. "That looks like somethin' from outer space. I hope you apologized to the spirit of the tree before stickin' them tin feathers in its hair!" she admonished.

"What are you talkin' about, old woman? That tree is honored by the task I have given it. That's the first antenna on the reservation. It ain't gonna be the last, ya know. It's a magic thing. If you were a shaman, you would know that scientific things are magic . . . just like visions . . . and this vision comes right into my living room and talks to me. Come on in and see!" Saddles retorted.

"You wanna make the new village into San Francisco! The next thing I know you'll have a pink neon sign on your house that reads *Man of Two Souls*", the elder Mrs. Redwing grunted.

I had the feeling Grandmother Redwing could have criticized the antenna all night without dampening any interest the rest of us had to see the shaman's newest electronic gadget. We followed Saddles into his home and gathered around the television set as if it had appeared in a blaze of light from outer space. It looked remarkably like the floor model radio at the Harding farm. It stood about three and a half feet high with an arched top. Like the radio, it sported about an eight-inch round glass screen near its top but unlike the radio, behind whose glass screen one could see a long thin, red arrow and a circular pattern of radio call numbers, one could see nothing behind the television glass except the grayish-green of the television tube.

"Does it work? Are you gonna turn it on for us?" Willie asked.

"Of course, it works. I'll turn it on. There's a cartoon show comin' on in just a minute or two, and then the news. They'll stop broadcasting after that until eight o'clock tonight. Then there will be another show on," Saddles answered, clicking the power switch on.

A bright dot appeared at the center of the little round screen. Then, slowly, the whole tube lit up revealing nothing more than a series of jagged lines flipping about in horizontal and vertical patters. Grandmother Redwing gave a little gasp. Saddles reached behind the television set and began fiddling with little knobs and buttons. Eventually the rapidly jiggling lines slowed down until the picture came into focus revealing a portrait of an Indian in full headdress above a series of vertical and horizontal line patterns.

"Would you look at that!" Audrey commented

"I'll be damned," Clarence remarked.

"It's got an Indian on it . . . he looks like my grandpa! How did you do that, Saddles?" Grandmother Redwing questioned.

"I didn't do it . . . the people in Seattle did it. That's the test pattern. They have that on the air for an hour before a show comes on so you can adjust your set to get the best picture. Think of it, old woman, they use a picture of a great Indian chief for their test pattern. That means that the first thing people see when they warm up their television sets is an Indian. It's a sign, Old Lady Redwing, don'tcha see? It's a sign and I'm told that same test pattern is shown all over America. That means an Indian leads the way before the white man's vision gets into the set. That's why I don't apologize to the tree . . . that tree helps bring that Indian's picture into the house . . . I think it is powerful magic. Tell me that isn't good magic!" Saddles beamed.

Grandmother Redwing didn't respond right away. No one did. We were all mesmerized by the test pattern glowing in front of us. The boys and I sat down on the living room rug and stared into the flickering picture as if we expected to see or hear the voice and face of God come from it. Finally, after

397

taking a seat on the couch, the old woman spoke. "When they supposed to start sendin' a show?" she asked.

"Just about now. They don't always start right on time. You want some tea? I gotta go check my oven," Saddles answered.

"Yea . . . tea . . . maybe a cookie . . . that'll be fine. You think the picture gonna come on right away, huh?"

"Right away," Saddles assured her.

Just as he disappeared down the hall to his kitchen, the test pattern on the television set flickered and was replaced with a man's face. "Good evening, ladies and gentlemen. You are watching K-I-N-G Television, the first television station in the Pacific Northwest. Please stand by for our national anthem."

Immediately an orchestra began playing *The Star Spangled Banner*, but on the screen we saw a picture of an American bald eagle flying through the sky until it landed on the high branch of a Douglas fir tree. After that, a picture of the Capitol in Washington, D.C. was shown, followed by a picture of the State Capitol building in Olympia.

"This contraption begins with the image of my grandfather and then brings Brother Eagle into your lodge. I think this must be a very good magic and a very powerful magic," Grandmother Redwing said, more to herself than to anyone in the room.

Saddles Seatco served the adults tea, glasses of lemonade to each of us kids, and made sure everyone had one of his biscuits as we silently watched the cartoon as if we had never seen one before. It was an old cartoon. Mickey Mouse didn't quite look like himself and his voice was squeakier than the one we had all heard in cartoons seen at the Cosmo Theater in Perkins Prairie. Still, it was a cartoon and it was in Saddles Seatco's living room. We were mesmerized.

After the cartoon was over, we watched fifteen minutes of news read by a newscaster who only looked up from his script to greet us when he began, to introduce an advertisement, and then again when he signed off. The moment he said goodnight, the screen flickered for a few seconds until the test pattern reappeared.

"That's absolutely fascinating!" Grandmother Redwing announced.

"I can't believe we can actually see a guy clear away in Seattle read the news to us," Audrey exclaimed.

"Do they gots more cartoons?" Darleen asked.

"Nope, just one before the news. I think they show that just so people can get their sets better adjusted before the news comes on, because sometimes they show the same one a couple a days in a row," Saddles answered.

"I've got to get me one of those," Clarence muttered.

"You're all welcome to come back at eight o'clock, if you like. They always show a movie every night at just about eight. They interrupt it lots of times with advertisements for toothpaste and cigarettes and stuff . . . but you can still follow the movie real good," Saddles suggested.

"I just can't believe it," Grandmother Redwing

commented. "I wonder how they do that?"

"I don't know . . . it has something to do with radio waves that the television set turns into lines of different shades of light . . . and that makes the pictures. It is real magic, huh?" Saddles responded.

"And it begins with a picture of my grandpa and Brother Eagle flying above the earth. I got the feelin' the Great Spirit approves of this new magic," the old woman asserted.

"They say, eventually, there'll be a television set in every home, maybe even more than one . . . just like radios," Saddles added.

"You think I could get one for me down on the flats?" Grandmother Redwing asked.

"You gotta have electricity to get television," Audrey observed.

"Well, wouldn't cha know there'd be a catch to it. Maybe I'll get me a goldfish then. They're kinda interesting to watch too," her mother-in-law responded.

"No goldfish is gunna give you the news," Saddles said as we headed back out to the car.

"I didn't hear no news about Indians," Grandmother Redwing noted.

"And how often do you hear news about Indians on the radio?" Saddles asked.

"It depends on which station I'm listening to."

"Don't ya need electricity to turn on the radio too?" I sked as I helped her down the steps on the front porch.

"Not when I'm visiting folks that's got one." She answered.

"Well, you could certainly have your own TV set

400

if you move into one of these little white houses like the rest of us," Saddles pointed out.

"Oh fiddlesticks, Saddles. I'll just hike up the hill and watch your contraption if I get in the mood. And I might just do that. I ain't seen a movie since the last time somebody drove me into Olympia one night for a dinner birthday at Mr. Lee's chicken place. What was the name of that movie, Clarence?"

"*The Wizard of Oz*, Mother. We saw *The Wizard of Oz*."

Chapter Twelve

Good Magic

The scalps sent by Grandmother Sunfield arrived at the post office Saturday morning before we left. Saddles carried them from house to house in one hand and a small clay pot of smoldering bark in the other, chanting ancient formulas and special prayers until he had visited the site of each new house being built above the old village. He permitted the boys and I to follow close behind to observe but made us promise not to say a word, even if we saw a spirit or anything unusual. "Even if I should turn into another animal while I do the ritual, you must remain silent or the magic cannot happen. Understood?"

We assured him we understood and trailed behind him. We were also to watch for the government agent who worked on the reservation. Saturday was his usual day off, but Saddles wanted us to watch for him anyway. Only if we saw him were we allowed to say anything.

When he finished, Clarence drove Saddles and the rest of us down the dirt road that led to Grandmother Redwing's little house on the flats. "Do you think the magic worked?" she asked as we walked into the house through the back door without knocking.

"There is no way to know if magic works until

you see it workin'. I did my best," he answered. :"The rest is up to the powers that be."

"Clarence will take the scalps back with him so he can return them to Audrey's mother, unless you think you'll be needin' them again," the old woman commented.

"If you think it will be okay with Mrs. Sunfield, I think we should just keep them right here at your house for a while," Saddles answered.

"Will that help the magic?" I asked.

"It can't hurt," Saddles responded.

"I doubt that Audrey's mother will mind. I'll ask her when we drive back up the hill," Clarence offered.

"Then I think I'll just keep them right here. I gotta feelin' I'm gonna need them before this ordeal is over," Mrs. Redwing observed.

§§§§

By the end of April, all ten of the new houses were finished. A few were occupied by newly married couples, and three were taken by families who had moved from the reservation as part of the government's relocation program but who had either become dissatisfied with life in the American mainstream, or because the business ventures upon which they embarked had failed. Two of the houses were kept in reserve for future expansion of the tribe's population. The house at the end of the block, next to the woods with the magnificent view of the lake and the property upon which the old village once stood, was reserved for Grandmother Redwing.

403

The second week of May, Randy and I, along with the other sixth-graders who would be entering junior high school the following fall, were permitted to register for our new classes as seventh-graders. It would be our first trip to the buildings that housed the junior and high school classes across town. Earlier that year my family had moved from Perkins Street to A Street, just a few houses down from the buildings in which we would be attending school. They were impressive structures built for $10,000 in 1910. A fortune in those days. There was a cafeteria in the basement staffed by local women who prepared lunches so good, a few of the towns people managed to eat there occasionally. There was a gymnasium next to the building that housed an Olympic sized swimming pool and a basket ball court upstairs that doubled as an indoor track when the weather was too cold or stormy to use the one that surrounded the football field out behind the buildings. There was a large grandstand area so students and parents could watch the games and two tennis courts; one next to the football field and one beside the building that housed the science labs, shop and home economics class rooms. The school was as good as anything built in Tacoma or larger cities on the western slope of the state.

Randy and I decided to take all the same classes if possible. We were to choose a minimum of six classes and one study hall. Three of the classes had to be in the areas of math or science, history, and English, and if we didn't turn out for one of the sport teams, we would have to sign up for a gym class. That left us with two elective classes of our choice. We had never been given that privilege in grade school. Both of us were very excited about the prospect and spent hours going over our schedules in an attempt to take all the same classes. But conflicts arose. The difficulty was over the two electives. We had no problem choosing between a math class or a science class because we both wanted to take a course in human biology. Willie had taken it and told us the teacher talked a lot about sex in that class. If there was anything we were interested in at that moment in time, it was sex.

But while I wanted to take band and shop for my two electives, Randy wanted to take home economics and theater arts. Not only would that put us in two different classes, it would also put us in different study halls. I tried everything to persuade him to change his mind. I even pointed out that Jerry Cotton was also taking theater arts and suggested there would be more problems than fun in that class for him. Randy just shrugged his shoulders and said: "I'll betcha a buck I'm a better actor right now than Cotton will ever be."

"But if you take band, you can get some of the best seats at the games, and you get to wear a uniform and march around and be in the spring concert," I argued.

"I hate sports. You know that. They don't make any sense to me. All that fuss over who has the ball seems to me to be an utter waste of time. All that excitement over how far a guy can hit or kick or throw a ball seems pretty juvenile to me when you compare that sort of talent to acting or becoming a great chef.

405

So being in the band would mean being at all those dumb sports games. That's not for me. Besides, if I don't make it as an actor or a chef, I plan to become a cosmetologist."

"What the hell is a cosmetologist?" I asked.

"A makeup artist and a hairdresser. I think about it all the time. I'd love to be a makeup artist in the movies or style hair for actresses like Hedy Lamarr or Veronica Lake. I dream of that all the time, but I'd settle for working in a nice beauty salon someday," Randy sighed dreamingly.

"I never knew you went for that stuff," I told him, trying to mask my surprise.

"I've dreamed about it for years. That's why I looked so great last Halloween. Doin' makeup just comes natural for me. Sometimes I think I should have been born a girl."

"What sport are you gonna take?" I asked, deciding to ignore his comment.

"Which one are you?"

"Track. I like runnin'. I'm real good at it. I don't much like the other games. I'm not much of a team player," I answered.

"How about swimming?" Randy asked.

"All swimming is for me is staying alive in the water."

"You're kidding!"

"Not an ounce."

"Well, I sure wish I could get gym credit for skating; I hate all the other sports," Randy confided. "But I like swimming."

"Skating is a sport . . . maybe they'll let you

practice during gym class."

"I already asked. They said the basketball court could get ruined by my skates and that I'd have to play volleyball, gymnastics, wrestling, or swimming. I'm gonna do the swimming. I just love bein' in the water."

"It's too bad swimming isn't coed, isn't it?" I observed.

"Oh, I wouldn't want to swim with girls . . . it's much more fun being in the pool with just a bunch of guys. I love bathing suits on guys . . . men look much better than women when they swim, don't cha think?"

"I guess I never thought about it," I answered.

"I think about it all the time," Randy whispered. "I think I'm like Saddles. A man with two souls."

"You mean to tell me that a man with two souls is queer?"

"Well 'gay' is the polite word to use, but yes that's what it means."

"So you like boys. Not girls?"

"Well of course. I thought you knew."

"It never crossed my mind. Do you think about me that way?"

"No."

"Well what's wrong with me. I'm pretty damn good look'n."

"Yes, you are. But I think of you like I do Willie. Like a brother."

Our conversation got nipped in the bud when one of the teachers came over and offered to help us finish our plans for the next school year.

After registration, we rode our bikes over to his house to see if his Grandmother Sunfield had arrived by bus yet. She was scheduled to spend the weekend with the Redwings and help Audrey plant bedding flowers and herbs in a plot behind the house the boys and I had helped Clarence spade the week before. When we walked in the back door, we could hear Audrey and her mother talking.

"I'm so upset with that woman, I could just scream!" Audrey fussed.

"She's set in her ways, Audrey, and I think she is right. If I had to do it all over again, I might have put up more of a fight myself. She has more guts than I did then. I miss the old ways myself," Grandmother Sunfield responded.

"What's up?" Randy asked.

"Grandma Redwing has had another fight with the government agent. Saddles just called Mom and told her all about it," Willie answered.

"Your Aunt Alice called too. Grandma Redwing has been shouting at the government people each time they try to see her, and she tore up some letters they sent to her and mailed them back unread. Alice wants us to drive up to see if we can't convince her to move. She wants us to bring some empty boxes," Audrey added.

"Are we going?" Randy asked.

"I don't know if we can. Your father doesn't want to shut down the shop on a Friday. It's not good for business. He wants me to drive up tomorrow. Sometimes his mother will listen to me when she'll listen to no one else. I just don't know what to do."

"You have to go, Mom," Willie declared. Dad said he would drive up in the delivery truck Saturday night and join us after he closes the shop."

"And I'll stay here and watch the rest of the kids. You should take Randy and Willie just in case you need their help. Strong boys like that always come in handy. I can plant them flowers and herbs with the girls help. You should go. Willie is right," Grandmother Sunfield insisted.

"Me and Randy could take tomorrow off from school and go with you, Mom. We can tell them we have a family emergency. They don't have to know what it is. They always let kids out of school for family emergencies," Willie said.

§§§§

Somehow I managed to convince my parents that I should go along with the Redwings. Mother was opposed but when Dad pointed out that everybody needs a mental health day away from his usual routines once in a while, that my grades had been very good, and that I had only missed two days of school all year because of illness, she finally relented and said she would write me an excuse when I returned to school Monday morning.

We left for the Quinault Reservation early the next morning. Audrey packed sandwiches and filled a small cooler with two quarts of lemonade so we wouldn't have to waste time stopping for lunch on the way. We arrived at Bill and Alice's home in the new village about noon. Alice was weeding her flower and herb beds when we pulled up to their small white frame house. "Have you been down to see Bill's mother yet?" she asked, looking up from her work.

"No. I thought I should come here first and see what's happened since I spoke to you last night. I hope you don't mind. I brought the boys and their friend, Fritz, along. I hate making that trip alone."

"The more the merrier. You know we enjoy the boys and their friend. But perhaps it is a good idea you came here first. Saddles and I are just beside ourselves with worry. That old woman is acting crazy. Bill's worried that she's slipped off the deep end this time. When Albert Radford went down tryin' to talk with her this morning, she wouldn't open the door to him. All she did was stand in front of her window shaking those scalps at him and cursing in Quinault. He thinks she's nuts and has threatened to call one of those psychologist fellows from the city and have her committed. She told Albert she has an old musket in the house and knows how to use it. You can't talk to government people like that . . . she's going to get herself killed or locked up. You've just got to go down there and see if she'll listen to you. Lord knows she won't listen to me or Bill anymore. She's even been yellin' at poor Saddles." Alice stood up, took off her garden gloves and put them in her apron pocket. "Push is getting very close to shove," Audrey."

"Well, I'm not at all sure she'll listen to me. I'm just the daughter-in-law," Audrey responded.

"She has always listened to you in the past. Mothers-in-law can be like that. She used to listen to me . . . but I've just pressed too hard this time. She

410

thinks I'm in cahoots with the government and the truth is I am, I guess. There is no alternative. She must move!"

"I never thought it would come to this either. I guess I just thought she would see the inevitability of all this and give in," Audrey said.

"Well, it has come to this. When will Clarence get here?"

"He'll be up sometime tomorrow evening. He may close the shop early if business slows down. But you know how it is when you own your own business."

"I'm sure he's doing his best. It will give us all a chance to see that new delivery truck of his. Do you want me to drive on down with you. She's pretty upset with me right now."

"No. I'll take the boys and go down. I'll try to be back in time to help you with dinner."

"See if Mother Redwing will come with you. I've got three nice pheasants that Bill shot this morning. There'll be plenty. Maybe she'll come. She loves pheasant. Tell her I'm fixing them just the way she likes them . . . stuffed with cattail roots, mushrooms and ground acorns. Tell her I promise not to talk about the move to the new village unless she brings it up herself."

"I'll tell her," Audrey assured. The two women embraced before Audrey got back in the car and drove down the hill to the old village site.

Grandmother Redwing must have seen us coming because she was out on her porch and walking down the front steps when we pulled up in front of her little house. Audrey pulled the emergency brake,

411

turned off the engine, and reached to open the door. Her mother-in-law opened it for her. "I'm glad you're here, Audrey, but if you've come to try and change my mind, you might as well drive back to Perkins Prairie because I ain't gonna change my mind!" she said firmly.

"Mother Redwing, the agent is talking about having you committed to some sort of an asylum or something. He can do that. He can have troops come down here and take you to Steilacoom. Is that what you want? At least in the new village you are still on the reservation and close to your family. If you keep acting crazy with scalps and yelling at people about having a gun in the house, you're going to be in very hot water and you won't be living in any house . . . you'll be living in a big room filled with twelve guys who think they're Jesus and some woman who runs around biting people because she thinks she a spider!" Audrey stepped out of the car. It was only then I began to understand how frustrated she had become. "Of course I'm here to try and talk you into moving up to the new house. I wouldn't be a very good daughter-in-law if I didn't try . . . and you know it!"

The two women looked into each other's eyes for several long seconds without either saying a word. The boys and I slipped out of the car on the other side so we wouldn't be in the way.

"You shouldn't have brought the kids into this mess," Grandmother Redwing chided, looking at the three of us.

"They are already in the middle of this mess. Do you think for five minutes that any of these boys want to see you dragged physically from your home by state troopers or worse yet, men in white jackets!" Audrey shouted.

"I got me some real strong magic. I just gotta stick with it and hold out until it overcomes that Albert Radford," the old woman retorted.

"It's not just Albert Radford! The government has decided you can't live down here anymore. They are going to move you physically if you don't move on your own. They are going to come down here with bulldozers and smash your house to smithereens and if you don't stop acting crazy, they're going to put you in a straitjacket and take you by ambulance to the state home for the delirious and nuts!" Audrey was still shouting.

"I don't like it when you shout at me, girl. You got no business shoutin' at me."

"I'm sorry, Mother Redwing . . . but you're driving me and everybody else crazy with all this," Audrey replied more softly. "Times have changed. We Salishans and Quinaults are no longer in charge of our own destiny . . . not unless we move into the new world and learn how to survive in it. The old world is gone. It will never come back! I'm sorry about that. I wish I could change that. Saddles wishes he could change that for you . . . but we can't! And if you keep shaking those scalps through the window at government people and yelling at them in Quinault, they're going to put you away. That's all there is to it. I don't want that to happen. These boys don't want that to happen. Alice and Bill don't want that to happen. Saddles doesn't want that to happen. Clarence doesn't want that to happen. There isn't a person in the village who wants that to happen. That's why I'm here. I want to prevent that from happening. Don't you see? Mother Redwing, you've got to move."

"Grandma, We're a-scared for you," Willie interjected.

"The old woman slowly turned from Audrey to her grandson. The wrinkles in her face relaxed and I could see that Willie's comment had softened her. "I know you are, dear, and I'm sorry about that. But sometimes adults got to stand up and fight, even when children are afraid for them. Maybe especially when children are afraid for them."

"I don't want them to put you in a rubber room somewhere, Grandma," Randy said, bursting into tears.

"Oh, dear," Grandmother Redwing said, walking over to her him and placing her arms around him. "You come in the house with Grandma. I've got wild honey cookies with hazelnuts in the soda box and a couple of huckleberry pies in the oven. You come in and let Grandma feed those tears away."

"You're going to have to move, Grandma . . . that's all there is to it," Randy said into her neck as he continued to weep.

"I don't think so, Randy. But you come in the house. Everybody come in the house. We'll have some tea and talk like human beings instead of banshees," she said, throwing Audrey a scolding glance.

The boys and I set the table while Grandmother Redwing made us tea and checked her pies. Audrey carefully arranged cookies in the cedar bowl Willie had made for his grandmother in shop class the year before.

"The pies need to bake a bit longer," the old

woman said, putting the steaming pot of seeping tea on the kitchen table. "Fritz . . . you bring cups from the rack, okay?" she directed.

I brought the cups to the table and set one in front of each person.

"I'm gonna let those pies bake about ten more minutes. You take a cookie," the old woman politely commanded everyone.

We each reached for a cookie.

"Will you at least stop shouting at the government people when they come down to talk with you . . . and stop waving those scalps in their faces?" Audrey pleaded.

"I don't know if I can do that, Audrey. All I know is that I will never move from this house unless they carry me out. I made up my mind . . . not unless they carry me out. I ain't' never gonna move of my own free will and I'm gonna fight like I was a warrior. If they take me to that new house, they gotta take me like a prisoner . . . 'cause as far as I'm concerned, it would be a prison. Don't you see, Audrey, if I give in and go up there of my own free will . . . then they win. But if they gotta carry me up there shoutin' and screamin' and fightin' back . . . then they don't really win. Then my spirit is still free. Besides, tomorrow I go to the cave and ask for guidance. Who knows? Maybe the Great Spirit wants me to move, and maybe this is that prankster Kwatee just tryin' to cause trouble for everybody. I'm goin' to the cave to find out."

"Mother Redwing, you're too old to go to the cave. You can barely walk down to the lake and back anymore. You haven't been able to walk up the hill to

415

town in over two years. You can't get up to that cave anymore!" Audrey argued.

"We could pull you up there in that little red wagon Uncle Bill bought his girls for Christmas last year. You'd have to get out and climb over a couple of logs, but Fritz and Randy and I could help you," Willie suggested.

"That's a terrible idea," Audrey said in alarm.

"It sounds like a damn good idea to me. We'll make an adventure out of it. That little red wagon ain't that little. It's pretty long, and it gots sidebars that can go on it. I could put a blanket in there and a pillow for my butt. I think I'd be very comfortable riding in that thing. Do you boys really think you can pull it up the hill?"

"Not a problem, Grandma. We can take turns and if there are some real steep places, two can push and one can pull," Willie said.

"This is getting more ridiculous by the minute. You can't go five miles into the woods in a little red wagon. What will you do if it gets stuck in the mud? What will people think? What will the government people say? What will they think? They'll think all three of you have gone crazy," Audrey admonished.

"They won't say nothin' about it if you don't tell them," her mother-in-law answered. Ain't nobody gotta know about this 'cept us."

"Being pulled up a mountain in a little red wagon could be very dangerous, side bars or not," Audrey cautioned.

"Look, Audrey, I'm goin' to the cave one way or another. I think the little red wagon is a good idea . . .

416

but if you forbid the boys to pull me up there in it . . . then I'll walk like I was plannin' on doin' n the first place . . . either way I'm gonna go."

Audrey looked exasperated. "Oh, all right . . . if you insist . . . but I'm coming along just to make sure nothing happens. You could wait until Clarence gets here."

"Clarence won't be here until Saturday night. I'm goin' up in the morning and that's that!"

"Well, at least let me tell Bill and Alice what you're planning to do so they'll know why I'm borrowing the wagon. Maybe Bill should come along too," Audrey suggested.

"I don't want the whole damn tribe goin' up the mountain with me. You can tell Bill and Alice . . . but I want they should stay home. Besides, Bill has to work this Saturday."

"All right, Mother, you win. I absolutely do not want you going up there alone. I'll let the boys help you. I'll decide tonight whether I'll come along as well. What time do you want us here in the morning?"

"About seven. I gotta get back so I can be here when Clarence arrives. And don't you say nothin' to him about this 'till he gets here," the old woman admonished.

"I'll do nothing of the kind. I'll be here with the boys to help you but I will also inform Clarence if we speak on the telephone. By the way, Alice would like you to come with us to her place for dinner. She's fixing pheasants just the way you like them. Okay?"

"Okay with me. I love the way she fixes pheasant for me. I'll take my pies for dessert. But you're a hard woman, Audrey. It is the way of the Quinault that the grandmother has the final say so."

"Not when it comes to conversations between a wife and a husband, and you know it . . . so don't try to pull made-up traditions on me. I don't approve of your going into the woods alone. That's the only reason I'm going to let the boys help you."

"We was gonna go over and see if Saddles would let us watch television after supper. You wanna come too, Grandma," Randy asked.

"Nope. I watched that fool thing with him a couple of times. Them movies is full of white people killin' each other. And one night he coaxed me to watch a cowboy and Indian movie. It was terrible. And the Indians was played by white guys with black wigs on. No more TV for me for a while. But I do like watchin' the news. They've hooked up with the big shots in New York now. King TV shows local and national news now. We see it clear from New York City. They fly it out here in can in an airplane. Don't that beat all. Now that's good magic."

§§§§

The four of us arrived back at Grandmother Redwing's about seven the next morning. Bill had insisted on securing the sidebars to the wagon to make sure the old woman wouldn't fall out when we pulled it over bumps and tree roots along the path. Alice stuffed two oversized pillows in the wagon to ensure that her mother-in-law would be comfortable. She also brought along a lunch of sandwiches and lemonade that could be carried along inside the wagon so we could stay our hunger during the trip.

Grandmother Redwing insisted on walking until we were far enough around the lake so that no one could see her get into the little red wagon unless they had very high- powered binoculars. "It's nobody's business," she said.

"What do you care what they think?" Audrey asked. "You certainly haven't given much thought to what they think about waving scalps at the agent or talking about guns."

"They're already callin' me crazy. I don't want them to think I'm physically incompetent as well. It's nobody's business but ours," she insisted.

Randy and Willie had dressed in tennis shoes, blue jeans and white T-shirts. I wore my breechcloth, moccasins and headgear. Randy thought I was carrying things too far and said so. "You don't have to dress like an Indian from the old days all the time. The Great Spirit knows Willie and I are Indians no matter what we wear."

"We're on a vision quest. Why wouldn't I dress this way?"

"I think you just like walking around half naked in the woods," he quipped.

"Nothin' wrong with that, Randy," his grandmother scolded, settling herself in the wagon. "Our people lived in outfits like that for as long as anyone can remember. The Great Spirit don't give two farts in a wind storm over who wears what. A costume is a costume and we is all in a costume unless we're naked as the day we entered the world."

"He's just worried that Fritz will be a better Indian than he is," Willie commented.

"I am not. I just think he carries things too far sometimes," Randy retorted.

"Oh, stop fussing, Randy," his mother admonished.

"The Great Spirit doesn't give three broken sea shells and a splinter about what anyone wears during a quest. It is the condition of the heart that matters. So if it helps Fritz's heart to dress in the old ways, then it is right for him. Everybody's different, Randy. You gotta keep that in mind. Everybody's different and we gotta respect them differences. Now, if you braves don't mind, I'm tryin' to pray. You all know this journey is to be made in mostly silence and prayer. Now hush up or I'll leave you right here with your little red wagon and walk up to the cave by myself. If you can't pray with me, then don't stay with me," she scolded.

"Yes, Grandmother," the three of us responded in unison.

We made our way along the rest of the trail in silence. We took turns pulling the wagon. When we came to hills, all four of us helped out. A couple of the hills were steeper than I remembered. We were all glad Audrey had come along.

Grandmother Redwing insisted on getting out of the wagon when we came to creeks and small rivers. She would take off her shoes and anklets and wade barefooted across each rivulet and stream. "Nothin' feels so good on the toes as ice-cold water flowin' down from the mountains," she said each time. The rest of us jumped the creeks or got across by stepping on stones that were large enough to be partially exposed to the air. Once we almost turned the little red wagon over and came close to having the pillows spill out. After that we were more careful about getting the wagon across the streams.

Eventually we arrived at the short path that led to the cave. "This is the place," Willie said, panting slightly. The hill to the path had proven to be much steeper than any of us had remembered. We were all out of breath and panting.

"You boys did a good job. I like okay comin' to the cave in a little red wagon. I feel like Claudette Colbert when she was carried into Rome in that movie about Cleopatra I seen one time when Saddles took me with him to Tacoma. Your grandma thanks you. You too, Audrey. I know this can be a rough climb, and pullin' and pushin' me in this little wagon was real work. It'll be easier going back. It's mostly downhill. You're a good daughter-in-law. But now it is time for me to go on alone. You guys wait here until I come back. If you whisper, you can talk. But the cave ain't far from here, so don't be talkin' and laughin' loud enough for me to hear you. I don't want you chasin' the spirits away. Of course, it would be even nicer if you prayed quietly."

"I think I'll take the boys back a piece on the trail. I saw a whole bunch of salmonberries back there. We'll pick them and have a little bit of our lunch. You can give us a yell when you're finished," Audrey commented.

"You do what you want. Just don't make no noise." The old woman turned, and using her walking stick, disappeared into the bushes down the little trail that led to the cave of visions.

"I think we should pray first," Willie whispered.

"Me too," I whispered back.

The four of us found comfortable places to sit or stretch out and pray. I decided to lie on my back on a bed of moss not far from the entrance of the cave. Randy found a place to sit about fifty feet away where he could lean his back against a moss-covered log. Willie stretched out on the top of the same log. Audrey sat down next to Randy and closed her eyes.

I looked up through the trees to the white and grayish clouds making their way across the sky. A grove of birch and cascara trees made their home around and in front of the entrance to the cave. The green canopy they provided made the colors of the sky even more vivid. I prayed silently in thanks for the bounty and glory of trees, the mystery of clouds and leaves, and the soft moss upon which I had found such a comfortable bed. I thanked the Great Spirit for bringing Willie and Randy to Perkins Prairie and into my life. I prayed that Grandmother Redwing would find the answer she needed to do whatever it would take to survive the government's intrusion into her life. I was lost in my thoughts when I became aware of the smell of smoke from the old woman's fire in the cave. I wondered what visions she would see in its coals and if the One Who Changes was already speaking with her.

I don't remember falling asleep, but nearly two hours had passed when I felt Grandmother Redwing's walking stick nudging my shoulder. "Wake up, boy," she whispered. "It's time to put this old lady back in that little red wagon and take her home."

I looked around; everyone was still asleep. "Did you have your vision?" I whispered back.

"I'll tell you all about it as soon as we're on our way. Help me get the others up . . . and don't whisper. They've been sleepin' long enough."

"Oh, Mother Redwing, you're back. I must have dozed off," Audrey said, getting to her feet. "Willie, Randy!" she shouted. "Grandma is back. Wake up. It's time for us to have our lunch and get back."

Willie slid off the log and ran over to his grandmother." Did you have your vision?" he asked.

"A very strange vision. I'll tell you about it as we eat," she answered.

Grandmother Redwing sat on the moss-covered log with her sandwich after taking a drink from the lemonade in one of the quart jars Audrey had brought along. The rest of us sat on the ground in front of her. "Did One Who Changes come to you?" I asked.

"Yes. One Who Changes came to me as three yellow finches . . . and then as my grandmother . . . but she wouldn't talk to me . . . and then One Who Changes came to me as a coyote, and finally as an old man. The old man did some talkin'. He told me that if I would remember the ways of coyote, the three yellow finches would sing just for me. He told me the old woman I saw was not my grandmother. It was me. I was lookin' at myself; only it wasn't like in a mirror

423

where she did everything I did. It was more like she was on television or somebody else. That old lady had a mind of her own. That's why I didn't realize I was lookin' at myself."

"What do you think it all means?" Randy questioned with a mouth full of sandwich.

"I'll be damned if I know what it all means. I wanna get back and ask Saddles. Maybe that old fool will know what this is all about if he hasn't spent so much time watching his own television set he's forgotten how to read visions."

"Didn't you find out what you should do?" Audrey queried.

"Nope. I couldn't figure it out. I must be losin' my touch."

"Maybe Saddles will know what it's all about," Willie offered.

"Well, I certainly hope so, boy. You kids done with your sandwiches?"

We each confirmed that we had finished.

"Okay, then. Let's get back down to the flats and go find Saddles," the old woman said, settling herself back in the wagon. "This thing ain't half bad to ride in."

The trip back went much faster. It helped that it was mostly downhill all the way. It also helped that we could talk this time. For all her confusion over her vision in the cave, Grandmother Redwing seemed especially relaxed and talkative after the experience. "I should have gone back up there a long time ago. I feel better all over. I do believe that cave's a kinda tonic. How about you, Talks With Eagles. Did you have a

424

vision?" she asked.

"Nope. I did me some prayin' . . . but I fell asleep."

"Did you have a dream, boy?"

"No, ma'am. I don't recall no dream."

"Hmmm. A sleep without a dream . . . maybe that's some kinda sign. To sleep and not dream is kinda like havin' a vision but not gettin' no answer."

By the time we reached her house on the flats, I had learned two new legends of the Quinaults and the medicinal uses of a few more plants. We no sooner got back to her home than she asked Audrey to drive her up to the shaman's house in the new village.

Saddles Seatco was sitting on his porch petting a calico cat when we drove up.

"Where did you get the cat?" Grandmother Redwing asked as she and her walking stick made their way up his walk.

"She just started comin' around. I feed her fresh cream and tuna and scraps from the table. She's a real good cat. Good company too," Saddles answered.

"What'cha gonna name her?" Willie asked.

"Already did. I call this cat Dorothy Parker."

"Dorothy Parker. That's a funny name for a cat," Randy observed.

"She's one of my favorite poets."

"Saddles has all her books. She's a kind of witty New York City poet. Very sophisticated, they tell me. Saddles used to read me her witticisms all the time when he lived down on the flats. Don't they teach you about Dorothy Parker in school?" Grandmother Redwing asked.

425

"I didn't know you liked American poetry," I commented.

"Don't know too much about it . . . but I used to have a friend in San Francisco who read Dorothy Parker to me. He even took me to a reading she gave in San Francisco. She was witty but sort of a bitchy wit. I loved her. He gave me a copy of her poems for my birthday one year. I love them poems. Sometimes they're funny and sometimes they're very dark and scary . . . but almost all the time they're funny . . . sarcastic, I guess is the word for it. Anyhow . . . I love them poems and I love this cat . . . she's kind of bitchy too, so I named her Dorothy Parker."

"You're such a sentimental old fool," Grandmother Redwing teased.

"It takes one to know one," Saddles quipped.

"Grandma had a vision up in the cave but she don't know what it means," Willie interrupted.

"Well, it wouldn't have hurt if you'd had me bless you before you took off, old woman," Saddles told her.

"I plum forgot about that part," the elder Mrs. Redwing admitted.

"Well, tell me what happened. What did ya see and what did ya hear when you was up in the cave?"

Grandmother Redwing related her experience in the cave with even more vivid details than she had given when she discussed it with us earlier. Saddles listened with genuine interest, petting Dorothy Parker with one hand and rolling a Bull Durham cigarette with the other.

"What'cha think it all means?" the old woman

426

asked when she finished. "It means that if you treat this situation like coyote would treat it . . . you'll overcome an evil spirit as no one in this village has done for a damn long time," Saddles answered.

"But how do I treat this situation like coyote? Coyotes aren't asked to move into government houses," Grandmother Redwing persisted.

"No . . . but neither can coyote live on the land the way he once did. Now there are roads and highways and cars and airplane fields and cities . . . coyote has had to learn new ways to adjust to new landscapes and territory. In some ways, moving to the government house is a new territory and a new landscape."

"Yeah, but I ain't movin' to no new damn landscape. Not me. And now I went all the way up to the cave and I still don't know what I'm supposed to do . . . and you ain't helpin' much. There may be lots of road and cities and airplane fields out there that coyote has to deal with these days . . . but he still lives free in the woods and in the den of his choosing. I can't make heads or tails of this damn vision . . . and I don't much understand what you're sayin' either."

"I think you gotta wait and listen. Evidently the Great Spirit ain't done explainin'. You'll just have to wait and listen."

Grandmother Redwing straightened her back and held her head high. "Ya know, Saddles . . . you ain't the shaman you used to be. In the old days you would'a told me exactly what the vision meant."

"In the old days things were simpler. I still say

you gotta wait and listen. My hunch is that it's all gonna work out no matter what you do. In the end, you will know what the vision means."

"Okay. But I'm gonna wait and listen in my house on the flats and not in the little government house they want me to move into . . . and that's that."

"You are the most stubborn women I have ever known," Saddles told her. "Look at me. I love my little house and all the comforts it gives me."

"You was spoiled by live'n in the big city so long. You got yourself citified."

"Oh give me a break, you old hen, I lived down there in the flats near you for years and years and years. I had me a good time down there. But I'm old. Older than you. That's a hard life down there without a village of people around you to pitch in and help out. If the boys didn't come down and get you wood and water you wouldn't be able to stay there and you know it. Up here you get running water inside the house and nice hot water for a bath or shower. Change is good."

"It's a pain in the ass, Saddles, and so are you." She turned on her heels and headed down the sidewalk towards Alice and Bill's house and her supper.

§§§§

That evening, after dinner at Alice and Bill's, all of us including Clarence drove over to Saddles' house to watch a movie. Even Grandmother Redwing went along after Saddles assured her there would be no white people killing one another and no fake Indians in black wigs.

Saddles served a mixture of roasted pumpkin seeds and hazelnuts and gave everyone a tall glass of lemonade just before the movie came on.

"I wonder if that fella that reads the news over at the KING Television Station would be interested in the fact that my mother is being forced from her home with threats of state troopers taking her screaming and kicking from her house?" Clarence speculated.

"That might just be a very good idea," Audrey mused.

"You mean give the government some adverse publicity?" Saddles asked.

"Why not? They like human interest stories. I'll bet Mother's story would interest a lot of people'.

"You really think a bunch of white people give a damn about what happens to an old lady they don't know, livin' on a reservation they probably ain't never heard of?" Grandmother Redwing asked.

"Why wouldn't they? I bet no one else has ever stood up to the government as long as you have. And I'll just bet there are a lot of people out there who would be sympathetic to what's happening to you. I think Clarence has come up with a very good suggestion. They say you gotta fight fire with fire. Why not use the white man's ways to fight the white man's ways?" Audrey speculated.

"I for one think it's a damn good idea. I'm gonna call that fella up and ask him right now. I'll bet he ain't had time to get out of the television station yet," Saddles said. He got up from the couch and walked into the kitchen where he kept his telephone.

About that same moment, the test pattern on the glowing screen flickered and the movie began without so much as an introduction. "Oh, it's a Topper movie! I love these," Audrey commented.

"Who the hell is Topper?" Grandmother Redwing asked.

"A ghost . . . and a pretty dapper ghost at that," Audrey replied.

"So it's a Halloween movie?"

"No, no . . . it's a comedy," Clarence answered.

"A comedy about a ghost. Well, this I gotta see."

As the movie unfolded and we were introduced to its main characters, Grandmother Redwing suddenly interrupted. "Hey, I've seen Topper's wife before. Ain't she the good witch in the movie with Judy Garland?"

"Yes. That's Billie Burke," Audrey answered.

"Well, you'd think that if she's the good witch, she'd know what the hell is goin' on right off the bat. She's sure actin' kinda dumb right now," Grandmother Redwing noted.

"She's not the good witch, Mother. She played the good witch in *The Wizard of Oz.* This is a different movie. This time she's playing Topper's wife. Just like the same dancer can do either the *Whale Dance* or the *Dog Dance.* We know it's the same dancer and we also know it's a completely different dance and story. Same thing here. Billie Burke is an actress. She's playing a different part in this movie. In real life she's neither a witch nor dumb. She's a professional actress," Audrey instructed.

"Well, I'll be damned."

430

"Shh. Let's just watch and save our chatter for later. Okay?" Clarence pleaded.

About ten minutes into the movie, Saddles came back and asked Grandmother Redwing to come into the kitchen to speak to someone on the telephone. I think only Audrey and I saw her get up from her place on the couch and follow him. It was nearly twenty minutes later before they returned to finish watching it with us. With the exception of a few trips to the bathroom, we pretty much watched the rest of the movie without interruption.

When it was over, Grandmother Redwing made an announcement. "I have changed my mind 'bout TV, at least about that Topper movie and the news. The news is good magic and that Topper is a funny guy. He acts downright stupid but ya know he's pretty smart. But I got a big surprise for all of you. I'm maybe gonna be on the television myself. Me!"

"You got through to the news man at KING TV?" Clarence asked.

"Not only did I get through to him, he talked with Bertha and then we called *The Seattle Times* and *The Tacoma News Tribune*. That was the news fella's idea. I think they're all sendin' folks out here tomorrow to get the story. And I'd be willing to bet everyone of you twenty bucks that it's Albert who's gonna end up lookin' like the bad guy in all this. He said they would do a news show about Bertha on Sunday night. Now how's that for new fangled contraptions like the telephone, Bertha? Huh? You gotta admit it . . . these electronic gadgets are terrific. Good magic!"

"Okay, okay, okay . . . rub it in a little deeper,

why don't cha? So they come in handy. Don't you forget that it is the Great Spirit who inspired somebody to invent them contraptions . . . and He belongs just as much to us as to them white eyes! What matters is that this news fella is gonna be here to see me in the mornin'. He said he is gonna try and talk with Albert Radford too," she said victoriously.

"This is really going to piss off the government people," Audrey exclaimed.

"Well, so what, Audrey! They've been pissin' me off for over three years now. It's their turn to stew in their juices for a while. That fella from KING TV is gonna come right to Saddles' house . . . he's gonna show him how to get to my place in the mornin'. I plan to show them my house and how clean I keep it. I'll talk about how healthy I am and about my traditions and the spirit of our people. And if that piss's off the government, I don't care. I hope it makes them look like the miserable land-stealers they are and makes them ashamed."

"I do hope you won't wave those scalps of Mother Sunfield's in his face. Those scalps belonged to white people you know," Audrey reminded her.

"I'm pissed, Audrey . . . not stupid!"

Suddenly, to everyone's surprise, we heard Grandmother Redwing's name announced on the late news.

Bertha Redwing, an elderly Indian woman living on the Quinault Reservation, is giving government officials a taste of Quinault tenacity. It seems Mrs. Redwing

432

doesn't want to move from her lifelong home in the old village to a new government house in the new village. The agent there has evidently threatened to have her declared insane and have her committed to a mental hospital and even threatened to send in state troopers to move her to the new house after which they plan to bulldoze her old home to the ground. We have been told by friends of Mrs. Redwing that she is sound as a dollar and as sane as the rest of us and simply wants to live out her years as close to the ways of her ancestors as possible. We'll report more on this story in tomorrow night's news, right here on KING TV, first in the Northwest.

"Well, I'll be damned. They sure didn't waste any time," Clarence noted with surprise.

"This is very good magic. This means that announcer man believed me and believed Saddles. And you said not to use the magic of the scalps, Audrey . . . what do you think now?"

"If they will keep you in your old home . . . then I say okay . . . but I still think you would be makin' a big mistake if you showed them to the news fella on TV."

"I ain't gonna show them - but I think it was their magic that got us to this point, and don't you forget it."

"What matters right now is that we're gonna see some changes. Public opinion has just gotta go in this old lady's direction," Saddles commented.

"It means something else too, Grandma," Randy said.

"And what is that, boy?"

"It means that you are now further out in the main stream that we are."

"I'm just usin' fire to fight fire, boy. When the smoke clears from all this . . . I'll go back to my old ways."

"No more movies?" Saddles asked.

"Well . . . I might walk up here once in a while to see another Topper movie," she conceded. "Ya know, Saddles, life ain't always a matter of this or that. Sometimes it's a matter of this AND that. We gotta find the balance. That's the meaning of the sacred circle. Blance."

"You don't need ta be tell'n me about the sacred circle. I may be a citified shaman but I got my finger on the pulse of the sacred circle and I don't need no advice from an old fool who shakes white men's scalps in the face of Indian agents."

§§§§

Audrey woke the boys and me early the next morning. "Saddle says there's already about ten different news people at his place and the KING Television people ain't even here yet. I thought you might wanna go with the rest of us down to Mother Redwing's to let her know what's going on," she informed us. We were up and dressed in seconds.

Clarence drove past Saddles' place just to see how many news cars had arrived. I counted five, but that number faded by comparison when we drove past the government agent's office on our way to the old village site. There were so many cars and reporters, the place looked like the parking lot at the Sears Building in Seattle. I'm not sure how Albert Radford was notified about all this . . . but we saw him standing on the steps in front of his office talking to the news people. One of them took a photograph of him as we passed by.

I could see smoke coming from the chimney of Grandmother Redwing's little house as we drove down the hill toward the old Indian village. She was up and fixing breakfast when we arrived. "I'm fixin' biscuits and gravy - anybody want some?" she asked.

"Clarence and I ate but the boys may be hungry. I left the girls up with Alice," Audrey answered.

"You should see all the news people gathering up in the new village," Willie told his grandmother.

"How many people I gotta talk to?" she asked.

"They were still comin' when we drove down here," Clarence answered.

"It looks like a lot of small town newspaper fellas came besides the big city guys," Randy interjected.

"When is Saddles gonna bring them down here?" the old woman asked.

"I suppose just as soon as the folks from KING Television arrive," Audrey responded.

"Well, help me get the boys served their breakfast so I can get this place cleaned up. I never

435

expected them to be here so early. My goodness, you'd think I was the Queen of England or something. I just thought there would be the fellow from TV and some guys from the *Times* and the *Tribune*."

We had just begun eating our biscuits and gravy when I looked out the front window and saw a large white van followed by a string of cars coming down the hill into the old village site. "I think they're on their way right now," I announced.

Grandmother Redwing walked to the window and looked out. "Gracious me, did you ever see so many cars? You'd think I was givin' away ten-dollar bills."

"You are. Advertising pays for the news time and the newsprint," Clarence said.

"I wonder how they all heard about it?" the old woman asked.

"They were probably watchin' TV last night just like the rest of us," Randy answered.

"How I'm gonna talk to so many people?"

"You'll hold a news conference," I advised her.

"What'cha mean?"

"We could put a chair on the porch for you and have all the reporters stand in front of the porch and ask you questions. I seen it in the Silver Tone News at the movies," I answered.

"Sounds like a good idea to me," she said.

"Well, I want you all to come out there with me. Clarence, you go out and tell them how we gonna do this, okay?"

"Sure, Ma," he answered. He took a slug of coffee and walked out on the porch followed by his brother, Bill. The boys and I huddled around the window, watching.

The white van had the words KING Television and a huge red crown painted on both sides of it. They stopped first. The rest of the cars parked alongside or behind it. Saddles got out of the van along with a man dressed in a business suit. They were followed by two other guys. One carried a large television camera and the other a stand to mount it on. Saddles introduced the newsman to Clarence and Bill. I couldn't stay my curiosity by watching out the window anymore, so I opened the door and walked out onto the small porch. "This here is Robert Benchworthy. He's the newscaster from the television," Saddles was saying. A crowd of other reporters began gathering at the foot of the steps behind Mr. Benchworthy.

"How do you do?" Clarence asked.

"I'm just fine, Mr. Redwing. I've come to speak to Mrs. Redwing," the reporter said.

"Evidently you and the rest of the world," Bill responded.

"Yes, evidently a lot of people heard our newscast last night. I was hoping to get an exclusive interview."

"Mother is a little nervous over the number of people here . . . "

Clarence was interrupted by a reporter who shouted: "Have you contacted the governor's office for help?"

"No, sir, we haven't. We didn't even think about doing that," Clarence answered.

"When can we see the old lady?" another

reporter yelled out.

"One question at a time, please," Clarence shouted. Then, looking at Mr. Benchworthy, he said: "I don't see how a private interview is possible, do you?"

"Maybe we could be allowed to take our camera inside the house to talk," he answered.

"That's a possibility. But Mother doesn't have any electricity for you to plug that stuff into," Bill told him.

"We've got a generator in the van . . . and some battery packs. We'll just have to hope we've enough power. But considering that . . . we'd better just do the interview out here. I don't have enough power with me to run lights and the camera," Mr. Benchworthy informed him.

"Could you speak up so the rest of us can hear!" a woman reporter shouted from the crowd.

"I was just tellin' this fella that we're gonna bring out a chair for my mother to sit on, and then you people can ask her questions. But please remember, my Mother is in her eighties and she's already under a lot of stress over this entire situation. She wasn't expecting so many of you this morning. I hope we can count on you to be ladies and gentlemen about all this," Clarence said, loud enough to be heard.

Would it be all right for us to set up our microphones before she comes out?" another reporter asked.

"Yes, I suppose so. I never thought about that either, but I'm sure that will be okay," Clarence answered.

438

Willie brought out one of the kitchen chairs to the porch for his grandmother. Mrs. Redwing remained in the house until the reporters had set up their microphones and the cameraman from the television station had set up his camera. Randy and I counted thirty-two people waiting for his grandmother to emerge from the house. Not all were reporters. They seemed to be in teams of one reporter and one photographer. Two reporters placed wire recorders on the porch. When everything was in place, Saddles went in the house and brought his old friend out onto the porch. Audrey and Randy followed but remained in the doorway. Grandmother Redwing walked to the chair, looked out over the crowd, returned smiles to those who gave them to her, and took her seat.

Everyone began asking questions at once.

"One at a time!" Saddles shouted. "You people raise your hands like in school, and I'll point to you when you can talk, okay." He pointed to the man from KING Television first.

"Mrs. Redwing, when I spoke with you on the telephone last night, you told me you have attempted to convince the local Indian agents for three years to allow you to remain living in your home here in the old village. Could you tell us about that?"

"Three years," she affirmed.

After a few moments of silence, the reporters asked her if she would elaborate and try to speak directly toward the battery of microphones in front of her.

"For three years I been tellin' them fools that I wanna live out my years right here where I grew up.

This is my home. I don't want no little white house up on the hill. I just wanna live down here with my garden and my memories. I don't need no flush toilets, no 'lectricity, no radio, no washin' machine . . . Quinault people been livin' without that stuff for thousands of years. That's how I wanna live. What's wrong with that?"

Saddles recognized a woman reporter.

"Mrs. Redwing, I'm Sarah Holmes from KOMO Radio. We spoke to the agent this morning by telephone. He tells us all the houses down here on the flats were condemned by the Department of Health and Sanitation and that he is only following orders. He says you must comply with those orders for your own health's sake. Can you respond to that?"

"My health is excellent. I'm in better shape than Saddles Seatco, and he's been livin' up in the new village for some time now. Quinault people know how to keep their lodges clean without vacuum cleaners, Ajax the foaming cleanser, and all that stuff. They just want me to live like Europeans live. I guess that's fine with the rest of the tribe, but it ain't fine with me. I wanna stay right here and live like I have always lived. I'm in good health. Hell, there weren't no Department of Health and Sanitation back in the old days and the Quinaults lived to be old people just like me. Who says my house is condemned? Somebody who ain't a Quinault, that's who. Maybe if I inspected his home, I'd find it unsuitable for habitation too . . . who knows. I wanna stay put."

"But wouldn't you be more comfortable without having to do all the extra work you have to do to remain down here. I mean . . . don't you have to lug water form the lake and chop your own wood . . . and what about electricity? Don't you want electricity?" the woman pressed.

"How's 'lectricity gonna help me weave a basket, or peel cattail roots, or do my bead work. I don't need no 'lectricity. I don't need nothin' like that. I'm fine just the way I am. Besides, I like hard work. That's how's-a-come I'm so healthy! I'll bet I can chop more wood that you can, young lady," she retorted. A wave of laughter passed through the crowd.

"I'll bet you can too," the woman agreed.

Saddles recognized another hand.

"Mrs. Redwing, my name is Garold Storm. I'm a reporter for the *Tacoma News Tribune* . . ."

"How do you do, Mr. Storm?" Grandmother Redwing interrupted.

"Very well, thank you, ma'am. I was wondering what you plan to do if the government actually sends state troopers down here to physically remove you from your home?"

"Well, I been givin' that a lot of thought too. Most folks here on the rez know what I would do. I can tell you this: I won't walk out of the house on my own two feet. They'll haveta carry me out. I even thought about tyin' myself to the old wood stove in the kitchen . . . but they'd just untie me. But I ain't never gonna leave by my own physical self. Maybe you can help me. Why don't you go talk to that Albert Radford and see if you can talk some sense into him?"

"I tried to speak with him on the telephone this morning but he refused an interview. He told me he has already said all he has to say on the subject."

"That's because he don't gotta move! He gets to do what he wants. Every one of you gets to do what you want. Freedom of choice. That's why you people moved away from Europe and chased us off our lands . . . so you could have freedom of choice. But I don't get no freedom of choice. You want to chase us out of everything. It is very arrogant of Albert Radford and the government to think that they know better than me how I should live. They think they know more about everything than we do. They even tried to stop our shaman, Saddles Seatco, from doin' his magic and healin' people. For a long time they said they would arrest old Saddles if he continued to practice his medicine and his magic. Can you imagine that? Arrest him! Well, the people kept sneekin' over to him anyway. What was they to do? Them damn agents didn't know nothin' about gettin' a kid ready for a vision quest and they certainly didn't know nothin' about how to talk to the spirits. Saddles went right ahead and did it in secret. Can you imagine that? We had to live in secret right on our own rez. We even had missionaries come into our homes and tell us Saddles was doing the work of some devil creature they believe in. And the doctors would have a fit if they thought he was usin' herbs and stuff from the woods to heal people. Like he didn't know how to heal people just as good as they did. That was arrogant and stupid! You want us to respect you and your traditions . . . but you don't wanna respect ours. What's wrong with an old lady livin' out her life like she has always lived. Do you see anything wrong in that? I'm healthy. Saddles is healthy. The people he fixed up is healthy . . . and the children who went on vision quests are all fine upstanding citizens of the tribe. Do you see anything wrong with that at all?

"No, ma'am, I don't . . . and I wish you well," Mr. Storm sympathized.

Saddles recognized another hand.

"Mrs. Redwing, I'm Mike Marshal from the *Seattle Post Intelligencer.* Would you mind telling us the history of how all this came about?"

"I don't mind at all, young man. But I wonder if someone would get me a cup of tea or something. My throat is dry as an old buffalo hide from all this talkin' . . . and I'm a little bit nervous. Any of you people need something to drink?"

"Most of us brought thermoses of coffee, ma'am. We're all used to this sort of thing," Marshal answered.

"Then how 'bout somebody brings me a cup of coffee," the old woman instructed. Another wave a gentle laughter filled the crowd as Sarah Holmes brought a thermos cup filled with coffee up to the porch. Grandmother Redwing took a sip. "That nice and hot, thank you, dear" she said, smiling.

"You're welcome, ma'am," Holmes answered.

"The history of how I come to be talkin' with you people is very long and very old. I cannot tell you all of it, we'd be here until you were an old lady like me," she gestured at Sara Holmes . . . but many moons ago . . . many years ago . . . for thousands of years the fine lodges of my people covered these flats. We lived in them and raised our children for more years than there's been a Europe. I was born into such a lodge. My parents and brothers and sisters and some of my mother's people lived in the lodge with us. It was a big lodge. They were all big in those days. Not like these little smoke shacks we've converted into houses. Each one of our lodges had many carvings on the outside walls around the front door and they was always painted up real fancy. Oh, they were a sight to see . . . and there were great totem poles in front of each lodge. You could tell the whole history of the clan that lived in that lodge just by seein' who the animals on their totems were. I'll tell ya it was really somethin' to see. Each lodge was so big that many families lived comfortably in just one. We had lofts in them for sleepin', and private places for people. But we almost always came together for our meals. All the women pitched in. Each night was a feast in those days. Sometimes a family would eat alone at their private hearth but mostly we all ate together around the big hearth that belongs to everybody. In the summer the women always cooked outside, unless it was rainin'. The young men would go out huntin' or fishin' or diggin' for clams. The woman picked greens and nuts and roots and berries from the woods and us kids used to play all over the place. We had plenty of old ones to watch after us when we was kids. Many of them were good storytellers. Life was good in them days. And they was good right up until I got my husband and we lived in my mother's lodge. I think I was fourteen or fifteen. I forget. It was a long time ago. Then, one day, without any notice or explanation, the white eyes came down to these flats and set fire to almost everything. We had a bunch of little smokehouses down here closer to the lake. For some reason, they didn't burn any of them. .   I watched in terror as Europeans burned our lodges to the ground and forced some of our people to move into the first houses built up on the hill. They sent off many of the children to schools run by white people. The kids even had to live there until the summer months when they were allowed to come back to the rez for a while. Many people ran away into the woods. Some went up to the Makah and lived with them. A good many made their way up through the mountains into Nootka territory. Lotta Nootka still lived in the old ways back in them days. My husband and I hadn't been married very long when all this happened. We was still livin' in my mother's lodge but we was fixin' to build our own lodge. Then, when they burned down the big lodges . . . a lot of us fixed up the smoke shacks down here to live in. This is the one my husband and I fixed up. He built that little lean-to out back all by himself. This porch too. When we first seen them buildin' the first few houses up on the hill, we thought they was buildin' them for themselves . . . you know . . . homes for the government agents. But they was for Indians. Most people refused to go. Lots more ran off into the woods. My husband and I just plain refused to move. Lots of us did. The rest moved into the new houses. Then . . . every so many years, they built a few more up there. Each time they did . . . more and more people left their little shacks down here on the flats until finally there were only about twenty people livin' down here."

"That must have been very difficult for you,"

one of the reporters interrupted.

"Well, of course, it was difficult for me   But I got used to it.   Now I'm the only one left.   I like it down here. This is my home and I ain't movin'."

"But, Mrs. Redwing, the government says that by June 15th, if you're not out of here, they're going to move you physically up to your new house. Some of us have talked to Mr. Radford. He says it will happen. How do you feel about that?" Sarah Holmes persisted.

"I just told you how I feel about that. I'm an old woman. In a few short years I will be gone. But until then, I want to live as close to the ways of my people as possible. I don't want to live in a house on the hill. I want to remain here. Your government claims to stand for freedom.   Where, I ask, is freedom for Bertha Redwing?"

Chapter Thirteen

Testing the Spirits

After Grandmother Redwing's press conference, the television people did some filming inside her house. The news anchor from KING TV sat at the table and had tea with us while he and the old Quinault woman exchanged stories about their children. He agreed that he would much rather raise his in a small community like the village instead of in Seattle. "I'm a small town boy myself - raised close to nature. I have great sympathy for your cause, but I must report both sides of the story honestly and completely. You do understand that, don't you?" he asked.

"It was the same in the old days. If there was a problem, the tribal elders would listen to both sides of the story . . . sometimes even a third and fourth side. Only then did they make their decision. I understand and appreciate that in the magic of television where the great chief arrives first to each home in the test pattern, you will do the same. It is good." she answered.

Before long the crowd of reporters and technicians piled back into their vehicles and disappeared up the hill toward the new village and back to their cities and towns. By early afternoon several radio stations were carrying the story and that evening the *Seattle Times*, *The Post Intelligencer*, and the *Tacoma News Tribune* told her story in broad bold headlines with photographs of Grandmother Redwing and her small cedar shack down on the flats.

That night we, along with several friends of the Redwing family, gathered at Saddles Seatco's house to watch the six o'clock news on television. The report began with an overview of the situation along with a few pictures taken inside and outside of Grandmother Redwing's little house on the flats, as well as shots of the little white house in the new village. To our surprise, Robert Benchworthy announced that he had gotten a call through to the Governor of the state who claimed to be unaware of Grandmother Redwing's situation but promised to look into it.

When she first saw the black and white images of herself sitting on her porch answering the questions of the reporters, she gasped. "My goodness, but I look old on TV. Do I look that old in person," she asked, looking around at everyone.

"Wait until after you're finished talkin' on TV before you talk now . . . we wanna hear you on the news," Saddles shushed.

"Humph!" she grunted.

Our second surprise came when the face of Albert Radford flashed onto the screen.

"What's he doin' on there?" the old woman snapped.

"He's sayin' somethin' about them bringin' a psychologist out here to test you for bein' crazy. Now hush, so we can hear!" Saddles snapped back in a stage whisper.

We sat in shock and dismay as we listened to the young agent inform the news audience that a Dr. Lamb, a leading psychologist from the university, had been called in by the government to test Grandmother Redwing's mental capabilities. When Robert Benchworthy asked Albert Radford why he and the government felt a psychological evaluation was necessary, our hearts were further saddened by his description of the wonderful, spirited old woman at whose feet I sat and listened. "We are talking about a woman who defecates in the woods. She uses lake water to cook with and does her wash in the same place she gathers water for drinking. Her house is a firetrap and a sanitation nightmare! She refuses to speak with government officials when they drive in from Olympia and shakes some scalps or wigs at them through her window and cusses at them in Quinault when they knock on her door."

"I wasn't cussin' at them people, I was reciting chants and prayers . . . he don't know what he's talkin' 'bout!" Grandmother Redwing hissed.

"Shh . . . we can't hear what he's saying when you talk," Clarence admonished.

"His mother's face flashed back on the screen, then a few pictures of the inside of her home with her voice in the background saying: "In a few short years I will be gone. But until then, I wanna live as close to the ways of my people as possible. I don't want to live in a house up on the hill. I'm okay right where I am. Your government claims to stand for freedom. Where, I ask, is freedom for Bertha Redwing?"

Then the screen returned to the face of Robert Benchworthy. "There you have it, ladies and gentlemen. An old Indian woman wants to live out her years in her little converted smokehouse down on the flats of the Quinault Reservation, and it seems the government not only doesn't want her to remain there but also thinks she may not be mentally competent to make that decision for herself. A psychologist is being called in to determine her mental status, and the governor is looking into the matter. Check back with us tomorrow during the six o'clock news when we look further into this story. We hope you'll also listen to our news after the movie tonight. Until then, this is Robert Benchworthy saying . . . goodnight and good listening here on KING Television - first in the Northwest."

The screen flipped several times then returned to its test pattern.

"Who does that Albert Radford think he is sending a psychologist in here. Doesn't the family have any rights in this matter?" Clarence asked.

"Maybe the governor can set the matter straight," Audrey suggested.

"The governor is the government," Saddles retorted. "I wouldn't trust him as far as I can throw him."

"I think I should talk to this psychologist fella. I ain't nuts. If he's a real psychologist, he'll figure that out in no time. I ain't afraid of talkin' to the man," Grandmother Redwing announced.

"Ya know, I was just thinkin'. This is an election year. I think the governor will either back away from this whole thing or step in and use this moment to show the voters he is for the underdog. Maybe we should try to talk to him ourselves," Saddles suggested.

"How many Indians do you know who vote? I'll

bet you and Clarence haven't even registered yet," Audrey quipped.

"There you go make'n sense again," Grandmother Redwing quipped back.

"She's got a point. Governors play up to voters . . . I'll bet there aren't four people registered to vote on the whole reservation," Saddles agreed.

Grandmother Redwing got up from the couch and walked over to the closet in which Saddles had put her wrap. "I don't wanna speak with no governor. I first gotta think about talkin' with this other fella."

"Maybe the governor can keep him from coming," Willie suggested.

"I doubt that. He might be able to keep them from moving her up the hill but the psychologist will be seen as a necessary part of this whole thing," Audrey said.

"And what if he finds her incompetent?" Randy asked.

"I ain't incompetent!"

"We know that . . . but can't you see how white folks will see this? You're runnin' around shaking scalps in people's faces and refusing a free house. White folks is bound to see that as nuts! You gotta knock all that stuff off and prove to that Dr. Lamb fella that you're a competent adult, and that your actions and decision to remain in your little house is the result of good clear thinking. Whether you like it or not, you gotta play the game by their rules," Saddles asserted.

"Why we all the time gotta play by their rules?" Grandmother Redwing pouted as she slipped her wrap

451

around her shoulders.

"Because it's their game and in the government's eyes, you're just a cantankerous old lady who might be crazy trying to cause trouble. You're in a bit of a pickle right now. Don't take any scalps or sacred bones or anything with you to that interview that makes you appear different or deviant," Audrey admonished.

"So, I'm in a pickle?"

"You're in a pickle, Bertha. For all we know, this psychologist works for the government. He is coming from the university and it's run by the state. Who knows what's goin' on behind the scenes right now. You gotta out white-eyes this guy when he gets here.," Saddles agreed.

§§§§

At school the following Tuesday I learned that Dr. Lamb would visit the Quinault Reservation the following Saturday to conduct his evaluation of Grandmother Redwing.

"I guess he wanted her to meet him at the agent's office about ten that morning, but she said he had to come to her house. Mom said that Aunt Alice called Dr. Lamb at his office and told him what Grandma said, and he agreed, but the agent gets to sit out on the front porch to make sure nothin' happens to Dr. Lamb," Willie told me.

"Like he expects her to scalp him or something?" I suggested.

"I guess he doesn't know what to expect.

452

Anyway, we're goin' up Friday night so we can be there to give Grandma support. You wanna come?" Randy inquired.

"I'll ask. That would be two weekends in a row. My dad may have chores for me to do. And we're gettin' real close to school bein' out for the summer. Tests are comin' up."

"Are you doin' okay in all your classes?" Willie asked.

"Oh, yeah . . I'm doing fine."

"Then beg to come. This is gonna be real interesting," Randy pointed out.

At first Mother said I shouldn't go and Dad went along with her decision. But later that evening while she was preparing dinner, Mom heard Grandmother Redwing's story over the radio and the confirmation that the psychologist from the university would be evaluating her the following Saturday. She relented and I was allowed to accompany the Redwings back to the Quinault Reservation.

Dad was as surprised as I was by her change of heart. "I thought you were against the idea," he said.

"I was. But this is history actually happening. It's gotta be more interesting than reading history from a book. I think that as long as he is already involved in the story, he should go."

The morning of the psychologist's visit, we drove down to the little house on the flats. Gramdmother Redwing was just putting some cornmeal muffins in her oven. "Whatchu all doin' down here?" she asked.

"We wanted to be with you when the

psychologist got here," Alice answered.

"We wanna be supportive, Grandma," Willie echoed.

"Well, you can't be in here . . . Albert came down and told me that just this Dr. Lamb fella and me can be here during our talk."

"We figured that. We'll wait outside until you're finished. We wanna be here just in case," Audrey replied.

"Besides, we'll want to know exactly what went on and what this psychologist fella thinks right away," Clarence said, kissing his mother on the cheek.

"Well, I ain't got nothin' to serve you. I'm makin' these muffins to serve Dr. Lamb when he gets here."

"We already ate. Fritz brought up some Polish sausage for us," Bill explained.

"Did you bring me some too?"

"You bet I did, Grandmother. Grandma and Grandpa Harding sent a whole one just for you. I forgot to bring it over to Saddle's house last night," I said, handing her a small package wrapped in butcher paper and tied with a string.

"Go put it in the screened cooler out in the lean-to for me. I gotta get this place cleaned up before that fella from the university gets here."

"The place looks fine, Mother. Just relax," Clarence suggested.

"Well, it's a good thing. Looks like that's him comin' down the hill in that blue car behind Albert's pickup," Audrey said, looking out the window.

"Well. Let's go outside and greet my guest. You

454

guys can sit out there on the porch if you wanna. But I ain't got no idea how long this is gonna take. If he's got half a brain in his head, he'll figure out right away that I'm as fit as a fiddle."

I placed the package of sausage in the old woman's cooler and stepped back into the kitchen. She was out on the porch with the rest of her family, waiting for Dr. Lamb's car to pull up. I'm not sure what made me do what I did next, but I saw the fresh tablecloth she had placed on her table and recalled the time I hid under my grandparents' table to eavesdrop on a family meeting. Without giving it a second thought, I slipped under the table and drew myself up as small as possible so I couldn't be seen.

It seemed like an eternity before the old woman reentered her home. I lowered my head to the floor in order to see. Out on the porch Dr. Lamb was being introduced to everyone. When the elder Mrs. Redwing turned and led the man into the house, I sat bolt upright for fear of being seen.

"It's very kind of you to see me, Mrs. Redwing," the man said.

"I ain't had no choice in this, so it ain't really kind of me. But to show you I can be a good host, even when held hostage in my own home, I put some water on for tea. You can sit there at the table if you wanna."

"Tea won't really be necessary," the man responded.

"It would be bad manners of me not to offer you tea, and even worse on your part if you refused it," Grandmother Redwing instructed. "It is the way of the Quinault. Strangers are always offered tea. You afraid I'm gonna poison ya?"

"Not at all. I'll take mine with sugar."

"Will wild honey do?"

"Even better. May I put my papers and things here on the table?"

"Make yourself comfortable, young man. I'll get the tea."

I listened as the man snapped open his briefcase and rustled a few papers. After a few seconds he closed his briefcase and set it down on the floor beside him. "How long have you lived here?" he asked.

"Since they burned down the lodges where my people used to live," she answered.

"How many years ago was that?"

"Oh, my . . . long time ago . . . It wasn't yet the 1900's. I don't remember exactly. I didn't use white man's way of counting years in them days . . . so I can't tell you exactly. Maybe 1897. I'm eighty-three now. I was just married a short time when all that happened. It could have been much earlier than 1897. I was about sixteen." I could hear her place their cups on the table.

"I understand this little house used to be a smokehouse," the man remarked.

"Yes. There were about twenty good smokehouses down here before the lodges were burned down. Just about every lodge had one. We kept them down here so the smoke wouldn't get in our lodges. We was always smokin' fish and game in them days. I still like smoked bear better than fresh fried. Me and my husband fixed this place up for a house. There was Indians in each of the old smokehouses back in them

456

days. I raised all my kids here. I think they all turned out pretty good. Everybody who moved in down here raised their kids from these houses. But the kids - they all wanted houses up on the hill with separate bedrooms and stuff. They weren't used to livin' in lodges with all their kin. So, one by one, all the old people died off or moved up to the new village to be closer to their kids, 'specially since them brand new houses was built. Of course, some of the folks from the first houses they put up on the hill moved into them new ones too. Lots of families have even moved off the reservation. My own son now owns a dry cleaning place in Perkins Prairie. Times change."

"Yes, I understand that all those older houses are being brought up to code so that future families can move back into them," the man commented.

"Yeah, I guess so. It's beginnin' to look like a small city here, ain't it. It sure don't much look like a village no more. Anyways, down here . . . well, finally it was just Redhawk, Saddles and me livin' in these houses. Redhawk fell and broke his hip . . . so he moved up with his daughter and her husband though he wasn't too happy about it. Neither was they. They're gettin' old now too, and Redhawk is pretty set in his ways. But it is as it should be. In the old days the young always took care of the old. Then it was just Saddles and me. Saddles moved up as soon as those first new houses was ready. He lived in San Francisco when he was a young man. He got real used to livin' like white people. But he stayed down here a long time. He's got arthritis, ya know. Claims he needs better heating these days. Now I'm the only one left who wants to live in the old ways."

"How come your friend, Saddles, moved back to the reservation from San Francisco?"

"His papa got sick. His ma and pa lived in that other old smokehouse you seen when you drove down here. Saddles lived in it after they died until he moved up the hill. I guess they'll be burnin' or bulldozing it to the ground someday soon too. Anyway, Saddles' mother was dead by the time his papa got sick. His papa was shaman to this tribe for many years like his papa before him. Long line of shamans in that clan goin' way back to the days when our people lived much farther north. So . . . Saddles' papa taught him about herbs and plants and magic and he became the new shaman. He never did move back to San Francisco, but he use'ta go down there on visits in the old days. All his friends died off. He stopped goin' down there then. He's outlived them all, ya know. Which tells ya something about life on the rez compared to life in a big city." I could hear her pour hot water in the gentleman's cup.

"How do you feel about them burning or bulldozing these old houses down?"

"Makes me wanna cry. And it makes me mad. That's out history. Let the earth take them back naturally. That's what I say. Oh, let that tea seep a bit before you taste it. I got some muffins in the oven. I'll get them out now. They should be finished. Then we can get down to business."

"So, your friend Saddles could have moved up to the new houses earlier if he had wanted too?"

"Not really. At first you had to be married to get

one of them houses or move in with some relatives that lived in one. Saddles didn't have no relatives and it was damn sure he wasn't gonna get married, at least not in the traditional way . . . so he just stayed on down here. Then they changed the rules. I think they only changed them rules so they could try to force me into movin'. They've been tryin' to push one off on me for years now. Well, I guess you know that." I heard her place the tray of muffins on the table before sitting down. "We can have some of these once they cool a little. She sat now, I'm ready to prove to you I ain't nuts."

"I never said I thought you were nuts. That's what the agent said. So . . . is that how you see all this . . . as the government trying to push off one of those new houses on you?"

"There's a lot more to it than that, young man. You wanna try some of my salmonberry jam on these muffins? A friend of mine sends it up to me with my daughter-in-law."

"I'd be delighted, Mrs. Redwing. I've never had salmonberry jam before."

"You can call me Bertha if you want to," the old woman said, getting up and bringing a jar of the jam to the table and a couple of plates.

"And you may call me Robert if you like."

"Robert Lamb. That's a good soundin' name. It's always good to be named after an animal. Our names come from the red-winged blackbird. The red-winged blackbird is a very powerful symbol in Quinault ways."

"Is a lamb an Indian symbol for anything?" the

psychologist asked.

"We didn't have no lambs. We didn't raise animals like the Indians in the south did. We hunted. So we ain't got no stories about lambs. We got some about fawns but none about lambs. Still, it don't hurt none to be named after animal. You're supposed to inherit the animal's spirit when you're named after one. Are you gentle as a lamb, Dr. Lamb?"

"The lamb is actually a pretty powerful symbol in the ways of my people," he told her.

"Yeah? How?"

"My wife and I are Episcopalians. For us, Jesus was the Lamb of God . . . so the lamb is a very powerful symbol to us."

"Oh, I know plenty about Jesus."

"I don't know much about the red-winged blackbird. Perhaps you could instruct me."

"Muffins first. Oh, I forgot to bring some butter. I'll bet you like butter on your muffins."

"I do. Let me get it for you. Where do you keep it?"

"In the pantry out in the lean-to. It's in a screened box out there so the flies can't get to it.

"I'd be delighted," Lamb said, scooting his chair back. I listened as he walked through the kitchen door out into the lean-to. Grandmother Redwing got up and brought something back to the table.

"Here it is. Your pantry seems very well stocked," Lamb said, bringing the butter dish to the table.

I don't like to go to the store very often. I usually just get stuff like flour and salt and coffee.

460

Sometimes I get pepper. But I don't much like white sugar. Most of the stuff out there comes from the woods."

"I noticed. Why don't you tell me about the red-winged blackbird?"

"Okay. It begins many years ago when there was no Salishan people livin' in these parts. Our ancestors lived way up North. They was snow people. But it was a hard life. No berries grew in the snow and they hadda build their lodges out of ice. One day the father and mother of all the Salishans led a group of people to look for berries. They had a small son who was born sickly. Their shaman told them the only thing that would make him strong was if he ate berries with every meal. It didn't matter if they was fresh or dried . . . as long as they was berries. So the father and mother of all the Salishans and their little group walked and walked and searched and searched . . . "

"How did their sickly son travel with them?" Dr. Lamb interrupted.

"They lugged two poles behind them. All their belongings lashed to them poles and a reindeer hide was used as a sort of big sack. The boy rode on top of that. Anyway, they walked and walked until the world was too dark for them to see anything. Suddenly a red-winged blackbird come to the father and mother and screamed at them for comin' into his territory. He asked them what they was doin' in the dark. The father told the red-winged blackbird that they was lookin' for berries 'cause there was none up in the snow country. He explained that his little son hadda have some to get well and grow strong. The red-winged blackbird called

461

all his brothers and sisters together and flocked into the sky above the travelers. Their red feathers caught the beams of the moon and filled the night sky with lights. The father and mother of the Salishans could see well enough to keep walkin'. They walked until they came to this place right here at Quinault Lake. There was berries everywhere. All kinds. Blackberries, huckleberries, salmonberries, wild strawberries . . . every kinda berry you can think of. They're still here. This is the best place in the world to pick berries. And they picked plenty. And at every meal the boy ate, there was berries. The boy got well and grew strong and one day became the leader of his people. The mother and father of all the Salishans were so grateful when they saw the boy getting better and better, they prepared a huge feast and invited all the red-winged blackbirds to join them. The blackbirds were so touched by the generosity of my ancestors, they promised to bring the sacred lights to the sky every year . . . and my ancestors were so grateful for the health of their son, they gave up snow names and took the name of the red-winged blackbirds. And now, I am the last Redwing livin' on these flats. It all happened right here. I worry every year that the spirits of the ancestors of that original red-winged blackbird will be offended by what the government has done to my people and that the lights won't come some year."

"That's a very good story. I think I like it almost better than mine," Dr. Lamb observed.

"We got a rich tradition here. I hate to see it all end. Did ya know that most of them berries used to grow up where that new village is. They built them

462

houses right on top of the best berry patches. There's still a lot around - but you gotta look hard for them. It's a good thing not everybody likes to eat them berries these days 'cause there ain't enough to go around anymore. And if you ask me, Dr. Lamb . . . I think that explains why our people are beginnin' to look so sickly. They're not eatin' berries with every meal anymore - only me. The rest of them is eatin' chocolate cakes and ice cream and sugar frosted donuts."

"You might be right. Bertha, I have to ask you about those scalps you shook in the faces of the government people and your refusal to discuss moving to the new village with them each time they have tried to talk with you about this."

"My kids say I shouldn't of used the scalps in that way. I got bawled out plenty by everybody about it. They might be right. But them scalps is to me like a crucifix is to a nun."

"You mean they're sacred?"

"Why sure. Both them scalps and the crucifix represent the sacrifice of human life for a cause. They ain't even my scalps. They belong to my son's mother-in-law. She loaned them to me for good luck. I used them wrong and brought myself some bad luck. But I was mad."

Perhaps if you had made them tea and talked to them the way we're talking things would have gone better for all of you," Dr. Lamb suggested.

"I talked to them until I got blue in the face. I said everything I got to say. I mean, how many times do I gotta say no before they understand that I mean no. And who knows? Maybe if I go live up on the hill, the northern lights will go out forever. You want another muffin?"

"Don't mind if I do . . . they're very good muffins."

"I put some ground camas root in the batter. It makes them sweeter and gives them a nutty taste."

"Camas root?"

"It's a plant. It grows all over these parts. It's in the lily family. It's got blue flowers. They grow all over in the lowlands and meadows. The bulbs use'ta be a staple food of my people before you guys brought us pasta. The word camas means sweet fruit . . . but it's more like a potato but not as big. I gather them whenever I can. I like to make flour out of them and add it to my cornmeal muffins. We grow some potatoes too. We got starts from some people in the south who came tradin' stuff. But I always like the camas better."

"I must be honest with you, Bertha . . . I don't think there is anything you can do to stop the government from moving you up to the new village. What will you do if that happens?"

"I don't really know. I ain't gonna kill myself, if that's what you're wonderin' about. I got a lotta life left in these old bones. But I sure don't wanna leave my home. Is that why you're here - to try and talk me into movin'?"

"No, ma'am, I'm here to see if you're mentally competent enough to live on your own."

"Well, what'cha think?"

"I think you're quite sane. I doubt seriously if you have any sort of dementia. Your memory seems

464

especially good, and I think your reasons for wanting to stay in this little house are fairly well justified . . . perhaps even legitimate. But I do have a few more questions I must ask you."

"Let me warm up our tea . . . then you can fire away."

The old woman went back to the stove, brought the hot water kettle to the table and poured additional water into the teapot. "I can usually get two good pots from one batch of dried greens," she said proudly.

"Bertha, don't you think you would have an easier time of it in the new house? You'd be up there closer to your family in case of an emergency, you wouldn't have to burn wood to keep warm, and you'd have running water and would no longer have to carry buckets in from the lake."

"I don't need no easy way. I like things the way they are. It keeps me healthy."

""The government's position is that this house is not sanitary . . . it doesn't come up to present codes."

"Do you feel like you're eatin' in a pig pen?"

"No ma'am, I don't. You keep your place very tidy."

"Did you see me on the TV the other night?"

"Yes, my wife and I watched."

"Did I sound nuts to you?"

"No, Bertha, you did not sound nuts. In fact, both my wife and I were very impressed with your speech."

"Then what'chu gonna tell them government people out there?"

"I'm going to tell them I believe you are

competent but I don't think that will affect their plans to move you to the new house. Sometimes you just can't fight city hall. Ya know what I mean?"

"I ain't done fightin' yet."

"How many days before your deadline is up?"

"They say if I ain't outta here by the 15th of next month, they gonna come down here and move me out."

"I'll speak to them on your behalf if you like, but I don't think it will do any good."

"That would be nice of you, Robert. Who knows, it might help. The truth is what holds up the sky, ya know. But let me tell you this, Robert Lamb; they gonna have'ta carry me out of here! I ain't walkin' out of my own free will. They gonna have to carry me. I seen a vision. In the vision I got three yellow finches. That means I'm gonna overcome an evil spirit. You watch and see . . . I got me twenty-one days left to fight . . . and I'm gonna fight."

"I wish you well, Bertha. It was certainly a pleasure making your acquaintance. I hope you win."

"Well, there's some press people out there, and Albert's been pacin' back and forth. I can hear his boots out on the porch. It was a pleasure meetin' you too. You're a nice young fella. You help hold up the sky, I think. You do what you gotta do and I'll do what I gotta do."

"I will. And I will tell my wife to see if she can find some camas flour to put in her cornbread the next time she makes muffins. They were very good."

"You wanna take the rest home with you? If your wife tastes them, she'll know how much camas to use. Tell her only wild honey . . . no white sugar."

"You wouldn't mind?"

"I baked them for you," she said. Suddenly she lifted up the tablecloth. "Talks With Eagles, you get out from under there and go into the lean-to and get me one of them little brown paper bags over by the pickle barrel, so I can send the rest of these muffins home with Dr. Lamb," she ordered.

I crawled out from under the table, surprised that she knew I had been there all along. "Yes, Grandmother," Said, scrambling to my feet.

"This here is Talks With Eagles," the old woman said.

"He doesn't look very Indian. He looks like a white boy," Dr. Lamb observed.

"He's part Micmac and part too nosy for his own good."

"How do you do, Dr. Lamb," I blushed. "How long have you known I was under there?" I asked.

"I saw you when I walked back in the house. I figured if you was that curious, I'd just let you stay and listen."

"I'm just fine, young man."

"Now, you go get me that paper sack and make yourself useful before I decide to get me a switch," she commanded again.

I darted into the lean-to and brought back the sack as instructed and handed it to her.

"Now you go on outside with everybody else. I got a few things to say to Dr. Lamb in private."

When I stepped out onto the porch, Willie ran over to me. "There you are. Were you in there all the time?" he asked.

"I hid under the table."

"What did ya find out?' Clarence inquired.

"I found out she knew I was there all the time."

"You must of learned more than that," Audry insisted.

"I learned all about the legend of the Redwing clan and the Quanult story for the northern lights. It's really a cool story."

"I mean what did you find out about the doctor's opinion of Ma," Clarence quipped.

"Dr. Lamb doesn't think Grandmother Redwing is nuts. He's taking some of her muffins home to his wife."

"He's what?" Albert Radford asked.

Before I could repeat what I had said, the old Indian woman and the psychologist from the University of Washington stepped out onto the porch and joined us.

"Dr. Lamb, how did things go?" Albert asked.

"Things went very well, Mr. Radford."

"I'm glad to hear that," Radford smiled.

"Mrs. Redwing is as sane as I am and her memory is sharp as a tack. I'm afraid you'll have to force this woman out of her home without my help," Dr. Lamb informed him.

Suddenly there was a scurry of press people walking up to the porch asking all sorts of questions.

"When did they get here?" I asked Randy.

"They started driving up while you were in the house. How come Grandma let you stay and made the rest of us wait outside?"

"I hid under the table. I didn't think she knew I was there, but I guess she knew all the time."

"Well, later you gotta tell us what happened . . . in full," Clarence insisted.

"I've got the feelin' your mother will be able to do that without much assistance from me," I answered. My admiration for his mother's intellect and skill at conversation had gone up another notch or two. It looked to me like she might win the battle after all.

§§§§

That evening after dinner, we all gathered again at Saddles' to watch the six o'clock news. Even though the cameraman for Channel Five News wasn't among the reporters that day, they had sent a representative. To our surprise, the cameraman and Robert Benchworthy had visited the governor's office. After reporting Dr. Lamb's findings, parts of an interview with Governor William J. Debore were flashed across the little eight-inch screen of Saddles Seatco's Philco television set. The governor's words were introduced by Benchworthy asking him if he planned to intervene for Mrs. Redwing now that Dr. Lamb had found her to be sane and capable of living on her own.

"No, Mr. Benchworthy, I am not going to intervene. Being sane is not what is at question here. The fact that Mrs. Redwing is sane in no way removes her responsibility to comply with the law. This is 1950. Civilized societies must insist for the sake of the general health of all its citizens that every home in every community have proper sanitation methods around it. Mrs. Redwing's home was condemned over three years ago. A very nice house in the upper village that meets all legal codes has been built for her at absolutely no cost to her. I will not intervene in this matter. The Department of Indian Affairs is a federal office, not a state office. I have no real jurisdiction in this matter anyway."

"Well, there you have it, ladies and gentlemen. Governor Debore will not intervene in this matter. Stay tuned to KING Television as we approach the day Mrs. Redwing must actually move to her new home. We'll keep you posted. In other news . . ."

Saddles reached over and turned down the volume. "I can't believe that. I thought after the psychologist fella was here, things would change," he sighed.

"The governor could do something if he wanted to. He's just sluffing it off on the federal government so he's off the hook," Bill noted.

"I'm afraid you're right," Audrey agreed.

Grandmother Redwing took a handkerchief from her apron pocket and dabbed her eyes with it.

"Mother Redwing, you're crying," Alice noted sympathetically. She walked to her mother-in-law and put her arms around her.

"I guess I thought gettin' my story on the TV would make a difference. I thought it was good magic.

I guess there ain't any magic powerful enough to overcome these guys," the old woman whispered through her tears.

"Well, it ain't the 15th of June yet!" Saddles declared. I'm gonna try some more magic. Maybe I should go up to the cave myself and see what's goin' on."

"You're too old to go up to that cave anymore. You got worse arthritis than me. No, Saddles, the time for magic is over. Now we just gotta be brave and wait," Grandmother Redwing said emphatically.

"Mother Redwing, now that you know it's inevitable, won't you please just let us move you up to the new house without any fuss? What good will it do to wait for the state troopers to come in and force you out of the house? It's going to upset the whole village. What if some of the young men decide to fight them off? Someone could get hurt," Audrey said.

"Oh, Audrey, don't you see? If I move outta my place willingly . . . then it looks like I gave in. I'm not givin' in. I'm gonna force them to send them big strappin' boys down here to move one old willowy Indian lady from her house . . . 'cause that's what it's gonna take. They're gonna have to treat me like I was Geronimo. I ain't gonna cooperate with them!"

"They shot Geronimo, Grandma," Randy noted.

"Sometimes I think I'd be better of if they did shoot me than have to live up here in these new houses."

"But you come up here all the time for dinner and parties. And you've come to visit Saddles many times since he moved. You're up here all the time," Bill interjected.

"Just because I love my family and friends don't mean I'm gonna give up the ways of my ancestors. You all did what you hadda do . . . and I ain't turned my back on one of ya . . . I'm still just as much your friend or mother or grandmother or mother-in-law as I was before all these changes began. I have respected your choices. I think you should respect mine."

"I just hate it when you make so much sense, Ma," Bill admitted.

"I gotta go up to that cave . . . maybe the boys could take me up in that little red wagon they got you up there in," Saddles insisted.

"You just stop that foolishness, old man. There is no more magic. Besides . . . it's time you started teachin' somebody new to be the man with two souls around here. You should be puttin' your efforts into teachin' the old ways to somebody new or it's all gonna die when you die. What's gonna happen to the Quinault people if nobody even knows our sacred history and our medicines and our ways. What's gonna happen to future generations if nobody knows about the spirits that live near the cave? What's gonna happen if nobody knows how to heal the sick. It's a damn sure thing you can't write worth nothin' . . . if you can't write it down in a book, you gotta find somebody and start teachin' them. We're gonna need a new shaman when you go . . . and you ain't even got no prospects," Grandmother Redwing said, spreading her handkerchief across her knees and lap.

"That's not true, Bertha . . . I do have a new prospect, and I been already teachin' him stuff. I ain't said nothin' 'cause he don't want nobody to know yet, but I think we got us a new candidate for a man with two souls," Saddles retorted.

I noticed Randy squirm in his chair.

"And who would that be?" his old friend asked.

"I promised I wouldn't let that cat out of the bag until he was ready . . . until he was sure," Saddles answered.

"It's okay, Saddles, you can tell them," Randy whispered. He was looking down at the floor.

"You sure, boy?" Saddles asked.

"Randy looked around the room at each of us, then shook his head in the affirmative.

"Your grandson, Randy; he's gonna be our new shaman. He's been comin' around when nobody was lookin' and we been talkin' about these things. I already been teachin' him about herbs and stuff. And both you and Grandma Sunfield have already taught him lots about what's out in the woods. He's a fast learner. I just been waitin' 'til all this movin' stuff blew over before I approached his mama and papa and the village chief about the subject," Saddles told her.

"Randy?" Willie said, sounding as surprised as the rest of us felt.

"Randy," Saddles repeated.

"Why son, you never said a word about thinking you might be a person of two souls," Clarence said.

"And not all shamans have two souls . . . my father was a damn good shaman and he was not a man of two souls in the strictest sense of that word," Saddles commented.

"Well, I ain't sure, Papa . . . but I sorta think so.

That's why I've been talkin' to Saddles about it. He even let me call him on his telephone collect so we could talk about it some times. He thinks I might could be a shaman. And he thinks, for sure, I'm gonna be a man of two souls. I was even thinkin' I would like to live in San Francisco . . . but Saddles said it's better to skip that part and go right into my studies with him."

The adults all grew silent. Clarence cleared his throat and looked at the floor. Audrey reached for her own handkerchief. Alice and Bill looked at each other. Grandmother Redwing folded her handkerchief, put it back in her apron pocket, stood up, and walked to Randy. "I been thinkin' this was the case since you was five. You was all the time more interested in herbs and healin' plants than playin' ball . . . and you was all the time more interested in how Grandma fixes food than how to hunt. You always been more gentle than the other boys. Bein' gentle is sometimes a sure sign but not always. It means you're sensitive to the spirits that live around here and to the spirits of the people. I ain't one bit surprised, boy . . . in fact, I'd be damn proud to have one of my grandsons become the shaman of the Quinaults. There ain't never been a Redwing who was a shaman of our people . . . and I think you'd make a really good one. I'd be damn proud, boy, damn proud to have a man of two souls in the family. You get up and let your grandma give you a hug, boy . . . this news lightens my burden today and makes my heart glad."

Randy stood up and fell into his grandmother's arms.

"Don't you worry none about none of it.

Saddles is one of the best shamans all up and down the coast. He's gonna teach ya good, boy. Don't you worry none about none of it. Bein' a man of two souls is somethin' Saddles knows a lot about too. You ain't got nothin' to worry about," she said, patting him gently on the back. Randy was crying. So was the old woman. It wasn't a deep mournful cry and they weren't the kind of tears that come from joy. It was something else. I could not name it. When I looked over at Clarence and Audrey, they had tears in their eyes as well. I wasn't sure what it all meant at the time. All I knew was that one of my best friends was going to become the shaman of the Quinault tribe. I was filled with pride for him. I thought he and his tears looked noble.

§§§§

The next two weeks were fraught with frustration over Grandmother Redwing's situation. It seemed that everyone in Perkins Prairie had an opinion on the subject. Debates broke out all over town. I imagined they were breaking out all over the state. The town newspaper even interviewed Clarence and Audrey the week after we returned from Grandmother Redwing's evaluation by Dr. Lamb. Letters to the editor contained such a variety of opinions and comments, the paper expanded by two whole pages that week. Most favored letting the old woman remain in her little house on the flats, although a surprising number thought her refusal to accept the modern house proved there was something wrong with her. I read three of the negative letters aloud to my mother while she did the dinner dishes one night.

Jack and I will be making payments on this house and the stuff in it until our grandchildren start coming for visits in their own cars! Get a clue, Bertha. Take the money and run with it.

- Velma Olson
Perkins Prairie

Anybody who refuses a free house and running water belongs in rubber room somewhere.

Jim Koval
Enumclaw

If God had intended for us to lug water to our houses from nearby lakes and streams for all time and eternity, he wouldn't have let us invent pipes and water faucets. If Bertha Redwing was a Christian, she would understand these things.

Thelma Farkington
Perkins Prairie

"How can people be so unable to see her point of view?" I asked.

"If most people could understand everyone else's point of view in the world, we wouldn't have

476

wars, wouldn't need lawyers, and we wouldn't need governments. Diversity is the name of the game, Fritz. Until you learn that, you will never learn how to live at peace with the world," she answered.

"I think people should live and let live. That's my motto."

"And that's a good motto to have. Unfortunately it is not everyone's motto. Take for example that Christian woman's comment. If you take her logic to its obvious conclusion, we could say that because God inspired man to invent cigarettes, smoking is a divine calling!"

Jerry Cotton also had an opinion. I bumped into him at the feed store while purchasing some small salt licks for the rabbits my father raised in hutches he had built on the north side of our garage.

"Hi, Jerry," I said, attempting to sound polite but not overtly friendly.

"Good afternoon, Mr. Harding. Looking for work?" The sarcasm in his voice was as obvious as the new pimple waiting to be popped on his chin.

"Just picking up some salt licks for the bunnies," I noted, stepping up to the counter.

"I'm picking up some very special fertilizers. They had to ship them to me all the way from Southern California. This stuff is so good it's going to make my orchids look like Goliath at the fair this year. Everyone else's orchids will look little and puny by comparison. My orchids will be like Goliath. Other's will look like the boy David. I'm sure to walk off with first, second and third prizes this year."

"Will all the members of The Orchid

Appreciation Society be using this special new fertilizer?" I asked, more in an attempt to continue the conversation than out of real interest.

"It's too expensive. There won't be enough for everyone," he answered.

"Oh . . . so the other members of the Orchid Appreciation Society won't really stand a chance next to the ones you grow. That doesn't sound very fair."

"All is fair in love and war and raising orchids, dear boy. Now, if you'll excuse me, I have blue ribbons to win."

"Jerry, if I remember correctly, didn't David slay Goliath?"

"I was speaking metaphorically."

"I know a metaphor when I hear one. I was just pointing out that it wasn't your best possible choice."

"I think my choices in metaphor are much better than your choices in friends. I hear tell that Randy Redwing is queer as a three dollar bill."

"Where did you hear garbage like that?"

"From Suzie Clogston, the Presbyterian minister's daughter. She's a member of The Orchid Appreciation Society, you know. We're very close. She tells me everything."

"Well, Suzie Clogston doesn't know what she's talkin' about," I asserted.

"She should know. Your little Indian friend is having sex with her brother, Ray. Her dad caught them in the basement of the church. She overheard her mom and dad talking about it. Reverend Clogston is thinkin' about sending Ray off to live with his brother in Montana. He thinks working with horses and cattle will make a man of him. I know it's true. Whenever Randy isn't hanging out with you, he and that Clogston boy are always hiking out into the woods. You know damn well what they're doing out there. Suzie said she caught them kissing up in Ray's bedroom one afternoon after school. Oh, it's true all right; your friend Randy is a fairy. Who knows, maybe you're kissing him after school too."

"You take that back, Jerry Cotton. You know damn well I ain't no fairy . . . and neither is Randy!"

"He went dressed as a girl to the Halloween party, didn't he. Come on, Fritz, open your eyes . . . that boy is as weird as his grandmother. The two of them ought to be locked up someplace before they bite somebody."

"You're just jealous because Randy skates better than you do. You don't know nothin' about what you're talkin' about. You don't know nothin' about Randy Redwing, and you know even less about his grandmother. You're just a spiteful, hateful, little boy who likes to make up stories about people."

"Why don't you ask Randy? If he's such a good friend of yours, maybe he'll confide in you. All I can tell you is that Suzie Clogston is a good friend of mine and she told me it's true. Suzie tells me everything. And everybody thinks his grandmother is an old kook. Anybody who turns down a free house has got bats in their belfry."

"And you've got fertilizer for a brain! How'd you like me to beat the shit out of ya?"

"I know you're bigger and stronger than me, Fritz Harding. But slugging me won't change the fact that your little Redskin is a fairy . . . and it won't change the fact that his grandmother ought to be locked up in a funny farm somewhere."

I was giving some serious thought to belting him when Hite Thornton, the owner of the feed store, came up to the counter with Jerry's package. "Here you are, young Mr. Cotton, all the way from Southern California. That will be $1.25 for the fertilizer and 39 cents for the shipping fee, and a penny for tax. Let's see, that comes to $1.65."

Jerry handed him two one dollar bills. Mr. Thornton rang up the sale on his cash register, wrapped Jerry's purchase in a sheet of brown paper, and slid it across the counter to him. "How can I help you, Fritz," he asked.

"I'd like to buy four salt licks for our rabbit hutches."

"Well, I've got to be off, Fritz. You be sure and give my regards to your friend," Jerry quipped.

I stared at him in disbelief and made sure I didn't smile.

"Do you want the large economy size? They're 15 cents each. I also have the regular size. They're 7 cents each."

"I've just got enough money for the regular size," I told him.

After helping Dad secure the salt licks in the cages, I asked if I could ride my bike over to the Redwings.

"Be back in time for dinner. You don't want to upset your mom anymore than she is about your going back up to the reservation on the day those troopers are supposed to move Mrs. Redwing. She really doesn't want you to go, you know."

"I know."

§§§

When I arrived at the Redwings, Willie was chopping wood. "Where's Randy?" I asked.

"Don't know. He took off on his bike about an hour ago."

"Shouldn't he be helping you chop and carry in the wood?"

"Naw, we've been takin' turns lately."

"I wasn't sure how to bring up Jerry's accusation. I wasn't sure I should. But curiosity and stress over the whole idea was getting the best of me. "Who does Randy hang out with when he's not with us?" I asked, trying to sound as nonchalant as possible.

Willie looked up from the piece of wood he was about to strike with the axe. "Ray Clogston," he said.

"Why?"

"I heard somethin' at the feed store that kinda upset me. I don't know what to make of it. Jerry Cotton was the one who said it and who knows if he tells the truth about anything anymore?"

"What did Jerry say?"

"Well, of course, he thinks your grandmother is a kook for not taking a free house. He also said that Randy is a . . . that Randy is . . . that Randy and Ray. He said that Randy was . . ."

"A man of two souls?" Willie interjected.

"No. He said Randy is a fairy. He said

481

everybody knows he's queer." I answered, finally able to get the words out of my mouth.

"That's what a man with two souls is."

"A man with two souls is a fairy? Saddles is a fairy?"

"Well, *fairy* isn't a very nice word. It's sort of like the word *Jap* or *Chink*. Words like that rob people of their dignity. Indians don't use words like that. We don't even have words that slur another person's identity in the Salishan language. Calling a person with two souls a *fairy* or a *queer* would be like calling a Jewish person a *kike*."

I was flabbergasted. I sat down on the pile of wood he had chopped to catch my breath. "How come he never told me and how come it seems perfectly okay to you?"

"I sort of suspected it all along but I didn't know until we were all told," Willie replied.

"When were we all told. I don't remember Randy telling me he was a queer."

"When Randy told the family he wanted to study to be the next shaman for the tribe and told us that Saddles was sure he was a person with two souls . . . that's what he meant. That's what us Indians call it. We believe that some people are born with two souls. One is a male soul and one is a female soul. It don't much matter if the person is in a man's body or a woman's body . . . eventually, if they got two souls, one of them takes over as the boss of the body. At least most of the time. Sometimes they remain both. But in Randy and Saddles' bodies the female soul is stronger. That means that when Randy falls in love, he's gonna fall in love with another boy. Surely you've heard of such things before?"

"Yeah, I have. I've got a cousin, Raymond. He lives with another man. He even brought him to the party you attended. And my dad has a cousin, a woman . . . she lives with another woman in Seattle. I heard tell rumors about them too."

"Well, if you can have a person with two souls in your family . . . you shouldn't be surprised that we have one in ours," Willie said, striking another chunk from the block of wood he was chopping.

"And that's okay with you?"

"Why shouldn't it be?"

"Because he's queer. Well, it might be okay for you. You're his brother. But I been skinny-dippin' with Randy. Now I'm wonderin' if he was lusting after my body all that time."

"That body?"

"Why, what's wrong with my body?"

"You're as skinny as a bean pole. You sure ain't no Tarzan. Ray Clogston works out. He plays football. He lifts weights. Now, he looks like Tarzan."

"You sound like you're hot for him yourself."

"I wouldn't mind havin' his body. I'm too plump."

"So, Randy and Ray are . . . datin'?"

"I've got the feeling they're doing a hell of a lot more than datin'. You wanna give me a hand carryin' some of this wood into the house?"

"Sure. So you think they're doin' it?"

"Probably."

"Have you ever done it?" I asked, starting to load

my left arm with wood.

"Only with old lady Thumb and her four daughters."

"You been doin' it with an older woman and her daughters?"

"No . . . I mean with my hand. You know, jerkin' off."

"I don't do that."

"Everybody does that, Fritz. Get real."

"Well, it ain't nothin' I've ever talked about. And I don't understand what Randy and Ray do. I mean, do you suppose they kiss, just like boys and girls? And what can they do anyhow? My dad told me how babies get into the world. Randy and Ray are both guys. I mean, they both got things that go into things . . . and ain't neither of them got the thing they're supposed to be goin' into."

"Your dad sure didn't tell you very much, did he."

"What'cha mean?"

"I mean there are lots more things to do than just put it in the baby factory. They can play with each other. They both got mouths and they both got bun-holes. Figure it out."

"Mouths! You gotta be kiddin'!"

"Even men and women do that, Fritz. It's called oral sex."

"I'll bet my mom and dad don't do that."

"Everybody does it, Fritz."

"Ya know, I just got used to the fact that babies don't get here by storks. I ain't never heard about any of these other messy details. Why would people wanna do stuff like that?"

"Probably because it feels good."

"I ain't ready yet to even get naked in front of a girl. I sure don't wanna start thinkin' about putting my tongue anyplace strange. I'm not sure I even like the idea of French kissing."

"Why, Fritz Harding, you're a genuine prude."

"I ain't no prude. It's just that all that stuff seems so messy."

"Well, it won't when you're older. Besides, you saw those French postcards we looked at in your grandmother's barn. They was do'n some oral sex in those cards."

"Yeah but I thought that was just because they're French."

"Everybody does it, Fritz. Everybody."

"Doesn't it seem messy to you?"

"Nope. I can hardly wait."

"Yuk! You actually wanna stick your thing in a girl's mouth?"

"Under the right circumstances, yes."

"I'm just sure my parents don't do anything like that."

"Well they did something. You're here aren't you?"

"Yes, but I'm sure they did it the old fashioned way."

"There is nothing new fashioned about oral sex, Fritz. It's just part of love making. Love is a verb, ya know. It's something you do."

"Well, I ain't never gunna do anything like that."

"You'll change."

"And I sure wouldn't ask no girl to do noth'n like that."

"You are a genuine prude, Fritz."

"And now I don't know what to say when I see Randy again. I don't know how to behave. I mean, what if he wants to kiss me?"

"Has he tried to kiss you?"

"No." We dumped our loads of wood neatly in the wood box on his parents back porch.

"You're not his type. Like I said, you ain't no Tarzan. Besides, you said you knew your cousin, Raymond, lived with another guy. How do you treat him when you see him?"

"Just like I do all the rest of my cousins. But he's a lot older than me. He's got a job in Seattle and everything."

"Well, maybe you should treat Randy the same as you do your cousin, Raymond . . . you know . . . just like always. It really don't change nothin', Fritz. Randy is still Randy. He ain't one ounce different today than he was two months ago. The only difference is that now you know he's a person with two souls. In Quinault ways he is very special. That's why Grandma Redwing said she was so proud to have him for a grandson."

"So in Quinault ways, this is a good thing?"

"Yes. It is an unexpected thing but a good thing. The Great Spirit makes people like Randy so they can understand men and women. They are shaman to each. Besides, I'll bet it's the same with Micmac ways. Most of the time it's always people with two souls who are the shamans for a tribe. You're just makin' a big deal out of nothin'. How does your family act when your cousin comes around?"

"They don't act no different toward him. They know he's a fairy . . . a person with two souls . . . but they don't much talk about it. He and his friend come up and go fishin' with my dad once in a while. So I guess it don't much bother my dad."

"It shouldn't bother anybody, Fritz. We Quinault believe there are many ways for people to live on this earth . . . being a person with two souls is just one of them"

"I don't think very many white people think like that."

"The Hardings don't seem to be having much of a problem."

"I guess you're right. I guess I can get used to the idea . . . only I ain't gonna dance with him or nothin'."

"You already did."

"When?"

"On the reservation."

"You're right. I can be a real poop, can't I?"

"I don't think you're a poop at all. I think you're becoming a damn good Indian."

"And you're becoming better and better at livin' like a European."

"That's because there are lots of ways to live on this earth, Fritz. Lots of ways."

"You're pretty wise, Willie."

"That's because I'm almost two years older than you.

"Maybe there's a bit of shaman in you too."

"I don't think so, Fritz. I'm pretty sure I've only got one soul."

Chapter Fourteen

Troopers on the Flats

On Friday, the 14th of June, right after lunch, I climbed into the Redwing's new delivery wagon with Randy and Willie and headed for the Quinault Reservation. Clarence had decided to drive the wagon because his Ford had been acting up and was at the repair shop. The boys and I were delighted to have the chance for a long ride in the delivery wagon, but Audrey complained that the seats weren't nearly so comfortable as those in the car. We waved our good-byes to Grandmother Sunfield, who came up to watch the girls so Audrey could be there for the final confrontation between Grandmother Redwing and the government officials. Sonja Hackman, who was always glad to get extra hours at the cleaning shop, would fill in for Clarence while he was gone.

I had decided not to mention Randy's two souls to my parents right away, at least not until after I knew for sure whether Grandmother Redwing had actually been moved from her home on the flats by state troopers. Such a revelation might have been just the straw to break my mother's reluctant permission to let me keep going along on the trips to the reservation. I had no idea how she or my dad might react to the information that both Saddles Seatco and Randy Redwing were fairies.

I had seen Randy on many occasions since my

conversation with Willie but decided against bringing up the subject unless he did. I found myself watching his every gesture and move. As far as I could see, there was no apparent change in him, but the image of him and Ray Clogston kissing romantically was something I couldn't get out of my mind. I wondered if they kissed the way I sometimes dreamed of kissing Lily Whitedove or the way Hollywood stars kiss in the movies. The recurring image of the two boys locked in embrace just seemed downright weird to me. I was convinced I should be able to find some visible physical or behavioral hint of fairyness in Randy and caught myself staring at him whenever he wasn't aware I was around. I'm not sure what I expected to see. Randy was no more girlish than the rest of the boys our age, he didn't speak with a lisp and despite his lack of interest in football and baseball, he was an avid swimmer and tennis player.

Saddles was a different story. The more I thought about it the more I realized that he more swished into a room than walked into it. He was what my dad called "limp wristed" and when he spoke he often seemed to reach for a broach he wasn't wearing. No doubt about it, Saddles was girlish even if he was an old man.

"Have I got a new pimple on my face or somethin', Fritz?" Randy asked as his father turned the wagon onto the highway that would take us out toward the Washington Peninsula and to his grandmother's home on the reservation.

"No," I answered sheepishly.

"Then how come you're staring at me like that?

Seems to me you're always starin' at me anymore."

"I wasn't starin' at you. I was lookin' out the window on the other side of you," I lied.

Once we arrived at the reservation, it was decided that Saddles would let Bill and Alice's kids spend the night at his place so they along with Clarence and Audrey could spend the night in Grandmother Redwing's house just in case anything unusual happened. The boys and I got permission to stay up with Saddles and watch the Friday night movie as well as permission to sleep in the back of the delivery truck since there wouldn't be any room left for us in Grandmother Redwing's little house with the four adults sleeping in it that night.

After the movie the three of us hiked down the hill toward the little house down by the lake. Willie, who loved to jog and who, I thought, wanted to make sure he got the best place to sleep in the back of the van, ran ahead of us. "I haven't seen much of you the past few weeks," I told Randy as we walked.

"Yeah, I been sort of busy. . . you know . . . helpin' Dad in the shop and all."

"I thought that's why he hired Sonja Hackman. I guess ya just been busy," I speculated.

"I've been spendin' a lot of time over at the Presbyterian church."

"You gettin' religion?"

"Na . . . I'm . . . I've . . . I've been hangin' out with the minister's son, Ray."

"Is he your new best friend?"

"Oh, no, Fritz . . . you're still my best friend. Ray is . . . well, Ray is . . . him and me is . . . I mean, Ray and

491

me have been . . . you know . . . hangin' out."

"Did I ever tell you about my cousin Raymond and his friend who live in Seattle?" I asked.

"Yeah, I met them at the big shindig at your grandparents' place last Thanksgiving. He's a real nice guy. I talked to them quite a bit, ya know."

"I didn't know, but I saw you was pretty friendly to him."

"Yeah, he's a real nice guy . . . they're both real nice guys."

"They're lovers, ya know," I blurted out.

"Yeah . . . I know."

"What do you think of that?"

"I think they were lucky to find each other."

"That's what I think too," I murmured.

We walked several yards before either of us spoke again. I wasn't sure what to say next, but what I wanted was for Randy to be more honest with me than he was being. I had thought the whole thing over and decided that it didn't matter to me if he was a fairy. He was my friend and that was all that mattered. Finally, I broke the silence. "Randy . . ."

"Yeah."

"Are we best friends or not?"

"Well, of course we are, Fritz. Why do you ask?"

"Then how's-a-come you ain't told me about . . . about you and Ray? I mean the real story?"

"Tell you what?"

"You know . . . that you're both . . . you know . . . that you're both . . . boys with two souls."

Randy stopped in his tracks. He looked down at the ground. "I guess I was afraid you wouldn't like me anymore. Mama said she didn't think you knew what havin' two souls really meant . . . so I just didn't say nothin'."

"Well, your mom was right. I didn't know what it meant. Willie told me."

"Well, now ya know."

"Yeah, now I know."

"Does it make a difference?"

"I thought it was gonna. At first, I mean. Then, after I had time to think about it. Well, my cousin Raymond and his friend, they come up and go fishin' with my dad all the time and it don't seem to bother him that they're . . . ah . . . "

"Gay?" Randy said.

"Gay? No, that they're . . . you know . . . fairies."

"We don't use that word. We don't use the word *queer, fruit, faggot, Nancy-boy,* or any of those derogatory words. We call ourselves *gay,* and if you don't like that word you can just say *homosexual* or *people with two souls.* We like *gay* best."

"Who started that?"

"I don't know. Saddles told me that's the term everybody uses in San Francisco. It's a pretty good word. I mean, I ain't ashamed of who I am. I'm actually pretty happy to finally understand why I've always felt so different. So, *gay* seems like a good word to use. I guess it used to be sort of a secret code word. But now everybody uses it in the big cities."

"Well, I'm still your best friend . . . but I guess you won't have nearly so much time for me now that you got Ray."

"I really do like bein' with him, Fritz. He's so

neat," Randy sighed.

"Is it different kissin' a boy than a girl?" I asked.

"I don't know. I never kissed any girls except for my mom and my grandmas and my little sisters."

"Never!"

"Oh, like you've kissed that many girls and have become the world's best kisser. You ain't even got a real girl friend yet so don't be actin' like some kind of specialist."

"But you really like kissin' him?"

"Oh, yeah . . bein' with him is like bein' in heaven."

"Well, how come you never tried to kiss me?"

"I don't think about you in that way, Fritz. You're kinda like another brother to me. And I never kissed anybody that way until I first kissed Ray. Well, actually he kissed me the first time. He's the one that taught me how to kiss. You know . . . deep kissin'."

"Deep kissin? What the hell is that?"

"You know, with the tongue."

"He sticks his tongue in your mouth? Now that sounds downright messy."

"Sex is messy."

"It sure sounds like it. I don't think I want anybody to stick their tongue in my mouth."

"You will when the time comes."

"Well, maybe. But did you ever want to kiss me? Am I ugly or somethin'?"

"No, Fritz . . . you ain't ugly. Actually I'd give anything to look like you. I think you're real cute and I'd love to be tall like you. You're just not my type."

"Type? You already been gay long enough to

494

have a type? What's that all about?"

"I don't know. Some guys just have a certain way of walkin' or talkin' or lookin' at you. Ray is like that. I don't really understand it myself. I like the way he swaggers when he walks . . . and he's got the most beautiful shoulders and back I've ever seen . . . and those freckles and blue eyes and red hair of his . . . he just drives me nuts. There's somethin' about the way he smiles and talks and stands and looks . . . I don't know, Fritz. He just my type."

"Well, maybe the three of us can hang out sometime," I suggested.

"Oh, maybe, Fritz, but right now, whenever we can get together . . . well, we really like bein' alone right now. You know how it is when you're in love."

"No, I don't know. I ain't never been in love. You think you're in love with Ray?"

"Oh, I'm sure of it . . . and what's even better, he says he's in love with me too!"

"I hear tell his dad caught you guys in the church basement."

"Who told you that?"

"Jerry Cotton. Ray's sister overheard their parents talkin' about it. Jerry has probably told everyone in town by now. He's such a gossip."

"He's an asshole."

"An asshole and a gossip. That was just awful when his dad caught us."

"Jerry said you was doin' a lot more than kissin'."

"We was."

"Was that your first time?"

"No . . . the first time was at the old swimmin'

hole up at Spikton Creek. We rode our bikes up there just to have somethin' to do one day, and Ray suggested we go skinny-dippin'. He kissed me while we was in the water . . . and then . . . and then it was my first time."

"Except for the fact that it's two guys, it sounds almost romantic."

"Oh, it was very romantic. There's a little mossy place back in the trees just up from the swimming hole . . ."

"I know where that spot it. It's a great place to take a nap."

"It's a great place to do just about anything. It's so soft there . . .and you can hear the birds singing and the water splashing by and all the sounds of the forest. We go back to that spot whenever we can. It's just perfect."

"So you ain't a virgin anymore, huh?"
"Guess not."

"Jerry says that Ray's dad is thinkin' of sending him to live in Montana on a ranch. He thinks it will make a man out of him."

"Well, his dad ain't got nothin' to worry about in that department. Ray is already a real man. But he told me about it. He said he would just run away and come back to me. He said no matter how many time his father sends him away . . . he's gonna run away and come back to me. He told his dad that too. I think his dad has changed his mind about sending him away. Ray said he ain't brought up the subject for a couple of days."

"Well, I hope he don't send him away for your

sake. I guess that would break your heart."

"For a while, but lately Earl Vanderfleet, you know, the guy who's the captain of the senior swim team . . . he's been flirtin' with me. I can tell. He's got such a body on him, and he's so cute . . . and I don't know if you've seen him in the shower or not, but he's very okay in the man department, if you know what I mean."

"Why, Randy Redwing . . . you're startin' to sound like a slut," I said, only half joking."

"I tell ya, Fritz . . . sometimes I think bein' a slut might be a lot of fun. Don't get me wrong . . I really love Ray . . . but I've got a lot of wild oats to sow before I settle down and let some guy brand me and put me out to pasture."

"Well, if you ask me, you're too young for all that stuff. I think I'm too young for it."

"You live a very sheltered life. Why you even told me your grandparents were married when your grandma was just 14. I'll bet she had done some kiss'n before she got married."

"You watch how you talk about my grandmother."

"I ain't say'n she's a slut. I'm just say'n people do what comes naturally and kiss'n comes naturally."

"Willie told me about all the stuff you do together. You really think it's fun. I mean oral sex sounds pretty messy to me."

"Sex is messy. It's supposed to be messy. I'll tell you this, Fritz, it's more than fun. It's delicious. One day you'll have a girlfriend . . . you'll see."

"Yeah, but I don't think girls think about sex the

way guys do. I think guys are always ready to do it . . . at least I am."

"That's one of the reasons I like datin' guys . . . we're supposed to do it lots. Girls are supposed to wait until they're married. Most don't according to Saddles, but they're supposed to. Guys are supposed to be like butterflies and go from flower to flower to flower."

"I don't know, Randy; I think we're too young to be doin' stuff like that yet."

"Don't be such a prude, Fritz. I'm almost thirteen. My grandma was married by the time she was fourteen too. Even Romeo and Juliet were our age. We ain't too young. The machinery works just fine."

"I don't know, Randy . . . that's how girls get pregnant before they get married. I think people are supposed to wait until they get married before they have sex."

"Well, number one, neither Ray nor I are gonna get pregnant. And number two, people have sex before they get married all the time. Wake up, Fritz. This is the 1950's. You're livin' in the dark ages."

"Maybe so, Randy . . . but just the idea of havin' sex with another person kinda scares me. I mean, you gotta get naked and everything."

"You get naked in front of other people in gym class all the time."

"Yeah, but not in front of girls . . . oh, my god . . . everytime you get naked with guys in gym class, you're havin' a ball, ain't cha?"

"You bet. I love skin."

"Do you guys do the other thing too?"

"What other thing?"

498

"You know . . . butt-fuck."

"Of course."

"Doesn't it hurt?"

"A little the first time . . . but not after that. I love it. Ray don't like it though. It's not for everybody. I mean, Ray don't like to receive, if ya know what I mean. He jokes about it . . . he says it's better to give than receive."

"Well, I think I'm on Ray's side of that argument."

§§§§

That night I dreamed of bears. Huge bears growling and sniffing around the delivery van in which the Redwing boys and I slept. Suddenly one of the bears shot flames from his mouth the way they say dragons do. He stood up and looked into the van through the driver's window and growled so loudly I woke up. There were lights flickering in through the windows and the dull growl of trucks shifting into low gear as they made their way down the hill toward the old village. I turned on my flashlight and checked my watch. It was only 2:30 in the morning. I reached over and shook Willie and then Randy.

"What's up?" Willie asked.

"There're a couple of trucks comin' down the hill. I think it might be the state troopers."

"It's pretty damn early in the morning for anybody to be up and about," Randy yawned.

"Do you think it's a sneak attack," Willie whispered.

"I don't know but somethin' goin' on out there."

"We better go wake Mom and Dad," Randy said, reaching for the door handle.

The three of us hurried into the house as the lights of the trucks came closer.

"Bill Redwing was sleeping closest to the door. Willie shook him. "Uncle Bill . . . there're some trucks comin' down the hill," he whispered.

Bill got up, walked out onto the porch and then returned to the small living room. "Wake up everybody. We got trouble comin' down the hill!" he ordered under his breath.

Clarence got up and lit a kerosene lamp on the kitchen table. Audrey and Alice went into the bedroom to wake their mother-in-law. Bill pulled back the curtain on the living room window and looked out toward the lights coming down the hill.

"How many vehicles are there?" Clarence asked.

"Not as many as I thought. Looks like two trucks and a couple of cars. Maybe a van.. Yup, most of the noise is coming from a big van . . . that guy's obviously got transmission problems," Bill answered.

"Do you think it's the troopers," Willie asked.

"I don't know. I don't know how many troopers they plan to send. It's kinda odd that they're coming here in the dark. What time is it? I can't see much out there but the lights. They're almost here," Clarence responded.

"It's just a little after two-thirty," Audrey answered.

"Grandmother Redwing slipped under Clarence's arm and stepped out onto the porch.

500

"Mother, what do you think you're doing?" he asked.

"I don't think they're gonna shoot us, Clarence. I'm gonna find out what these rascals are doin' here so damn early in the morning," she mumbled, stepping off the porch and walking toward the lights of the largest vehicle. The rest of us ran out onto the porch and followed her. Someone opened the door to the largest vehicle and stepped into the night. "What's all this racket about? Can't a body even sleep 'til dawn anymore!" Grandmother Redwing shouted.

"I'm sorry ma'am, I'm from Channel Five news. Mr. Benchworthy wanted to get things set up to film just in case those troopers actually do come down here today," a young man's voice answered.

"You ain't troopers?" Grandmother Redwing yelled into the lights.

"No, ma'am, I'm Eric Couffman. I'm the cameraman. Mr. Benchworthy is in one of the cars behind me."

"Well, you scared the hell out of us and woke everybody up. You should a wrote and said you was comin'," the old woman scolded. Bill and Clarence walked up and stood on either side of their mother. The rest of us huddled behind them like a flock of chicks.

"Yes, ma'am."

Benchworthy walked into the lights of the van. "Mrs. Redwing . . . I'm sorry we didn't let you know we were coming. The station manager didn't agree to let us come until about ten last night."

"Who is in all the other cars?" Clarence asked.

"Other news people. I think both papers sent

reporters and camera people, and a car from KOMO radio kept passing me so I know at least one radio station will be here. Maybe our presence will scare off the troopers."

"Well, you just about scared us into the next world. You scared the hell out of my grandsons. They was sleepin' in Clarence's new van. You be sure and get a picture of that on the TV. It's for his dry cleanin' shop in Perkins Prairie. He drove it all the way up here."

"Is he going to use it to help move your things?" one of the reporters walking up to them asked.

"Me and mine ain't movin' nothin'. Not one spoon. If my stuff is gonna get torn from my home . . . they're gonna have to do it all by themselves."

"Wish we had that on film, Eric. Get the camera out and get it rolling," Benchworthy said over his shoulder.

Grandmother Redwing sent Audrey and Alice into the house to stir the fire and make some tea. She, her sons, the boys and I, sat on the front porch visiting with the reporters. When the women returned, they brought with them two large pots of tea and a tray of cups. The reporters produced donuts and other snacks from their vehicles and the lot of us shared an unexpected breakfast and talked about the possible events of the coming day until the sun began peeking over the Olympic Mountain Range. Grandmother Redwing excused herself and went into the house to change from her nightgown and robe into day clothes. When she returned she was dressed in traditional Quinault attire except for a well worn pink sweater she

502

threw over her shoulders to keep the chill off.

"Do you plan to pack any sentimental or especially personal items so the troopers can't damage them?" one of the reporters asked.

"Stuff like that is in trunks anyway. But don't be soundin' like it's for sure them troopers is gonna be movin' me outta here today. I ain't through fightin' and so far they ain't nowhere in sight," the old woman chided. I couldn't help but notice that she spoke directly into the camera.

"I'm afraid that isn't true, Mrs. Redwing," Benchworthy said, looking up the road to the top of the hill. "That sounds like the troopers now."

We all looked up the hill just in time to see a khaki colored truck with a canvas cover come into view and start down the hill. It was followed by three others.

"It begins," the old woman said, turning to walk back into her house.

"Wonder why they've got four trucks? Mother doesn't own enough to fill one of them," Audrey asked.

"My hunch is that one truck is for Mrs. Redwing's things and the others are full of troopers," a reporter suggested.

"My god, look at that!" Bill announced.

Grandmother Redwing turned around just in time to see a bulldozer turn onto the hill road and begin to inch its way down toward the flats. She watched in stoic silence as the trucks and troopers and the bulldozer moved slowly and deliberately in our direction. "Looks like somethin' from a World War II movie, don't it?" she finally mumbled before turning around and going back into her house.

To our surprise, the trucks stopped as soon as they were close enough to see the news vehicles and the van from the KING television station. "Looks like you fellas have given them a bit of a surprise," Clarence noted.

Several of the reporters, including Robert Benchworthy, walked up to the trucks and spoke with the drivers. Several troopers got out of their trucks and milled around, smoking cigarettes. Occasionally they would look toward the house. Eventually one of the reporters came back to let us know what was going on. "You were right. Finding the news here surprised them. They're waiting for the agent to arrive to see if he wants Mrs. Redwing evicted in front of the press," he told us.

"Well, they're going to have a long wait; it's only a little after six. Albert Radford don't usually get to the office until about eight," Bill noted.

"He's up at his office making phone calls right now. Radford is on duty, it's his superiors that can't be reached at the moment. It's a Saturday . . . he may have real problems," the reported informed us.

It took about forty-five minutes before Agent Radford's pickup drove down the hill to join the troopers. After conferring for a few minutes with who we supposed were the leaders, he got back into his truck and drove to where we were standing. In the past, Albert had always parked his truck down by the mail box and walked to the house. Today he drove right up to the porch. He didn't get out of his vehicle. He just rolled down his window and spoke directly to Clarence.

504

"I'm here to ask you, one more time, to gather up your mother and move her things to the house in the new village. If you are not demonstrating compliance with this request in thirty minutes, and by that I mean if it is not visibly certain to me that you are loading her things into your van, I will give the order for the troopers to move down here and move them for her. You've got to be out by noon. Having these troopers here is costing a fortune. If necessary, they are prepared to use military force to accomplish their task," he said.

"You mean they would shoot us?" Audrey asked.

"Of course not. I mean they will do everything short of shooting you. They will form into squads and march on the building."

"Right here in front of all these news people?" Clarence asked.

"Right here in front of all these news people. The law is the law, Clarence. The presence of the news does not change that. I must also tell you that once the troopers get the order to empty the house and remove Mrs. Redwing, any of you or the reporters who block their way or attempt to stop them will be arrested."

"You can't arrest us. We have press cards," Benchworthy protested as Grandmother Redwing stepped out of the house and walked up to Radford's truck.

"I have a special dispensation from the governor's office to arrest anyone who gets in the way of today's operation. This is a military operation now. Reporters don't get special rights. I hope you will all accept this request as quickly as possible. You have thirty minutes."

"You're makin' a terrible mistake, Albert. I ain't gonna do anything but bake some muffins for a snack," the old woman said in a slow calm voice.

"Thirty minutes. That's all you have," he repeated. Albert rolled his window up, lit a cigarette, and drove back to the waiting troopers and bulldozer down the road. Robert Benchworthy and a few other reporters followed after him on foot.

Thirty minutes later the troopers were still down the road, and we could smell fresh muffins baking in the oven on the inside of the house.

An hour later Albert Radford returned. Grandmother Redwing went out on the porch to talk with him. "Thank you for giving me time to fix the muffins, Albert. There are a few left. Are you hungry?"

"I didn't give you time to fix your muffins, Mrs. Redwing; I had difficulty getting through to the powers that be. Most government offices are closed today."

"Poor plannin' on your part, I'd say," she quipped.

"Mrs. Redwing, as we stand here, a load of new furniture . . . all gifts from the governor . . . is being moved into your new home. You'll have a new kitchen table with four new chairs, a complete living room set in early American, a new bedroom set complete with mirrored vanity, and something only Saddles has so far - a brand new television set and the best antenna money can buy. What do you think of that!" he beamed.

"I think it's a pretty obvious bribe, Albert. It's

not stuff I'm lookin' for. I got stuff. What I want is geography and spirit. I want to stay down here on the flats like my people before me. I don't need no TV or mirrored vanity. I need this dirt to live on and that lake to drink from."

"The furniture isn't a bribe. It's yours whether you move up to the new house willingly or whether my men carry you up there kicking and screaming. Either way, all that stuff is yours. It's the governor's way of making this whole ordeal less traumatic for you. He knows you don't have a lot of money to buy things with."

"I don't need no money to buy things with. I got everything I want right here!"

"Mrs. Redwing, please tell me to send the troopers back to their families. Tell me you are willing to move up to the new house willingly," Albert pleaded.

"Now you know that ain't gonna happen, Albert."

"You leave me no choice," the agent told her.

"And you don't leave me none either." She lifted the plate of muffins to the open window of his truck. "Now take one of these muffins and eat it. I'm sure you ain't been bright enough to eat you some breakfast," she told him.

He took one, nodded his head in thanks, took a bite and drove away.

§§§§

Nearly two hours went by before the next event happened. We were all out on the porch sipping some

507

fresh-made lemonade, visiting with some of the reporters and a few of few of the folks from the upper village who had walked down to see what was going on when we saw Agent Radford's pickup coming back down the hill. He was being followed by a paddy wagon. As they drove up to the house, two of the military trucks and most of the troopers fell in behind them. The driver of the bulldozer fired up the engine, although it didn't move from where it had been parked. At that same moment a seaplane flew over the house. We watched in amazement as it circled the lake and prepared to land.

"Now nothin' like that has ever happened in these parts. Wonder who that is?" the old woman asked. Several young people walked around the house to get a better view of the landing.

"Probably the governor," one of the reporters suggested.

"Looks like they're fixin' to move us out for sure this time," Clarence noted.

"You boys get back up here on the porch," Alice ordered.

I noticed that several more tribal members began walking down the hill to see what was going on. The crest of the hill was lined with people watching the activity on the flats. A few boys threw pebbles as the agent's truck passed them.

"That's not a good sign," Audrey said.

The press formed a sort of shield between us and the oncoming vehicles. When the troopers reached the house, there was an entire wall of reporters between them and us. One of the troopers spoke up

508

and called out to us. "Which one of you is Bertha Redwing?" he hollered.

"I am Bertha Redwing," the old woman answered as a few flash cameras went off.

"Requesting permission to come forward and speak to you, ma'am," he petitioned.

"Your request is granted, young man," she answered, folding her dish towel over the porch railing.

The reporters stepped aside, forming a break through which the trooper could approach the house. At that same moment a station wagon with a canoe strapped to the top went past the house and headed for the lake. Saddles Seatco yelled out the window as it drove past. "Just hang on, Bertha . . . we got some strong magic happenin' here in a few minutes!"

"Mrs. Redwing, I'm Major Daryl Traster. It's my responsibility to move you, your family, and your belongings from this condemned residence up the hill to your new house in the upper village. I'm giving you one last opportunity to avoid any unpleasantness and move from these premises of your own free will. Now, how do your respond?"

"Now how do you think I'm gonna respond, Major Traster?"

"I would hope in the affirmative, ma'am," he said, walking up to the porch.

"Well, you might as well hope in one hand and spit in the other. I can tell you which one is gonna fill up the fastest," she replied.

"Is that a no, Ma'am?"

"Well of course it's a no. You don't know much about me, do ya young man? I ain't move'n from this house of my own free will. You'll have to pick me up and carry me and then I can't promise I won't bite ya."

"Then you are leaving me no alternative but to order my men to remove you and your family physically from this place. If you resist, we will use force. Is that understood?"

"My family ain't gonna give you no resistance. Just me." She sat down on the wooden planks of the porch, stretched her legs out in front of her and folded her hands in her lap. Several tribal members were now walking past the bulldozer and getting closer and closer to the little house on the flats.

Major Traster turned around in a military fashion and bellowed to his troops. "Company B, attention!"

At just that moment the station wagon we had seen pass by the house returned and came to a screeching halt. The canoe was no longer strapped to the top of it. "Stop!" a voice boomed as someone stepped out of the vehicle. It was Saddles.

"Bertha, Bertha! That airplane that just landed on the lake 'sgot Edward R. Murrow aboard. He's come all the way from New York City. He wants to interview you for a national TV and radio show," Saddles panted as he ran up to the porch. The station wagon backed up and headed back for the lake.

"Who the hell is Edward R. Murrow?" Grandmother Redwing asked. She motioned for Randy to help her get back up on her feet.

"He's that fella on the national news. He wants to take some film while he's here and fly it back to New York City. That plane out there brought him in from Boeing Field where an even bigger plane brought him from the East Coast. They're gonna put you on national TV and radio!" Saddles said excitedly.

"He flew here in that little plane?" she asked, getting her balance and walking toward the old shaman.

"Yes. They called me from Seattle just minutes before he got here. That's why I got the Blackhawk boys to come down here with their canoe strapped to the top of their station wagon. So they can bring him to shore. He'll be here any minute. The Blackhawk boys just went back down to bring him up here."

Agent Radford stepped forward. "Somebody call the governor's office and get him on the line for me, please I've got to let him know Mr. Murrow is here. Major Traster, I think we should postpone our plans until I hear from the governor on this matter. Murrow will bring national attention to this." he directed.

"Yes, sir," he said quietly. 'Company B, at ease!" he bellowed.

Within a few minutes the station wagon was back. In it was Edward R. Murrow, a sound technician, and a cameraman. "I'm looking for Bertha Redwing," a distinguished looking gentlemen in a pinstriped suit said through a cigarette held in the corner of his mouth."

"I am Bertha Redwing," the old woman responded.

"How do you do, Ma'am. I'm Edward R. Murrow. We've heard about you all the way back in New York City. I would like to talk with you, if you don't mind. I would have called to make an appointment, but you don't seem to have a telephone," Murrow said.

"Don't need no telephone and you don't need no appointment to talk to me. Talk."

"Could we go inside? I'd like this to be a private interview."

"It's okay with me, but I think this young army fella here is about to throw me over his shoulder and pack me off to the new village in one of those trucks," she responded.

"No, ma'am, I've been directed to pull back. If you want to speak with Mr. Murrow inside, you go right ahead," Major Traster advised.

"When I'm finished speaking with Mrs. Redwing, I'd like to interview Agent Radford. Is he here?" Murrow asked.

"That would be me, Mr. Murrow. I'll be up at my office. I have a few telephone calls to make," Albert responded.

Grandmother Redwing, Mr. Murrow, his cameraman and sound technician went into the house and closed the door. A young trooper ran up to Albert. "Agent Radford, we just spoke to the governor's office. They advise that the troops, the trucks and the bulldozer retreat back up the hill at this time. They don't want any eviction or destruction of property to occur while Mr. Murrow is here," he said.

"He doesn't mind if the local press is here?" Albert asked.

"I guess not, sir . . . he just doesn't want this going national."

"Very well, Major Traster, would you be so kind as to direct your men and trucks and the bulldozer driver to go back up the hill! There's a large vacant lot behind my office. They can all park there for the time being. There's a restroom in my office they can use if they need to relieve themselves."

Major Traster gave the orders, and within a few minutes only the reporters, the Redwings, a few people from the village, and I were left in the front yard of the little house on the flats. Some of the reporters got in their cars and followed the troopers back up the hill. The KING TV people all stayed near the house. Robert Benchworthy said he hoped to get a chance to obtain additional film of Murrow speaking with Grandmother Redwing. I hoped she heard some of the villagers applauding when the troopers left and drove back up the hill.

I'm not sure how long the old Indian woman and the reporter from New York City spoke to one another in the house, but when they finally emerged it was getting on into the afternoon. Murrow asked the Blackhawk boys to drive him and his team to the agent's office so he could speak with Albert Radford and Major Traster. Saddles remained behind to visit with the rest of us. He walked over to where I was sitting on the porch by myself. "I've got a good feelin' about all this," he said, sitting on the railing next to me.

"You think that big-time television reporter sacred them off forever?" I asked.

"It wouldn't surprise me," Saddles noted, pulling out his sack of Bull Durham.

"I hope you're right," I responded.

"Fritz, I hear tell you didn't know what the term *a man of two souls* meant until you learned accidentally from some smart-aleck back in Perkins Prairie. Is that true?"

"Yes, sir. I just thought it meant something magical. You know, something spiritual."

"Well, I think it is spiritual. Most spiritual things have physical manifestations. You, for example, are the visible manifestation of an eternal reality called life. The life force is invisible stuff, spiritual stuff. But it inhabits your body. Your body don't so much possess life. It's more like life possesses your body . . . and when life becomes dissatisfied with its resting place, it will move on. You will move on. But your body will return to the elements from which life took it. You understand?"

"Sort of, but I don't much know what that has to do with bein' . . .with bein', you know, a guy who falls in love with other guys."

"Sometimes life is filled with surprises . . . with things we do not expect. The surprises are not as important as the ways we learn to deal with them. How are you dealing with the fact that Randy will love other boys or that in my younger days, I did too?"

"Okay, I guess. I'm gettin' used to it. Willie talked to me a lot and I got a cousin up in Seattle who is that way. It don't seem to bother my dad much so I'm sort of takin' it a day at a time. How's-a-come you don't live with no guy now?"

"I'm an old man. My man died when I was still livin' in San Francisco. I just ain't never found nobody who could take his place. Oh, I had a fling here and there . . . even since I moved back here and became the shaman to my people. But it was never the same. I finally figured out that I was to live with my memories.

514

And they're damn good memories, Fritz . . . damn good. And part of what makes them good is that me and him had good friends, friends like your mom and dad who treated us good and like equals. So, if you can remain a good friend to Randy . . . his memories will be good too. I know finding out he's gay was a surprise to you. But it's how you deal with that surprise that matters. You understand?"

"Yes, sir, I think I do. Besides, I ain't never gonna stop bein' Randy's friend. I don't much like that Ray fella he's so in love with . . . but I ain't never gonna stop bein' Randy's friend."

"Bein' his friend means stickin' up for him and keepin' his secret when you can. You understand that part too, don't cha?"

"Yes, sir, I do. I already stuck up for him. And I ain't gonna tell nobody unless they ask. Even then I might just say that's something they should talk to Randy about, not me."

"You got the picture, boy. You're gonna be just fine and you're gonna be a good friend to Randy. Believe me, he's gonna need one."

Bill came back up on the porch after speaking to a few of the villagers. "I hear tell the governor's got political ambitions to run for president soon. It might not look so good for him in the eyes of the American people if he ran an old lady from her home," he said.

"Let's not get our hopes built up just to have them dashed to smithereens again," Alice warned.

"We've got to think positively," Saddles chided.

"I want to think realistically and positively at the same time," Alice answered.

"I think we should start thinkin' about what we're gonna fix ourselves for dinner. I got me a stash of canned deer meat out in the pantry. How's about I fix us some good old fashioned stew?" Grandmother Redwing suggested.

"You think we've got time to fix dinner and eat it?" Alice asked.

"Well, girl, it's gonna get to be supper time whether we fix somethin' to eat or not. I say we fix . . . and see what life brings us for the rest of the day. Clarence, you and Bill and the boys go cut me some firewood. There's a dry log that washed up on the beach a few weeks ago. You can busy yourselves with that while we ladies start fixin' supper. I have a feelin' them trucks won't be back until after Mr. Murrow leaves. We gots plenty of time."

"I think you're right, Bertha. I got a plum pudding upside-down cake I baked last night up at the house. If somebody will run me up there, I'll get it for our dessert," Saddles responded.

"Plum pudding upside-down cake don't sound very Indian," I teased.

"It ain't. It's something I learned to fix when I lived in California. It'll melt in your mouth and make your tummy say howdy," Saddles beamed.

"Saddles, did you ever fix real Indian food for that guy you lived with in San Francisco?" I asked.

"Well sure I did, boy. Everyone in a while I'd go out into the streets and pick me up a stray dog and fix him dog stew. He loved it. Especially if I could find me one of them little stray poodles."

"You gotta be kid'n me, Saddles. That sounds

516

disgusting."

"Of course I'm kidding you, Fritz. I was just see'n if you were pay'n attention. But I did fix some traditional foods for him. We ate out a lot. You know, Chinese, Italian, burgers. But he liked good old fashioned American food. Steak and potatoes. But sometimes I did something fancy. A little French cooking and sometimes a plum pudding upside down cake."

§§§§

When Saddles returned with his cake, he was so excited he almost dropped it while getting out of the car. Clarence, the boys and I had just finished filling Grandmother Redwing's wood box when he drove up with Alice from the upper village.

"What's with you, old man? You look like you just fell in love!" the old woman told him.

"The troopers and their trucks and the bulldozer were all drivin' off the reservation when we got up there. I tell ya, they're all gone!" he said breathlessly.

"It's true, Mother Redwing, I saw it with my own eyes," Alice affirmed.

"I knew them scalps would work! Where is Mr. Murrow? Did you see him?" her mother-in-law asked.

"Yes, that's him in the station wagon right behind us," Saddles said, still trying to catch his breath.

"I hope this ain't some sort of trick," Bill commented.

"It wouldn't be the first time government agents

have tricked us," Clarence responded.

Murrow got out of the vehicle as soon as it came to a stop and walked directly to the porch and Grandmother Redwing. "I think they've decided to postpone moving you. I don't know for how long but Agent Radford said that the governor's office was emphatic about believing this whole thing has gotten out of hand. Thank you for speaking with me, ma'am. I'll be going back to the plane," he said, extending his hand to her.

"You gonna put me on TV back in New York City?" she asked.

"I'll be filing my radio report as soon as we reach Boeing Field. I assure you that you will be on TV next week and on national radio this evening. Next week you will be one of the features on the new show titled *Omnibus*. I think your story belongs there. Most of Americans with TV sets watch that show. But what I don't know is whether it will do any real good to keep you here in your little house on the flats. Only time will tell us that."

"I got me a TV set . . . it's one of only four in the whole village," Saddles noted with pride.

"No, sir, it is not. It's now one of five. We did a little filming at the house the government wants Mrs. Redwing to move into. There's a nice Philco TV in the living room of that house," the cameraman responded.

"Well, since it ain't my house . . . yet, anyways . . . then ain't nobody owns a TV set up there 'ceptin' Saddles and three other people," Grandmother Redwing asserted.

"Well, at least I'll always be the first to have

one," Saddles mumbled.

We all walked down to the lake and watched as one of the Blackhawk boys paddled Mr. Murrow and his crew out to the plane. Saddles pointed out that this was the first time in the history of the Quinault Reservation that an airplane of any kind had been in the village, let alone a plane with pontoons that could land on the lake. It turned out that the soundman was also the pilot. He skillfully guided the small yellow plane into a perfect takeoff, swooped back over us one time as if to say good-bye, and then disappeared in the direction of Seattle.

"Did anybody besides me notice that that their airplane is the same color as a yellow finch?" Grandmother Redwing asked as we walked back up to her house.

"I didn't even think about it," Saddles noted.

"A good shaman would have noticed," the old woman tesed.

"You suggest'n I'm not a good shaman?"

"Not really, dear, but some days you're better fed than observant."

Once all the reporters and villagers left the flats, we gathered around on the porch and enjoyed the fine stew the women had prepared. Saddles was right about his plum pudding upside down-cake. It was delicious and melted in our mouths.

After dinner we all drove up to Saddles' house to watch the evening news. Grandmother Redwing was a little worried the troopers would come back if she left her house again, but the rest of us convinced her the battle was over, at least for now. When we arrived at

Saddles', several people from the village were waiting on his porch in hopes of watching the news as well. The air was filled with congratulations and good wishes.

"Thank you for all your kind words, but I ain't sure the battle is over yet. I think we still gotta watch and wait. I'm scared to death them trucks is gonna go back down there while I'm up here watchin' TV and knock down my house," she told them.

"Even if the war isn't over, what you have done here is the stuff legends is spun from, Bertha. If our people are still storytellers in the future . . . the story of Grandmother Redwing will be told over and over again," Saddles said as we walked into the house.

"Oh, you old coot, you don't know what you're talkin' about," the old woman blushed. "Don't be carryin' on like that in front of all these people. I'm just a cantankerous old lady who ain't afraid to stand up to the government. Hell, if this was 1895 and they still shot Indians for causing an uprising, who knows . . . I might not be nearly so brave

"No, it's true Bertha. Hell, everybody on this whole reservation knows what a cantankerous old bat you can be. But this is different. You are an old woman who embraces with all her heart the heritage and spirit of her people. Your soul contains their souls . . . you are their Geronimo. And even if havin' to move to the top of the hill kills ya, it will still be true that them trucks is gone for now. You got the governor thinkin' about you and your ancestors. Edward R. Murrow and KING TV was right here in this village making history with you. And look at the sign the Great Spirit sent you."

"What sign?" I asked, almost afraid my question might break the awesome spell with which his portrayal of the old woman filled the room.

"That yellow airplane is the thunderbird of the new world. And if you noticed, it was a yellow thunderbird. Old woman, if you think there is power in the feather of a yellow finch . . . imagine the power in the wings of thunderbird from the new world. I tell you . . . today is the first day of the telling of a sacred story . . . a story that will be told as long as there are shamans to remember it and Quinault who want to listen to the legends and history of their tribe. In the old days, a totem bearing a red winged blackbird would be added to the next carving, and your story would become part of our history."

"I could carve such a totem," Randy said. The comment surprised all of us.

"What makes you think you can be a shaman and a woodcarver?" Willie asked.

"I been whittlin' on little pieces of wood. I'm pretty good. I keep them hidden in my bedroom. Ray got me started. He makes model airplanes out of balsa wood. It's real soft and easy to carve on. I practiced on them first. Then I tried some in cedar. It ain't as soft and it's stringier but it works real good. Besides, it grows around here and balsa wood has to be shipped in from someplace. I can get cedar for free. Ray has to pay about a quarter for just a little bit of balsa wood. I already did some little totem poles. Ray says I got a real talent. I don't know how I do it but my hands just seem to know how much wood to carve away to make

521

a face appear. I did a real good wolf on one of them and a bear turned out real good on one of them too. I got them all hidden in my bedroom. When we get back I'll show them to you if you like. I think I could do a big one . . . a regular sized one. In fact I think workin' on a big log would be lots easier than tryin' to carve a little skinny piece of wood. I think I could put a red winged blackbird on the family totem real easy. Ray says I got a real knack for it."

"That don't surprise me one bit, boy. Lotta shaman could carve. It ain't unusual for a man to have more than one talent," Saddles commented.

"When am I gonna get some sort of talent. I'm not even especially good at school," Willie stated.

"Come now, older brother, don't get green in the eyes over this. Besides you have many talents. One of the best of them is asking good questions. Without good questions life don't mean squat. Besides, any boy who dances like you can and skates like you do ain't got no business bein' jealous over a brother who can carve a piece of wood. In the eyes of the Great Spirit it is all good." Saddles look straight at Willie as he spoke. He had a way of looking at, into, and through a person when he talked. That was one of the reasons I loved listening to him.

"Well, if you're gonna carve me as a red winged blackbird . . . just don't give me a beak that looks like a hawk's. I don't want my ancestors thinkin' I was a nosy old woman."

"Oh, Bertha, how's-a-come you can't never be serious when folks is sayin' somethin' good about cha? You always turn it into a joke," Saddles chided.

"Hush, you old fool, and stop that test pattern from flippin' . . . I want to see how my nose looks on the TV," she teased.

Saddles walked over to the TV set, fiddled with the knobs on the back, and stopped the test pattern from flipping. In seconds the news came. Everyone sat quietly listening to Robert Benchworthy retell Grandmother Redwing's story and show pictures of the troopers down by her little house on the flats. He concluded his program by inviting everyone to tune in the following Sunday at three to watch Omnibus from New York City, where, the story of Grandmother Redwing would be broadcast all over the nation.

The room went wild with applause when the news ended and the test pattern returned to the screen. Saddles walked over and turned down the sound. "They wouldn't dare force you to move into that new little house now," he noted.

"I ain't so sure, Saddles. I think, just to be on the safe side, I'd like my boys to stay with me down there tonight. I got a feelin' in my gut that the worst is yet to come," Bertha said quietly. The entire mood of the room changed. Everyone turned to look at her.

"I don't really think you have anything to worry about, Mother Redwing," Audrey said. "But if it will make you feel any better, I'd be happy to stay with you as well."

"I would like that," her mother-in-law responded.

"That means we get to sleep in the back of Dad's van again tonight!" Willie whispered excitedly.

"I got a crick in my neck from sleepin' in that

thing last night," Randy complained.

"Oh, don't be so delicate," his brother chided.

"I am not delicate. A moose would have gotten a crick in his neck sleepin' in that van last night. Just because I'm a man with two souls don't mean I'm delicate."

"Well, I ain't no moose, and I didn't get a crick in my neck," Willie boasted.

"Yes, and you slept all curled up on the front seat. You practically had a mattress. The rest of us just had our sleeping blankets between us and the metal floor. "

"Give him a break, Willie . . . a crick is a crick. I didn't sleep none too good myself," I retorted in a loud stage whisper. Saddles gave me a quick look and winked.

After drinking some daisy tea which Grandmother Redwing insisted would help all of us sleep better, the boys and I went out to the van. I had wild and vivid dreams that night. In one of them Randy and Earl Vanderfleet got married in the high school gymnasium during a Halloween celebration and Jerry Cotton supplied fresh orchids for the occasion. The gymnasium was literally filled with bouquets and wreaths of orchids. I walked up to Jerry and said, "I thought you didn't approve of guys bein' fairies!" to which he responded, "Business is business, Fritz. Business is business."

Randy was dressed like Mae West. Earl Vanderfleet wore nothing but a tight blue bathing suit. An orchestra played a Strauss waltz for the newlyweds who glided across the floor for a few seconds and then separated and chose new dance partners from among the guests. Earl asked me to dance. He pressed his body so close to mine I could feel the buttons on my shirt press into his skin and mine. Then, all of the sudden, he turned into Lily Whitedove and the two of us started spinning and spinning until we became a tornado and spun right up through the ceiling of the gym and out into the stars. Instantly we were riding on the back of a huge yellow bird that was zooming toward, among and around hundreds of explosive lights in the sky. Some of the lights from the stars were so bright they hurt my eyes. Some of the stars seemed to be surrounded by flying debris that made a rumbling noise as they spun past us.

Suddenly I was awake and the dream of dancing with Lily Whitedove dissipated like so much confetti caught by a breeze. Lights were flashing through the windows of the delivery truck. I could hear the distinct sound of trucks shifting their gears and the low grinding sound of the bulldozer coming back down the hill. I sat bolt upright and for a few seconds was quiet as a stone.

Chapter Fifteen

Assault of the Weasels

"Randy! Willie! They're back! The troopers are back!" I yelled, slipping into my jeans.

"Willie sat bolt upright and looked out the window. "Oh, my god, you're right. Grab your clothes, we can get dressed in the house. Randy, wake up! The troopers are back!" he hollered.

The three of us grabbed our clothes and dashed for the house. Bill opened the door for us. "They're back!" Willie whispered.

"We know. I was just comin' out to get you boys," his uncle told us.

"Is Grandmother awake?" Randy asked.

"The women are getting her up now," Clarence said, lighting a second kerosene lamp.

"The boys and I ran to the window to watch the state troopers assemble in front of their truck lights. Seeing them stand in the illuminated exhaust of their vehicles reminded me of stories I had heard about the Jews in Germany when they were taken from their homes in the middle of the night. I couldn't believe the same thing was actually going to happen to us in America.

"Can you see any of the press out there?" Audrey asked behind us.

"Nope, it's just the troopers and the bulldozer,"

Willie answered.

"Albert Radford is out there. See, he's over there with that Major Traster. I don't see no press people either," Randy reported.

"What skunks," I moaned.

"Grandmother Redwing came up behind us, pushed Willie aside, and looked out the window. "They're not skunks. Skunks are not sneaky. A skunk always lets you know what it's about to do. And if you don't let them do what they want to do, they'll put up quite a stink, but they always do it right in front of ya the first time. They never sneak back to spray ya later in the day or while you're asleep. There's only one animal tries to make you think it's doin' one thing when all the while it has something else on its mind and that's the weasel. I never figured Albert Radford to be no weasel. But we shoulda seen it comin'. The government has always been a weasel to us."

"What's goin' on out there now, Ma?" Bill asked.

"The major and the weasel and a few troopers is walkin' up to the house," she answered, closing the curtain. She walked to one of the kitchen chairs, sat down, folded her hands in her lap, and let out a long sigh.

"Looks like this is it," Clarence whispered.

"I think I'm gonna go back to bed," his mother announced.

"Bed? But the troopers are here," Randy observed.

"Well, it's too damn early for them to be here and I'm goin' back to bed." She stood up and walked into the little room that served as both her closet and bedroom.

We heard the heavy steps of boots come up the wooden stairs and march to the door. After a few seconds of silence, three loud knocks came on the door. Clarence walked over and opened it. Major Traster and Albert Radford stood side by side in the doorway. "I'm here to ask you and the rest of your family to leave now. If you do not leave, I am prepared and empowered by the United States Government to arrest you. Which do you choose?" Traster asked with surprising politeness.

"We'll leave," Clarence answered despondently. He motioned for the rest of us to step out of the house.

"What about Mother Redwing?" Alice asked.

"She must leave too, of course," Traster responded.

"She's gone back to bed," Audrey told him.

"Perhaps you will ask her to get up?" Albert Radford suggested.

"It won't do no damn good. You know my mother, Albert. She's not going to do what we tell her to do, and she's not going to do what you tell her to do," Bill responded.

The major stepped into the room and stood next to the door as the five of us filed out onto the porch. "You are to go to your vehicles. You may drive to Bill and Alice's home or to the house in the new village that has been built for Mrs. Redwing. The choice is yours."

"We're not going anywhere until we see that my mother is safely out of this house. And I warn you . . . if you harm her in any way . . . you'll have to shoot me.

528

You can count on that," Bill answered.

"We have no intentions of harming your mother. We're just here to do our job and that is to evict Mrs. Redwing from this condemned building. If I or my men are forced to employ physical guidance to remove her from this structure, you may be assured that no harm will be done to her," Major Traster asserted. "Now, would one of you please go back into the house and tell her we're here and we want her to come out."

"She knows you're here and she's not going to come out no matter how any or all of us plead," Audrey informed him.

"I need two able-bodied men!" Traster barked at the troops.

Two men stepped forward and came up onto the porch. "Sir, yes, sir, how can we help," the older of the two said, snapping to attention.

"I want you two men to go into the house and bring Mrs. Redwing out here. Carry her if you must. Do not hurt her. Understood?"

"Sir, yes, sir," the two men answered in unison.

We watched as they disappeared into the house with their flashlights.

"You're probably going to have to find a way to carry that bed out here. I doubt that my mother will budge, and if I know her, she has tied herself to her bed or to a chair," Clarence informed the major.

"If necessary, Mr. Redwing, my men will be instructed to carry the bed out here. It will be no more difficult to transport your mother to her new home if she chooses to tie herself to her bed or a chair."

The two troopers came back empty-handed.

"Where's the old woman?" Traster asked.

'She's stark naked in there, sir! Do you expect us to pick up a naked old lady and bring her out here in front of all those troops?" the older trooper reported.

'Can't you throw a blanket over her?"

'Yes, sir! But we would still have to place our hands on her nakedness. But if that's what you want, sir, we'll do it."

"No, no . . . that wouldn't be appropriate. Radford, you go down to the radio truck and phone the jail down in Aberdeen. They've got matrons working there. See if you can get two or three up here to help out. Ask for husky matrons. Tell them what will be expected of them. Tell whoever is in charge that this is not to get out to the news," Traster ordered.

"While we're waiting for them to get here, may we go back in and visit with my mother?" Clarence asked.

"No, sir, I can't allow that. Maybe being in there alone will encourage her to come out on her own two feet."

"It won't happen," Alice told him.

"Then the matrons will carry her out," Traster asserted.

By the time Albert Radford returned from telephoning the jail in Aberdeen, the sun was beginning to come up. A pink glow lifted from the lake. "It will take nearly an hour before the matrons can get here. Maybe longer," he reported.

"Tell the men to be at ease," Traster ordered a sergeant standing next to him.

"The men were called to ease and began milling

about.

"There's coffee and donuts in the back of one of the trucks, if you're interested," Traster told us.

"I don't want any refreshment if my Mother can't have some as well," Clarence told him.

"Well, would you at least let the boys have some?" Traster asked.

"You boys hungry?" Clarence asked.

I was starving.

"We're not eatin' until Grandma can eat," Randy answered.

"Oh, very well. Take some donuts and coffee in to the old lady and have some yourselves. I'm not trying to be your enemy, Mr. Redwing. I'm only doing what I've been ordered to do. Orders are orders. Believe me when I tell you I understand how your mother feels. I have great empathy for this situation. I'm a Jew. My grandparents lost their lives in the Hitler death camps. I deeply appreciate how difficult this is for all of you. But orders are orders," Traster said.

"Isn't that what Hitler's officers said?" Alice remarked.

"Yes, it is. But this is a very different situation. Mrs. Redwing is not going to be gassed or hurt in any way. She is simply going to be removed from this condemned building and taken up to a new house on the hill. Nothing more."

"Well, she is also losing her heritage and traditions. Don't Jews have heritage and traditions?" Audrey observed.

"Yes. Yes. I know. Please, just take some coffee and donuts into the house and visit with your mother-in-law. I'll let you know when the matrons from the Aberdeen jail have arrived."

"Why Major Traster . . . you do have a heart. You don't like this anymore than I do, do you?"

"My job is to enforce the law. The law is very important to me . . . both the civil laws and the religious laws. Believe me when I tell you, Mrs. Redwing, there are religious laws that are as difficult for me to keep as it is for me to enforce the law that will move your mother-in-law from her home. Just because I'm going to do my job and enforce the law, doesn't mean my heart is made of stone. The law will win, you know."

"I know."

"Then, please, take some donuts and have one of the boys carry one of those large thermoses of coffee . . . and go inside and visit with your mother-in-law and try to enjoy your last minutes in there together. I hope you thought to bring a camera or have taken some nice pictures of the place for her to keep in an album," Traster said.

"Me and Randy did that, sir, a couple of weeks ago," I interrupted.

"You and Randy did the right thing. Now if you will excuse me, I have to radio the current situation to my commanding officer."

"And what is the current situation, Major Traster?" Audrey asked.

"That you mother-in-law is sitting in there naked as a jay bird and that two matrons from the Aberdeen jail are on their way to help us out . . . and that I have sent in donuts and coffee."

532

"Do you think your commanding officer will approve of that?" Audrey asked.

"Mrs. Redwing, my commanding officer's name is Harvey Blackwater. He is a full-blooded Yakima Indian who just happens to be a full-bird colonel. I am only a major. Believe me when I tell you that my commanding officer will care very much that I have sent in donuts."

"My goodness. I know that man. He has come to Potlatch," Clarence said.

"Yes. But like me and like you and like the old lady in the shack, he will follow the law."

§§§§

Saddles Seatco arrived on the scene at about six-thirty. One of the Blackhawk boys drove him down in their station wagon. Saddles conferred with Clarence and Bill momentarily before starting up the stairs to the porch.

"One minute, sir. I should warn you that Mrs. Redwing is naked in there. We've had to call for some matrons to help us remove her from the house," one of the soldiers sitting with the boys and me near the steps said.

"Young man, I am Saddles Seatco, a man with two souls and the shaman of this tribe. There is nothin' about the nakedness of that old woman that will either offend or embarrass me or her. The Great Spirit invented skin a long time before he invented clothes. The truth is, we Indians don't wear clothes to cover up our nakedness . . . we wear them to keep from catching cold and to keep the nettles from gettin' us. We ain't like you Europeans. Nakedness don't bother us one bit." The old shaman opened the door to the house and walked in.

In less than an hour, the matrons from the jail in Aberdeen drove down the hill and pulled up in front of the house. Three husky women in uniforms got out of the state patrol car that brought them to the reservation and walked directly to Major Traster. After a few moments of conversation, they walked into the house. In a matter of seconds Audrey, Alice and Saddles walked out onto the porch. A silence fell over the entire body of onlookers. The troopers had gathered just beyond the house, except for a few who had been talking with Clarence and Bill. The boys and I walked over to Saddles but said nothing. The sun had yet to warm the chill from the morning and a thin layer of fog was still lingering just above the lake. It was so quiet we could hear the bullfrogs calling to one another down there and the calls of birds busy looking for tidbits for their fledglings. In the distance we suddenly heard the screech of a mountain lion somewhere in the woods at the end of the lake. It amazed me that the world continued to conduct its usual business at this tragic and momentous moment in human history.

Within only a few moments one of the matrons opened the front door of the little house on the flats and the other two carried Grandmother Redwing, wrapped in a blanket, out of her house and down the steps. She looked something like a small, thick rug being carried out to be cleaned. The two matrons tried to stand her up, but the old woman bent her knees and

534

sat down on the morning grass.

"Are you okay, Mother?" Clarence asked.

"I'm just fine. But now I know how a rabbit feels when it's surrounded by wolves."

"You're a brave old bird," Saddles said, reaching down and squeezing her shoulder.

Major Traster walked over to us. "Ma'am, will you please get up and come with us to the car? We have to drive you up to the new house now."

"I ain't walking off this property."

"Please, ma'am, cooperate with the major," one of the matrons interjected.

"If you ladies want me in that weasel's car . . . you'll just have to carry me over there," she snapped.

"And that's exactly what we will do. Ma'am, we're just doing our job. We're trying to make this as pleasant as possible. Believe it or not, each of us is on your side in this matter. We're just doing our jobs," another of the matrons said. Her voice was amazingly gentle, very unlike the image she presented in her uniform with the pistol, holster, handcuffs, and billy club attached to the side of her belt.

"I appreciate that, young lady, but I ain't gonna help you do that job. I can't. Under other circumstances I might fix ya cookies and tea . . . but today, my job is to be the last of the Quinault to leave these flats. If you want me in that car, you're gonna have to stuff me into it feet first."

"Understood, ma'am," the woman answered. She gave a sign to the other two women. They formed a sort of chair with their arms. The matron with the kindly voice stepped in front of Grandmother

Redwing, put her arms around her, lifted her gently into the air, then sat her down in the armchair provided by the other two.

We watched in silence as they carried her to the waiting state car and carefully placed her in the back seat. All three of the matrons then got into the car. Major Traster walked over to it, got into the drivers side, closed the door, started up the engine, and turned toward the upper village.

"They're going to drive her to the new house now. You folks can follow up in your own vehicles if you'd like to. The men and I will go in and carefully pack her things, including that pile of wood we saw out behind the house. Once we've got it all in our trucks, we'll bring it up to the new house and unload it," one of the troopers told us.

"Thanks for nothing," Bill said.

"Please believe me when I tell you we're just following orders, sir. I myself am one-eighth Ogallala Sioux," the young soldier said.

"Just following orders, huh?" Bill repeated.

"Yes, sir."

"That's what Hitler's people said. They were just following orders too," Bill answered.

"Hitler was trying to wipe out an entire culture," the soldier noted.

"And what is it you think just happened here?" Bill asked.

§§§§

When we arrived at Grandmother Redwing's new

536

house in the upper village, she was sitting on the porch wrapped in her blanket. The three matrons were climbing back into their car.

"I should have gone in your old house and gotten you something to wear," Audrey told her.

"I'm just fine. It's plenty warm under here. This blanket is okay by me for a while. I feel very traditional wearing it."

"Traditional? I'd hardly call what's happened here this morning traditional," Clarence suggested.

"Do you want to go inside and see your new furniture and TV set?" Randy asked.

"No, honey, not right now. You and the boys go in if you like. I'm gonna sit right here for a few minutes. In fact, all of ya go on in. I'd like to be alone out here for a little bit, if ya don't mind. Anybody got a cigarette?"

"I've gone some Wings. You want one, Mother? You don't usuall smoke," Clarance said.

"I know I don't usually smoke, Clarence. I don't usually sit in front of a new house in a blanket either. Just give me a smoke and light it for me and give me some time to myself."

He did as instructed.

We all drifted into the house and began looking around. "It really looks nice," Willie said, absentmindedly.

"Yeah, it looks just like one of them pictures in the magazines. They even put fresh flowers in here," Randy noted.

We walked through the living room, down the little hall past the bathroom, and into the bedroom.

There, across the bed, was a new buckskin dress trimmed in beads and sea shells, a matching pair of new moccasins, and an envelope upon which the old woman's name was written. "Who do you suppose this is from?" I asked.

"Don't know," Willie answered. "But I think we should go back outside and let Grandma know that not everything in this new house is European."

"Let's give her a few minutes. At least time to finish that cigarette." I suggested.

When we walked back out on the porch, Saddles was just getting out of the Blackhawk's station wagon. He waved, rubbed his hands together, gave out a little giggle, and hurried up the walk to where his old friend sat wrapped in her blanket. "Haven't you gone in yet,?" he asked excitedly.

"Not yet, Saddles. I'm not ready" said Grandma Redwing.

"You ain't never gonna be ready, old woman. That's how's-a-come you're sittin' there wrapped in a blanket. Come on now . . . you've proved your point. You stood your ground. But now it's over and you're here. Now it is time to dance with Kwatee. That old changer has changed everything . . . you might as well get used to it. Piss him off! Show him you can adapt to change as easily as he can."

"They're gonna bulldoze down my house, Saddles. How I'm gonna live with that change, huh?"

Saddles sat down beside her and put his arm around her. "Just like you lived through the death of your husband and the death of your mother and father. The old house is gonna die today, Bertha. The old ways is gonna die today. It is not the Quinault way to let them die alone. You must get dressed now and prepare for the death of that little smoke house on the flats. There are prayers to be said, and we must smoke a pipe of long farewells, and you must dress appropriately to meet death when it comes for your house. This is not time to stop being a Quinault," he admonished.

"Sometimes I think you are Kwatee incarnate," Grandmother Redwing snapped.

"Now you listen to me, you stubborn old woman. You ain't got much time. Them boys will have your things packed and up here in no time . . . and that bulldozer is gonna fire up and push your house to the ground whether we make magic or not. They have already pushed my old house over. Albert told me they're gonna bulldoze them together in one pile and burn them to ashes. Come on, Bertha, you got stuff to do. You come in your new house. I got a surprise in there for you myself."

"You are one pushy old man, Saddles," his old friend said, extending her right hand to Randy for help to her feet.

"I brought along my binoculars. You wanna go out into the backyard and see what's goin' on before you go into the house?" Saddles asked.

"I got time?"

"Yeah. It will take those boys at least an hour to pack those trucks. You got a lotta wood out back and they're takin' extra special care to wrap everything so nothin' gets scratched or broken or cracked. We got just enough time to go out back and take a look."

539

We all went into the backyard taking turns so that each of us could watch the activity going on around the little house on the flats. After Grandmother Redwing had looked twice through the binoculars, Randy walked up to her. "Saddles is right, Grandma. You gotta face this like a good Quinault woman. There is stuff we can do to make sure that old house of yours goes into the next world the way it should. This ain't no different than when our people left their homes in the snow country. There is a proper way to say good-by and a proper way to leave a village . . . the Quinault way. Right?" he admonished almost in a whisper.

Grandmother Redwing turned and looked at her grandson face to face. "So, you are already givin' advice like a true shaman?"

"You know I'm right, Grandma."

"Yes, I know in my mind you are right. It is my heart that doesn't want to listen."

"Come on, Bertha, let's go into the new house. I got somethin' in there for ya. If you hurry you can see what it is, and we can all get back out here before your old house is sent to the Great Spirit." Saddles said, taking her by the arm and guiding her toward the back door of her new home.

The rest of us filed in behind them. Grandmother Redwing stopped in the kitchen and looked around. The room looked like an ad in a Sears Roebuck catalog. She walked over and felt the yellow surface of the Formica table top. "Hmmm," she said.

"Look, Mother Redwing, they've even put a little radio on the kitchen counter for you. They've thought

540

of everything," Audrey commented.

"Everything but my heart, girl. Everything but my heart," the old woman answered. "Where is my surprise from Saddles?"

"Don't you want to see your new living room first," Alice asked.

"Only if I gotta go through it to see my surprise from Saddles," her mother-in-law answered.

"Your surprise is in the master bedroom," Saddles instructed, pointing to the door that led to the dining room and living room.

"Master bedroom?" the elder Mrs. Redwing questioned.

"You got a master bedroom and a guest bedroom on the main floor, so's the grandkids can stay over. And you got another one up in the attic area. It's got a window and everything. You got enough room here for Audrey and Clarence to bring their whole clan and stay with ya," Saddles answered.

"We better hurry," Bill said. "I don't want to miss what's going on down on the flats."

"We got time," Saddles assured.

Grandmother Redwing walked into the dining room and without stopping to look around, walked through the living room and into the short hallway that led to the two bedrooms and bathroom. Saddles followed after her. The rest of us trailed after him. Before I could enter the master bedroom, I heard the old woman's voice give a gasp of surprise. "This here's beautiful. Why this is the most beautiful Quinault dress I ever did see. Where did it come from?"

"I made it for you . . . the old-fashioned way. I

541

even used bone needles to do all the work. The Blackhawk boys brought me the skins of two bucks they shot when they was huntin'. I tanned them skins myself . . . just like our ancestors used to do. I used whale blubber mixed with mint leaf to make the skins soft as silk and fragrant as all out doors."

"When did you learn to do all that?" his old friend asked, picking up the dress and holding it over her body.

"I remembered from when we was kids. Just because I was more interested in gatherin' flowers than huntin' didn't mean I didn't pay attention to what was goin' on around me," the shaman replied.

"And you did the beadwork too?"

"That was the easy part . . . you know how I like to design clothes. But I'm tellin' ya, Bertha, I thought I would bust my fingers trying to sew the lining to that dress to the buckskin. I was all the time thinkin' I should just use my sewing machine. But I stuck to it and did it all the old-fashioned way."

"Traditional Quinault ceremony dresses didn't have cloth linings," Grandmother Redwing noted.

"I know that! I said I made it the old-fashioned way. I didn't say I didn't make some improvements. You're gonna love it. Put on your new ceremony dress. We gotta get back out there."

"What's a ceremony dress?" I asked.

"When a person moves to a new village, even if they are kidnapped by another tribe, the new village must give that person a new set of clothes as a welcoming gift. The clothes must never be simple or old. They must be very special to show the high status the person is given by the tribe. That way nobody moves into a new village as low man on the totem pole, so to speak," Clarence answered.

"Well, this is certainly the most beautiful dress I've ever owned," Grandmother Redwing said. She had tears in her eyes.

"Then you like?"

"I love it."

"And you'll put it on?"

"Yes. I will put it on."

"Then, on behalf of the new village, we thank you for accepting our gift and welcome you to your new life," Saddles said.

"Just so," Grandmother Redwing affirmed. Then a scowl swept across her face. "Now you folks get out of here so an old lady don't have to get dressed in front of an audience!" The scolding tone in her voice was more playful than demanding. It was the first time I had seen her smile in weeks.

We all went into the living room to wait while she dressed. Bill and Clarence developed an instant interest in the new Philco television set at one end of the room. Audrey and Alice began admiring the bouquets of flowers and the way the room was decorated. "This looks like a room from a fancy magazine," one of them noted.

"I decorated the house a little," Saddles admitted.

"A little . . . it looks like you spent hours at it," Alice commented.

"Well . . . when the governor decided to send a house full of furniture and trimmings up here as a peace offering, Albert Radford brought me a Sears catalogue and told me to order whatever I thought Bertha would really like from it. You don't think it's too lush?"

"It's beautiful," Audrey said, looking around in admiration.

"It's pretty fancy, Saddles . . . almost like a movie set," Bill noted.

"And the great thing is that there's plenty of room for her stuff. I designed it that way. And with three bedrooms, she can store whatever she don't wanna use right away."

Grandmother Redwing stepped into the room wearing her new dress and moccasins. "How do I look?" she beamed.

"Mother, you look beautiful," Clarence said lovingly.

"Like a princess," Randy cooed.

"I feel pretty good in it. Just as wrinkled . . . but pretty good. These moccasins is a perfect fit, Saddles. You done yourself proud," she said, opening her arms to him.

"I'm glad you like them, Bertha. You look like a movie star," Saddles answered, embracing her.

"And look at this house. It looks like somethin' out of a movie, don't it. I ain't never seen so much new stuff in one place at one time except at one of them big furniture stores . . . and it all fits together real nice. You must have had something to do with that too, you old window dresser, you."

"I helped the governor decide what to buy you."

"So . . . the whole time you was encouragin' me

to stand firm and fight, you was also out picking up fancy chairs and TV sets for this house?"

"Why, Bertha Redwing, I'm surprised at you. I am a man of two souls. I can see into the past as well as into the future. I am the bridge between the Great Spirit and the great Quinault woman who caused an army to assemble on the flats just to move her up the hill. Of course, I did both. And don't act like you don't like all this . . . I know you, old woman . . . you're stubborn but you're no dummy."

"I like it. I ain't happy about losin' my old place . . . but now that that part of the battle is over . . . this place will do me just fine. It's as pretty as this dress, Saddles. You are a good friend."

"Good. Now, let's all go outside and see if they're ready to push down that old house," Saddles said as a knock came at the front door.

"Get that, would you Clarence. You're closest to the door," Grandmother Redwing requested.

I looked at my watch. It was ten-thirty in the morning.

"It's Major Traster," Clarence said.

"Well, come on in," the old woman told him, motioning for him to enter the room.

"Ma'am, we've got all your stuff in the trucks out there. We're about to unload them. Where do you want everything?"

"I don't rightly know right now. This place is pretty full of stuff as it is. You can put the wood in the shed out back. Maybe a little of it in the wood box on the back porch. You can put the furniture on the porch for now. The men will help me move it around when the time comes. All the little stuff you can put in the kitchen. I'll get to it when I can. Right now we're goin' outside to watch you weasels push down my house, if you haven't already done so."

"No, ma'am, we haven't bulldozed it yet. I wanted to let you know we're about to. The men are waiting for my order. I told them I wanted to give you a chance to watch if you wanted to and I thought, perhaps, Saddles might want to say a few words or do some sort of ritual thing before we actually bulldoze it down."

"Give us time to go out in the back, then you can give your order," Clarence said.

"Yes, sir," Traster answered. He gave a polite salute and left the house.

As we stepped onto the back porch, Randy and Saddles began chanting in Quinault. I was surprised to see Randy participating in the ritual. "What is this song. I don't remember hearing it before," I whispered to his grandmother.

"It's a song we sing for the dying. They're helpin' me say good-bye to my old place. There's a lot dyin' today, Fritz. More than you'll know."

"Do you really like what Saddles did with your new house?" I asked as I helped her down the back steps.

"It's a little fancy. But don't say nothin'. I'll get used to it . . . and I'm gonna fix it up with some of my stuff . . . so it's gonna be okay."

The troopers started piling wood in the little shed at the end of Grandmother Redwing's property even before we reached the area to watch what was

546

going on down on the flats. Within a few minutes we saw Major Traster's car moving towards the bulldozer which was already pushing the remains of Saddles old place toward the one remaining tribal smokehouse below. Within seconds the bulldozer backed up, turned toward Grandmother Redwing's little house and slowly moved forward.

"I don't know if I can watch," Grandmother Redwing said as Saddles lit a long stemmed pipe.

"Come on up here, Grandma. It's time to smoke the pipe of farewells. You gotta take the first puffs," Randy instructed. Saddles walked up to his old friend and took her by the hand.

"He's gonna make a fine shaman, ain't he, Saddles," I heard her whisper. Saddles only nodded his head in the affirmative.

Randy handed the pipe to his grandmother. I noticed that several yellow feathers hung from a string at the end of the bowl. Grandmother Redwing took the pipe to her lips and took a puff. She blew the first smoke in her mouth to the east where the little house waited for the oncoming bulldozer. A second puff was blown to the west, a third to the north, and a fourth to the south. Saddles Seatco, shaman of the Quinault, stood in front of her with his arms outstretched to the heavens, chanting along with Randy.

When she finished blowing smoke to the four major directions, the old woman took the pipe to Saddles and handed it to him. Saddles repeated the ritual, then handed the pipe to Randy who did the same thing.

I tried to imagine the intensity of emotion that

547

must have been surging through the old woman. I remembered the year my parents moved us from our house on Perkins Street to a larger home in the more expensive end of town across from the high school. I turned ten that year. I so missed the old house, I went back to visit it every day until the new people moved into it. I would go in through the bathroom window, open the back door to let in my old dog, Butch, and then together, we would haunt the rooms and miss the history we had lived there. Inevitably we would crawl into my old childhood hiding place under the steps in the kitchen that led to bedrooms upstairs. We would remain there until I could no longer bear the loss and reluctantly walk out locking the door behind me. I was young when it happened yet my love of the place was deep and real. I couldn't help wondering how much deeper the emotions and feelings of loss must be in the old Indian woman standing beside me. Just reflecting on how I felt when we moved from Perkins Street brought tears to my eyes.

"There it goes!" Grandmother Redwing announced.

I placed my hand above my eyes and squinted into the morning sun to better see the events below. It was difficult to see much without the binoculars the old woman was using. Still, I was able to make out the old structure collapse under the weight of the bulldozer. Not so much as a puff of dust went into the air. The little house just dropped to the ground like a deer whose heart had been Perced by an arrow.

"There go the ways of the Quinault," Grandmother Redwing whispered.

"Only the old ways, Grandma," Randy said, wrapping his arm around her waist and resting his head on her shoulder. "And not even the oldest of the ways of our people. The oldest of the ways were left in the snow country, and the ways of the old village were left behind even when you moved into that little house. The ways of the Quinault are not really lost, they have just changed. It is Kwatee's privilege. Change is always with us . . . but the *ways* do not change. Look at us. I live in a white man's town, my father runs a dry cleaning establishment, you've got a brand new Philco TV in your new house . . . and yet I will be the shaman to this tribe when I am old enough. The magic in the pipe of farewells will not be lost to our people, nor the sacred stories that unite us with them. No, Grandmother, the ways of the Quinault have not been lost this day. If I could wave a magic wand and restore your little house to you, pick you up and place you back in its kitchen . . . I would do it gleefully. But I cannot do that. What I can do is remind you that change is always with us. From the snow country to your new little house behind us, it is all change. But we are the same and the Great Spirit has already moved into your new house. He waits there now to welcome you."

I was dumbstruck by the wisdom and profundity with which my boyhood chum comforted the old woman. In that second all the concerns I had for Randy's love of boys vanished. I knew I was privileged to be in the presence of a being destined to be a holy man, a man of two souls, a shaman who, like Saddles and the shamans before him, would become a bridge that linked the old ways to the new, the ancient

549

memories to dreams that would carry the tribe into a future none of us could yet see. My heart filled with as much pride for Randy as it held sorrow for the old woman he was comforting.

"What's he doing now?" Alice asked, interrupting my train of thought.

"He's pushin' the debris of my old house over to the debris that was Saddles' place. It looks like we'll be goin' up in flames together," Grandmother Redwing answered, putting her free arm around her grandson.

"It is fittin'. You and me is the oldest in the tribe now. I'm gonna smoke the pipe one last time now. This time for my place. You know the words, Randy, please chant them to Tyee Sahale while I light up," Saddles responded.

"Randy kissed his grandmother's cheek, released his arm from her waist, and walked back to the edge of the hill overlooking the flats. He dropped to his knees, lifted his arms to the heavens, and began to chant. Saddles lit the pipe, blew smoke into the four directions, closed his eyes, and joined Randy in the song of final farewells.

When they finished we watched as the bulldozer retreated far enough away from the wreckage of the two houses to be safe from the flames that would soon engulf them. A truck drove over to the pile of destruction and stopped. Several troopers took something from behind the truck and poured it over the timbers and logs that had once been the two old Indian's homes. The truck pulled away, and within seconds we saw an enormous tongue of flame leap into the air followed by a cloud of black smoke. The cloud lifted above the vestiges of the two old buildings until it formed a column of smoke that seemed to reach into the very heavens. Once it was as high as the hill upon which we stood watching, a breeze caught it and pushed the thick black smoke out above the forests that separated the Quinault Reservation from Puget Sound, the metropolis cities of Seattle and Tacoma, and the little town near Mt. Rainier called Perkins Prairie.

"Okay. I seen enough," Grandmother Redwing announced in a somewhat broken and choppy voice. "I wanna go in and get outta this dress. Don't wanna ruin it while I'm puttin' my stuff away. Clarence, I want you to take the boys and drive over to the coast and dig us some fresh clams. I wanna make a nice late lunch - early dinner for you folks before you head back home. We got plenty of time. Alice and Audrey, I want you two to help me put my things away."

"I should go too, Ma. Ain't nobody as good a clam digger as me," Bill told his mother as we followed her back up to the house.

"I got plans for you right here. I need one able-bodied man to do the heavy stuff. We women can do the rest," she instructed.

§§§§

I loved digging clams almost as much as I enjoyed being at the ocean. The sound of the surf licking its way along the sandy shore and the deep roar of the waves crashing far out at sea filled the air with earth's own music. I loved listening to it because I knew it was a music that played long before people walked the earth

- perhaps before dinosaurs walked the earth. That music connected me to all the history of the planet. And that was one of the reasons I loved digging clams. I knew they were prehistoric creatures upon which our ancestors and their ancestors and the creatures that gave them birth once feasted. The simple clam connected me to all that history. We might just as easily have been apes with digging sticks or long-necked lizards poking our long sharp beaks into the sand to catch the tasty shell-lined mussels below. I picked up my shovel, took a deep breath of the husky ocean air, and was about to thrust into the sand where a tiny air bubble indicated I would find my first clam when Randy stopped me. "We pray first," he said, lifting his arms and face to the heavens.

"The clam is our brother, our fellow earth-dweller, our companion in the sand. We ask Father Spirit and Mother Earth to witness that we take no one's life for mere sport. We are here to find food for our table. All clams taken here today will become our celebration of life, our sustenance. We ask the spirit of the clams to forgive us."

"Well said, little shaman," Clarence responded with obvious pride.

"You pray real good," I told him.

"Saddles has been teaching me. I could never have done that prayer all on my own."

"Is there a prayer for each animal taken for food?" I asked.

"There is a prayer for everything taken from the earth. Even the tree has its own spirit. It's the same with rocks and the ocean itself."

"So everything has its own spirit?"

"Yes, that is one way of saying it. The more accurate way of understanding it is that the Great Spirit, God, is in everything, being it, experiencing it, finding new ways to experience Himself."

"So, when we eat clams we're eatin' God?"

"We are always eating God. God is in us too. Because of that we are always eating God, and hugging God, and kissing God, and taking God out to lunch."

"That's way over my head," I said.

"It's almost over mine," Clarence observed. "But we are not here for a lesson in religion, we're here to dig clams. Let's get to it," he said. And although he did not say so out loud, I could tell that he was very impressed with his younger son's explanation of the ways of the Quinault. There was a distinct aura of pride about him.

Digging clams on reservation property proved to be an experience of bounty. Unlike the public beaches which were constantly being harvested of their clams and mussels, the reservation beaches, which stretched for hundreds of miles around the peninsula, were only dug when a family wanted a meal of clams. There were clams everywhere and almost all of them were much larger than those found farther south on the public beaches. In less than thirty minutes, which was about as long it took us to drive from the village to the beach, both of the large buckets Grandmother Redwing had sent with us were full of succulent clams.

As we drove back into the village we noticed several vehicles parked outside the agent's office. One was from the KOMO radio station. Two were from

553

newspapers. "I expected them to be back," Clarence told us as we turned onto the street that led to Grandmother Redwing's new house. It surprised none of us to discover that Robert Benchworthy and his crew, along with several other reporters, had already set up their equipment and were speaking with the old woman on her porch. Clarence stopped the van in the middle of the street and instructed us to take the buckets of clams out from the back so we wouldn't have to lug them from where he would have to park. Willie lifted one bucket by himself. Randy and I helped with the other just as Grandmother Redwing walked over to us. "Take those buckets around to the side of the house. There's an outside faucet over there. Me and Alice put the old kitchen table next to it and a wash tub. We can clean them over there soon as I can shoo off these reporter fellas," she instructed.

"Too bad the news people weren't here to witness the burning of your grandma's old house," I mumbled as we struggled to carry our bucket of clams to the side of the house.

"It was planned that way," Randy observed. That's why we had a sneak attack. Now all they can film or photograph are the ashes or Grandma in her new house. As far as the public is concerned . . . this will look like a happy ending."

"It's not a very happy ending, is it?" I observed.

"No, it's not," Randy said, helping me settle our bucket under the faucet. "But that's no reason why Grandma shouldn't have a happy beginning in this new place. That's what I was prayin' for when me and Saddles helped Grandma through the ceremony of the pipe. I was prayin' for a happy beginning."

"You been studyin' this shaman stuff for a long time, ain't'cha?" I asked.

"About two years. I started just before we moved to Perkins Prairie."

"You were a man of two souls even then?"

"Oh, I knew that when I was five."

"How can you know that when you're five? When I was five, the only difference I knew about in boys and girls was that girls wore dresses and had longer hair. How could you tell when you was five?"

"I don't know how I knew. I just knew I was different and then one day I knew why. How did you know you liked girls and wasn't different than most other guys?"

"I don't know. I just knew," I said.

"Well, it was the same for me. I'll bet you had your first girlfriend when you were about five."

"I did. Her name was Sybil Rometo. She was six," I said.

"Ah, an older woman."

"Yeah, I guess you could say that. Did you have your first boyfriend when you was five too?"

"Yup. Only he was almost eleven."

"It was here on the reservation?"

"Yup, right here. And I ain't' tellin' you who it was neither, 'causes he still lives here and just got married," Randy said as Saddles came around the corner of the house wearing an apron.

"What good lookin' clams. We're gonna have a real feast before you boys head back for home. One of the neighbors brought over a whole sack of camas root for us, and I've got a cake in the oven. If you boys go in the house, don't you stomp your feet or nothin' near that stove. I'm worried sick with all those press people walking around in there."

"How long those press people gonna stay," Randy asked.

"They got here just after you guys left for the beach. Bertha told them she's too busy to talk much. Some of them have already gone up to the agent's office to speak with him. The troopers left the reservation right after you guys left for the beach. Things will get back to normal soon enough," Saddles answered.

"How's Mother doing?" Clarence asked, coming around the side of the house.

"She's just fine. A tear or two in the house . . . but you know your mother . . . when there's work to do . . . that's what gets done. That's one of the reasons she's so healthy at her age. She keeps busy," Saddles responded.

Once the last of the news people had gone, Grandmother Redwing came around the side of the house to make sure we were cleaning the clams to suit her. "I'm gonna fry them the old way . . . dipped in camas root batter. Alice went home and got some store-bought stuff for a nice salad from her refrigerator. It's gonna take me a week to put everything where I want it, but we made a good dent on the work while you was gone," she said, roughing up Randy's hair.

"We can stick these in your refrigerator to keep cool until you're ready to cook them," Randy pointed

556

out.

"My land, so we can. I ain't got nothin' in there yet except some pop and beer that Alice brought back with her. Now that thing is gonna take some time to get used to. I'm used to keepin' stuff in a window cooler or eatin' it up or feedin' it to the birds. Did you know that thing makes ice cubes too. It's got two trays in there. I had me some ice water a while back. I could get used to that real quick."

"So you like your new place," I asked.

"Let's just say I'm gonna get used to it. What's done is done and what is, is. Soon as you boys got the rest of them clams cleaned, you bring them on into the house. Come in the back door. I don't want you draggin' no sand across my new carpet. I'll try to have the meal fixed by two. Audrey said you should get back on the road for home by three, three-thirty. Clarence, how about you run up to the store and get me some sugar and one of them Kool Aid packages. I want to fix some for the boys. Now that I got ice cubes in my refrigerator, I can try out all sorts of things. I even made a pot of coffee for our break in that brand new electric percolator the governor sent over. Saddles showed me how. It makes real good coffee and ya don't have to drop egg shells in it to get the grounds to settle to the bottom cause there ain't no grounds in it. Ain't that somethin'? And my new tea kettle's got a whistle on it so ya know when the water is boilin'. I tell ya, all these newfangled things ain't half bad."

"Why, Bertha Redwing, I do believe you're becomin' a city girl," Saddles teased.

"Ain't none of that happenin', you old coot. I'm

just tellin' the truth about a few newfangled thing I ain't never used before."

"You like them. Admit it!" he squealed.

"I ain't admittin' nothin' of the kind. But it is nice not to have to keep egg shells around to clear up the coffee before you pour a cup."

"Oh you like it and you know you do," Saddles taunted.

"Maybe I do and maybe I don't. If I was half the shaman you claim to be, you'd know the answer to that without askin'."

"Well, you'll notice, old woman, I ain't askin' . . . I'm tellin'. And that's a sure sign of a super good shaman."

"Next thing I know, you'll be wantin' me to buy a car and learn how to drive it," Grandmother Redwing said as she turned to go back into the house.

"And that ain't a half bad idea either," Saddles shouted after her.

§§§§

Once the clams were cleaned, Randy and I carried them into the house and placed them on the kitchen counter. Saddles was dressing out the small carcass of what I thought was a rabbit. "You shoot yourself a rabbit?" I asked, watching him skillfully slice through the joint between the leg and thigh.

"Nope, this here's a possum. Delbert Longfeather's wife brought it over as a house warming gift for Bertha while you boys was diggin' clams. I'm just dressing it out for her. You ever eat possum?"

"Unfortunately , yes," I answered.

"Good, ain't they?" he asserted, rinsing his hands under the faucet in the sink.

"I don't remember. All I know is that I remember having to choke it down. Possums are too cute to eat."

"Nothin's too cute to eat, boy. Whoever heard of a squeamish Indian?"

"I'm not squeamish."

"You don't much care for dog stew," Randy interjected.

"Well, that was dog meat. My dad is a real hunter and we ain't rich. My dad is always draggin' something home from the woods. I've eaten bear, all sorts of game birds, just about every fish that exists in these parts, squirrels, mountain goat, deer, moose, elk. I've even had horse meat over at my Aunt Ladeans. But I draw the line at possum and dog."

"Ain't no different than squirrel 'cept maybe there's a little more meat on its bones and they taste a bit like pig. You is a squeamish boy. Admit it," Saddles said.

"I hear tell you don't like boxin' because you don't like to see people bleed. Is that true, Saddles?" I asked.

"I don't much care for any of the beat'm-up sports. Punchin' a guy in the face until his eyes bleed don't seem like no sport to me."

"Then you're just as squeamish as me."

"Then maybe you're a man with two souls yourself," Randy teased.

"Right now I ain't even sure I'm a man of one soul . . . but I am sure that I don't wanna eat none of that possum."

"Good! All the more for me," Grandmother Redwing noted, coming into the room. "Hurry up, Saddles, I wanna rinse these clams one more time before I batter them up for fryin'."

"Can we play the radio, Grandma?" Randy asked.

"If you like. I can't figure out how to make it say anything yet. I clicked that button that says *off* and *on* but nothin' happened."

"You gotta select a station and turn up the volume," Saddles told her.

"Come on, Grandma, I'll show you," Randy said. He walked his grandmother over to the little portable radio at the other end of the counter. "It's real simple. Watch me," he instructed. Randy clicked the radio on, turned the knob that selected stations until he found KOMO radio, and adjusted the volume. "The Arthur Godfrey Show should be on now," he said. Within seconds the room filled with Godfrey's voice singing *Hawaiian War Chant*, accompanying himself on his ukulele. "Oh, I do love listening to Arthur Godfrey sing," Saddles commented.

"Who is Arthur Godfrey?" Grandmother Redwing asked.

"That's him singin'. He's got a talk show on the radio every day. He talks about the news and everyday things and he sings and has other singers on his show. He advertises Lipton Tea. You've heard of Lipton Tea, haven't you?" Randy explained

"I heard about the tea. I got me some

560

someplace in one of them boxes. But I sure never heard of no Arthur Godfrey."

"I don't even answer the telephone when his show is on. I just know he's a kind man. I love Hawaiian music anyway, and Arthur is always playing it. Here, Bertha, I'm finished with the sink. You can rinse them clams now. I'll wrap this possum in some butcher paper I brought over from my place. It will keep about two months in the freezer compartment of your refrigerator. After that it will start to get freezer burn so be sure you don't forget to cook it before that."

"I plan on savin' him for when I got some company but are you sure that little chest in the refrigerator can freeze him solid. I ain't never froze nothin' before 'cept in the winter."

"Solid as those ice cubes you've fallen in love with," Saddles assured her.

The boys and I went out back to see what remained of the two burned residences down on the flats. Saddles loaned us his binoculars. Willie looked first. "Ain't nothin' down there but some smoldering black spots," he commented, handing the binoculars to Randy.

"I'm sure gonna miss that place," Randy said. I don't know why they couldn't just let the buildings slowly rot back into the land. That way at least we could have visited there once in a while."

"If they had left it standing, Grandma would have moved back in," Willie reminded him.

"Oh, yeah."

I was the last to look down at the charcoaled remains of the two homes. I was struck with the sudden barrenness of the place. "It's hard to believe they actually went through with it, ain't it?" I mused.

"It's a damn shame," Willie agreed.

"Yes and no," Randy commented. "On the one hand the whites won another battle. Another Indian has been screwed over by the American Government. But I was always worried about Grandma livin' down there by herself. She's at the age where she could fall and break a hip or somethin' real easy. I think it's gonna be better for her to be up here closer to Bill and Alice . . . especially now that Saddles is livin' up here. The Great Spirit knows what he's doin'. We got to trust that if we're gonna keep the true spirit of the Quinault alive in the world."

"You're gonna be a good teacher someday, Randy," I commented.

"All shamans are teachers, Fritz," Willie told me.

"Really?"

"Yeah. It's sort of like bein' a rabbi for the Jews. A shaman is like a priest, a teacher, a medicine man, a counselor, and a spirit guide . . . all in one."

"I hope I'm up to it. Most of the time all I think about are boys," Randy said more to himself than aloud.

"If Saddles says you're gonna be a good shaman, then all you got to do is study," his brother assured him.

"I got to do more than that. I've got to saddle Seatco someday myself."

"When the day comes, you'll be up to it. Now, how 'bout us guys carry some wood from the shed up to the wood box on the back porch for Grandma. I

562

noticed them troopers only filled it about half full."

"Sounds okay to me," I said.

We walked over to the little shed at the end of the property, opened the door and stepped inside. There against the wall across from the neatly piled wood was a brand new porcelain toilet. "Wonder what that's doin' here?" I queried.

"Probably an extra," Willie suggested.

We each loaded our arms with wood and carried it to the wood box on the back porch, then went into the house through the back door to see how close we were to eating. "You boys go on in and wash your hands. By the time you get back, we'll have lunch on the table," Alice instructed. The rich fragrance of fried clams and clam chowder filled the kitchen.

The three of us walked down the hall to the bathroom. When we stepped inside, I was dumbfounded. The toilet had been removed. A small scatter rug had been placed over the floor where it had stood and a kitchen chair was placed over the rug to keep anyone from stepping in the hole. "What's this all about?" I asked, stepping up to the sink.

"Beats me," Willie noted.

"Me, too," Randy agreed.

As soon as I walked back into the kitchen, I walked over to Grandmother Redwing. "How come you had somebody take the toilet out and put it in the shed?" I asked.

The old woman set a platter of fried clams on the table, wiped her hands with her apron, and gave me a long friendly look. "I don't want to insult your European ways, Fritz, so I'm gonna tell you the same thing I told my kids when I told Bill to take that fool contraption outta my house." She sat down on one of the kitchen chairs. "I have done what the government made me do. I have moved to the upper village. I'm gonna learn some new ways and start doin' lots of things I ain't never done before like cook coffee in a percolator and make toast in a little electric hotbox instead of on the stove. I'm gonna have television and radio programs talkin' to me in my house and learn to use a telephone. But first and foremost I am a Quinault . . . the oldest Quinault livin' in this here village. I am gonna keep the Quinault ways and do my duty out in the woods just like I always did, just like my own mother and father did, and all the Quinaults before me. Them weasels may have chased me away from my old place . . . but they ain't gonna turn me into no European. Fritz, even the coyote knows better than to poop in his own den."

Chapter Sixteen

Learning the Ways of Coyote

"She did what?" my mother asked.

"She had Bill unhook the toilet from her new bathroom and put it out in the shed."

"I tell you, that old woman is crazy. I thought the reason they moved her to the village was because her old place didn't meet governmental standards of sanitation?"

"She says that even the coyote knows better than to poop in its own cave"

"Does she have an outhouse?"

"Nope."

"Then where, in the name of mercy, is the woman going to defecate?" Mother asked.

"Out in the woods," I answered.

"In the woods!? That cinches it. Any old woman who would rather take a dump in the woods when she can sit on a comfortable toilet, has bats in her belfry. They should have put that old woman in Stelicoom when they had the chance."

"Oh, Marjorie, people have been going to the bathroom outdoors far longer than indoors. Don't be so critical." Dad admonished.

"People used to also live in caves and eat their meat raw. Any person who would willingly trudge out into the rain and snow to take care of something that can much more easily be done indoors is nuttier than a fruit cake."

"Just because the woman doesn't want a toilet in her house doesn't make her insane, Marjorie."

"I don't know why you always take sides with that old lady. One would think you were an Indian instead of Polish!" Mother admonished.

"It don't make no never mind," I said, dumping my dirty clothes into the hamper.

"What sort of English is that?" Mother chided.

"What'cha mean?" I answered.

"Whether you are aware of it or not, your grammar is beginning to sound as if you were born to urchins living under a bridge somewhere. Is that the kind of English they speak up on that reservation?"

"They speak English just as good as us," I answered.

"*They speak English just as well as we do* would be the correct way to say that, dear. You will kindly use only correct diction and sentence structure while in my presence. Is that understood?"

"I'm just talkin' the way Saddles and Grandma Redwing talk. Even Grandma and Grandpa Harding talk like that. It's faster. What's wrong with it?"

"English is a second language for your friends, Saddles Seatco and Grandmother Redwing. The same is true for your grandparents. But English is not your second language. You have no excuse for using such poor language skills and I won't have it in my home. This isn't a debatable issue. Is that clear?"

"Yes, ma'am. But Randy and Willie do it when they're up there too. And sometimes here."

"If Randy and Willie jumped off a mountain, would you?"

"No, ma'am."

"Then let's use the language as it is meant to be used and not in ways that abuse that process. Okay?"

"Okay. Grandmother Redwing's birthday is in two weeks. I've been invited. Can I go?"

"You're spending a great deal of time up there, dear."

"But he isn't getting into any trouble. I see no reason why he shouldn't go," Dad countered.

"Well, make sure your chores are done. I suppose you'll be up there the whole weekend again?"

"Yes, ma'am."

"Okay. But you haven't seen much of Jerry Cotton in a long time. His feelings must be very hurt," she observed.

"He's busy with his Orchid Appreciation Society. The Redwing boys and me was thinkin' 'bout bringin' Saddles Seatco to town to teach us how to start a Vision Appreciation Society," I answered.

"There you go again . . . speaking English like an uneducated ruffian. I will not have it! On my side of the family we've been English and have spoken English for hundreds and hundreds of years. If you're so much into traditions, I don't understand why you don't embrace the tradition of speaking good English! Now once again, try that bit about the Vision Appreciation Society using only proper word endings and acceptable syntax."

"And when you get done . . . there's something in the living room I think you'll be interested in seeing?" Dad interjected.

"What's in the living room?" I asked.

"Oh, your father has gone off the deep end again. He thinks money grows on trees. He purchased a television set. We'll be paying for it for the next three years!"

"Really! Our own television set? Grandmother Redwing is gonna be on some show called Omnibus next Sunday. Edward R. Murrow was out to see her and everything!"

"Grandmother Redwing is *going* to be on some show," Mother corrected.

"Yeah, next Sunday. Can we invite the Redwings over to watch?"

"If you like," Mother agreed.

"Edward R. Murrow was on the Quinault Reservation this weekend?" Dad asked.

"Didn't you see him on the Channel Five news?"

"We just got the antenna hooked up about an hour before you got home. All we've seen so far is the test pattern. I bought the TV Friday night when I got off work but Al Pederson down at the furniture store couldn't deliver it until today," Dad answered.

"Well, Murrow was there all right. Lots of reporters were there. But they all left before the government bulldozed down her house and forced her up to the new place. We was tricked."

"*Were* tricked," Mother corrected

"Yup. They tricked everyone into thinking they weren't gonna do anything. The troopers and the bulldozer all left the reservation. Then while we were asleep . . . they came back and forced her out of the

568

house. They had to send for two matrons from the jailhouse over in Shelton though. Grandma Redwing took off all her clothes so that when the troopers burst into the house to carry her to the truck . . . they found her naked as a jay bird! You should have seen their faces when they came out! Then the major sent for the matrons. They was the ones who actually carried her outside wrapped in a blanket."

"They *were* the ones," Mother corrected again. This time through an exasperated sigh.

"We were tricked. I'm getting to the point where I can hardly stand white people anymore," I said.

"Well, that's not going to work very well for you," Mother sighed again.

"Oh, Mom, that's not what I mean. I mean I just don't get it. I still don't understand why they wouldn't just let her live out her life the way she wanted to. It just isn't fair."

"Life is not fair. You'd better get used to that. Believe me. It is not fair," she responded.

"Yeah, I been figurin' that out all on my own."

"But you'll be back up there in two weeks and you can find out how the old woman is doing and what happened with that toilet. I think I'll call Audrey and invite the Redwings to watch Omnibus with us next Sunday. We might as well share."

"Oh, Mom, that would be great."

§§§§

We arrived later than usual at the Quinault Reservation the weekend of Grandmother Redwing's birthday

569

party. Clarence had some last minute deliveries to make. But now that his mother had extra bedrooms, the boys and I would no longer be permitted to sleep in the little travel-trailer out behind Bill and Alice's place. Saddles had ordered double-sized bunk beds for one of the rooms so we all had comfortable places to sleep in the old woman's new house in the upper village. It was nearly nine-thirty when Clarence pulled his Ford up in front of his mother's house. A white picket fence now graced the perimeters of her property. Clarence honked the horn to let her know we had arrived. Within seconds Grandmother Redwing opened the door and walked out onto the porch.

"Where did the nice fence come from?" Audrey asked as she stepped out of the car.

"Bill put it up for me as a birthday present this week. The Blackhawk boys helped him."

"It's sure nice," Clarence noted as a large puppy nosed its way out onto the porch. Grandmother Redwing stooped over and picked the creature up and cradled it in her arms.

"A puppy! I thought you didn't like having a dog around the house," Clarence said.

"He's why I got the fence. That fool Saddles got me this dog for my birthday. He said he thought I needed some company and that the dog would help take my mind off my old house. I wasn't gonna take him. But Saddles brought her over and put her in my lap. I don't know what got into me but I liked her right away. She sort of wormed her way into my spirit. Well, there's too many cars goin' up and down these streets and I didn't want to keep the puppy chained up in the backyard. That ain't no kinda life for a dog. So Bill offered to build me a fence for my birthday present. I think him and Saddles was in on the whole thing all the time," she said, walking down the steps toward the gate at the end of her sidewalk.

"What did you name the puppy," I asked, helping the boys remove some suitcases and birthday presents from the trunk of the car.

"I was just gonna call her Dog . . . but Saddles said she should get a name and have a naming ceremony just like any other member of the family. I named her Abby, 'cause she's white like them monks that live over in that monastery near Olympia. I seen them out walkin' around when we go by. And I kinda just like the name.

"She's sure big for a puppy. What kind of dog is she?" Randy asked as his sisters scurried through the gate to pet the young creature in their grandmother's arms.

"He says this here's a Great Pyrenees, whatever that is. She's gonna get real big. She's already heavy to lift."

"She's beautiful," I said, putting down a suitcase so I could pet her too.

"Well, she sure ain't no coyote. I've gotta keep papers down on the kitchen floor until she learns to go outside. She's finally learned to pee and poop just on them papers, but I still ain't got her trained to go out in the yard like she's supposed to. But she does go in the woods when I take her for his walks. She'll figure it out soon enough. And she knows her name, don'tcha, Abby," she said, lifting the puppy to her face. The dog licked the old woman's nose, and wagged her tail.

"Looks like you've got a real friend there, Mother," Clarence told her.

"Well, I didn't really want her at first. I scolded Saddles for even buyin' her without first talkin' to me, 'specially a dog that's gonna get bigger than a wolf when she's done growin'. But ya know, this little girl is so damn cute, I couldn't resist her. And appetite! Land, this girl can eat! I went up to the store and bought a big bag of dog food for her. It was such a big bag the store had to deliver it for me . . . weighed fifty pounds. But she prefers table scraps. I usually mix whatever's left of my supper with her kibble. She eats it right down. 'Course I fix extra now that I got her. I gotta keep kibble down all the time. This girl always seems to be hungry. Close that gate after yourselves, boys. I wanna put this heavy galoot down. I don't want her gettin' out in the street. Bill put a gate out back for me too. That way I can take Abby with me when I go out into the woods without havin' to go to the front gate all the time."

"Looks like this is going to be a pretty nice birthday year for you, Mother Redwing," Audrey noted.

"Yup. Pretty good. Anybody hungry? I got cookies and I've got a couple of quarts of milk in the refrigerator. I had Hollis from the store bring them by today. It keeps milk sweet and cold for nearly a week," she said, putting the pup down. She walked back into the house with Abby close behind her.

Once we put everything away, the boys and I went straight for the kitchen to take their grandmother up on the offer of cold milk and cookies. As we

572

walked in, a telephone on the kitchen wall near the back door rang.

"I don't remember there bein' no phone in the kitchen," Clarence noted.

"'Twern't. I had the telephone people come and put one in here and one in the bedroom too so's I won't miss any calls. That's probably Saddles. I was supposed to call him when you folks got here. He wants to walk over and see what you think of Abby."

The old woman walked over to the telephone. "Hello," she shouted into the receiver. "Oh, I'm sorry, Saddles. I keep forgettin' I don't have to yell atcha through this contraption. Yeah, they're here. They just unpacked. I'm about to serve the boys some cookies and milk. See ya." She carefully placed the telephone back on its hook and walked to the cookie jar.

"My, my . . . three telephones. Sounds to me like you're adjusting just fine to livin' in the new village," Audrey teased.

"Well . . . Saddles and Bill talked me into gettin' them . . . just in case there's an emergency or somethin'. They just installed the two new ones yesterday.

"With all those phones, how's-a-come you don't call us?" Clarence asked.

"It's long distance. Besides, I don't much like talkin' on the thing yet. Not that that bothers Saddles in any way. He must call over here five or six times a day. Same thing with Alice and Bill. Why, you'd think they're afraid they'll forget what my voice sounds like the way they carry on."

"You say you called Hollis down at the store to have him deliver the milk?" Audrey asked.

"Well, Audrey, what's the point in havin' a nice newfangled thing like a telephone if it don't come in handy. Besides, I don't much like leavin' Abby alone and I sure ain't taken her to the store until she learns not to pee in the aisles. Home delivery don't cost no extra and local calls is free."

"You're movin' into the new world, Grandma," Randy asserted.

"I'm doin' okay but I think you'll find these cookies are better than anything you can buy up at Hollis' new world grocery store. These here are old world cookies," she teased.

"Indians didn't bake cookies in the old days, Grandma. We didn't have white flour or cookie sheets. Even cookies are new world." Randy was quick to point out.

We had our own flour and we made a kind of cookie sweetened with honey and fresh fruit and sometimes nuts. We may not have called them cookies but us kids ate them just as fast." His grandmother assured him.

"Well, you didn't eat them with a glass of cold milk you had delivered special to the house." Randy pointed out.

"That's true. Not with cold milk or any kind of milk. But we did have tea. Cookies and tea." the old woman agreed.

"Sweet cakes and tea," Randy contradicted. "They weren't cookies. Cookies are not traditional Indian foods."

"I will not argue with the young shaman providing the young shaman will not argue with his grandmother."

§§§§

The next morning I awoke to the smell of hot Ovaltine. I slipped into my jeans and T shirt and headed for the kitchen. I could hear Audrey and Clarence whispering down the hall. "Is that Ovaltine I smell?" I hinted.

"Shh. Mother Redwing is still sleeping. I'll get you a cup. I want to get her birthday cake in the oven right away. Saddles is bringing over a batch of quail for me to roast for her birthday dinner, and he plans to roast his cattail and camas casserole over here too. This oven is going to be busy all day," she whispered.

"I sure hope she likes what I got her for her birthday," I said, sitting down at the table.

"What did you get her," Clarence whispered.

"Well, I was gonna give her a bag of peacock feathers, but Jerry said he was fresh out. I'm sure he was lying. So, that put me in a real dilemma. I ended up buying her a bunch of beads. I know how much she likes to do beadwork. My dad took me to all the thrift shops along Pacific Avenue in Tacoma. I must have three pounds of different kinds of beads. All kinds. Every color you can think of. Even some colors I never seen before."

"*Saw* before," Audrey corrected.

"Did my mom talk to you about my grammar?"

"She did . . . and she was right too. Willie and Randy need to improve their grammar as well. From now on you boys are all going to be expected to speak properly."

"I wonder how's-a-come bad grammar comes so easily and it's so hard to learn good grammar?" I pondered.

"It's all the more difficult when you have grandparents and older friends for whom English is not their first language. Your mother and I had quite a nice talk about all this. We understand that you want to emulate those who are grandparent figures in your lives . . . but if you hope to succeed in the world . . . you and the boys are going to have to learn to speak more appropriately. That goes for Clarence and me too. We're all gong to try to be better examples."

"Are you gonna correct Grandmother Redwing too?"

"*Going* to correct . . . and no. Mother Redwing and Saddles, just like your grandparents, probably don't even think in English. Besides it is never appropriate for a child to correct a parent in such matters."

"In what matters?" her mother-in-law asked, stepping into the room.

"Oh, we didn't mean to wake you," Audrey apologized.

"I shoulda been up a long time ago. That Philco keeps me up too late on nights they show a movie. I gotta learn to shut that thing off at bedtime. Sometimes I fall asleep right in my chair with the fool thing on. Then I wake up in the wee hours of the morning with the white screen flickin' at me."

"Nothing wrong with sleeping in a little later at your age. You're not a spring chicken anymore,"

Clarence observed.

"Thank you for remindin' me I'm another year older. You drinkin' that sweet stuff so early in the mornin'?"

"Clarence has a cup or two of hot Ovaltine every morning since we moved to Perkins Prairie," Audrey answered.

"It'll ruin your teeth," the old woman chided.

"I have perfect teeth, Mother. Happy birthday," Clarence said kissing The old woman on the cheek.

"I've got your tea kettle on and your coffee all perked" Audrey pointed out. "I didn't know which you would prefer this morning."

"I usually have coffee. I like that coffee machine. I can plug it in, go wash my face and brush my teeth, get dressed, take Abby out in the back for a while, and by the time I'm done . . . so is the coffee."

"Happy birthday," I said warmly.

"Thank you, Talks With Eagles. I been now eighty-five times around the sun . . . and that's exactly how many old bones ache this mornin'."

"I brought up sweet rolls and maple bars from Fox's Bakery. Would you like one with your coffee?" Audrey asked.

"You know how partial I am to them maple bars. That old Mr. Fox is a real good pastry maker. Did you bring the ones that got that cream fillin' in them too?"

"I certainly did," Audrey answered, taking one of the pastries out and placing it on a plate for her mother-in law.

"It will ruin your teeth," Clarence teased.

"Sure wish you hadn't put that toilet out in the

shed. I gotta go in the worst way," I mumbled.

"Well, you'll just have to go out in the woods like everybody else," Grandmother Redwing observed.

"I gotta go number two," I pointed out.

"There's a roll of toilet paper on the back porch. Just follow the path on the other side of the back gate out into the woods. There's plenty of places to poop out there," the old woman instructed.

"I'm going over to Saddles' place to do my duty, Fritz . . . I'll drive you over if you like," Clarence told me.

"Ya know, Clarence, every creature live'n in these parts poops in the woods. That's how's a come the woods is so lush. Poop is good for green things. Everybody knows that."

"I prefer to sit in a warm room where I can wash my hands afterwards and be comfortable while I poop. One of these days you're going to lose your balance out there try'n to poop in the woods and you're gunna fall in your own crap. Maybe then you'll wish you had left that toilet in the house. And you should have left it in at least for company."

"You're gettin' more white all the time," his mother admonished.

"I don't mind slingin' my ass over a log if I'm out hunting or something. But I am not going to use the woods for my bathroom on a regular basis. Besides, Saddles said we could use his facilities anytime we wanted," Clarence noted.

"I need to go too, Clarence. Let's drive on over. Fritz, you can bring along your Ovaltine if you like. I have a feeling there will be a line."

§§§§

When we returned from Saddles' place, Grandmother Redwing and her grandsons were eating pastry and talking in the kitchen. Audrey began taking ingredients for the cake frosting out of a bag of groceries she had brought along for the weekend.

"That cake sure smells good. Lemon, ain't it?" Grandmother Redwing asked.

"Your favorite. Would I bake anything else?" her daughter-in-law commented as a knock came at the front door.

"I wonder who that can be at this hour? It's way too early for Saddles to be movin' in this direction," Grandmother Redwing said, wiping her hands on her apron and going down the hall to the front door. I followed after her hoping it might be Lily Whitedove who I knew had also been invited to the party. When she opened the door, Albert Radford was standing there with a dozen white roses in his hand. "You!" she said, disapprovingly.

"I came to wish you a happy birthday," Radford said, extending the flowers to her. "I brought these as a peace offering."

I knew enough about Quinault traditions to know that a gift of white flowers was always a plea for forgiveness and a sign of peace. To refuse such a gift could bring bad medicine to one's lodge unless the refusal was truly justified.

"You're as clever as a coyote," Grandmother Redwing said, accepting the flowers.

"I prefer to call it the wisdom of the ancestors," the agent told her.

"Well, don't just stand there lettin' dust blow in. Come on in and shut the door and say hello to Clarence and Audrey and the boys. They're out in the kitchen," the old woman mumbled.

"Well, actually, Mrs. Redwing, I need to talk to you about something."

"You can talk to me in the kitchen. I got lots to do before company starts gettin' here for my party. You want some coffee, Albert?"

"Please," he answered. The two of us followed her into the kitchen.

"And how are you, young Mr. Harding?" Albert asked.

"Just fine. I came up for the party."

"Good morning, Albert. Burned down any houses lately?" Clarence said as we stepped into the kitchen.

"That's all water under the bridge now, Clarence . . . no need to bring it up no more. Albert was just followin' orders. That battle is over and done with. No sense openin' old wounds," his mother chastised. "Albert is just here to wish me a happy birthday. He brought white flowers." She walked over to the cupboard and took out a cup and saucer.

"Well, actually, as I said, I do need to speak to you about something," Radford said, leaning up against the kitchen counter as he accepted a cup of coffee from the old Indian woman.

"What is it, Albert?" she said, sitting back down at her place at the table.

"We've had some complaints . . . "

"About my Abby?"

"Oh, no ma'am. Everybody loves Abby. She's a beautiful puppy. No . . . we've had some complaints from some parents and a couple of tourists who say . . . well, they say their kids have seen you . . . have caught you out in the woods defecating. Is that true?"

"Well of course, it's true. I have pooped in the woods all my life, just as my mother did and her mother before her. It is the way of the Quinault just as it is the way of all the Great Spirit's creatures."

Radford took a sip of his coffee. I suspected he was trying to create a little time in which to frame his words. "Mrs. Redwing, there's a perfectly good toilet in the bathroom of this house. It was put in this house so you wouldn't have to use the woods for such things anymore. It is, in fact, against the law to use the woods for such things."

"Oh, that's a crock of shit, Albert. You know damn well hunters and fisherman crap in the woods all the time. There ain't no such law and you know it!" Clarence said angrily.

"I had Bill take that damn thing out to the little shed the very day I moved in here. I am Quinault, Albert Radford, and in Quinault ways - even coyote knows better than to poop in his own cave. I'm gonna use the woods like always and don't give me no nonsense about it bein' against the law to poop in the woods. You gonna arrest all the critters that live out there?"

"No, ma'am . . . and you're right . . . it is not against the law to defecate in the woods. But that stand of trees out behind your place is now part of city property. Those are city owned woods and it is against the law to defecate on city property."

"So, you're just here to start another fight!" the old woman snapped. She got up, took the white roses from the kitchen counter, and handed them back to him.

"Oh, Bertha, please don't be like this. There's a city ordinance about this. The tribe voted it in when the upper village was first incorporated. Those woods were left standing so people could enjoy walking in them . . . so children could play out there . . . so the place would still look pristine and woodsy. I'm just here asking you to keep the law. If you like, I can reinstall that toilet for you. There's nothing to it. But you can't continue to use that wooded area for such things. This is now an incorporated township. It has laws and rules of sanitation that must be followed by all its citizens. That's why you were forced to move from that little house on the flats . . . it was not up to sanitation codes. And as long as your toilet is out in the shed, neither is this house. It must be put back."

"Albert Radford, I been poopin' out in them woods since I moved in and it's gonna take more than some damn fool white man's law to force me to poop in my own lodge."

"The law was voted in by the tribe," Radford insisted.

"The law was forced down the peoples' throats and you know it. Just like all these little houses and the destruction of our village was pushed down their throats. You didn't give me no choice but to move up here on the hill, but unless you plan on be'n with me twenty-four hours a day to catch me poopin' . . . I don't think there's a damn thing you can do about this! Now if you don't mind, I got better things to do than stand around talkin' to you about when, where, and how I'm gonna poop."

"But, Mother Redwing, when you visit us in Perkins Prairie, you use the toilet at our house and you did the same when you visited the Hardings at their farm last year at Thanksgiving," her daughter-in-law noted.

"Audrey, whose side are you on?" the old woman admonished.

"I'm on your side, Mother Redwing. But the law is the law . . . and you accepted the lovely dress Saddles made for you on the day you moved into the upper village. Part of Quinault tradition is to follow the ways of the new village. Isn't that right, Clarence?"

"Don't pull me into this argument. I'm not going to start a fight with my mother on her birthday," Clarence responded.

"Bertha, the law is the law. Are we going to have to have another long battle?" Radford asked.

"Tell me, Albert, do you ever poop in the woods?" Grandmother Redwing asked.

"Only if I'm away from my office and the township, like if I'm out fishing or hunting. Only when I have a good reason for being out in the woods when the need arises," he answered.

"Well, as far as I'm concerned, I've got a damn good reason for goin' out in the woods. Now I think you should leave so I can get back to gettin' ready for my party."

"Clarence, she's your mother. Talk to her," Albert requested.

"I've already talked to her. She will hear none of it. What real difference does it make, Albert. What if Mother promises to be more careful and make sure there aren't any other folks around when she needs to go?"

"Everybody else in the tribe is using their bathrooms appropriately," the agent pointed out."

"Well, I ain't everybody else. If ya ain't figured that out by now, ya ain't never gonna."

"Can't we dig her an outhouse down by the shed? Wouldn't that solve the problem?" Clarence asked.

"You can't have an outhouse inside the city limits. It's the law," Radford replied.

"The law, the law, the law. Is that all you can talk about?" the old woman snapped.

"That's my job, Bertha."

"Well, then I'll just start hikin' down to the flats and go back to doin' my duty in the woods down there. The exercise will be good for me."

"You're too old to make that trip all the time. And what about in the winter or when it's raining?" Audrey pointed out.

"That won't change the fact that you must reinstall that toilet in the house. Without a flush toilet in the bathroom, this house no longer comes up to city sanitation codes. You can hike anywhere down on the flats to do your duty you want to . . . but the toilet has to come back in . . . no matter what. That's the law!"

584

"I ain't gonna have that contraption in my house, Albert Radford, and that's that. You try puttin' it back in here and if I have to take it out myself, that's what I'll do. But I ain't havin' that thing in my house and that is final!"

"You're an impossible old woman. I'm going to have to call Olympia about this," Radford said, swallowing the rest of his coffee and setting the empty cup on the counter.

"I don't care if you call the president of the United States."

"Why do you have to make everything so difficult, Bertha?" the agent asked.

"Look here, Albert. I was perfectly happy until you got here this mornin'. And I'm tellin' you right now . . . even if Olympia says I gotta have that contraption in my house and even if they send troopers down here to put it back in . . . I ain't so old that I can't fill it up with dirt and put house plants in it. You may have forced me to move from the flats, Albert, but not you or nobody else is gonna make me poop in my own lodge. I'll let you arrest me and lug me off to prison before that will happen!"

Clarence walked the agent to the front door just as Saddles arrived with a basket filled with cattail and camas roots. The two men exchanged brief greetings as the old shaman walked into the house. "I see that your mother has turned down an offering of white flowers," he noted once the door was closed.

"Albert is insisting Mother bring the toilet back into the house," Clarence said as they walked into the kitchen.

585

"How did he find learn it was out in the shed?" Saddles asked.

"He said some people caught me poopin' out in the woods and complained about it," the elder Mrs. Redwing said without looking up from her work.

"Well, I'd complain if I was walkin' around out in them woods and stumbled across you poopin' out there. Good Lord, Bertha, this is the 1950's. I don't see the difference between using a modern device to brew your coffee or mix your cake batter and using a modern device to do your poopin' on. Yer bein' real contradictory here, Bertha!" Saddles chided.

"You know what I've said about coyote not goin' in his own cave. Besides if you can't tell the difference between poopin' in your own cave and making a pot of coffee, you're gettin' a little touched in the head, you old coot!"

"Bertha Redwing, you know damn well that if coyote could figure a way to put a flush toilet in his den, he would be happy to use it. You're just pushin' this thing too far. I knew this was gonna happen. You've always been the most cantankerous, stubborn person I have ever known," he responded, putting his camas roots and cattails on the counter.

"You tryin' to ruin my birthday party, Saddles?"

"No, Bertha, I am not. But don't you think you've proved your point by now?"

"I ain't proved my point until I am free to poop someplace besides in my own lodge. Our people have been usin' the woods for millions of years. How can there be laws against somethin' like that? Why it's like makin' it against the law to dig camas root or go

586

swimmin'. The next thing ya know they're gonna pass a law that says it's illegal for fish to pee in the lake."

"Mother . . . parents here in the upper village don't want their children seein' your bare butt out in those woods. Children play out there. Doesn't that mean anything to you?" Clarence said. His mother flashed him a disapproving glance.

"When I was a girl . . . a bare butt was nothin' to be ashamed of. Butts was just a natural part of a person. Folks use'ta go swimming in the lake naked all the time. Old people, young people, children. Hell, we seen a lot more than butts in those days and it sure didn't pervert any of us or send us off to see a psychologist. What's happenin' to the world when somethin' as simple as a bare butt causes all this fuss. Seems to me this white man's civilization is nuts. I ain't movin' that toilet back into this house, and that's that! I will try to make sure there ain't no kids around the next time I do my duty out in them woods . . . but I'll be damned if I'm gonna let them make me poop in my own lodge. I've drawn a line, people, and I ain't lettin' no white man's government cross it. I may be livin' up here with all kinds a fancy new contraptions, but on this one issue I ain't budgin'. Now, are we gonna get things ready for my birthday party or are we gonna have an Indian war right here in my kitchen!"

"We're going to celebrate your birthday, Grandma," Willie said.

"And you, Saddles? What you gonna do?" she asked.

"I'm gonna fix this pile of camas root and cattails into a casserole that will be so good it will knock you on that cantankerous butt of yours," Saddles quipped.

"Now that's a challenge I don't mind takin'," she quipped back.

§§§§

During the next several weeks, we heard very little about agent Radford's insistence that the flush toilet had to be taken back into Grandmother Redwing's house in the new village. There was so much going on, I had forgotten about the situation for a while. Tahola Days and the next Dog Dance were swiftly approaching. Saddles had given me some very soft buckskin fragments when I told him I wanted to make my own costume for the upcoming celebration. I figured I didn't have much chance of winning a prize, but I did want to make a good showing.

Because my new Indian name was Talks With Eagles, I decided to do a dance that commemorated my namesake. I had been designing my costume secretly but knew I would have to approach Mother and ask her to teach me how to use her Singer sewing machine. My design called for two sleeves held together by only two leather straps, a breechcloth, and three-inch leather ankle and wrist bracelets, moccasins, and a headpiece. Onto each of these I planned to sew white peacock feathers that had been dyed a pale blue. I had been gathering blue jay feathers for months to use as a darker contrasting blue for the headpiece. I had only two things left to do before I could execute my design. I had to convince my mother to teach me how to use her sewing machine, and I had to procure additional feathers from Jerry Cotton. If Mother said no, I had a second plan. I would ask Audrey to teach me how to use her sewing machine. But Mother was my first choice. If possible, I wanted to keep my costume a secret from the Redwings. I wanted to keep it a surprise until I actually put it on at the Tahola Days celebration.

I decided to deal with Jerry first. I figured there was no point in asking anyone to teach me how to sew if I didn't have feathers for my costume. Jerry wasn't particularly friendly when I called, but because business was business, he agreed to sell me what I needed. I rode my bicycle to his place right after I finished speaking with him on the telephone.

"You're sure using a lot of feathers," Jerry noted as we rode our bikes over to his grandmother's farm.

"I gave the others away as gifts. These are actually for me. I really only need to buy your white ones this time," I responded.

"Well, I need to sell all of them. I got two bags of colored ones and one bag of white ones. I need the cash for all three right now so I can have some up-front money for the Orchid Appreciation Society's booth at the Puyallup Fair this fall."

"Can't you sell the other two bags to those folks in Tacoma?"

"They don't want to bother with less than three bags at a time. So if you want the white ones, you gotta buy the colored ones too, or I'm takin' the whole batch into Tacoma. Make up your mind."

"I'll buy the whole batch. There's always plenty

to do with feathers."

"What you gonna do with these feathers? Stuff pillows with them?"

"I'm making a costume for Tahola Days. I'm gonna dance this year."

"You goin' as some kinda bird?"

"Yes . . . a blue eagle. That's why I need the white feathers. I'm gonna dye them blue. I've gathered a lot of blue jay feathers for the headpiece. It's going to be a real neat costume. I'm going to wear it at the Dog Dance."

"So you're gonna dress up in feathers and dance for a bunch of Indians. What's happening to you, Fritz? You used to be so normal."

"This is normal. I'm going to dance for my spirit guide . . . for my namesake . . . there'll be folks watchin', but I won't really be dancing for them. I'll be dancing for the Great Spirit . . . for the eagle."

"So now you believe God is an eagle. If I recall my Sunday school lessons correctly, that's blasphemy."

"No, I don't think God is an eagle. But I do think the eagle can be a symbol for God, just like the dove is a symbol for God."

"Well that dove was around for Noah and was also there for the baptism of Jesus. I don't recall no eagles in either story."

"You're such a literalist, Jerry. God is in everything. Even in feathers. After all, He created feathers."

"What'chu gonna do, glue them onto your body?"

"No, no. I'm gonna have Mom show me how to

590

use her Singer sewing machine and make a costume. I seen how Audrey and Willie sew feathers onto a costume. I know I can do it once I learn how to run the thing. Mom's got one of those peddle sewing machines she inherited from her mother. She makes all sorts of things on it."

"God! The next thing I know you'll be tellin' me you're gonna dress up like a Hoochie-Koochie girl this Halloween like Randy did last year. You ain't becomin' no queer like him, are ya?"

"No, I'm fairly sure I'm a man with just one soul."

"Man with one soul?"

"Indians say that people who fall in love with members of their own gender have two souls. They don't use words like *queer* or *faggot*. They're much more civilized about it than white folks are. People with two souls are deeply respected by the Quinault. Many times people with two souls become shamans and medicine women."

"Well, I'm sure glad old Doc Wilson ain't got two souls. I'm always havin' to bare my butt to him to get some kinda shot, it seems. So how's-a-come your spirit guide is an eagle?"

"That's the animal that came to me on my vision quest."

"You had a vision quest? I'll bet the Presbyterian minister ain't gonna approve of that. You know, Fritz, they're gonna put you in a rubber room some day. I don't know why you just don't do something more sane . . . like join the Orchid Appreciation Society."

"I just ain't into orchids like you are. I like

learnin' stuff about Indians. They've got a history every bit as interesting as the English, or the Polish or anybody else. You know how much you like readin' about the ancient Gods of Greece and Rome? Well, the stories the Quinault tell about their spirits and gods is just as interesting. Maybe more. Yeah, come to think of it . . . lots more."

"What makes you think the Quinault stories are more interesting than the myths of the Greeks and Romans?"

"'Cause we live right where all these stories took place. The Greek and Roman stories took place clear over in the Mediterranean Sea. The Quinault stories are all about stuff that happened right in our backyard."

"The Greek and Roman stories were written by people who actually built civilizations, cities, paved roads, stadiums, theatres, public bath houses. What have you Indians contributed to architecture and archeology?"

"They left the land the way God made it. I think God is a better architect than people are, no matter where they live in history. You could learn a lot about history if you weren't so against Indians."

"Well, I prefer my orchids. Did I tell you we're going to have our own booth at the fair this year? I'm going to run it every day. Members of the society are even going to get out of school for it just like the 4-H kids do. And we all get special discounts on all the rides. Everyone in the society gets discounts, even on food, and we never have to pay to go in and out of the front gate. We'll all have special passes just like the performers. If you'd join the society, you'd get extra privileges too. . . . although I don't think I could talk the other members into letting you cover your body with peacock feathers when you come to meetings."

"I won't have time for your meetings. And if I did, I know how to dress the for occasion. Just because I'm learn'n Indian ways doesn't mean I have forgotten how to be a regular American."

"Regular Americans don't dress up like blue eagles."

"Neither do most regular Americans raise orchids."

§§§§

Mother was ironing when I came into the house. "Can I use the washtub to dye some feathers?" I asked.

If you take it out in the backyard. Why do you need something as big as the washtub. How many feathers are you planning to dye?"

"A big gunny sack full . . . and I was wonderin' . . . I mean, I was wondering if you would teach me to use your sewing machine?"

"Why on earth would you want to learn how to sew. Men don't sew."

"The best tailors and dress designers in the world are men," I argued.

"Who told you that?"

"I saw it on television. Besides, you taught me how to iron. You said if I wanted the creases in my pants so perfect, I could just learn to do my own ironing. So what's the difference?"

She turned off her iron, set it on the iron shaped cooling rack at the end of the ironing board and walked to the windowsill where she kept her Raleigh cigarettes, eyeing me peculiarly. Then she poured herself a cup of coffee, sat down at the kitchen table, lit her cigarette, blew smoke toward the ceiling, and repeated the question: "Why on earth are you interesting in learning how to sew?"

"I want to make a costume for the Dog Dance."

"Are you planning on skipping the family Fourth of July celebration again this year?"

"I'd much rather go to Tahola Days and the Dog Dance. I'll be at the family reunion for Grandma Harding's birthday. That's less than a month away from the fourth. I'll still see everybody."

"Well, I'm glad to hear that you haven't forgotten that you have real relatives on this planet."

"Will you teach me?"

"Why don't you tell me what you want done and I'll do the sewing for you. What will your father think if you take up sewing. What will other people think?"

"Lots of men sew, Mom. Besides, Saddles says there is a special magic that comes to a costume if it is made by the person who will dance in it."

"Well I certainly hope you aren't going to end up in a costume that makes you look like some feathered floozy in a Las Vegas nightclub!"

"You might have to worry about Randy wearing that kind of costume . . . but not me. I just want to honor the eagle in my dance."

"Oh, yes . . . I remember. You are Talks With Eagles on the reservation."

594

"I am Talks With Eagles all the time. It's my second name," I said very seriously.

"Well, as long as you don't forget how to spell *Harding*. Why should I worry about Randy wearing a feathered floozy costume?"

Suddenly I realized I had almost slipped up. I wasn't ready for my parents to know that Randy was a person with two souls . . . at least not yet. I had almost let the cat out of the bag. It was one thing having a cousin living in Seattle who was romantically involved with another man but perhaps quite another thing to have a best friend, especially one with whom I frequently spent weekends out of town, being similarly inclined. "He likes pretty frilly costumes," I ad-libbed.

"Well, every man to himself, I always say. Come on into the bedroom. I'll set up the machine and show you how to use it if you insist. You can practice on some scraps I've got in there."

"Will the machine sew pretty thick material?" I asked.

"How thick?"

"Saddles gave me some real soft buckskin."

"I think so . . . but buckskin is expensive. I wouldn't try sewing on it until after you've learned how to run the machine."

"Oh, I wouldn't," I said, watching her open the hinged lid to the sewing machine and set it up.

"Okay . . . I've got some old towels I've cut up for washcloths. I'll show you how to put edges on them so they don't fray. You can also sew some scraps together for practice first. If you manage to make washcloths that actually look like washcloths without sewing your fingers or shirt sleeves to them . . . then I'll leave you to your feathers and buckskin. But if you break a needle or my pedal or the little leather belt that turns it, you'll have to repay me out of your allowance or berry money. Deal?"

"Deal!" I said.

"Did the Redwings tell you that the boys' grandmother up at the Quinault Reservation was on the news again. I guess they're going to force her to put that flush toilet back into the house whether she wants it there or not," she said as she worked the thread through the needle and locked it in place.

"I haven't talked to them yet today. But they probably know. Clarence keeps the radio on at his shop all the time. You'll have to show me how to change the spool of thread. I want to use a color that matches the buckskin when I actually start working on my costume."

"That's easy. I'll show you when the time comes. I'll bet you a dollar she'll have to comply this time."

"I'll take that bet. I've really got to know that old woman. She's a lot like Grandma Harding. She don't let nobody push her around."

"She *doesn't* let *anyone* push her around," she corrected.

"Yes, ma'am."

By the time Dad arrived home from work, I had sewn two wads of cloth more suited for scrubbing pots and pans than fingers and toes, one oblong but usable washcloth, and five that were so close to being perfect, I was sure Mother wouldn't be able to tell them from the store-bought kind.

She was just complimenting my efforts when Dad, home early from work, popped into the bedroom. "I got off early. Wanna go out to Third Pond and go fishin' with me? I'm hungry for sunfish tonight," he invited. Then he stopped dead in his tracks when he saw that I was sitting at the sewing machine. His facial expression changed from excitement to something between shock and confusion. "Are you sewing?" he asked.

"Yeah! Mom's teaching me how to make washcloths out of old towels. Neat, huh?"

"Why on earth would you want to know how to make washcloths out of old towels? Sewing is woman's work."

"The best tailors are almost always men," Mother quipped.

"I only know the name of one clothing designer and that's Edith Head . . . and the last time I looked, she was a woman."

"Oh, stop fussing. You didn't say a word when I taught him to iron. What is it you're always saying? *This is the 1950s*, isn't that it? There's just too much to do around here for me to be expected to do it all without help. If he can learn to iron, he can learn to sew."

"Mom's teaching me to use her Singer so I can make my own costume for the Dog Dance this year. I'm going as a Blue Eagle. I'm gonna dye some peacock feathers blue, and I've already got a whole bunch of blue jay feathers and . . ."

"Well, how about we go fishin' right now. We can talk about your new found talent out at Third

Pond."

"Thanks, Dad, but I really don't want to go right now. Why don't you take Dinah? She loves to fish. I really need to learn how to sew right now. I'm gonna . . . *going* to make pouches with the leftover buckskin to give away at potlatch. It's going to take me most of the two weeks before Potlatch to get this all done, what with my chores and berry picking . . . "

"You'd rather sew than fish?"

"Right now. I just gotta get this done, Dad. This is real important to me. I want to enter into competition for the Dog Dance and I don't want to make the costume over at the Redwings 'cause I wanna surprise them."

"I don't get it, but if that's really what you would rather do . . . I guess it's okay. Where is Dinah?"

"She's out back playing with her dolls under the pear tree," Mother answered.

"I swear, Marjorie, I don't know what the world's coming to these days. Half the boys in this town are raising orchids and the other half are sewing feathers on their dance costumes."

"Yeah, and there's a lot of fierce competition between the Orchid Appreciation Society and the Dog Dancers," I agreed.

"At least they aren't getting drunk and getting all dirty fixing up old cars, dear," Mother responded.

Chapter Seventeen

Dancing With Kwatee

One afternoon after berry picking, the boys and I decided to pedal our bikes around the Cascade State School for the Mentally Retarded instead of going directly home to do our chores. The Quinault celebration was still a week away and I had yet to put all the finishing touches on my costume, but a bicycle ride around the state institution was one of our favorite pastimes. We all enjoyed looking at the spacious manicured lawns and beautifully landscaped trees and flower gardens. With its white adobe buildings, red tile roofs and covered walkways, the place looked like an enormous Spanish villa and seemed to us to have the ambiance of old world charm.

And as if just seeing the beauty of the sprawling institution wasn't enough, there were other things to enjoy along the way, as well. A long slow hill waited for us just after we would pass the old Bunker farm. For the next mile and a half, all we would have to do is coast and relax in the cool breeze caused by the speed of our bicycles, no matter how hot or still the day was for the rest of the town.

"Sometimes I wish I was retarded just so I could live in such a fancy place," Randy said as we rode single file past the town library.

"My mom says it ain't so nice on the inside as it

is on the outside except in the visitor rooms, the main entrance and some of the offices. I guess the halls themselves are kinda like military barracks. Nobody's got a private bedroom," I advised.

"She been in there?" Willie asked.

"No, but her friend Maryella Madden works out there. She says some of the stuff that goes on behind the walls is pretty scary. I guess some of the kids that live out there are pretty strange. Maryella told Mom that sometimes they have to beat the kids to keep them in line and some of them are really strange . . . you know . . . they smear poop on the walls in' stuff like that. Sometimes the staff has to put them in straitjackets."

"They'd have to put me in a straitjacket to keep me in a place like that," Willie observed.

"Maryella says they got a whole bunch of people who are really deformed . . . you know, people with more arms and legs than they're supposed to have. She says they even got one boy out there they call the lizard boy 'cause his skin looks like a lizard's. He has to stay in water a lot to keep his skin healthy. But I guess other than that he's normal. Maryella says he can play the piano real good," I said as we came to the end of Main Street and veered to the right to follow the paved road leading out to the school.

"I don't want to hear any more. I don't want my illusion of the place shattered by any secondhand reality. Let's just pretend it's the gigantic home of Janet Gaynor or one of them other Hollywood stars and that we're all invited to lunch today," Willie interrupted.

"I wanna know more about the kids that smear

poop on the walls," Randy asserted.

"Oh, spare me the details," Willie moaned.

"Well . . . Maryella says only some of the kids are that bad. Not many I guess. Most of the kids are real good. Some of them even come into town to buy things and shop or have a soda at the Sweet Shop. The kids that live there keep up the lawns; they got their own dairy and vegetable gardens . . . and they raise all their own chicken and eggs. They're almost self-sufficient," I said as we turned to the right toward the long hill that descended into the shallow valley where the state institution, its farms, orchards, and gardens sprawled in either direction for hundreds of acres.

"Did ya ever talk with any of them kids that come into town?" Willie asked.

"Naw . . . I was always afraid to. But two of them sat in the booth next to me at the Sweet Shop and I listened to them talk."

"Did they talk just like us guys?" Randy inquired.

"Far as I could tell."

"That's sounds pretty normal. I wonder how's-a-come they're out there if it's okay for them to come into town. Was they by themselves?" Randy asked.

"Far as I could tell."

"Then I wonder how's-a-come they're out there in the first place?"

"Did ya ever see that guy who sits out on the low stone wall on the southeast corner of the grounds and plays his ukulele?" Willie asked as we approached that point in the road where the pavement began its descend into the valley below.

"Yeah. He's sometimes out there when me and

my Dad drive by on the way to my grandparent's farm. I wave at him every once in a while."

"Does he ever wave back?" Randy asked.

"Oh, yeah, almost all the time."

"I hear they've got their own movie theater and sweet shop out there . . . and that they hold dances for them and bring in outside entertainment," Willie noted.

"Yeah, the year before you guys moved to town, my class went out and sang Christmas carols for them and there was other people there singin' for them too. It looked to me like they was all having a great time," I said as our bikes began picking up speed on their own and started coasting down the hill.

We glided down the hill in silence enjoying the sheer exhilaration of traveling faster and faster without exerting any energy at all. With any luck we wouldn't have to begin pedaling our bicycle again, until we were halfway around the corner at the bottom of the hill.

Once we began peddling again Willie put his right hand up to his eyes to shield the sun. "Isn't that somebody sittin' alongside the fence down there? I wonder if that's the guy you was talkin' about who plays the ukulele?"

The closer we pedaled our bikes to the figure, the more I was convinced that it was the boy I had told them about earlier. "Yup, that's him," I said as we came into easy view of him. I waved. The boy waved back.

"Shall we stop and say hello?" Randy asked.

"Sure. Ain't no law against that," I said, noticing for the first time that the boy had an elongated head, almost as if he were wearing a modified dunce cap. He wasn't ugly though. The rest of him seemed just fine.

His face was pleasant enough and he looked as if he was about our age. I stopped my bike first. The Redwing boys followed suit. The four of us stood there staring at each other for almost a full minute before anyone spoke anything. The boy sitting on the road side of the low stone wall was the first to speak.

"Afternoon," he said with a smile.

"Hi. My name is Fritz Harding. These are my friends, Randy and Willie Redwing. They're Quinault Indians," I said, pointing to the boys as I said their names.

"Everybody here calls me Old Pinhead," the boy responded.

"On account your head is shaped like that?" Randy asked.

"I guess," the boy answered.

"You live here all the time?" Willie asked.

"Yeah. I've been here for a about ten years.. My mom died and none of my brothers or sisters wanted me to live at their house. So they sent me here."

"What'cha doin' out here by the road all by yourself?" Randy asked.

"I'm a trustee. I can pretty much go where I want . . . 'cept I ain't supposed to leave the grounds without permission and I ain't supposed to talk to no outsiders."

"Will ya get into trouble for talkin' to us?" Randy asked.

"Only if they catch me."

"Ain't you technically off the grounds just sittin' there on this side of the wall?" Willie asked.

"I guess. I don't care. I like to watch the cars go

603

by. If I sit up on the wall they can see me and then they're always yellin' at me to come and clean up something."

"So, you're kinda hidin' out?" I observed.

"Yeah. They make me do lots a hard work. I work in the kitchen mostly, but in-between the meals they make me do lots of other stuff too. The regular kitchen staff get to relax between meals for a while. Not me. I gotta work all the time. So I come out here and hide out. That way they think I'm someplace workin' for somebody else if they can't find me."

"That's pretty smart," Randy said.

"I ain't dumb. I'm just a little bit retarded and I look funny. I can read. My mom taught me."

"Did you go to school before you came here?" I asked.

"Nope. They wouldn't take me."

"They got a school in there you can go to?" Randy asked.

"Not really. I don't know why. Some kids get to go. But if you can work real good, you don't go. Mostly the little kids go. They teach them to eat and stuff like that."

"What's it like livin' in there. It's sure beautiful from out here," Randy said.

"It's sort of like a prison, if ya ask me. I work all the time except when I sleep. I even gotta help set up for when there's a movie or a party n' stuff. It looks okay when ya drive around the place, but you wouldn't wanna live here."

"What'cha like least about it?" Willie asked.

"It ain't like livin' at home. I'm always with a

604

whole bunch of people. That's why I come out here . . . to get away from all them people once in a while. You can't even take a pee in there without somebody watchin' ya. We don't have our own bedrooms. There's just people everywhere. That's the part I don't like. No privacy. And I don't get to choose nothin' for myself . . . not my clothes, my toothpaste . . . nothin'. I don't much like that."

"Why don't you run away?" Randy asked.

"Where I'm gonna go lookin' like I look. I can't hide very easy and they don't let us have no money."

"Does it bother ya by bein' here and talkin' to us about it?" Willie asked.

"Nope. There's a whole lotta kids on the inside who don't talk at all, and most don't know nothin' to talk about, and the staff hardly ever talks to me unless they're tellin' me what to do. Most everybody sort of ignores me 'cause of the shape of my head, I guess. But I don't much mind. I'm gettin' used to it after all these years."

"Ain't cha got no friends in there?" Willie asked.

"The cook lady is real nice to me. She gives me extras. I like workin' for her. But she's about it. I ain't been here very long."

"Somebody said there's a kid in there that looks like a lizard. They call him Lizard Boy. You met him yet?" Randy asked.

"Yeah, but he don't look much like no lizard. He's just got real wrinkly skin. But he don't have much to do with me. He lives in another building, and he don't never go out unless it's real dark out."

"How long you gonna stay here?" I asked.

"I think I gotta stay forever."

"Do your brothers and sisters come and take you to town or to their place for dinner once in a while?" Willie inquired.

"They live clear in Tacoma. I think it must be a long ways away from here 'cause they ain't never been to see me since they brought me here."

"My grandparents own a farm on the other end of this road. That's where we're going when we leave here. The transparent apples are just perfect right now. We're gonna go pick some and eat 'em. Do you like transparent apples? We could bring some back for you, if you like," I said as a large delivery van made the turn at the bottom of the road and headed our way.

"We got a bunch in the orchards out here too. They make real good pies. I pick apples here all the time too. I'm always workin' unless I sneak over here by the fence. But I gotta get back and start helpin' with supper. If I'm late, I get demerits and then I won't be a trustee no more. So I gotta get back," the boy said, standing up and jumping up onto the fence.

"That's Dad's delivery truck," Willie noted. I wonder what he's doin' way out here?"

"Well, it was nice meetin' you," I said to the boy as he swung his legs over the fence and dropped to the other side.

"It was nice meetin' you too. Maybe I'll see you guys again sometime," the boy said as Clarence's truck pulled up alongside us.

"I hope so. Maybe you'll play your ukulele for us sometime. Randy knows how to harmonize," I responded.

606

"Maybe," the boy answered.

"You got laundry to deliver out here, Dad?" Randy asked.

"No. Saddles called. I was lookin' for you guys. Grandmother Redwing had another big fight with Albert Radford up at the reservation. She got so excited she swung at him with her garden shovel . . ."

"Did she hit him?" Willie interrupted.

"No, she missed him. But she dislocated her shoulder. Bill took her in to Tacoma to see a specialist at Indian Hospital. They said she can't lift anything for a few days so he brought her up to our place since he and Alice are taking the kids over to Yakima for a few days and won't be around to watch after her. I want you boys to go on home and make sure she doesn't try to lift anything. Your mom has to help out in the store this week because Sonja Hackman and her husband are out of town. You'll have to watch out for your grandmother until we close the shop each day."

"We were gonna give Fritz a hand and get some apples so Mom could bake a pie. Have we got time to pick a few transparent apples over at the Harding farm before we go home?" Willie asked.

"If you hurry. Bill and Alice and the kids said they would sit with her until you two get home. Don't take more than an hour."

"I was gonna go swimmin' with the Wells boy after we picked apples," Randy whined. "His dad finally said we could be friends again and this is the first time we've been able to see each other in a long time."

"Well, one of you has to be there. You can go swimming with the Wells boy if Willie doesn't mind

607

watching Mother by himself. You know how rambunctious she can be."

"I don't mind, Dad," Willie answered.

"Okay, you go pick apples but no longer than an hour. Randy, when you've finished swimmin', you go on home and help your brother."

"It won't even take an hour with all three of us pickin'," I said, looking back to see if Old Pinhead was still standing on the other side of the fence so I could introduce him to Mr. Redwing. But when I looked, the boy was gone.

We arrived at the Redwing home with apples enough for everyone to enjoy one or two fresh ones from the bag with plenty left over for two large pies. "This is my favorite apple," Bill said as he joined the boys and me on the front porch.

"Mine too," I admitted.

"I think they're too sour when they're hard like this. I like them when they become soft and get really sweet," Randy told us.

"Oh, yuk! I hate them like that. They're pithy and flat tasting," I disagreed.

"To each his own," Randy commented.

"You gonna pick apples while you're over in Yakima?" Willie asked his uncle.

Bill Redwing looked over his shoulder to make sure his mother hadn't walked out onto the porch. "We're not really going to Yakima," he whispered.

"Then how come you brought Grandma up to stay with us?" Randy asked.

"Me and Saddles and Albert have come up with an idea that might just keep your grandma happy and satisfy the requirements of the law. We ain't got it all worked out yet, but if we get what we want, we don't want Mother on the reservation for a few days. This thing with her shoulder happened at just the right time."

"That's a terrible thing to say," Randy said.

"Well, I don't mean that it's good that she hurt herself. But it is good that it happened at this particular moment in time. Sometimes the Great Spirit makes things happen so other things can happen," Bill answered.

"And Albert Radford is in on this? I thought he'd be mad at Grandma for tryin' to hit him with a shovel," Randy speculated.

"He's no madder than usual. Besides, she missed him more than a mile is what he said. But the main thing is he wants a solution to all this as bad as Alice and I do . . . so he's workin' with us on the project."

"Project? What'cha gonna do?" I asked.

"It's a secret. If it works, I want everyone to be surprised at the same time," Bill answered.

"Does Dad know?" Willie asked.

"Nope. Nobody but those of us that are plannin' it."

"It's not like you to be so filled with mystery," Randy noted.

"Well, the times is a changin'," Bill responded.

§§§§

The moment my grandmother learned that Clarence's mother was in town, she called over to invite the old

609

woman and Audrey to lunch. Audrey declined because of having to work in her husband's shop so Grandma included Randy, Willie and me in the invitation. I rode my bike to the farm early that day to help Grandpa split some wood for the coming winter. His arthritis was getting worse and worse, and now that all his sons had married and moved from the farm, it was up to him to stock the woodshed with enough dry wood to last through the long Cascade winters. Grandpa and I were just getting ready to go up to the house to wash up for lunch when Audrey drove up to drop off her mother-in-law and the boys. By the time we got up to the house, Grandma Harding was already walking down the steps to greet the elder Mrs. Redwing.

"Bertha . . . it is so good to see you again. Thank you for coming," my grandmother said, extending her arms to the old Indian woman.

"Is good to see you too, Martha. You won't believe what I been through since we was here for your Thanksgiving party," she said, stepping into my grandmother's embrace.

"I heard plenty. The radio talks about you every once in a while. You've become a celebrity just like that Dagmar somebody that's always in the news."

"They pushed my house down, Martha, and then they burned it to the ground. Now I'm fightin' with them again. That's how I threw my shoulder out . . . fightin'. You think I'm stupid for not lettin' them put that flush toilet back in my house, Martha?"

"You gotcher reasons. It's good enough. People think I'm nuts 'causes I don't buy store-bought bread. It's cheap. It takes lotta time to bake my own bread and it's damn hot in the kitchen if I do it in the summer. But I don't care. I don't like them store-bought breads. They're like eatin' air . . . so how am I to judge you," my grandmother answered.

"I'm actually glad to be away from that place for a few days. I'm pretendin' that when I go back . . . it will be to my little house on the flats. I ain't never really been so glad to be away in all my life."

"Well, we're certainly glad you can stop by for a visit. I fixed some Polish sausage salad and some pierogi for dinner last night. We got plenty left over for a nice lunch."

"Ain't that the salad with horseradish in it?"

"That's the one."

"I like Polish food, Martha. It's of the earth like Indian food. Saddles been havin' me up for a lot a French cookin' he's doin' these days. He got himself a book about it. It's good stuff but most of it's like eatin' dessert. Creamy and light stuff. It's fluffy food. Give me earthy food any day. I like stuff to be not so fancy."

"You got any big celebrations come' up real soon?" Grandpa asked me.

"Potlatch is comin' up real soon. Same time as your Fourth of July," I answered.

"Oh, yes, I think your mother told me you planned on goin' up there instead of bein' here on the farm," my grandmother noted.

"Yeah . . . I'm gonna dance to honor Brother Eagle. But I'll be here for your birthday celebration. I like your birthday party even better than Christmas," I said, wondering if she could tell I was stretching the truth more than just a little.

"I'm thinkin' about stayin' home from Potlatch this year," Grandmother Redwing announced.

"Stay home! But you can't, Grandma . . . we want you to see us dance. And besides, you're the oldest Quinault person alive today. You just gotta come," Randy pleaded.

"I don't know, boy. I been thinkin' about it lots. I don't much feel like celebratin' this year. I know I'm puttin' on a good front about likin' all the new fangled stuff in that house . . . but the truth is . . . I ain't happy. Everybody knows I lost that battle. And now they're tryin' to force me to put that damn flush toilet back in the house. I'm losin' face fast boy. How'my gonna hold my head up and celebrate in front of everyone when they all know I been beat like dog?"

"That's how we felt when we left the old country," Grandpa said.

"Yeah, but the new country has been real good to us," my grandmother pointed out.

"Grandmother, please think about this real hard. It won't be any fun at Potlatch unless you're there," Willie pleaded.

"In a few years I won't be there anyway. I can't last forever, boy. But there ain't no sense in me goin' if I won't have any fun. Nope, I think maybe I'll just stay home and watch TV."

"A person has to do what they have to do," my grandfather said, helping Mrs. Redwing to the table.

"I think old Kwattee has beat me this time, John,"

"Kwatee?" my grandmother asked.

"He's the changer. He makes all the changes, and when he's done doin' them, he makes us dance with him even if we're too tired to dance . . . and I'm too tired to dance. Ever since this happened, it's like my spirit ain't got no get-up-and-go."

"Personally, I was glad when we could stop poopin' in the woods. When John and I first came to this place, we didn't even have a cabin and certainly not an outhouse. We used the woods a lot in them days," Grandma pointed out.

"You and Grandpa pooped in the woods?" I asked.

"We sure did. Why, when I came across the country by ox cart, we had'ta poop in the woods or behind a bush in a meadow all the time. People been poopin' a long time before there was outhouses, Fritz."

"Well, my own people been complainin' to the agent about me. I was hikin' up into some trees above my house. Ain't nobody told me they was part of the town. I guess some kids saw me . . . couple of tourists once too. People complained. That's part of why I don't much care if I go to Potlatch or not this year. Even some of my own people have turned against me. They could'a come and talked to me instead of runnin' and bein' tattletales to Albert Radford."

"That must just break your heart," my grandmother said, placing the last of the dishes on the table and sitting down next to the old Indian woman.

"Well, it sure don't make me feel much like a real member of the new village. It's like I'm the only one left who remembers the ways of the tribe. My people ain't a nation no more, Bertha, they're just people living in government housing."

"I didn't know you felt like that, Grandma," Randy said

"Well, I do. I meant to hit Alfred with that shovel. I thought maybe if I hit him and hurt him a little, they'd take me off to some funny farm. In the old days people respected the old ones. Not any more. Now-a-days they complain to the Indian agent even though they know the old ways but don't live them themselves. I'm tellin' ya, I ain't gonna stop fightin' on this one. They'll either have to move me off the reservation or keep that damn flush toilet down in that little shed 'cause I ain't havin' it in the house and that's that!"

"Well, if it comes to that . . . havin' to move from the reservation . . . you know that John and I would be happy to make room for you here. Lord knows we've got plenty of bedrooms now that the kids is all gone . . . and here you can use the flush toilet or hike out into the woods and ain't nobody gonna say a damn thing about it. I can promise ya that!" my grandmother said.

"Martha, you're a good woman," Mrs. Redwing told her.

"Us old people got to stick together, Bertha."

"Yes, indeed, Martha, us old people got to stick together."

§§§§

On the fourth day of her visit, Grandmother Redwing's shoulder was doing much better and she was becoming bored just sitting around Audrey and Clarence's house with nothing to do. I had gone over to the Redwings that afternoon to help the boys pack their things for the trip to the Tahola Days celebration but we got side tracked because the old woman decided to tell us the story of how raven ate the night. We all listened in silence as she wove the ancient Quinault tale for us when a sudden knock came to the front door.

"Wonder who that could be?" Willie asked, getting up to see.

"Well, I sure ain't expectin' no company," his grandmother noted.

"Neither are we," Randy agreed.

"It's Saddles," Willie said even before opening the door.

The old shaman hugged the boy and stepped into the living room.

"Why, Saddles, you old fool, how did you get up here? Did you take the bus?" Mrs. Redwing asked.

"Nope. I drove Bill's car."

"I'm surprised you remembered how to drive. How come Bill loaned you his station wagon?"

"Well, he figured there wouldn't be room in Clarence's car for everyone with you here when he drives on up for Potlatch day after tomorrow . . . so he asked me if I'd mind driving his car up here to lighten the load. I come a couple of days early so I could visit with the family for a few days. I love drivin'. Ain't done it in a long time."

"Well, I'm glad you're here. I'm about to go stir-crazy sittin' in this house day after day. I been tellin' the kids stories. Martha Harding had me over for lunch

615

one day, but other than that I've just sat here with these boys refusin' to let me lift much more than my fork."

"How is your shoulder, Bertha?"

"Much better. I can lift my arm way over my head now. I suspect I'm just about well . . . but these young rascals won't let me so much as bake cookies for them."

"They're just tryin' to help you get well."

"Besides, Grandmother, you didn't offer to bake cookies," Randy joked.

"Well, at first I didn't feel up to it and then it sort of just slipped my mind."

"The boys were just trying to take good care of you, old woman." Saddles said, taking out his bag of tobacco to fill his pipe.

"I know . . . and I love them for it . . . but, damn, I'm gettin' real bored. Clarence promised to take me down to the Cosmo Theatre tonight. Somebody by the name of Doris Day is in a movie. Clarence says she's his favorite actress."

"Oh, I adore Doris Day. She sings too. I would love to come along. I love movies," Saddles squealed.

"We're all goin'," Willie noted.

"Do they sell popcorn and cola at the Cosmo?" Saddles asked.

"Of course," I answered.

"Oh, my . . . it will be just like San Francisco . . . except, of course, the theater will be smaller."

"Well, in the meantime . . . how's about takin' me for a ride someplace. I just gotta get out of this house."

"Where would you like to go? I could drive

616

twenty-four hours a day. You wanna drive up and see the mountains more closely or maybe go out to one of the lakes?"

"Actually, I'd like to drive over to that place where Fritz gets them peacock feathers," she answered.

"Oh, I got plenty of peacock feathers if you want them, Grandmother. Jerry Cotton made me buy two bags of regular ones before he'd sell me the white ones I wanted for my costume. You're welcome to them."

"That's right generous of you, Talks With Eagles, and I'm gonna take you up on that offer. But what I'd really like to see me a peacock. I ain't' never seen one except in picture books."

"Ain't you never been to the zoo, Grandma?" Darleen asked.

"No . . . and I don't wanna go to no zoo. The very idea of pennin' them animals up in cages just so's people can come and gawk at them ain't right. How'd you like to be all penned up behind bars? I seen a copy of *Life Magazine* once that showed Brother Bear and Brother Wolf livin' behind bars. It broke my heart. No siree, no zoos for me. My hunch is that them peacocks that live on some farm up here is pretty much free. Am I right, little Mr. Harding?"

"Yup. Jerry's grandparents let the peacocks roam all around the farm. Lots of them sleep in the cedar trees in the woods that surround their place. Of course, some like to sleep in the rafters of their big old barn . . . but none of them are in cages. You want me to call Jerry and see if it's okay for us to drive out and see them?"

"I suspect you should call his grandparents," Saddles interjected. "The peacocks are at their home, not Jerry's, right?"

"Right."

"Why don't you call them, Fritz. I'd like to see them peacocks too," Randy urged.

"Me too," Darleen quipped.

"Me three," Amy-Lynn chimed in.

I went down the hall and into the kitchen where Clarence and Audrey kept their telephone and called the Cotton farm. After explaining what we would like to do, Jerry's grandmother informed me it would be all right for Saddles to drive the Redwings out to see the peacocks. "So, it would be okay if Saddles Seatco drives us all out so the boys' grandmother can see the birds? Randy, Willie and their sisters want to come along too," I explained.

"Well, sure, Fritz . . . that would be just fine. Jerry's mother is here helping me put up some applesauce from our transparent apple trees . . . so I won't be able to give your friends much of a tour . . . but you know your way around the farm. You feel free to take them anywhere you want. I'll try to step out and say hello and introduce myself . . . but if I can't, you explain to your friends, okay?"

"Okay, and thank you, ma'am."

"What time you folks plan on gettin' here?"

"I suppose we'll come just as soon as we pile into the station wagon," I answered.

"That'll be just fine. You can park over by the barn, if you like. That way I can see you pull up from the kitchen window."

618

"Okay. And thanks again, Mrs. Cotton," I answered.

We piled into Bill's station wagon and headed through town toward the Cotton farm. As we drove down Main Street, Grandmother Redwing turned to Saddles and said, "You got any money on ya, Saddles?"

"About twenty bucks," he replied. "Why?"

"I've got a hankerin' for one of them cream-filled maple bars at Fox's bakery. Can we stop and get some for us and the kids?"

"Why, Bertha Redwing, I'm surprised at you. Cream-filled maple bars are definitely a European delicacy. Wouldn't you rather I stop along the way so we can pick some licorice root to chew while we drive?" he admonished teasingly.

"Just park the car and go get some of them maple bars, you old coot. And don't forget to get some paper napkins. We don't want the kids gettin' stickum on Bill's nice clean upholstery."

"I'm gonna see if he's got any of them warm hotdogs in a bun. I ain't had my lunch yet. Anybody want one of them?" Saddles asked.

"Oh, I do. Mr. Fox makes the best hotdog in a bun I ever tasted. He bakes the mustard right inside the bun. I'll have one," I said.

"Just the maple bars for me," Mrs. Redwing answered.

"Anybody else?" Saddles asked, getting out of the station wagon.

§§§§

As Saddles pulled the vehicle up along the Cotton's enormous red barn, Jerry stepped out of his greenhouse with a puzzled look on his face. "Here comes trouble," Randy whispered in my ear.

"Well, we're here. Let's start lookin' for peacocks," I said excitedly as Jerry headed our way. I saw his grandmother step out onto her back porch behind him and begin walking toward us.

Willie was the first out of the car. He walked over and opened the door for his grandmother. The rest of us followed. Two white peacock hens came around the side of the barn just as the old woman stepped out of the vehicle. "There's two hens right over there," I pointed out.

"My, what pretty faces they have for birds . . . don'tcha think, Saddles?" she noted.

"I'm much more interested in the pretty face of that young man walkin' toward us," Saddles giggled.

"That's Jerry Cotton. His grandparents own this place. He's been a real pill lately," I observed.

"Well, hello, Mr. Harding . . . what are you and all these Ind . . . and all these people doing here?" Jerry asked.

"We've come to see the peacocks," the old shaman replied, stepping forward and extending his hand. "I'm Saddles Seatco, shaman and medicine man for the Quinault . . . and who might you be, my pretty?"

Jerry stopped dead in his tracks. A look of confusion and disdain swept across his face. "I'm Jerry Cotton, the president of the Orchid Appreciation Society and the grandson of the people who own this farm. Who gave you people permission to just drive out here and onto this farm? I'll have you know this is private property!" he said sarcastically.

"And who gave you permission to speak to my guests in that tone of voice, young man?" his grandmother asked from behind him.

"Oh, Grandma, I just figured they all came out here of their own accord."

"Well, they didn't. Fritz called and I invited them. And regardless of how they got here . . . you have no business speaking to adults in that tone of voice. I don't know where you think you learned your manners, but I'll tell you one thing. In my home, on my farm, you will address adults with respect! Have I made myself perfectly clear?" She spoke softly but firmly.

"I'm sorry, ma'am, we didn't mean to cause no fuss between you and your kin. I'm Bertha Redwing. I was the one who asked Fritz to call and see if it would be okay for me to come out and see your birds. I ain't never seen no live peacocks before," Grandmother Redwing said, stepping forward.

"How do you do, Mrs. Redwing. I'm Almira Cotton. This here whippersnapper's grandmother. You'll have to forgive Jerry . . . he can be very arrogant."

"I ain't arrogant! I just didn't want no batch of Indians attacking your farm, Grandma," Jerry mumbled.

"What a snippy thing for you to say. You apologize to my guests right now or I'll see to it you don't raise another orchid in that greenhouse I had built for you!"

Jerry didn't move and didn't say anything. He just looked down at his feet.

"Did you hear me, young man?" his grandmother asked as Jerry's mother came up behind them.

"What seems to be the problem, Mother Cotton?" she asked.

"Your son seems to think that these good people are invading our farm and he's been quite rude to them. I've asked him to apologize but so far all he's done is stand there looking at his shoes."

"Hello, everyone. I'm Cynthia Cotton. We're very pleased that you've come to see the birds. Now if you'll excuse me, I need to take my son inside and have a little chat with him." She reached out her right hand, took Jerry by the ear, and led him into the house.

"Oh, how upsetting," the elder Mrs. Cotton said.

"Think nothing of it. We might have frightened him," Mrs. Redwing offered.

"Jerry has been mad at me for a long time because I've made friends with the Redwing family. I think he's jealous." I told her.

"Truth is, there's a little Indian blood in our family too. My husbands grandmother was a member of the Puyallup tribe," the older Mrs. Cotton told us.

"Does Jerry know that?" I asked.

"I'm sure he does, dear. He's seen all the photos in the album."

"Well, I'll be darned." I commented.

"Do you ever eat these birds?" Grandmother Redwing asked.

"Oh, yes dear. All the time. I prefer them to a

622

turkey or a goose, but of course we eat those as well," Almira answered.

"Well, what's it taste like?" Saddles asked

"Hmmm. I'd say it's more like a turkey than a chicken, but more like a quail than a pheasant. Is that any help," Almira asked.

"Not really. But I know what you're saying. When I try to tell people what bear meat tastes like I tell them it's more like pork in flavor but more like beef in texture," Saddles answered.

"Have you ever eaten possum?" Almira asked

"Yes, of course. It tastes a lot like goose, doesn't it?" Saddles said.

"It does indeed. The next time you folks come up to visit have your kin let me know and we'll slaughter and dress a peacock out for you," Almira offered.

"That's very good of you, Mrs. Cotton. Thank you," Grandmother Redwing said, giving a little bow.

"Well, anyway, you are most welcome to look at my birds. I became fascinated with peacocks as a child and swore I'd have some one day. We must have fifty or sixty out here now. I hope Fritz told you that my daughter-in-law and I are canning applesauce today . . . so I can't offer you a guided tour. But . . ." At just that minute Jerry and his mother returned to where we were all standing.

"I'm sorry I was so rude," he mumbled. They were the right words but I saw nothing but fire in his eyes.

"Much better," Jerry's mother said. She excused herself and returned to the house.

"Well, now that Jerry is back and providing he can mind his manners, perhaps you won't mind if he shows you around the place. You might want to show them how you raise orchids as well," his grandmother said.

"That old Indian man called me *my pretty*," Jerry pouted.

"Well, you are pretty . . . too pretty to be a boy. I tell you that all the time and you don't get snippy with me. Now, are you going to behave yourself and be polite to my guests or shall I send you home and permit Fritz to walk them around the farm?"

"I'll be good," Jerry agreed.

"Jerry tells me you use the feathers from our birds to decorate some of your clothing," Mrs. Cotton smiled.

"People shouldn't wear feathers on their clothes," Jerry mumbled.

"Young man, I've had quite enough out of you. I'll have you know that I have never seen a man's hat worthy of its salt that didn't have a nice feather tucked into its brim . . . and I have several pieces of clothing myself that are made all the more lovely by the addition of feathers . . . some of them peacock. Now, you march your little butt into the kitchen and tell your mother I've sent you home for being rude to my guests. We'll just let Fritz guide this tour," Mrs. Cotton scolded.

Jerry took off in a huff.

"I'm so sorry, Mrs. Redwing, Saddles . . . I don't know what to say," Mrs. Cotton blushed.

"Think nothing of it, my dear. Sometimes kids can be just awful . . . even the ones related to me,"

624

Grandmother Redwing laughed.

"Well, I must get back in and help with the applesauce. There's still plenty of transparent on the trees if you'd like some . . . help yourself . . and enjoy the birds."

"I'm sure I will," Grandmother Redwing assured her.

§§§§

Later, when we were driving back to town, I asked Saddles why he had called Jerry *my pretty*. He giggled a little, then said, "To make him show his true colors."

"You knew he was gonna behave like that?"

"Why, Talks With Eagles, you forget . . . I am a shaman. Understanding human nature comes naturally for me. On such a glorious day . . . I simply was not in the mood to put up with any arrogant little piss ant. Who knows, maybe he learned something today."

By the time we arrived back at the Redwing residence, Audrey's mother, Stella Sunfield, had unexpectedly arrived and was waiting for us on the front porch.

"Stella! What a surprise! I'm so glad to see you," Saddles exclaimed, giving the old woman a smile. Her grandchildren scurried around to greet and touch her. So did I.

"I knew Bertha was here and that you still had a spare cot in the store room. So I figured I'd save you a drive to Auburn to pick me up for Potlatch and squeeze in an extra day or two of visitin'," her mother explained, smiling warmly to Grandmother Redwing.

"Well, it's damn good ta see ya," Saddles grinned.

"So you've decided to go to Potlatch this year?" Audrey more observed than questioned.

"I'm gettin' awfully old to make that trip and sleep in the back of a van anymore, but I figured one more year won't kill me. Besides, I wanna see this damn house after all the fuss that's been in the news. How are you, Bertha?" Stella asked, walking toward Clarence's mother with her arms extended.

"None the worse for wear. You're certainly a feast for sore eyes," Grandmother Redwing responded, wrapping her arms around Mrs. Sunfield.

"I hear you been givin' them state people a real run for their money," Stella commented. Her tone was decidedly congratulatory.

"I been tryin'."

"She's also been poopin' out in the trees behind her place and has gotten half the village in an uproar, not to mention the Indian agent and the folks down in Olympia," Saddles muttered.

"You're a born tattletale, you old coot," Grandmother Redwing quipped.

"Besides, I don't see nothin' wrong in that. I poop out in the trees all the time. I don't use that outhouse they built for me unless it's rainin' like hell, or there's too much snow on the ground to hike out in the woods. What's all the fuss about?" Mrs. Sunfield asked.

"Mother! You're kidding!" Audrey exclaimed.

"I am not. Hell, I'm out in them woods all the time. You know I'm always out there pickin' or gatherin' something for the table and a tea. Why on earth would I hike all the way back to that outhouse.

Our people been poopin' in the woods forever," Stella responded.

"Good girl, Stella. I'm glad to hear that at least one person besides me knows what's goin' on here," Clarence's mother responded.

"It's all about power, Bertha . . . that's all it is. That's all it ever is. They got the power and they don't want us to forget it," Audrey's mother said, pulling back a bit, then kissing Grandmother Redwing on both cheeks.

"Well, it's pretty damn petty of them to want to have power over where a body can poop," Bertha answered.

"Grandma, I don't like the outhouse either. It smells bad in there. But I don't think I'm any less an Indian just because I like to sit on a real toilet seat and flush my waste out into the sea. Isn't that also part of what people and the earth do?" Randy questioned.

"You tell 'em, boy," Saddles cheered.

"What kind of a shaman are you raisin' him to be, Saddles?" Bertha quipped.

"One that lives in the twentieth century," the old man answered.

"Do you all mind if we change the subject. I've heard just about all I want to hear about poop for a few days," Audrey requested.

"Well, if you're tired of hearin' about it, go call the governor and tell him he's the one makin' a big deal over this. All I'm doin' is what I been doin' all my life since these white people took over . . . I'm standin' up for my rights. I'm a Quinault, damn it, not a European and I'll be damned if I'm gonna live like one."

"I brung you something, Bertha. A little gift," Grandmother Sunfield announced to her old friend.

"Just seein' your face is all the gift I need, woman. But ya know how much I like a good surprise. What'cha got?" Clarence's mother asked.

"Elk jerky! Some of the boys down the road got themselves an elk in the hills up behind the reservation. They brung me some. I was always good to them when they was kids. Anyway, they brung me a nice slab of meat. I made jerky out of some of it . . . the old-fashioned way. If you look real close, you can even see some fly poop on some of the pieces," Stella said, winking at her old friend.

"Please! Enough talk about poop!" Audrey moaned.

"Do flies really poop on jerky when it's made the old fashioned way," Willie asked.

"Well, I don't even know if flies actually poop . . . but they certainly flock all over the meat while it's dryin' out," Stella answered.

"Oh, that's gross," Willie responded.

"It's worse than gross . . . it's unsanitary," Randy commented.

"I love elk jerky. It is absolutely my favorite. You still got a dryin' rack at your place?" Grandmother Redwing asked Audrey's mother.

"I keep it up on the roof above the back porch. I just climb up there on my ladder and lay out the meat for a couple of days . . . just like our mothers did . . . and presto, elk jerky. Course I always make my grandmother's sauce and marinate it first. Ain't nobody makes a jerky sauce like my grandmother did. She used rose hips and licorice root in it. That's the secret," Stella said proudly.

"Mother, I didn't know you climbed up and down on that old ladder and went to the roof," Audrey noted.

"Well, I can't leave it out on the ground. The raccoons and mice would get it. I got me a wire cage up on the roof that keeps the birds out. And I do lots of things I don't tell you about, Audrey. My goodness, you'd think I was ready for my death mat the way you carry on sometimes."

"A wire cage ain't exactly doin' it the old-fashioned way. In the old days, the women stood guard and chased off the birds," Saddles grunted.

"And in the old days, good shamans had the manners not to say nothin' that would ruin a good gift," Grandmother Redwing admonished.

"She didn't bring me no elk jerky," Saddles noted.

"She didn't know you was here. Besides, don't I always share with you. Ain't I always shared with you since we was kids?" Clarence's mother retorted.

"Yes. Yes, you do," Saddles agreed.

"Well, then forget about the damn wire cage. Besides, it ain't got nothin' to do with wire cages. It's got to do with the sauce and the slow dry in the sun. If a little thing like a wire cage makes the process easier, why even bring the matter up?" Bertha snapped.

"I swear to Kwatee, Bertha, sometimes you act just like you were my wife," Saddles sighed.

Grandmother Redwing let out a loud hurumph.

"And when it comes to a wire cage being okay to

use because it makes the process easier . . . why can't a flush toilet be used to make another process easier?" Saddles questioned.

"Don't be tryin' to confuse me, ya old fool," Grandmother Redwing snapped, opening the package of jerky and taking a deep breath of its perfume.

"Besides, Saddles, you need a wife, you old fool," Grandmother Sunfield teased. She walked up to him with extended arms. "How are you? I didn't expect to find you here. Talk about a sight for sore eyes. Come here, you old window dresser you and give an old lady a hug."

"It's good to see you too, Stella," Saddles said.

"How did ya get up here? Take the bus?" Stella asked.

"No, I drove Bill's station wagon up. I'm gonna help transport you folks to the Potlatch. What with Bertha here, Bill knew there wouldn't be room in Clarence's car unless he took the van, and that is not a very comfortable ride for anyone, I understand."

"You drove Bill's car up here all by yourself?" she asked.

"Sure did. It's like ridin' a bicycle. You don't forget how once you've learned."

"Hell, I didn't think you even saw well enough to cross the busy street by yourself these days. You must be as old as God by now," Stella teased. Teasing, I was beginning to understand, was Grandmother Sunfield's way of being affectionate.

"He still sees well enough to spot a pretty face at thirty yards," Grandmother Redwing bedeviled.

"Then he is graced by the Great Spirit and

Kwatee as well. May none of us live so long that we can no longer enjoy a pretty face," Grandmother Sunfield responded.

"And may none of us live so long that we forget how to dance with Kwatee."

"What do you mean by that, Saddles," Randy asked.

"That none of us lives so long that we forget how to change with the times."

Chapter Eighteen

Three Yellow Finch Feathers

The drive to the Quinault Reservation was filled with legends, lore and gossip. The boys and I rode up with Saddles and the two grandmothers in Bill's station wagon. I sat in the back between the two old women because each of them wanted to sit by a window. Willie and Randy sat up front with Saddles. To keep them from wrinkling, our costumes were stored in boxes in the back provided by Clarence's cleaning establishment.

There had been many questions about my costume but I had managed to keep it a secret. Dad had helped with that. He tied the box that held my costume with garden twine in knots only a seasoned seaman would know how to unravel. Dad's Uncle Todd was a Merchant Marine and taught him how to tie all sorts of fancy knots. We drove in silence until we reached the crest of the plateau that held Perkins Prairie and were about to drive to the valley below.

"Sure seems funny to see all them daffodil and tulip fields down there, don't it?" Grandmother Sunfield commented as Saddles drove the station wagon down Ely Hill toward the Puyallup Valley.

"It's a real pretty sight when all the flowers are in bloom. But I feel sorry for the Puyallups who used' a live here. I'm told the forest and flats just below this hill were rich in game and fulla all sorts of camas root and berries. There was so many different things livin' in this valley in those days; a whole bunch of tribes made their livin' from the valley, and nobody had to worry about there not bein' enough to go around. Now all they got down here is paved roads, all them fields of flowers and a bunch of small towns. It don't make no sense to me. Best huntin' and camas roots on the whole West Coast and they all but paved it over," Grandmother Redwing responded.

"Did either of you ever visit this place before it was daffodil and tulip fields?" I asked.

"We used to come and trade with the Puyallups all the time when I was a kid. We'd bring them all sorts of stuff and trade them for shells. Lots of shells in the bay in those days. My dad and some of the other men would bring them a couple of long cedar poles. We traded them for dried oysters and clams. My mother use'ta make the best clam chowder in the winter outta them dried clams. I ain't had that in maybe sixty years," Grandmother Sunfield replied.

"What other stuff did you trade with them?" I asked.

"Oh, we exchanged a lotta deer and bear skins for big shells . . . you know, big ones like the horse clams and some of them big fancy mussels; there use'ta be so many of them back in them days."

"I wouldn't give up nice deer and bear skins for a bunch of old clam and mussel shells," I mumbled.

"You would if you wanted some sturdy bowls and cups and spoons," Saddles interjected.

"You used shells for bowls and cups and spoons?"

"Well, hell, boy . . . you couldn't run over to the kitchen department at Sears and buy stuff like that in them days. There weren't no shops and there damn sure weren't no fancy glass and porcelain makers here. These was just woods and bay and hills," he answered.

"People made bowls, even water tight ones by weavin' grasses tight together, and every tribe had a couple of good pottery makers and a couple of people who could carve bowls and things out of wood . . . but if you wanted a really strong bowl or cup . . . you used shells. Pottery is good but it breaks easy. A good thick bowl made from horse-clam shell or a geoduck shell couldn't be beat. Shells was as good as dollars back in them days," Grandmother Sunfield explained.

"I was a boy of not much more than seven or eight the last time we came from Quinault to trade with the Puyallups. After that, there was too many whites movin' in and the government wouldn't let the tribes gather along the Puyallup River to trade no more. That was when the tribes started comin' to the peninsula. First it was to trade and have ceremonies . . . and then they started comin' for our Potlatch and Dog Dance. Course we don't do hardly any tradin' anymore. We go to Sears like everybody else. Times sure have changed, ain't they, girls?" the old shaman commented.

"Saddles, do you remember that summer we both turned fourteen and some tribal members all the way from Palouse country came to the reservation to trade? Grandmother Redwing asked.

"How can I forget it. That was the summer I

first fell in love," Saddles giggled.

"It was the first time I ever fell in love too!" Grandmother Redwing giggled back.

"I didn't know you fell in love, Saddles. I figured you was always a man with two souls," I commented.

"That was the summer I discovered I was a boy of two souls," Saddles remarked.

"Oh, you mean you . . . didn't fall in love with a . . . with a girl," I noted.

"He fell in love with the same boy I had a crush on," Grandmother Redwing interjected.

"Who did the boy fall in love with?" Randy asked.

"Saddles!" Grandmother Redwing harrumphed.

"Saddles beat your time with a Palouse boy?" Grandmother Sunfield questioned.

"I had been flirtin' with that boy for two days. My mother had scolded and scolded me for it. She was afraid the boy and I would fall in love and I would move east of the mountains. She wanted me to fall love with a boy from one of the coastal tribes . . . you know, somebody that spoke my language. But this boy, Spotted Eagle was his name, was so pretty and so beautifully built . . . I swooned every time he walked by. Well, I didn't know that Saddles, who in those days was still known as Chases Rainbows, was swoonin' too! And, of course, he had an advantage. Back in them days, boys could talk with other boys just like girls could talk with other girls . . . but boys couldn't talk with girls unless they asked permission of her parents, and it was unthinkable for a girl to speak first."

"So you could talk to him any time you wanted,

huh, Saddles?' I asked.

"Indeed, I could. I thought I was gonna faint the first time I saw him."

"He followed that boy all over the campsite for one whole day until he finally got up enough nerve to speak to him and get his attention," Grandmother Redwing laughed.

"Then what happened?" Randy asked.

"What happened is not for your ears right now," Saddles quipped.

"Well, did you at least kiss the boy?" Randy pressed.

"He did a hell of a lot more than kiss him. I caught the two of them billin' and cooin' when I went for a walk down along the river one night with my best friend, Little Doe. They was practically eatin' up each other's faces!" Grandmother Redwing exclaimed.

"Oh, how you talk, Bertha! Ain't nobody's business but mine and Spotted Eagle's what went on down by the river that night or any other time while he was on the reservation," Saddles admonished.

"Well, maybe so. But I still think I was prettier than you in them days. I still can't figure out how you got that boy to fall in love with you," Grandmother Redwing responded.

"He was also a boy with two souls. Ain't you ever figured that out? It wouldn't have mattered if you was Betty Grable. He wasn't gonna see you."

"He was a boy of two souls?" Grandmother Redwing asked. She sounded surprised.

"Well, of course," Saddles answered.

"But he was so . . . so . . ."

636

"*Butch* is the word you're lookin' for, Bertha," Saddles interrupted.

"Butch?"

"That's the word they used in San Francisco to describe a man with two souls who was . . . you know . . . super manly . . . like my longshoreman was."

"Butch, huh?" Grandmother Redwing repeated.

"How come you didn't follow him to the Palouse country?" Randy asked. "I would have followed him to the ends of the earth."

"The Palouse country was way past the ends of the earth in them days, boy," Saddles explained. "Besides, my father wasn't too pleased about it. Neither was Spotted Eagle's folks."

"You got caught?" Willie asked.

"Yes. We wasn't sneaky enough. He and his folks left the reservation two days before the rest of their party headed back over the mountains. It broke my heart."

"Did you ever see him again?" Randy asked.

"Oh, Randy, you're such a romantic," Willie sighed.

"Well, it's a romantic story, Willie, even if you don't think so. And I did see him again. I saw him years later in San Francisco. He was a chef in a fancy restaurant down on the wharf."

"Did you start datin' again?" Randy asked.

"No . . . by that time I had met somebody and was livin' with him . . . and Spotted Eagle had changed his name to Danny Eagle . . . he was livin' with a Swede who was a fisherman. They was both very beautiful men. Of course, me and mine weren't anything to poke fun at in them days either. We used to play cards with them once in a while. Then they moved up to Alaska where the fishin' was better. I'm told that Danny opened his own restaurant up there someplace. But I lost track. You know how it goes."

"I miss them days," Grandmother Sunfield commented.

"Me, too," Grandmother Redwing allowed.

"Did you ever go up to the Quinault Reservation with a trading party when you were younger, Grandmother Sunfield?" Willie asked.

"Well, of course, I did. I knew your Grandmother Redwing a long time before either of us was married and had kids. In fact, we sort of arranged for Audrey and Clarence to meet," she answered.

"I didn't know that!" Willie exclaimed.

"Me neither," Randy echoed.

"So you knew Saddles before he moved to San Francisco?" Willie asked.

"Well, sure. You couldn't visit the Redwings without Chases Rainbows hangin' around. He and Bertha was like brother and sister."

"Sisters and sister," Saddles joked.

"And I'm proud to say I have always liked the old fart even if I do think he's too damn old to be drivin' this here station wagon on his own," Grandmother Sunfield noted.

"You're forgettin' something, Stella Sunfield. I ain't Chases Rainbows no more. I'm Saddles Seatco, Shaman of the Quinault, and I could drive this damn station wagon with my eyes closed if I concentrated. I got powers!"

638

§§§§

We arrived at the village a little after three that afternoon. Saddles insisted on stopping for gas before he drove to Grandmother Redwing's house, permitting Clarence, Audrey and the girls to drive on ahead of us. "I'm gonna surprise Bill by returnin' his vehicle with a full tank of gas," the old shaman commented.

"Well, hurry up about it. I ain't seen my Abby since I left home and I been worried sick. You was gonna watch after her for me and then showed up at Clarence's place. I mean, I was glad ta see ya, Saddles . . . but I been worried sick. Poor thing . . . she's probably forgotten all about me," Grandmother Redwing complained.

"The Redhawks have been takin' turns carin' for your Abby. Everybody just loves her to pieces. And I made sure she's got one of your old dresses and an old sweater to sleep with. She ain't forgotten who you are. You wait and see . . . that pup will be so glad to see you, she'll probably knock you over when she jumps up on you."

Saddles was interrupted by the station attendant. "Fill'er up, Saddles?" he asked.

"To the brim, Kevin," the old shaman answered.

"Did ya hear that some of the tribe members are plannin' to give you a run for your money on the old religion?" the attendant asked.

"What you talkin' about, Kevin?" Saddles inquired.

"Well, you know how Clare Redstone and Selma

639

Blackwing are all the time going into Shelton to attend that Holy Roller church?"

"Yes."

"Well, they met some sort of tent evangelist that was brought into town by the pastor of that church they attend. What's it called? *The Church of the Flaming Fire and Saving Blood of Jesus?*"

"Somethin' like that."

"Well, now that evangelist fella wants to bring his tent on the reservation and hold some kind of meetin's here. Clare and Selma are behind it all. Ain't nobody else on the reservation very excited about it."

"What did the tribal council say?" Saddles asked.

"Is that tank full yet? I wanna see my Abby," Grandmother Redwing yelled out the window.

"Hush, Bertha, Kevin is tellin' me about some evangelist that wants to bring his tent onto the reservation. I can't hear him with you caterwaulin' in the rear seat and that pump grindin' out here." He turned back to the attendant. "What did you say the council said?"

"Well, it was sort of a tie. Half the council thought they should vote in the spirit of openness and trust and voted to let the man pitch his tent. That way folks could decide for themselves whether they wanted to go see what he's all about. The other half of the council didn't want him steppin' foot on the rez . . . first because he's bringin' the white mans religion with him . . . and second because they think too many impressionable kids will go just to hear the music and see the show . . . and get confused or sucked up in it. So, by tribal law . . . you get the deciding vote. They're

640

leavin' it up to you. The revival fella came up and talked to the council while you were gone. He stopped here and filled up his tank. I went to the meetin'. He told us he believed the fire of the spirit was waitin' to blaze through the hearts of the Quinault people. He told us God has told him he must pitch his tents here or souls will be lost to the pits of hell."

"So this revival fella talks directly to the Great Spirit and the Great Spirit talks back to him?" Saddles interjected.

"I guess. Anyway, I went down and listened to what he had to say. He's a real showman. You know, lots of drama and stuff. I think he missed his callin'. He could a been a real good actor. Anyway, the tribal council's vote was split right down the middle. By tribal law the shaman casts the determining vote. It's up to you."

"Oh, like I ain't got nothin' else to do but get some of the council members mad at me right now . . . just a matter of hours before Potlatch begins."

"To be honest, Saddles, I think the council purposely voted to be at a tie. I don't think none of them wanted to disappoint the folks who want the evangelist to come on the rez . . . even if they didn't think it was a good idea."

"So I'm supposed to do the dirty work, huh?"

"I'm afraid so. It is your job. Besides, bein' the shaman and all, you can look into this matter and ask the spirits what should be done."

"I suppose so . . . although I ain't very inclined to think we need any sort a Billy Sunday on the rez."

"That'll be $3.25, Saddles. It took thirteen

641

gallons even. You want the windows washed?"

"Thanks, no, Kevin. If I don't get this cantankerous old woman over to her house to see that dog of hers, she's gonna nag me into a nervous breakdown."

When Saddles turned the station wagon down the street toward Grandmother Redwing's house, I saw a small group of people gathered in the front yard. Looks like you've got company," I commented.

"Maybe folks was worried about you and are here to welcome you home," Randy speculated.

"Ain't that that scoundrel, Albert Radford standin' on the curb? Now what the hell do ya think he'll be wantin'?"

"Uncle Bill and Aunt Alice are there too," Willie pointed out.

"Is that huge white dog Alice has on a leash your Abby?" Grandmother Sunfield asked.

"That's her. Ain't she a beauty?"

"She's certainly big. You should have named her Avalanche!"

"I just might have if I'd thought of it. But she's used to Abby now. Actually, she's such a gentle dear, I could've called her Snowflake," Grandmother Redwing purred.

"She must eat you out of house and home?" Grandmother Sunfield commented.

"Naw . . . I feed her dry. I buy it in fifty pound bags. They deliver them right to the back porch for me. I always add table scraps for her. I even snared me a couple of rabbits and cooked them up for her. Boy, that girl really likes boiled rabbit!"

Saddles pulled the station wagon up alongside the white picket fence that separated the old woman's house and yard from the sidewalk and parking strip. Grandmother Redwing opened her door and sprang from the vehicle towards her large white dog. "Abby! I'm back home. Did you miss me?" she shouted while ignoring the fact that Albert Radford was walking toward her.

The dog, who had been busy watching a squirrel run along the fence, heard her master's voice and bolted toward her, breaking Alice's hold on the leash. Abby jumped up placing her front paws on the old woman's shoulders and began licking her face and whining.

"Well, I'd say that's proof positive she remembers you," Saddles quipped as he came around the car and joined the others.

Grandmother Redwing threw her arms around the large white creature and embraced her. "There, there . . . Mommie's home. Did you miss me, sugar?" The dog licked her face again, then dropped to the ground and began rubbing its head on her legs for additional attention. The old woman reached down and began scratching the dog's ears. "She really likes this," she told the crowd.

"That's one beautiful animal," Albert Radford commented.

"Whatchu doin' here? Ain't I had enough trouble with you to last me the rest of my life?"

"Who is this young man?" Grandmother Sunfield asked.

"This is our Indian agent, Albert Radford . . . the

643

young whippersnapper that's been givin' me such a hard time about poopin' in the woods."

"Pleased to meet you, ma'am," Albert said with a smile.

"Don't be too sure about that. I ain't heard one good word about you," Grandmother Sunfield grumbled.

"You ain't answered my question, Albert. What you doin' here and how's-a-come the rest of you is here to greet me. Is there somethin' goin' on I should know about?"

"We have a surprise for you, Bertha," Saddles cooed next to her.

""We? You been up with me in Perkins Prairie. What you talkin' 'bout *we*?"

"You'll see, Mother," Bill answered, taking his mother by the arm and guiding her to the steps leading to the front porch.

"Has somethin' happened, Bill . . . somethin' bad?"

"Well, something has happened . . . but it's a good thing," Clarence responded.

"How do you know . . . you in on this too?" his mother queried.

"No . . . but I was told what the surprise is when we got here and I think you're going to like it. That's why everyone is here. They know what the surprise is too."

"Well, now ya got me worried. What kind of a surprise?"

"You're going to love it!" Audrey assured her.

"Come on, Bertha, don't dally. The surprise is

out in the backyard," Saddles said, pulling her up the stairs of the porch.

"Well, if it's out in the backyard, I don't want this whole crowd of people marchin' through my house. I left it spank-dab clean as a whistle and I intend for it to be that way when I walk back in. We can just as easily walk around the house to the backyard," she instructed, breaking free of Saddles and heading around the house. "Somebody close that gate so I can take this leash off Abby," she ordered. The rest of us fell in behind her.

As she came around the corner of the house, the old woman suddenly stopped in her tracks. "What in tarnation is that?" she asked.

As we came around the corner we saw for ourselves what had caught her curiosity. There, before our eyes, was a covered walkway made of the same boards and painted the same color as the house. It was attached at one end to the back porch which was now also enclosed. The covered walkway led to a new building at the far end of her property. "What is this all about. What's happened while I was gone?"

Abby began barking.

"Ain't it excitin', Bertha!" Saddles said, dancing around in front of her. "The government paid to have a real bathroom placed at the far end of your property. It's got a flush toilet in there and a sink and a mirror . . . and it's got an electric heater and a light you can turn off and on from a switch on the wall, and there's electric lights in the hallway leading to it so you don't have to worry about tryin' to see in the dark should you need to go at night. And look'ee there . . . it's even got a door on the outside of the hall here in the backyard, so's you can get to and from the bathroom while you're workin' out here in your garden . . . and you won't have to traipse back into the house. It's a flush toilet . . . I'll grant'cha that . . . but it ain't in your house! It's outside your house! Now you can still keep the ways of Coyote and the laws of the township! Ain't it excitin'!"

"I think it satisfies your needs and our needs," Albert Radford said.

"It's the perfect solution, Mother," Bill told her.

"Well, I'll be damned! And they enclosed my porch as well. Whose idea was this?" the old woman asked as she walked to the back steps.

"It was Saddles' idea," Radford answered.

"Where did you ever come up with an idea like this, you old coot?" the old woman asked as she climbed the steps and opened the back door.

"It came to me in a dream. I had been prayin' hard for a vision to help fix all this for you . . . and it came to me in a dream the night you left the hospital and went up to Perkins Prairie to stay with the kids while you got well. They had twenty men here buildin' and puttin' this thing together for you. I ain't never seen men work so hard and so fast on nothin' like this before. It was almost like it was a war effort. They done it all in about three days and didn't mess up nothin' but a long patch of lawn that use'ta grow where that enclosed hallway stands now. Ain't that somethin'?"

"Well, it appears to be. Come on, Stella, you come explore this new hallway tunnel with me," she shouted over her shoulder. Stella Sunfield climbed up the steps and joined her old friend at the entrance of the covered walkway. The boys and I followed after her.

"Why the thing has windows all along the outside wall. You can see the woods from here," Bertha commented.

"And what about them curtains.?" Saddles asked.

"Why, they're red and white checkerboard . . . my favorite."

"I made them on my new electric Singer . . . they make the place look real homey, don't they?"

"Well, they certainly do."

"And I hung up a few posters I had from old movies I like. I thought they kinda spruced up the place a bit. I think you'll be real comfortable walkin' down this nice hallway," the old shaman assured.

"And look . . . there'sa long shelf running along both sides of the wall. I can store stuff out here if I want."

"And it makes a great place to dry clothes on rainy days," Stella commented.

"I could even hang my herbs and spices out here to dry."

"And look at that floor. Ain't that linoleum?" Stella asked.

"I believe it is," Bertha answered.

"Easy to keep clean. And ya don't have to wax this kind if ya don't wanna. It's got the shine built right in to it. Ain't that somethin'?" Saddles noted.

"The linoleum was Alice's idea," Bill said, following us down the hall.

"It's a might sight bigger on the inside than it looks from the outside," Grandmother Redwing observed. "It's like havin' another house - only a long skinny one."

"This here hallway is wide enough you can put a couple of chairs and a thin table along one wall and do your weaving out here. There's a dozen things you can do with all the extra space," Saddles said excitedly.

"Well, it certainly does provide a lot of extra space," she responded.

"Do you like it, Mother Redwing?" Audrey asked.

"I think I do. Course I ain't seen the bathroom yet . . . but I do like this here hallway." She walked up to the door at the end of the hall and opened it. Inside the small room was a flush toilet, a built-in cabinet for washcloths and other bathroom necessities, a white porcelain sink with a medicine cabinet and mirror above it, a fancy towel rack attached to the wall and another curtained window.

"The windows all open and there's screens on the other side to keep flies and other bugs out," Radford said with pride.

"That's real important, Bertha. At my house I don't got no built in screens. I gotta put in them little slidin' wood-framed screens in my windows," Saddles pointed out.

"Yes, built-in screens. You seem to have thought 'bout everything."

"Well, watch'cha think, Bertha? We tried ta make it as perfect as possible. It ain't inside your lodge and there ain't gonna be any tourists complainin' about

648

this place. Does it meet with your approval?" Saddles asked.

"I just don't know what to think," she answered.

"Ya won't be poopin' in your own lodge by comin' out here, that's for sure," Grandmother Sunfield noted.

"By all the powers that be . . . I think you're right, Stella. I think havin' this here flush toilet down here at the end of the property . . . and that nice enclosed hallway . . . I think I can live with this just fine."

"Thank the good Lord," Radford said.

"And you won't have to hike down to the flats to poop when it's rainin' or snowin'," Saddles continued.

"Oh, quit tryin' to sell me on the idea, Saddles . . . I already said I could live with it just fine."

"And the facility comes up to code . . . it's a bit unusual, but your bathroom is perfectly legal," Radford added.

"That goes for you too, Albert. You can both stop tryin' to sell me on the idea."

"So, Mother, is the battle over poop over?" Bill asked.

Grandmother Redwing turned to her son, looked at him for a few long seconds, gave a wink to Saddles, and said: "Well, that all depends on what you mean by *over*. I suspect even Coyote would not confuse these two structures and think they are the same den. I will use this bathroom when the occasion arrives. But that does not meant I have given up on the woods. If I am down on the flats or out in the forest when nature calls . . . and you know damn well it's gonna call . . .

then I will be doin' what human bein's have been doin' since even before our people moved from the snow country. But this is okay with me. Whatchu done here is a good thing. But I want everybody, especially you, Albert, to understand that this ain't no compromise. As far as I am concerned, I out and out won this battle. I will still keep the ways of Coyote and honor my people. But now the war over poopin' is over."

"We are happy to concede that you have won the battle, Grandmother," Albert said.

"And it cost them a pretty penny too. These boards don't come cheap and they had'a run them pipes all the way out here. Those men brought a machine out to the rez and dug a trench slick as a whistle. Then, after they covered the pipes back over with dirt, they built the hallway right on top of where the pipes is. I ain't never seen nothin' like that before. And you can bet that machine cost a pretty penny too. No, ma'am . . . this didn't come cheap. Why you've got the most expensive bathroom on the whole reservation," Saddles exclaimed.

"Well, all that's fine and dandy, Saddles, but how 'bout you and the rest of these folks go back down the hall to the house and let an old lady try out this new bathroom. If I don't pee in a couple of minutes, we're gonna have to clean this linoleum," Grandmother Redwing instructed.

"Bertha, I have to go too," Stella whispered.
"I'm stayin'."

"We'll go down and unpack the cars. By the time you get back up to the house, you can decide what you want to take to Potlatch and we can get going. As

650

it is, we're probably not going to be able to set up camp very close to the celebration lodge," Bill responded.

"I need someone to come to my house and help carry out some stuff," Saddles requested.

"I'll help," I volunteered.

"Me too," Randy said.

"I'll drive over and pick you up as soon as the grandmothers are back in the car, Clarence told us.

"You still got that trailer hitch hooked up to your car, Clarence?" Saddles asked.

"Yeah, why?"

"I borrowed a little open trailer from the Blackhawk boys. I'm gonna need it to transport my gifts for Potlatch this year," Saddles answered.

"What'cha given' away?" Randy asked.

"You'll just have to wait and see. That's why I need help. I wanna get them from my shed into the trailer and covered with a canvass tarp before your dad comes by. I want everybody who's gettin' this particular gift to be surprised."

"Can we ride over to Tahola in Uncle Bill's station wagon?" Darleen asked.

"If he's got room," Audrey answered.

"Plenty of room for two such pretty little girls," Bill responded.

§§§§

We had just finished securing the canvass tarp over the little open trailer when Clarence parked his car in front of Saddles' place. After backing up as closely as possible to the trailer, he stepped out of his car. "You boys sure got that wagon filled to the brim with somethin'. I suppose you're are helpin' him keep the secret," he said.

"We're sworn to secrecy," Randy answered.

"I wonder if I'm gettin' one of whatever's in there?" he asked as Saddles came around the side of his house.

"Maybe, maybe not. This stuff is for the people livin' over by the coast . . . I can tell you that much," Saddles answered.

"Well, if I ain't gettin' one . . . why can't I know. It don't seem fittin' that these boys are informed and I don't know nothin' about it. After all, I am transporting them to Potlatch for you," Clarence said as a dark blue Cadillac pulled up and parked in front of the Redwing's Ford.

"Who said you wasn't gettin' one. Besides, I know you, Clarence Redwing; you got a mouth on you like a barn door with a broken hinge. You ain't never been able to keep a secret even when you was a kid. I know you. If I tell ya what's in there, you'll tell just one person. Then they'll tell someone else and they'll tell another someone else and the first thing ya know, all the tribes will know what my surprise is. So, I ain't tellin' ya a thing. I'm not even gonna let you lug them into the celebration hall for me," the old shaman responded with a twinkle in his eye. The boys and I pushed the trailer into position so Clarence could attach it to the hitch.

"But you trust the boys with your secret?"

"In this case, yes. Now stop your fussin', Clarence . . . you're gonna ruin my surprise."

652

"You boys be careful and don't strain anything," Audrey yelled from the car as a short man in a white suit got out of the Cadillac and began walking toward us.

"Which one of you is Saddles Seatco?" the man asked.

"My god, that's Pastor Wally Potts, the evangelist fella who gave us such a bad time up in Perkins Prairie," I whispered to Saddles. "He thinks Tyee Sahale is the devil!"

"I'm Saddles Seatco," the old man acknowledged without looking up from his supervision of our work. "What can I do for you?"

"Praise God! I'm glad I found you home. I was afraid you'd be gone down to that . . . that . . . that celebration goin' on down in Tahola," the man exclaimed.

"We're just on our way," Saddles responded, looking up at the man for the first time.

"Sir, I understand you hold the deciding vote in this town as to whether I can pitch my tents here and bring the gospel and the fire of the Holy Ghost to the spirit-starved creatures of this village who are in desperate need for the . . . "

"Isn't it customary to introduce yourself before you start asking for favors?" Saddles asked.

"Why, I'm the Reverend Wally Potts . . . the spirit-filled champion of God. I'm here to bring the cleansing power of Jeeesusss to the unsaved and vanquished souls livin' in this remote little town. God has sent me on a mission. Why there are members of your tribe prayin' right now that your vote will be for

653

Jeeesusss!" the evangelist boomed as both Grandmother Sunfield and Grandmother Redwing got out of Clarence's Ford to see what was going on.

"Members of my tribe should all be down in Tahola gettin' ready for the great religious events about to happen there," Saddles responded.

"Sir, half of the tribal council voted to let me pitch my tents and preach these people into the gates of heaven, into the fire of the Holy Ghost, into the lovin' arms of Jeeesusss! And you're the only man that can sway that vote in the direction of heaven. What'cha say, Mr. Seatco? Are you gonna vote for Jeeesusss!"

"Preachin' people into the gates of heaven must pay a pretty penny. That's one hell of a nice car you're drivin', white man," Grandmother Redwing observed.

"I make no apologies that the Lord has blessed me, ma'am. I may drive a Cadillac, but I live in a little trailer out behind my tents," Wally Potts responded.

"I seen that *little trailer* when you was up in Perkins Prairie. It's pretty damn fancy if you ask me, and I heard tell you got a real nice home in Southern California you return to every winter. Is that true?" I asked.

"I recognize you, boy. You're the lad that turned down the call of salvation and returned to the arms of Satan during the glorious revival fires I brought to that godforsaken little mountain town you live in . . . ain't'cha?" Potts bellowed.

"Don't you be usin' that tone of voice with Talks With Eagles," Grandmother Sunfield chided as she walked up and looked Potts in the face. Despite her aged and shrunken form, she was still a good two inches taller than the white-clad evangelist.

"Madam, this boy is not saved!" Potts blazed.

"Whatchu talkin' about, white man? This boy's had a vision . . . he's spoken with the Great Spirit . . . the Great Spirit gave him a new name. Don't you be tellin' me this boy ain't saved, you loudmouthed little man!" Grandmother Redwing vociferated.

"Madam . . . he can't be saved unless he's come down the sawdust trail and accepted Jeeesusss in his heart. That's why I want to bring my tents into this village. That's why I'm beggin' this Saddles Seatco fella to let me bring the light of the gospel to you people. Madam, if you had Jeeesusss in your heart . . . you'd know that the new name this boy has came straight from the pits of hellfire and brimstone! His new name should be written down in Glory . . . and in Glory . . . only God can talk with eagles!"

"He tried to get me to renounce my vision at that tent revival up in Perkins Prairie, Saddles. I refused to do that. Me and the boys had to run off to get away from him," I said.

"Mr. Potts," Saddles began.

"I am the Reverend Wally Potts, sir. I am not a mister. I am a man of God. You will kindly address me accordingly," the evangelist demanded.

"And I am Saddles Seatco, a man with two souls . . . and I'll have you know both of them are saved and as far as I'm concerned, your idea of Jesus and the tooth fairy have a lot more in common than my idea of Jesus. I am the shaman of the Quinault people. I am their spiritual leader and their medicine man. It is because of this high status that I am given the final vote on what is spiritually good for the Quinault people and what is bad for them. And I think that what you want to bring to this village is not good. You do not honor our ways. You are a man filled with himself. I don't see how the Great Spirit could possibly find any room to live inside you . . . you boisterous, overweight, bad-mannered little man . . . and you will kindly address me as Shaman Seatco."

"That's tellin' the son of a bitch," Grandmother Redwing exclaimed.

"I think you'd better get back in your fancy car and drive back out of town," Clarence said, standing up from having secured the little trailer filled with Saddles' gifts.

"If you don't let me pitch my tents and bring the gospel of Jeeesusss Christ to the poor unfortunates in this town . . . then their souls are gonna be on your hands," Potts snarled.

"And that's a good place for them," Randy asserted.

"And what do you know about spiritual things, boy?" Potts admonished.

"I am also one with two souls and with the grace of Tyee Sahale, I shall be the next shaman of the Quinault people. And I know as sure as I'm standin' here that the souls of my people are in good hands if those hands belong to Shaman Seatco. That's who I am . . . Potts."

"Ain't nobody on the planet got two souls!" the evangelist bellowed.

"That's for the Great Spirit to decide, Mr. Potts.

But I'll tell ya what there isn't. There isn't a chance in hell you're gonna prop up your tents on this reservation and bring your hateful, narrow-minded message here. Nope, ain't gonna be no money'grabin', Cadillac-drivin', fat little evangelist taken my people's hard-earned pay check back to his house in California for the winter," Saddles said firmly.

"You don't seem to understand, sir . . ." Potts began.

"No . . . you don't seem to understand. This interview has concluded. Your request has been denied. I have cast my vote against you. The answer is no. You ain't gonna preach on this reservation. It's time for you to leave. Is there anything I have just said that you do not understand, Mr. Potts?" Saddles said, shaking the crooked and arthritic finger of his right hand at the evangelist.

"I think we should push him in the mud and get his white suit all dirty before he goes home," Grandmother Redwing asserted.

"No, Bertha . . . we don't want to stoop to his level. Besides . . . wearin' a white suit don't cover up who this little devil is."

Pott's face was beet-red with anger.

"You go on and get back to your tents in the white man's city and gobble up his hard-earned cash in the name of your Jesus. As long as I live, you won't be pitchin' your tents here," Saddles instructed.

"And when I take Saddles' place . . . I'll keep the likes of you outta here too," Randy told him.

"You're all gonna burn in hell," Potts shouted as he walked back to his Cadillac.

"Sure hope you make it through Tahola before the war dance starts," Grandmother Sunfield said as Potts walked past her.

"What war dance?" the evangelist asked.

"It is customary to begin Potlatch with a war dance. Any white man found in town during the dance is sacrificed to the jaws of a grizzly bear we keep caged up out behind the celebration lodge," she told him.

Pott's eyes widened with fear. He slipped into his automobile, locked the door, started up the engine, and drove away from us at slightly above the speed limit.

"I don't remember any war dance at last year's Potlatch. Did we arrive late or something?" I asked.

"No, Fritz, you didn't arrive late . . . Stella was just puttin' a little fear in that little fart. She was tellin' a little white lie," Grandmother Redwing answered.

"Yes . . . and sometimes, to keep all things balanced in the sacred circle, it is important to tell an occasional little white lie to little men in white suits," Saddles said, winking at me.

"But you know I don't think Jesus is bad for people," I told him honestly.

"Oh son, neither do we. There are lots of folks on the rez who are Christians. We got Catholics and Protestants and even a Mormon or two. It's not Jesus I'm not let'n on the rez – it's Mr. Potts," Saddles told me.

"Actually, Fritz, we're gonna build us an all faith chapel. We got a priest gonna come up early on a Sunday and say mass for the Catholics and a young Methodist guy who I gonna come later and do a service for the other folks. Lots of Indians love Jesus. Don't you fus about that," Clarence informed me.

§§§§

Once our camps were set up, the boys and I began running around visiting their cousins and anticipating the feast waiting inside the pavilion. At one of the campsites I was able to visit with Lily Whitedove for a few minutes before she helped her parents carry baskets of roasted hazelnuts to the feast that would follow the dance. "I hear you made your own costume," she said, lowering her eyes and smiling warmly.

"Yes. I'm gonna wear it for the competition following the Dog Dance," I replied.

"I'm very anxious to see it. I love blue. It's my favorite color," she cooed.

"How did you know my costume is blue?" I asked.

"Saddles told Dad. He said you will dance to honor the Eagle."

"I'm not as good a dancer as Willie and Randy but I'm going to do my best."

"Will you dance with me afterwards?" she asked.

I looked quickly at the boys trying to mask the surprised look I was sure had swept across my face. "I would like nothing more," I answered, feeling clumsy and shy.

"Well . . . there may actually be more. I thought we might eat together too, if you don't mind."

"I would love that!" I answered.

"Well, I guess I'll see you inside," she said, picking up her basket and following after her parents.

I was still watching after her when the boys' little sister, Darleen, ran up to us. "Mom and Dad want you to come right back to camp. They have a surprise for you," she said breathlessly.

"What sort of surprise?" Willie asked.

"The kind I can't tell you until you get there and find out for yourself," his sister answered smugly.

We hurried back to where the station wagon and Ford were parked. It was indeed a surprise. Sitting on lawn chairs visiting with Audrey and Clarence were my parents. "What are you guys doin' here?" I asked.

"We wanted to see you dance," Mother answered.

"Where are Sonja and Dinah?"

"They're with Grandma and Grandpa Harding. We're just here for the day. But we wanted to see you dance in your new costume . . . so we drove up," Dad explained.

"We even brought something for Potlatch," Mother informed me.

"What's that?" I asked.

"Your father brought several bottles of his home-canned fish eggs and I brought along several half-pints of my homemade high mountain blackberry preserves."

"How come you didn't say nothin' about all this?" I asked.

"Don't you mean, *why didn't you say anything about all this?*" Mother corrected.

"Yeah. Why didn't you say anything?"

"They wanted to surprise you. We've known about it for weeks," Audrey answered.

"I can't believe it!" I said.

"Well, after all that work you put into making your costume, it would have been a shame to miss you dance in it to honor Brother Eagle," Dad noted as Saddles walked up to us.

"Look, Saddles! It's my mom and dad, they've come to watch me dance."

"And who do you think drew them the map to show them how to get here?" the shaman answered.

"Everybody knew but me?" I asked.

"We didn't know," Randy observed.

"Oh, and like you could have kept that a secret," Darleen admonished.

"Well, it's almost time for the Dog Dance. We better be hightailin' it into the pavilion or we'll miss something," Saddles prompted.

"Wait until you taste all the good food waiting for us after the dance," I told my parents as we followed the Redwings, Grandmother Sunfield and Saddles to the main entrance of the celebration lodge. Then, in a whisper, I told my dad about Saddles' special gifts that year. "He had totem poles carved to sit on the front porches of those living in the new village and one for Clarence and Audry. They were carved by a Nootka carver friend of his. The one for Grandmother Redwing is topped with a bobcat holding a finch in his mouth."

"That must have cost him a fortune," my dad whispered back.

"Nope. Saddles gave special lessons to the new

Nootka shaman about sacred things. It was a fair trade."

"Do the Redwings know yet?" he whispered.

"They will as soon as they walk into the hall and see the gifts spread out on the blankets. They're each just four feet long and painted in the traditional colors. I sure wish I was a Redwing. I'd love to have one," I whispered back.

"I'm afraid your mother would put her foot down on that one, son."

§§§§

I must confess that I spent more time watching the reactions of my parents to the Dog Dance than I did to the dancer that year. The look of approval, surprise and delight on their faces made the event all the more delicious for me.

When it came time for my dance, I was so nervous I could barely hear the beat of the drums. I had practiced and choreographed every step of my dance for weeks in the field out behind my grandparents' farm, but when Willie nudged me out onto the dance floor, every step faded from my memory and my mind went blank. I stood there staring across the floor into the eyes of Saddles Seatco, not knowing what to do. Saddles lifted his right arm and exposed his open palm to me. Suddenly the opening steps of the dance came back to me like a flash. I extended my arms, imitated the call of Brother Eagle, and began executing my steps to the rhythm of the drums. In that instant, I ceased being Fritz Harding from Perkins Prairie and understood, perhaps for the first time, how deeply ingrained my new name had become. I was Talks With Eagles celebrating the spirit of my namesake and spirit guide. I had the distinct feeling that the Micmac woman whose blood still lived in my veins was celebrating with me. I knew my dance should last about three or four minutes but it seemed to me at the time that it lasted only seconds. Somehow the drums stopped beating at exactly the moment my dance came to an end and I knew intuitively that I had done well. When I finished, the pavilion filled with whistles, applause, and wonderfully affirming hoots and hollers. I immediately looked for my parents and was pleased to see the proud expression on their faces. When I looked at Grandmother Redwing, she was giving me a thumbs up sign.

I only received an honorable mention that year, but I was pleased to have placed at all. A young Nootka carver took first place and a dancer from the Nez Perce tribe took third place. Randy Redwing's dance and costume won him the honor of second place. He had come dressed as an ancient shaman from the snow country and called his dance the Dance of Long Journeys. There were tears in the eyes of his grandmothers when he finished.

As soon as we changed back into our regular clothes, we returned to the pavilion to join in the feast that would precede the dance that would permit me to hold the lovely Lily Whitedove in my arms.

"That was very impressive," Mother said as we joined them.

"I had no idea you could look so . . . so Indian,"

Dad acknowledged.

"Let me dress you up in some war paint and some fine feathers and you'll look pretty Indian yourself," Saddles teased.

"You have a really good boy on your hands, Tony," Grandmother Redwing said. "He's truly learning the ways of Coyote."

"I'm not sure what that means," Mother answered, "but we're very proud of him ourselves."

After filling out plates and finding a place to sit, Lily Whitedove made her way through the crowd and joined us. I introduced her to my parents and made room for her at our table.

The time finally came for the dancing. The director of entertainment took the microphone and announced that at the request of Saddles Seatco, shaman and medicine man of the Quinault Tribe, the musicians had taken a great deal of time during the year to learn some of the most popular music of the Glenn Miller Band and would begin the dance by playing Miller's arrangement of *Moonlight Serenade.*

"Oh, I love that song," Mother whispered.

"Then allow me," Dad said, taking her hand and leading her onto the dance floor.

"I love this song too" Saddles said, watching the two of them disappear into the crowd.

"Well, come on then, you old fool, and I'll dance with you" Grandmother Redwing said, pulling him onto the dance floor.

Lily and I looked at one another for a few seconds. "You wanna dance this one?" I asked.

"Of course," she answered.

I slipped my right arm around her waist, took her right hand in my left, and tried my best to remember the box step I had learned at the Harding family dance the year before. As we moved among the other dancers, we eventually found ourselves dancing next to Saddles and Grandmother Redwing. For the first time I noticed she was wearing three yellow finch feathers, all pointed up, above her right ear. A sure sign to everyone at Potlatch that she had overcome an evil spirit.

The End

Fredrick Zydek is the author of eight collections of poems, a biography of Charles Taze Russell and a number of articles, reviews and essay that have appeared in a wide variety of religious, commercial and educational journals. Born and raised in the Pacific Northwest he taught at the University of Nebraska and later at the College of Saint Mary until his retirement. He lives in Nebraska where he divides his time between his home in Omaha and a small farm in Brunswick, Nebraska. He continues to write full time.